Praise for the Novels of Faith Hunter

Bloodring

"A bold interpretation of the what-might-be. . . . With a delicate weaving of magic and Scripture, Faith Hunter left me wondering: What's a woman to do when she falls in love with a seraph's child?"
—Kim Harrison

"Entertaining . . . outstanding supporting characters. . . . The strong cliff-hanger of an ending bodes well for future adventures."
—*Publishers Weekly*

"The cast is incredible. . . . Fans of postapocalypse fantasies will appreciate this superb interpretation of the endless end of days."
—*Midwest Book Review*

"Hunter's distinctive future vision offers a fresh though dark glimpse into a newly made postapocalyptic world. Bold and imaginative in approach, with appealing characters and a suspense-filled story, this belongs in most fantasy collections."
—*Library Journal*

"It's a pleasure to read this engaging tale about characters connected by strong bonds of friendship and family. Mixes romance, high fantasy, apocalyptic and postapocalyptic adventure to good effect."
—*Kirkus Reviews*

"Hunter's very professionally executed, tasty blend of dark fantasy, mystery, and romance should please fans of all three genres."
—*Booklist*

"Entertaining . . . a promising new series. . . . Steady pacing, dashes of humor, and a strong story line coupled with a great ending neatly setting up the next adventure make this take on the apocalypse worth checking out."
—Monsters and Critics

"Enjoyable . . . a tale of magic and secrets in a world gone mad."
—*Romantic Times*

continued . . .

Seraphs

"The world [Hunter] has created is unique and bleak . . . [an] exciting science fiction thriller."

—*Midwest Book Review*

"Continuing the story begun in *Bloodring*, Hunter expands on her darkly alluring vision of a future in which the armies of good and evil wage their eternal struggle in the world of flesh and blood. Strong characters and a compelling story."

—*Library Journal*

"This thrilling dark fantasy has elements of danger, adventure, and religious fanaticism, plus sexual overtones. Hunter's impressive narrative skills vividly describe a changed world, and she artfully weaves in social commentary . . . a well-written, exciting novel." —*Romantic Times*

Host

"Hunter's world continues to expand in this highly original fantasy with lively characters where nothing can ever be taken for granted." —*Publishers Weekly*

"Hunter has created a remarkable interpretation of the aftermath of Armageddon in which angels and devils once again walk the earth and humans struggle to find a place. Stylish storytelling and gripping drama make this a good addition to most fantasy collections." —*Library Journal*

"Readers will admire [Thorn's] sacrifice [in] placing others before herself. . . . Fans will enjoy reading about the continuing end of days." —*Midwest Book Review*

"With fast-paced action and the possibility of more romance, this is an enjoyable read with an alluring magical touch." —Darque Reviews

OTHER NOVELS BY FAITH HUNTER

The Rogue Mage Novels

Bloodring
Seraphs
Host

SKINWALKER

A Jane Yellowrock Novel

Faith Hunter

A ROC BOOK

ROC
Published by New American Library, a division of
Penguin Group (USA) Inc., 375 Hudson Street,
New York, New York 10014, USA
Penguin Group (Canada), 90 Eglinton Avenue East, Suite 700, Toronto,
Ontario M4P 2Y3, Canada (a division of Pearson Penguin Canada Inc.)
Penguin Books Ltd., 80 Strand, London WC2R 0RL, England
Penguin Ireland, 25 St. Stephen's Green, Dublin 2,
Ireland (a division of Penguin Books Ltd.)
Penguin Group (Australia), 250 Camberwell Road, Camberwell, Victoria 3124,
Australia (a division of Pearson Australia Group Pty. Ltd.)
Penguin Books India Pvt. Ltd., 11 Community Centre, Panchsheel Park,
New Delhi - 110 017, India
Penguin Group (NZ), 67 Apollo Drive, Rosedale, Auckland 0632,
New Zealand (a division of Pearson New Zealand Ltd.)
Penguin Books (South Africa) (Pty.) Ltd., 24 Sturdee Avenue,
Rosebank, Johannesburg 2196, South Africa

Penguin Books Ltd., Registered Offices:
80 Strand, London WC2R 0RL, England

First published by Roc, an imprint of New American Library,
a division of Penguin Group (USA) Inc.

First Printing, July 2009
10 9 8 7 6

Printed in the United States of America

To my Renaissance Man,
who knows the songs to sing and the rivers to run

ACKNOWLEDGMENTS

The Guy in the Leather Jacket, for telling me Jane needed a softer side.

Sarah Spieth for helping out with New Orleans settings.

Melanie Otto, for beta reading.

Holly McClure, for Cherokee stories, especially for allowing me to cull info from her Cherokee novel, *Lightning Creek*.

Randall Pruette, for gun info and for designing the vamp-killing ammo.

Mike Pruette, Web guru at www.FaithHunter.net and fan.

Judith Bienvenu, for coming up with the model for Jane's bike, and for beta reading.

Stephen Mullen, of Nightrider.com and TuneYourHar-ley.com for bike info and for creating a background for Jacob, Zen Harley Master.

Melissa Lee and Audrey Wilkinson for reading the first chapter and demanding more.

Rod Hunter, for the right word when my tired brain was stymied.

Joyce Wright, for reading everything I write, no matter how "weird."

Kim Harrison, Misty Massey, David B. Coe, C. E. Murphy, Tamar Myers, Greg Paxton, Raven Blackwell, Christina Stiles, and all my writer friends, for taking the writing journey with me.

My Yahoo fan group at www.groups.yahoo.com/group/the-enclave.

My cowriters at www.magicalwords.net.

Lucienne Diver, for doing what an agent does best, with grace and kindness.

And last but not least, my editor at Roc, Jessica Wade, who saw the multisouled Beast in Jane and bought this series.

Y'all ROCK!

CHAPTER 1

I travel light

I wheeled my bike down Decatur Street and eased deeper into the French Quarter, the bike's engine purring. My shotgun, a Benelli M4 Super 90, was slung over my back and loaded for vamp with hand-packed silver fléchette rounds. I carried a selection of silver crosses in my belt, hidden under my leather jacket, and stakes, secured in loops on my jeans-clad thighs. The saddlebags on my bike were filled with my meager travel belongings—clothes in one side, tools of the trade in the other. As a vamp killer for hire, I travel light.

I'd need to put the vamp-hunting tools out of sight for my interview. My hostess might be offended. Not a good thing when said hostess held my next paycheck in her hands and possessed a set of fangs of her own.

A guy, a good-looking Joe standing in a doorway, turned his head to follow my progress as I motored past. He wore leather boots, a jacket, and jeans, like me, though his dark hair was short and mine was down to my hips when not braided out of the way, tight to my head, for fighting. A Kawasaki motorbike leaned on a stand nearby. I didn't like his interest, but he didn't prick my predatory or territorial instincts.

I maneuvered the bike down St. Louis and then onto Dauphine, weaving between nervous-looking shop workers heading home for the evening and a few early revelers out for fun. I spotted the address in the fading light. Katie's

Ladies was the oldest continually operating whorehouse in the Quarter, in business since 1845, though at various locations, depending on hurricane, flood, the price of rent, and the agreeable nature of local law and its enforcement officers. I parked, set the kickstand, and unwound my long legs from the hog.

I had found two bikes in a junkyard in Charlotte, North Carolina, bodies rusted, rubber rotted. They were in bad shape. But Jacob, a semiretired Harley restoration mechanic/Zen Harley priest living along the Catawba River, took my money, fixing one up, using the other for parts, ordering what else he needed over the Net. It took six months.

During that time I'd hunted for him, keeping his wife and four kids supplied with venison, rabbit, turkey—whatever I could catch, as maimed as I was—restocked supplies from the city with my hoarded money, and rehabbed my damaged body back into shape. It was the best I could do for the months it took me to heal. Even someone with my rapid healing and variable metabolism takes a long while to totally mend from a near beheading.

Now that I was a hundred percent, I needed work. My best bet was a job killing off a rogue vampire that was terrorizing the city of New Orleans. It had taken down three tourists and left a squad of cops, drained and smiling, dead where it dropped them. Scuttlebutt said it hadn't been satisfied with just blood—it had eaten their internal organs. All that suggested the rogue was old, powerful, and deadly—a whacked-out vamp. The nutty ones were always the worst.

Just last week, Katherine "Katie" Fonteneau, the proprietress and namesake of Katie's Ladies, had e-mailed me. According to my Web site, I had successfully taken down an entire blood-family in the mountains near Asheville. And I had. No lies on the Web site or in the media reports, not bald-faced ones anyway. Truth is, I'd nearly died, but I'd done the job, made a rep for myself, and then taken off a few months to invest my legitimately gotten gains. Or to heal, but spin is everything. A lengthy vacation sounded better than the complete truth.

I took off my helmet and the clip that held my hair, pulling my braids out of my jacket collar and letting them fall around me, beads clicking. I palmed a few tools of the trade—one stake, ash wood and silver tipped; a tiny gun; and a cross—and tucked them into the braids, rearranging them to hang smoothly with no lumps or bulges. I also breathed deeply, seeking to relax, to assure my safety through the upcoming interview. I was nervous, and being nervous around a vamp was just plain dumb.

The sun was setting, casting a red glow on the horizon, limning the ancient buildings, shuttered windows, and wrought-iron balconies in fuchsia. It was pretty in a purely human way. I opened my senses and let my Beast taste the world. She liked the smells and wanted to prowl. *Later*, I promised her. Predators usually growl when irritated. *Soon*—she sent mental claws into my soul, kneading. It was uncomfortable, but the claw pricks kept me alert, which I'd need for the interview. I had never met a civilized vamp, certainly never done business with one. So far as I knew, vamps and skinwalkers had never met. I was about to change that. This could get interesting.

I clipped my sunglasses onto my collar, lenses hanging out. I glanced at the witchy-locks on my saddlebags and, satisfied, I walked to the narrow red door and pushed the buzzer. The bald-headed man who answered was definitely human, but big enough to be something else: professional wrestler, steroid-augmented bodybuilder, or troll. All of the above, maybe. The thought made me smile. He blocked the door, standing with arms loose and ready. "Something funny?" he asked, voice like a horse-hoof rasp on stone.

"Not really. Tell Katie that Jane Yellowrock is here." Tough always works best on first acquaintance. That my knees were knocking wasn't a consideration.

"Card?" Troll asked. A man of few words. I liked him already. My new best pal. With two gloved fingers, I unzipped my leather jacket, fished a business card from an inside pocket, and extended it to him. It read JANE YELLOWROCK, HAVE STAKES WILL TRAVEL. Vamp killing is a bloody business. I had discovered that a little humor went a long way to making it all bearable.

Troll took the card and closed the door in my face. I might have to teach my new pal a few manners. But that was nearly axiomatic for all the men of my acquaintance.

I heard a bike two blocks away. It wasn't a Harley. Maybe a Kawasaki, like the bright red crotch rocket I had seen earlier. I wasn't surprised when it came into view and it was the Joe from Decatur Street. He pulled his bike up beside mine, powered down, and sat there, eyes hidden behind sunglasses. He had a toothpick in his mouth and it twitched once as he pulled his helmet and glasses off.

The Joe was a looker. A little taller than my six feet even, he had olive skin, black hair, black brows. Black jacket and jeans. Black boots. Bit of overkill with all the black, but he made it work, with muscular legs wrapped around the red bike.

No silver in sight. No shotgun, but a suspicious bulge beneath his right arm. Made him a leftie. Something glinted in the back of his collar. A knife hilt, secured in a spine sheath. Maybe more than one blade. There were scuffs on his boots (Western, like mine, not Harley butt-stompers) but his were Fryes and mine were ostrich-skin Luccheses. I pulled in scents, my nostrils widening. His boots smelled of horse manure, fresh. Local boy, then, or one who had been in town long enough to find a mount. I smelled horse sweat and hay, a clean blend of scents. And cigar. It was the cigar that made me like him. The taint of steel, gun oil, and silver made me fall in love. Well, sorta. My Beast thought he was kinda cute, and maybe tough enough to be worthy of us. Yet there was a faint scent on the man, hidden beneath the surface smells, that made me wary.

The silence had lasted longer than expected. Since he had been the one to pull up, I just stared, and clearly our silence bothered the Joe, but it didn't bother me. I let a half grin curl my lip. He smiled back and eased off his bike. Behind me, inside Katie's, I heard footsteps. I maneuvered so that the Joe and the doorway were both visible. No way could I do it and be unobtrusive, but I raised a shoulder to show I had no hard feelings. Just playing it smart. Even for a pretty boy.

Troll opened the door and jerked his head to the side. I took it as the invitation it was and stepped inside. "You got interesting taste in friends," Troll said, as the door closed on the Joe.

"Never met him. Where you want the weapons?" Always better to offer than to have them removed. Power plays work all kinds of ways.

Troll opened an armoire. I unbuckled the shotgun holster and set it inside, pulling silver crosses from my belt and thighs and from beneath the coat until there was a nice pile. Thirteen crosses—excessive, but they distracted people from my backup weapons. Next came the wooden stakes and silver stakes. Thirteen of each. And the silver vial of holy water. One vial. If I carried thirteen, I'd slosh.

I hung the leather jacket on the hanger in the armoire and tucked the glasses in the inside pocket with the cell phone. I closed the armoire door and assumed the position so Troll could search me. He grunted as if surprised, but pleased, and did a thorough job. To give him credit, he didn't seem to enjoy it overmuch—used only the backs of his hands, no fingers, didn't linger or stroke where he shouldn't. Breathing didn't speed up, heart rate stayed regular; things I can sense if it's quiet enough. After a thorough feel inside the tops of my boots, he said, "This way."

I followed him down a narrow hallway that made two crooked turns toward the back of the house. We walked over old Persian carpets, past oils and watercolors done by famous and not-so-famous artists. The hallway was lit with stained-glass Lalique sconces, which looked real, not like reproductions, but maybe you can fake old; I didn't know. The walls were painted a soft butter color that worked with the sconces to illuminate the paintings. Classy joint for a whorehouse. The Christian children's home schoolgirl in me was both appalled and intrigued.

When Troll paused outside the red door at the end of the hallway, I stumbled, catching my foot on a rug. He caught me with one hand and I pushed off him with little body contact. I managed to look embarrassed; he shook his head. He knocked. I braced myself and palmed the cross he had missed. And the tiny two-shot derringer. Both hidden against my skull on the crown of my head, and covered by my braids, which men never, ever searched, as opposed to my boots, which men always had to stick their fingers in. He opened the door and stood aside. I stepped in.

The room was spartan but expensive, and each piece of furniture looked Spanish. Old Spanish. Like Queen-Isabella-and-Christopher-Columbus old. The woman, wearing a teal dress and soft slippers, standing beside the desk, could have passed for twenty until you looked in her eyes. Then she might have passed for said queen's older sister. Old, old,

old eyes. Peaceful as she stepped toward me. Until she caught my scent.

In a single instant her eyes bled red, pupils went wide and black, and her fangs snapped down. She leaped. I dodged under her jump as I pulled the cross and derringer, quickly moving to the far wall, where I held out the weapons. The cross was for the vamp, the gun for the Troll. She hissed at me, fangs fully extended. Her claws were bone white and two inches long. Troll had pulled a gun. A big gun. Men and their pissing contests. *Crap*. Why couldn't they ever just let me be the only one with a gun?

"Predator," she hissed. "In my territory." Vamp anger pheromones filled the air, bitter as wormwood.

"I'm not human," I said, my voice steady. "That's what you smell." I couldn't do anything about the tripping heart rate, which I knew would drive her further over the edge; I'm an animal. Biological factors always kick in. So much for trying not to be nervous. The cross in my hand glowed with a cold white light, and Katie, if that was her original name, tucked her head, shielding her eyes. Not attacking, which meant that she was thinking. Good.

"Katie?" Troll asked.

"I'm not human," I repeated. "I'll really hate shooting your Troll here, to bleed all over your rugs, but I will."

"Troll?" Katie asked. Her body froze with that inhuman stillness vamps possess when thinking, resting, or whatever else it is they do when they aren't hunting, eating, or killing. Her shoulders dropped and her fangs clicked back into the roof of her mouth with a sudden spurt of humor. Vampires can't laugh and go vampy at the same time. They're two distinct parts of them, one part still human, one part rabid hunter. Well, that's likely insulting, but then this was the first so-called civilized vamp I'd ever met. All the others I'd had personal contact with were sick, twisted killers. And then dead. Really dead.

Troll's eyes narrowed behind the .45 aimed my way. I figured he didn't like being compared to the bad guy in a children's fairy tale. I was better at fighting, but negotiation seemed wise. "Tell him to back off. Let me talk." I nudged it a bit. "Or I'll take you down and he'll never get a shot off." Unless he noticed that I had set the safety on his gun when I tripped. Then I'd *have* to shoot him. I wasn't betting on my .22 stopping him unless I got an eye shot. Chest hits wouldn't even slow him down. In fact they'd likely just make him mad.

When neither attacked, I said, "I'm not here to stake you. I'm Jane Yellowrock, here to interview for a job, to take out a rogue vamp that your own council declared an outlaw. But I don't smell human, so I take precautions. One cross, one stake, one two-shot derringer." The word "stake" didn't elude her. Or him. He'd missed three weapons. No Christmas bonus for Troll.

"What are you?" she asked.

"You tell me where you sleep during the day and I'll tell you what I am. Otherwise, we can agree to do business. Or I can leave."

Telling the location of a lair—where a vamp sleeps—is information for lovers, dearest friends, or family. Katie chuckled. It was one of the silky laughs that her kind can give, low and erotic, like vocal sex. My Beast purred. She liked the sound.

"Are you offering to be my toy for a while, intriguing nonhuman female?" When I didn't answer, she slid closer, despite the glowing cross, and said, "You are interesting. Tall, slender, young." She leaned in and breathed in my scent. "Or not so young. What are you?" she pressed, her voice heavy with fascination. Her eyes had gone back to their natural color, a sort of grayish hazel, but blood blush still marred her cheeks so I knew she was still primed for violence. That violence being my death.

"Secretive," she murmured, her voice taking on that tone they use to enthrall, a deep vibration that seems to stroke every gland. "Enticing scent. Likely tasty. Perhaps your blood would be worth the trade. Would you come to my bed if I offered?"

"No," I said. No inflection in my voice. No interest, no revulsion, no irritation, nothing. Nothing to tick off the vamp or her servant.

"Pity. Put down the gun, Tom. Get our guest something to drink."

I didn't wait for Tommy Troll to lower his weapon; I dropped mine. Beast wasn't happy, but she understood. I was the intruder in Katie's territory. While I couldn't show submission, I could show manners. Tom lowered his gun and his attitude at the same time and holstered the weapon as he moved into the room toward a well-stocked bar.

"Tom?" I said. "Uncheck your safety." He stopped mid-stride. "I set it when I fell against you in the hallway."

"Couldn't happen," he said.

"I'm fast. It's why your employer invited me for a job interview."

He inspected his .45 and nodded at his boss. Why anyone would want to go around with a holstered .45 with the safety off is beyond me. It smacks of either stupidity or quiet desperation, and Katie had lived too long to be stupid. I was guessing the rogue had made her truly apprehensive. I tucked the cross inside a little lead-foil-lined pocket in the leather belt holding up my Levi's, and eased the small gun in beside it, strapping it down. There was a safety, but on such a small gun, it was easy to knock the safety off with an accidental brush of my arm.

"Is that where you hid the weapons?" Katie asked. When I just looked at her, she shrugged as if my answer were unimportant and said, "Impressive. You are impressive."

Katie was one of those dark ash blondes with long straight hair so thick it whispered when she moved, falling across the teal silk that fit her like a second skin. She stood five feet and a smidge, but height was no measure of power in her kind. She could move as fast as I could and kill in an eyeblink. She had buffed nails that were short when she wasn't in killing mode, pale skin, and she wore exotic, Egyptian-style makeup around the eyes. Black liner overlaid with some kind of glitter. Not the kind of look I'd ever had the guts to try. I'd rather face down a grizzly than try to achieve "a look."

"What'll it be, Miz Yellowrock?" Tom asked.

"Cola's fine. No diet."

He popped the top on a Coke and poured it over ice that crackled and split when the liquid hit, placed a wedge of lime on the rim, and handed it to me. His employer got a tall fluted glass of something milky that smelled sharp and alcoholic. Well, at least it wasn't blood on ice. Ick.

"Thank you for coming such a distance," Katie said, taking one of two chairs and indicating the other for me. Both chairs were situated with backs to the door, which I didn't like, but I sat as she continued. "We never made proper introductions, and the In-ter-net," she said, separating the syllables as if the term was strange, "is no substitute for formal, proper introductions. I am Katherine Fonteneau." She offered the tips of her fingers, and I took them for a moment in my own before dropping them.

"Jane Yellowrock," I said, feeling as though it was all a little redundant. She sipped; I sipped. I figured that was enough etiquette. "Do I get the job?" I asked.

Katie waved away my impertinence. "I like to know the people with whom I do business. Tell me about yourself."

Cripes. The sun was down. I needed to be tooling around town, getting the smell and the feel of the place. I had errands to run, an apartment to rent, rocks to find, meat to buy. "You've been to my Web site, no doubt read my bio. It's all there in black and white." Well, in full color graphics, but still.

Katie's brows rose politely. "Your bio is dull and uninformative. For instance, there is no mention that you appeared out of the forest at age twelve, a feral child raised by wolves, without even the rudiments of human behavior. That you were placed in a children's home, where you spent the next six years. And that you again vanished until you reappeared two years ago and started killing my kind."

My hackles started to rise, but I forced them down. I'd been baited by a roomful of teenaged girls before I even learned to speak English. After that, nothing was too painful. I grinned and threw a leg over the chair arm. Which took Katie, of the elegant attack, aback. "I wasn't raised by wolves. At least I don't think so. I don't feel an urge to howl at the moon, anyway. I have no memories of my first twelve years of life, so I can't answer you about them, but I think I'm probably Cherokee." I touched my black hair, then my face with its golden brown skin and sharp American Indian nose in explanation. "After that, I was raised in a Christian children's home in the mountains of South Carolina. I left when I was eighteen, traveled around a while, and took up an apprenticeship with a security firm for two years. Then I hung out my shingle, and eventually drifted into the vamp-hunting business.

"What about you? You going to share all your own deep dark secrets, Katie of Katie's Ladies? Who is known to the world as Katherine Fonteneau, aka Katherine Louisa Dupre, Katherine Pearl Duplantis, and Katherine Vuillemont, among others I uncovered. Who renewed her liquor license in February, is a registered Republican, votes religiously, pardon the term, sits on the local full vampiric council, has numerous offshore accounts in various names, a half interest in two local hotels, at least three restaurants, and several bars, and has enough money to buy and sell this entire city if she wanted to."

"We have both done our research, I see."

I had a feeling Katie found me amusing. Must be hard to live a few centuries and find yourself in a modern world where everyone knows what you are and is either infatuated with you or scared silly by you. I was neither, which she liked, if the small smile was any indication. "So. Do I have the job?" I asked again.

Katie considered me for a moment, as if weighing my responses and attitude. "Yes," she said. "I've arranged a small house for you, per the requirements on your In-ter-net web place."

My brows went up despite myself. She must have been pretty sure she was gonna hire me, then.

"It backs up to this property." She waved vaguely at the back of the room. "The small L-shaped garden at the side and back is walled in brick, and I had the stones you require delivered two days ago."

Okay. Now I was impressed. My Web site says I require close proximity to boulders or a rock garden, and that I won't take a job if such a place can't be found. And the woman—the vamp—had made sure that nothing would keep me from accepting the job. I wondered what she would have done if I'd said no.

At her glance, Tr— Tom took up the narrative. "The gardener had a conniption, but he figured out a way to get boulders into the garden with a crane, and then blended them into his landscaping. Grumbled about it, but it's done."

"Would you tell me why you need piles of stone?" Katie asked.

"Meditation." When she looked blank I said, "I use stone for meditation. It helps prepare me for a hunt." I knew she had no idea what I was talking about. It sounded pretty lame even to me, and I had made up the lie. I'd have to work on that one.

Katie stood and so did I, setting aside my Coke. Katie had drained her foul-smelling libation. On her breath it smelled vaguely like licorice. "Tom will give you the contract and a packet of information, the compiled evidence gathered about the rogue by the police and our own investigators. Tonight you may rest or indulge in whatever pursuits appeal to you.

"Tomorrow, once you deliver the signed contract, you are invited to join my girls for dinner before business commences. They will be attending a private party, and dinner will be served at seven of the evening. I will not be present, that they may speak freely. Through them you may learn something of import." It was a strange way to say seven p.m., and an even stranger request for me to interrogate her employees right off the bat, but I didn't react. Maybe one of them knew something about the rogue. And maybe Katie knew it. "After dinner, you may initiate your inquiries.

"The council's offer of a bonus stands. An extra twenty percent if you dispatch the rogue inside of ten days, without the media taking a stronger note of *us*." The last word had an inflection that let me know the "us" wasn't Katie and me. She meant the vamps. "Human media attention has been . . . difficult. And the rogue's feeding has strained relations in the vampiric council. It is *important*," she said.

I nodded. *Sure. Whatever. I want to get paid, so I aim to please*. But I didn't say it.

Katie extended a folder to me and I tucked it under my arm. "The police photos of the crime scenes you requested. Three samples of bloodied cloth from the necks of the most recent victims, carefully wiped to gather saliva," she said.

Vamp saliva, I thought. *Full of vamp scent. Good for tracking*.

"On a card is my contact at the NOPD. She is expecting a call from you. Let Tom know if you need anything else." Katie settled cold eyes on me in obvious dismissal. She had already turned her mind to other things. Like dinner? Yep. Her cheeks had paled again and she suddenly looked drawn with hunger. Her eyes slipped to my neck. Time to leave.

CHAPTER 2

Okay, I was paranoid

"Where'dju hide the weapons?" Troll asked, his voice conversational.

I smiled as I slid into my jacket, not ignoring the barrel of the .45 pressed into my neck, but not reacting to it either. "You're human. Sure you want to risk standing so close to me?"

I felt him hesitate and whirled. Set my head to the side of the gun. Knocked his right arm across his body with my raised right fist. Twisting my hand, I took his wrist and lifted. And slammed against his left shoulder with my left hand, forcing him to the floor. It took maybe a half second. Deep in my bones, I felt my Beast spit. This was fun.

"Not bad," he said, his inflection still composed. I knew I'd been baited. Had known he would want to know if he could have taken me. "What discipline?"

He was asking what form of martial arts I studied. I thought a minute. "Dirty," I said. He chuckled. I pressed down just a bit on his shoulder joint. "Put the weapon down."

He placed the .45, a well-kept Smith & Wesson, on the floor and pushed it away. He could still get to it, but not before I hurt him bad. I took my weight off his shoulder and released his wrist, stepping back and setting my feet, balanced for his next move. But he didn't make one. He stood and tucked his thumbs into his waistband, a surer sign of peace than palms out. Thumbs in meant he couldn't strike out fast, while the universal gesture of peace was an easy way to mentally disarm an opponent and then kill him when he let down his guard.

"There's a hapkido black belt, second dan, practices after hours in the back of a jewelry store on St. Louis. I'll call in an intro if you want."

"That'd be nice." I waited, easing down a smidgen. Just enough for him to see it, but not enough to get sucker punched.

"Anything else I can do you for?" he asked companionably.

"Sure. Where can a girl buy a good steak for grilling?" Meaning where can I get good raw meat, but phrased in a socially acceptable way.

"Place I stocked your fridge from is the best. Thirty pounds of sirloin."

This time I controlled my reaction. My love of animal protein wasn't on my Web site. Not anywhere.

"I left directions to the butcher and a fresh market on your kitchen counter. Butcher delivers," he said, "seafood, beef, any kinda bird, alligator"—my Beast perked up at that—"mudbug, veggies, you name it."

"Mudbug?" I let a small smile cross my face, sure I was being baited again.

"Crawfish. Best steamed in beer, in my opinion. I left directions to eateries, too."

"Much appreciated."

He sighed and dropped his weight to one hip. I smothered my grin. "You're not going to tell me where you hid the weapons, are you?" he asked.

"Nope. But I promise not to break your knee if you'll reposition your weight back on both feet."

He laughed, the happy laugh of a contented man, and adjusted his weight back evenly. Still dangerous, but not sneaky dangerous. "Not bad, Jane Yellowrock."

"Right back at you, Tom."

"You can call me Troll. I kinda like it."

I nodded. "Sounds dangerous. Mean."

"Not me. I'm a pussycat."

I glanced at the armoire and back at him with a question in my eyes.

"Sorry," he said and took three steps back.

Without taking my eyes off him, I reached into the armoire and gathered my weapons in small batches, inserting them into the proper straps and sheaths, all but one stake, which I leaned into the darkest corner. I carried the shotgun. I had to work to get its harness strapped on and I wasn't taking chances with Tommy Troll. I grinned at the thought and he thought the smile was for him. Which it was, sorta. "Thanks for an interesting evening," I said.

"Welcome to New Orleans. See you tomorrow night." He lifted a large mailing envelope off a table at his side and handed it to me. I felt several things inside: what I took to be a stack of cash, trifolded papers (most likely the contract), flat pages, and a couple of keys. "Thanks," I said. I nodded and opened the narrow door, stepping into the night.

I stood with my back to Katie's, remembering to breathe, forcing down the fear I had controlled, subjugated, strangled till now. I grinned. I'd done it. I had faced down a civilized vamp, had lived to tell the tale, and had successfully taken away both cash and a job. Beast found my relief amusing. When I could walk without my knees shaking, I stuffed Katie's folder into the envelope and went to my bike.

The night wasn't dark, not in Jazz City. The glare of streetlights and neon beer signs fell in odd patterns and cast warped shadows across the cityscape, the effect of moisture in the air from the Mississippi River and Lake Pontchartrain. The bodies of water bracketed New Orleans, giving the city its famous stink and air so wet that rain sometimes fell from a blue sky. So I smelled the Joe before I saw him. But I knew where he was. Upwind, relaxed. The smell of gun oil and ammo no stronger than before.

He was sitting on a low brick wall one storefront over, a balcony above him, the old building at his back. He had one leg up, the other dangling, and the shadows hid the left side of his body. He could have a weapon hidden there. Okay, I was paranoid. But I had just bested a vamp on her home territory and then made nice-nice with her bodyguard. My glands still pumped adrenaline and my heart was suddenly pounding.

Keeping him to my side, I went around my bike and strapped the shotgun harness on top of my jacket, sliding the weapon into the special sheath made by a leathersmith in the mountains near Asheville. I checked the saddlebags and saw the finger smudges on the polished chrome. Gloved. No prints. But I bet touching my locks had hurt like a son of a gun. Making it look like I was getting a closer look, I bent and sniffed. The Joe's cigar scent was faint, but present. I raised my head and grinned at him. He touched the brim of an imaginary cowboy hat, a faint smile on his face.

I straddled the hog and sat. He slid off his glasses, and his eyes were dark, nearly black, a sign of mixed European and American Indian lineage. "Still hurting?" I asked, letting my voice carry on the damp air.

"A little tingly," he admitted easily. After all, if he had intended me not to guess it was him, he wouldn't have stayed around. "Witchy-lock?"

I nodded.

"Expensive. You get the job?" When I raised my brows politely he said, "With Katie. Word on the streets is the council brought in out-of-town talent to take down the rogue."

"I got the job." But I didn't like the fact that everyone in town knew why I was here. Rogue vamps were good hunters. The best. Beast snarled in disagreement but I ignored her.

He nodded and sighed. "I was hoping she'd can you. I wanted the contract."

I shrugged. What could I say? I kick-started the bike. Fumes and the roar drove Beast back down. She didn't like the smell, though she did approve of my method of travel. To her, hogs were totally cool. I wheeled and tooled away, keeping an eye on the Joe in the rearview. He never moved.

Moments later I switched off the Harley, sitting astride the too-warm leather seat as I looked over the narrow, two-story, old-brick French house. It was around the block and backed up to Katie's Ladies. The front door had a stained-glass oval window in the center and was protected from the elements by a three-foot-wide second-story veranda with a freshly painted black wrought-iron railing. A similar door opened on the upper porch, and neither looked particularly secure. There was a narrow lane down the right side, locked behind an ornate seven-foot-tall wrought-iron gate. Lots of wrought iron, half the spikes topped with fleur-de-lis, the rest with what could have been stakes. Tongue-in-cheek vamp humor. Before coming here, during the preliminary research phase of this job, I had learned that the fleur-de-lis was New Orleans' official city symbol and had been popular for ages in France, from whence many of the vamps had emigrated during the pre-Napoleonic purges of the French Revolution. Seemingly useless bits of knowledge often were the difference between success and failure.

House and gate had to be two, three hundred years old. I tried the larger, older of two keys, four inches in length, a heart shape on one end. The lock clicked and I squeezed the latch, two bars that compressed to unfasten the gate. It opened without a squeak. Boots on cobblestones, I walked my Harley inside and pulled the gate closed behind me. The latch clicked and I relocked it before walking the bike down the two-rut garden lane beside the house. Or storefront, or boardinghouse. From the smells, it had been lots of things at one time or another.

A careful driver could have gotten a car back here. A small car. But the lane was clearly intended for walkers, or maybe horseback riders. There were all kinds of plants, some with long stems and elephant ear–sized leaves of various color combinations. There were climbing roses and jasmine and a few other things I recognized, but my knowledge of botany was limited. Several plants were flowering and smelled heavenly. I caught a hint of catnip. Beast made a hacking sound deep inside. I wasn't always sure what that meant, but it was a reaction of some sort used during both positive and negative discoveries. In this case, maybe it was a sign of recognition.

The house was narrow on the street side, but long, with a deep second-story wooden balcony covering a ground-floor porch that overlooked the tiny side lane and back garden. I could see chairs on the porch, a few tables. More wrought-iron trellises and rails served to keep people from falling off. The porch on the lower level was slate floored, with more iron. The house had tall windows closed with French shutters, five windows on each story, and there was one door on each floor with stairs near the back leading between. Four doors total, all flimsy. Not much security.

I could check out the interior of the house later. The

back garden first. I pushed the Harley on around. The garden widened into a thirty-by-forty-foot rectangular space at the bottom of the lane, and was exquisite. It was surrounded by ornamental yet entirely functional brick walls fifteen feet high, and was lined with plants of all varieties. A big fountain splashed in a corner, water pouring from a huge marble tulip with a miniature naked woman sitting atop. The sculpture was finely detailed, a masterwork, and I noted the statue's resemblance to Katie. Tiny fangs were a dead giveaway. I wondered how many houses she owned on this block. Maybe all of them. You could do some powerful estate planning when you had lived over two hundred years. Maybe three hundred. Maybe more.

Over the city sounds and even with the roar of the Harley still affecting my ears, I could hear the tiny motor powering the pump. Other than that, and the sound of an unfamiliar night bird, the garden was silent.

Across from the fountain, sown with dozens of healthy plants, were three large boulders and half a dozen smaller ones brought in by the crane Troll had mentioned. Katie was right. The gardener had done a good job; the boulders looked like they had been here forever.

I set the kickstand and walked the garden, looking for wires, scuffs on the brick, signs of work other than the gardener's. I spotted them fast, a scuff near the left back corner, too high to be from a spade, and a well-concealed electrical line running from the security light down to the brick wall.

I pulled off the straps that secured my shotgun and set it aside. The jacket followed, and, sitting down on a conveniently placed bench, I tugged off my boots. I gathered three loose cobblestones and dropped them into my T-shirt. They landed against my skin at my waist, held in place by my belt. Then I pulled the bench to the wall, spat on my hands for effect more than necessity, and leaped.

The brick wall was irregular, with some bricks forming depressions and others sticking out just enough for a rock climber to know what to do with them. I hadn't climbed Everest, but I'd lived in the Appalachians and had taken a few classes. I had taken at least a few classes in lots of things.

I caught a slightly protuberant brick and swung out,

catching another with my toes, pushing up for a second handhold, another toehold. I reached the top of the fence and studied it. There was no barbed wire, no broken glass embedded in concrete, no trip wires. Nothing. A half-assed job, security-wise.

I pulled myself to the top and stood, surveying the yard next door. A small dog, more hair than meat, growled at me. Beast was rising in my mind as the moon rose and darkness fell, and she spat at it, not that the stupid little dog could tell. I reined her back and, because she understood that the safety of the den was paramount, she let me. I was better at human things, and she didn't mind me taking over as long as it wasn't dangerous. Then it got a bit harder to submerge her instincts.

I walked along the wall, taking in the scents of the place, the brick warm beneath my bare feet as I scrutinized the garden with eyes and nose and considered the walls on the houses adjacent to my freebie-house wall. I came to the back corner where the scuff was and toed a tiny lump, brushing away dirt that had been carefully sprinkled there. I reached down and pulled the miniature security camera from the duct tape holding it in place. The tape made little snapping sounds as it broke.

The electrical wires powering the camera came free as well, and I turned the camera lens to me, holding it level. I smiled at Katie, or maybe Troll. Or maybe a security firm. I shook my head. I held up the index finger of my free hand and shook it slowly side to side. Then I raised the camera and brought it down on the wall, lens first, and broke it into pieces. I did the same thing to the other two cameras.

I wasn't worried about ticking off Katie. My Web site was firm about my privacy requirement, and I insisted it be part of my contract. What could she say? "Oh, dearie me, I forgot they were there . . ."? Yeah, right.

When I was sure I had all the ones within easy reach, I positioned myself and studied the camera mounted on the neighbor's wall. I didn't want to smash the window next to it. I pulled my T-shirt out and caught the three cobblestones. I hefted them, getting their balance and weight. I had never been as good at throwing as I was at other sports. I threw like a girl. It took all three stones but I smashed the last camera.

Satisfied, I dropped from the wall, not bothering with the brick handholds. With the cameras gone I didn't need them. I gathered up my belongings and, barefoot, unlocked the door with the smaller key on the big ring. I went through the house fast, locating cameras. I busted two hidden behind grilles, one in an air return, one in a fanlight in the twelve-foot-high ceiling, which I hit with a broom handle. Several others. Finding security devices in a house was a lot harder than in a garden. I'd have to go over it later in better detail, but for now, I had a lot to do. First things first—a call to Molly.

Molly, a powerful earth witch and my very best friend, answered, children giggling and splashing water in the background. "Hey, witchy woman. I'm here. I got the gig," I said. Molly gave an ululating yell, and I laughed with her.

Vamps and witches came out of the closet in 1962, when Marilyn Monroe tried to turn the U.S. president in the Oval Office and was killed by the Secret Service. There was a witness, Beverly Stumpkin, a White House maid, who ran for her life. The Secret Service quickly set up a suicide scenario for the actress and staked her in her bedroom. Not that anyone believed she had offed herself with a wooden stake to the heart and a garroting wire that beheaded her. The government tried to track down the maid, but she got away clean. Sloppy work all the way around.

Some gossip rag got wind of the real Monroe story and managed to do what the Secret Service couldn't. They found the maid. Within weeks the lid was blown off the age-old myth. Vamps, and then witches, came out of the closet. If there had been other supernatural beings, it seemed like a good time for them to come out too, but so far no elves, pixies, wood nymphs, or merpeople had appeared. No weres or skinwalkers or shifters of any kind either. I was a singularity in a human world that wouldn't like me if it knew about me, which meant I had to keep my secret close. And that meant that I had to live without true backup. Except for Molly.

"I'm proud of you," she said. "Here, talk to the dirtiest child in the world. Maybe she'll let me finish her bath." The phone made muted rubbing noises, as if she held it under her arm. I waited patiently.

Molly Meagan Everhart Trueblood, the witch who had

spelled my saddlebags, knew all about me. Mol came from a long line of witches. Not the kind in a pointy black hat with a cauldron in the front yard, and not the kind like the *Bewitched* television show. Witches aren't human, though they can breed with humans, making little witches about fifty percent of the time, and normal humans the other fifty.

Young witches have a poor survival rate, especially the males, most dying before they reach the age of twenty from various kinds of cancers. The ones who live through puberty, however, tend to live into their early hundreds. Mol was forty, looked thirty, and was fearless.

I had wondered whether witches and skinwalkers had similar genetics. The witch trait is X linked, passed from generation to generation on the X chromosome. About ninety percent of the witches who live to maturity are female; only a few sorcerers, the term some call the male witch, survive in each generation. Nobody knows why witches have such a poor survival rate, but Molly was one of the lucky ones when it came to kids. So far. She had married a sorcerer, Evan, and they had a son, Little Evan, and a daughter, Angelina—Angie. Both have the witch X gene. The girl is a prodigy. And she is only six years old.

Most witches come into their gift slowly, around puberty. Angie came into her gift at age five, and it was atomic bomb potent. Mol postulated that her daughter has a witch gene on both of her X chromosomes, one from her dad, one from her mom, which, if true, would make the girl one of the most powerful witches on the planet, and someone that everyone would want, from the U.S. government's black ops programs, to the council of witches, to the Chinese, the Russians, you name it. And anyone who didn't have her would want her dead. Molly kept Angie's power level under wraps, a lot like I kept what I was under wraps. And she and Evan warded their children and their property with protection, healing, and lots of prayers.

A delicate, sweet voice said, "Hi, Aunt Jane." My heart started to melt. Beast stopped pushing and sat, panting, in my mind. *Kits*, she thought at me, happy.

"Hi, Angie. Are you giving your mother a hard time in the bath?"

"Yes. I'm being a bad girl." She giggled again. "I played in the mud. I miss you. When you coming home?"

"Soon. I hope. I'll bring you a doll. What kind do you want?"

"Long black hair and yellow eyes. Like you."

Cripes. My melting heart was a pile of goo. "I'll see if I can find one," I said past the lump in my throat. "For now, let your mama get you clean, okay?" Molly had needed backup when Angie's power erupted. I had been there for her and we had been friends ever since, back-to-back, including when I took down the rogue vamp's blood-family last year in the Appalachian Mountains, rescuing her sister in the process.

"Okay. Here, Mama. Aunt Jane wants you. And then she's gonna go play."

Into the phone Molly said, "Play, huh?"

"Yeah. You and Evan checked the wards around your house?"

Molly made a sound, half *pshaw*, half grunt, and I heard water falling into water as she lifted Angelina out of the bath. "Twice tonight. You have fun. Call me."

"I will." Feeling twenty pounds lighter, I left my belongings in the middle of the parlor floor and opened the fridge. Thirty pounds of fresh meat took up the center shelf. Beast hissed in anticipation, even though she hated to eat cold. I ripped the butcher paper off a five-pound stack, stuck it in the microwave for a bit, just enough to take the chill off, and, while it heated, gathered supplies. When the bell dinged, I carried the meat outside, a roll of paper towels under one arm, my travel pack and a zipper satchel under the other. Already it felt weird walking on two legs, as Beast moved up from the deeps into my thoughts.

I set the stack of raw, bloody steaks on the ground and wiped my hands. Beast wanted to lick them, but I refrained. I had that much control left. I stripped off my clothes, leaving them in a pile. My stomach was rumbling. I was panting, salivating. *Hungry*, she thought at me.

I am a skinwalker, and so far as I know, the last of my kind anywhere. If I have the right quantity of genetic material, I can take the shape of most any animal, though it's easier if the species is the same mass as I am. Borrowing mass to fill out the genetic requirements of a larger animal is painful and dangerous, and I haven't tried it often. It's equally difficult to skinwalk in the body of a smaller animal, as I have to release mass, dump it somewhere, and that always means dumping some of what I am, some of my consciousness, and leaving it behind. The fear that it won't be there when I return is enough to keep me my own size most of the time. Beast hissed at the thought; she didn't like it when I shifted into the form of another animal.

Beast. She is something outside my skinwalker nature—a whole other entity, sharing my body, and sometimes my mind. If I try to rein her in when she wants to come through, she sometimes forces her way in anyway; I don't have complete control over her. And I know, in my bones, that if other skinwalkers exist, they don't have a Beast soul living inside. I'm not sure how we ended up together, and thinking about it always leaves me feeling vaguely uneasy, though I have an inkling that Beast knows and is keeping it from me.

I pulled the travel pack over my head and positioned the gold nugget I wear around my neck on a double gold chain, usually under my clothes, but now swinging free. Together, they looked like an expensive collar and tote, like a Saint Bernard rescue dog might have carried in the Swiss Alps. I bent over and scraped the gold nugget across the uppermost rock, depositing a thin streak of gold. It was like, well, like a homing beacon, among other things.

Yesssss. Hunt, Beast thought at me. *Big!*

Beast was ready to scope out this new territory, but she had an unfortunate aggressive tendency and had, upon occasion, taken on a pack of dogs, a wild boar, or some other animal it might have been smarter to leave alone. When I first shifted in a strange place, her aggressive tendencies always came to the fore and she demanded that I take on mass, adding to my natural one-hundred-twenty-plus pounds, drawing on the fetish of the African lion to skinwalk. "Big is dangerous," I murmured to her. "We're just looking around tonight. Big later."

She panted in derision. *Big always better. Big now!*

But I could tell she wouldn't push the issue. Beast, while always present in the depths of my consciousness, was talking to me as a separate entity now, as a self-aware creature with desires of her own. And for her, hunting was more important than winning an argument tonight.

Going back to the steaks and the paper towels, I placed

the three bloody vamp cloths on the ground, securing them with a pot of geraniums. I climbed the boulders and sat, the rock warm beneath me. Mosquitoes swarmed, biting. I had forgotten about them. Beast hissed.

I opened the zipper bag and pulled out one of the bizarre necklaces inside, the one I used the most, like a totem or fetish, but so much more. The necklace of the mountain panther, commonly called the mountain lion. It was made of the claws, teeth, and small bones of the biggest female panther I had ever seen. The cat had been killed by a rancher in Montana during a legal hunt, the pelt and head mounted on his living room wall, the bones and teeth sold through a taxidermist. The mountain lion was hunted throughout the western United States but was extinct in the eastern states, or it had been. Some reports said panthers were making a comeback east of the Mississippi. One could hope. I didn't *have* to use the necklace to shift into this creature—unlike other species, the memory of Beast's form was always a part of me—but it was easier.

I held the necklace and closed my eyes. Relaxed. Listened to the wind, the pull of the moon, still sickle shaped, hiding below the horizon. I listened to the beat of my own heart. Beast rose in me, silent, predatory.

I slowed the functions of my body, slowed my heart rate, let my blood pressure drop, my muscles relax, as if I were going to sleep. I lay on the boulder, breasts and belly draping the cool stone in the humid air.

Mind slowing, I sank deep inside, my consciousness falling away, all but the purpose of this hunt. That purpose I set into the lining of my skin, into the deepest parts of my brain, so I wouldn't lose it when I *shifted*, when I *changed*. I dropped lower. Deeper. Into the darkness inside where ancient, nebulous memories swirled in a gray world of shadow, blood, uncertainty. I heard a distant drum, smelled herbed woodsmoke, and the night wind on my skin seemed to cool and freshen. As I dropped deeper, memories began to firm, memories that, at all other times, were half forgotten, both mine and Beast's.

As I had been taught so long ago—surely by a parent or perhaps a shaman?—I sought the inner snake lying inside the bones and teeth of the necklace, the coiled, curled snake, deep in the cells, in the remains of the marrow. Science had given it a name. RNA. DNA. Genetic sequences, specific to each species, each creature. For my people, for skinwalkers, it had always simply been "the inner snake," the phrase one of very few things that was certain in my past.

I took up the snake that rests in the depths of all beasts. And I dropped within. Like water flowing in a stream. Like snow falling, rolling down a mountainside. Grayness enveloped me, sparkling and cold as the world fell away. And I was in the gray place of the change.

My breathing deepened. Heart rate sped up. And my bones . . . slid. Skin rippled. Fur, tawny and gray, brown and tipped with black, sprouted. Pain, like a knife, slid between muscle and bone. My nostrils widened, drawing deep.

She fell away. Night came alive—wonderful, new scents, like mist on air, thick and dancing, like currents in stream, yet distinct. Salt. Humans. Alcohol. Fish. Mold. Human spices. *Blood*. I panted. Listened to sounds—cars, music from everywhere, voices talking over one another. Gathered limbs beneath, *lithe* and *lissome*—her words for me.

Ugly man-made light, shadow-stung vision. Yet clear, sharp. She never saw like this. Scented like this. I stretched. Front legs and chest. Pulling back legs, spine, belly. Little clicks fell away. Things from her hair rolled off boulders. Delicately, with killing teeth, lifted necklace she dropped. Hopped from boulders. Landed, four-footed, balanced. Studied garden. No predators. No thieves-of-meat. Dropped necklace near food. Sniffed. Hack of disgust. *Old meat. Dead prey. Long-cooled blood*. Tip of tail twitched, wanting chase. To taste hot blood. But stomach rumbled. Always so, after change. *Hunger*. She left this, an offering.

I ate. Long canines tearing into dead meat. Filled stomach. Cold food did not appease need to hunt. Afterward, licked blood from whiskers and face. Pack and collar in way, but . . . important. Her things.

Memory she buried under skin began to stir. *Ahhh. Hunt. For one of* them. Drew in night air. Delicate nostril membranes fluttering, expanding, relaxing. Many new smells, some with value, some without. Unimportant: close-by smell of flowers, fresh-turned earth, mouse cowering in boulders, small snake on brick. Important: fish, pungent, sour. Salt. Old, still water full of tiny living things. Houses, many, ancient wood and brick. Bike she rode. She—Jane.

Strolled to it, muscles long and supple. Foul smells: gasoline, rubber, metal, wax, fainter smell of new paint. Magic tingle on whiskers. Good bike. Silent-not-dead now, roaring heart still. I approved of it and of her, sitting in wind, smelling world. Fast speed, too swift for hunters to follow. Her territory wherever she wished it to be. Jane hunted wide.

Stepping with care, though new den was walled and safe from humans. Prowled garden and lower porch of house. Drank from water running over man-carved stone. A good place. I coughed softly, approving.

Hunt, the command came again, from her. Long hairs along shoulders lifted in anticipation. Scented air. Food on breeze. Human food, dead, cooked. Human urine. Dog. Domesticated cat. Hacked in disapproval of being *owned*. Even *she* didn't own *me*.

Smells of den grounds settled in olfactory memory. Went to pot. Sniffed cloth trapped there. Drew in scent. Blood. Fear. Humans, three. Alive when blood spilled. One female, ovulating, ready to mate. One man, old, wizened. Likely stringy, tough. New smell to skin.

Melanin, Jane whispered. *He was a black man.*

Last one was male, no melanin, young, healthy. All smelled of fear.

Beneath it all . . . was scent of rogue. Drew it in over tongue, over roof of mouth. Isolating. Parsing scent. Old. Very, *very* old. Anger. Madness. Many scents in layers, different parts of rogue.

Complex scent, she thought. *Like many scents overlapping, compounded. How strange. And what is* that *smell?* Image of her wrinkling weak, useless human nose.

Smell of madness, I thought at her. *Strong. Smell of decay, rot. Rot* . . . Ahhh. I remembered. *Liver-eater.* Long years since smelled a liver-eater. Felt her puzzlement. Pushed it away. Sucked in scent, opening mouth and pulling air over fluid-filled sacs in roof of mouth. Tongue extending, lips curling back. Tasting. Scenting.

Set liver-eater scent signature in memory. Named it *mad one*.

Complex, she thought. *Compounded scent signature,* many *individual scent molecules, pheromones and elements make up its essence. I've never smelled anything like it.*

Many, yes. Many scents for mad one. In a single bound, leaped to top of boulders. Small mountain. Nothing like my territory—no tall hills, deep crevasses. Easy hunt here in land of flatness. No challenge. Tail-twitching disdain for flatness, no tall trees and wild streams. Gathered self. Jumped to top of wall. Standing. Four feet in line on brick. Crouched, making smaller target. *There.* Scented vampire. Easy hunt. Only feet away.

No, her voice came.

Drew in night air again. Scent was wrong. This one female. *Kill it anyway?*

No. Hunt the rogue, her human memory whispered.

Dropped to ground, tail twitching. Eager. Liked hunt. Liked challenge. Liked danger. Moved through shadows of neighbor's yard to street. No dog scent. Good place to come and go. Sat beneath big leaves of low plant, watching. Learning. Scenting.

Saw him, hidden in shadows, sitting on stoop. Watching house, preying on new den. The male she liked, human with bike. Not hunting. Lazy, giving away position. Breathing smoke, scent like scat, marking territory. Strong enough to defend her? Possible mate? If he could catch her. If he could best her. Not likely. She was strong. Beast made her so, long ago.

Felt her puzzlement. Ignored it. Ignored her. Pondered, breath a soft, thrumming pant of throat tissues. Long past time for her to mate. If he could catch her. *Fun.*

Moved through shadows, into night. Humans and pets still about. Stupid little dogs barked. Hairy things, smelling of human perfume, dead food, rotten teeth. Scented me, scented *Beast.* All fell silent. Crouched, tails down. Scuttled away. I hunted, padding through darkness, feral and sleek. Night fully fallen. Humans never saw.

The French Quarter, territory she wanted to hunt, was small. Streets in squares. Buildings built close, squeezed together. Prey could not escape. Hidden gardens. Exhaust. Alcohol, fresh and sweet, and old and sour. Tar on streets, stinky human world.

Sound of music everywhere, loud, raucous. Horns,

drums—drums, like sound of beating heart, racing in fear, ready to be eaten. Smell of money, drugs. Pong of sex without mating. Lonely sex. Many female humans standing on tall spikes. Easy prey. Stores filled with paint and canvas, stone and metal. Much food and smell of sleeping. *Restaurants and hotel,* she thought at me. Smells of her world.

It stank. But underneath stink, other smells sat. Under reek of sewage and stench of dirty river. Under spices humans cook into food. Under odors of humans themselves, perfumed and breathing smoke. Scents of vampires. Many.

Vampire stench was part of ground, part of earth. Their ashes wafted along street, carried in air. Their bones, ground to powder, settled into cracks. Vampire territory, for longer than I lived, even counting time of hunger when I was alpha and Jane was beta. Didn't know numbers beyond five, but there were many more than five vampires. I marked their territories, setting *Beast* scent. A challenge.

Centuries, the thought came from her. *They have been here for centuries.* A long time by human reckoning. Too long for me to understand, or care. Turned back to hunt. Prowled, hiding often in night, scenting, searching. Finding hiding places as moon crossed sky. Crafty, silent, good hunter.

Saw/smelled vampire. Walking alone. Unnoticed by humans. Gliding. Predator. I hunched down in shadow. Jane wished for a cross and stake, Christian symbols to kill evil.

Not evil, I thought at her. *Predator. Like Beast.* She curled lips as if thought was spoiled meat. Together, we watched vampire stroll out of sight.

Long before dawn, scented old blood. Found street where mad one took down many humans, ate best parts. An alley. Narrow, confined. Walls, straight up like water gorge, but without bold river. Strong reek of blood, blood, blood, much blood. Pong of wasted meat. Scented mad one she hunted. Trying to drink enough to find health again. It was dying.

They cannot die, she whispered.

Dies, I thought back at her. *This one sick. Smell of rot.*

Above its reek I smelled angry, frightened humans morning after. Telltale stink of guns. Hacked softly at remembered smell. She liked guns. She hunted with guns. I remembered other. Long barrels, gunpowder, pain, fear, scream of big cat. Hated. Long ago in hunger times.

Placing paws carefully, walked through dark, under yellow ribbons, past dying flowers in tall piles. Along middle of narrow defile. Found place where ovulating female fell. And stringy old one, to her side, cobbles saturated with his need to protect, as if she were his kit, his cub. Healthy young male, three paces away. And more-than-five others. Mad one killed, ate slow.

She said, *It took its time.* She understood time when not measured by moon. Confusing.

Strolled back to alley entrance. Crouched low, belly held off dirty street. Humans walked past, singing, reeking of strong drink and vomit. Then gone. Searched for mad one's trail. Found none going in. None going out.

Looked up. Coughed approval. After mad one toyed with humans, after eating its fill, mad one went up, along wall like spider or squirrel. Tasty meat, squirrels. Not enough to fill belly. Mad one climbed wall like squirrel. Faint scratches where claws dug in. Worthy prey. Even I could not climb wall like this. I hacked excitement. Good hunt. Mad one powerful, smells captured in blood-stench memory. Humans tried to wash away. Could not hide it.

Heard more humans. Close. Two turned into alley. Dirty, reeking wine, sweat, filth. Humans moved in, trapping. I melted slowly into shadows. Soft warning hack. *Beast here. Not hunting, but will defend.*

They ignored warning. Stupid humans. They crawled into large paper box. Sounds of crackling cardboard, shifting humans. Dirty smells wafted. Their den. I had passed it without knowing. Dropped head. Shamed. Foolish as cub. Too intent on mad one and smells of hunt, blood, kills. Foolish. Stupid. Kitten mistake.

Two humans bedded down. Sleeping in open. Easy prey if I wanted diseased, sinewy meat. They talked. Quieted. One snored.

Crept along alley to opening. Dawn coming.

"Pretty pussy. Come here, pussycat."

Looked to side and saw human, eyes open, shining. Hand out. "Come here, pussycat. I got a treat for you."

Hacked, insulted. *Not* domesticated. Beast big. And free.

He held out hand, gesturing. *Come. Eat.* "Pretty pussy."

She was amused. Beast sniffed, mouth open. Beef. Hamburger. Dead, cooked. Jane liked them. I padded slowly to human, shoulders arching, belly low, pads silent. Human unafraid. Drunk. Sniffed offered treat. Stared at him with predator eyes, seeing Beast reflected, golden, in his. Prey should be afraid. Was *supposed* to be afraid.

"Pretty pussy, I know you're hungry. Have some."

Took offered hamburger. Flipped it back, into throat. Meat and mayonnaise. Swallowed. Walked away. She laughed.

I padded back along own scent trail before sun rose. Important, sun rising. She couldn't take back her skin once sun rose. She would be stuck in panther form—a good thing—but she would not be grateful. The night belonged to Beast. Only night. Daytime was hers.

Leaped to top of wall. Dropped down inside garden walls. Strolled, loose limbed and satisfied. Drew in scents. Smell of rotting blood was strong—old cattle, dead, killed by others. Rot, sped up by heat, trapped by wet air. Stench of blood in cloths—slain humans and mad one. Mad one had strange blend of scents, small parts of different things, some known, some not. Sniffed at aged blood on cloth. Familiar. The hunt. Yes, good hunt. With flex of muscles, leaped to top of rocks and lay flat, belly to stone. And thought of her.

Grayness covered me. Light and shadow. Bones and sinew flowed and shifted. Cracked and snapped. Pain stabbed deep and she/I groaned with pain. For a moment, we were one. We were Beast, together.

CHAPTER 3

I'm a tea snob

With a last slash of claws across my psyche, Beast was gone and I was left, my flesh and muscles aching, my nostrils deadened, vision drab and colorless, even as the sun lit the eastern sky. Human once again, my hair draped over me like a shawl. My bones ached as if I were old, in mind and soul.

The final slash of pain had been deliberate. Beast had occasionally referred to me as thief-of-soul, and I knew that I had stolen her, somehow, by accident, so long ago I couldn't remember it, though Beast remembered and sometimes punished me for it. I had feared Beast would not allow me to shift back. There had been times in the past when she held on to her form after dawn, which forced me to keep her shape until dusk or until the moon rose again, part of her punishment.

I don't know exactly how long I lived as Beast in the Appalachian Mountains, my human self subsumed, hiding from humans, from man with his guns and dogs and fire. It was a long time of danger, of hunger. I feared that it might have been decades, far longer than the normal human or big cat life span, and that my kin were all dead and gone, as lost to me as my own past.

I had vague memories of returning to human form several times over the long years, then shifting back to panther, until the final time I shifted to my human shape. It had happened a few days before I was discovered walking, naked and scarred, in the woods of the Appalachian Mountains. I had appeared to be about twelve and had total amnesia, unable to remember language, or how to think like a socialized human. Unable, at the time, to remember even Beast.

I think something had happened, something deadly. I had scars on my human body, bullet shaped. I think—have guessed—that a hunter found Beast. Shot her. And I changed back into my human form to survive, just as I had once shifted into Beast's to survive.

When the memory of Beast came back, other fractured, shattered memories came with it. I remembered her kits. I had memories of the hunger times, when Beast was alpha and I was beta. And before that, I remembered a few Cherokee words. Had memories of faces—elders, most of them. Memories that claimed I was a skinwalker. But that was all. I had no clear memories of time, or how or when I became what I—what we—were.

Since then, I had collected skins, claws, bones, teeth, feathers, and even scales of other animals. I had taught myself to skinwalk into other forms. And it always hurt like blue blazes to shift back into being human. Like now.

When I could breathe without pain, I unlatched the travel bag around my neck and rolled stiffly to my feet. I gathered my things and went into the house. Naked, I padded around my freebie-house kitchen, exploring. Like Beast, I was hungry after a shift, but unlike Beast, I wanted strong tea and cereal—caffeine, sugar, and carbs—to restore my sense of self. Comfort foods. I rinsed and filled a kettle and a pot with water, added salt to the pot. Opened a box of oatmeal from the supplies Troll had provided, and spotted the box I had shipped to Katie's last week. I'd been pretty hopeful about getting the job. Inside were travel supplies, including ziplocked black foil bags of loose tea. I chose a good, strong, single-estate Kenyan–Millma Estate tea. Searching through the drawers and cabinets for a strainer or a tea filter, I found a nook off the kitchen where china, silver, stoneware, and serving dishes were stored in glass-fronted cabinets.

There were a dozen teapots in one cabinet, some Chinese pots—a copper block Yixing teapot and a Summer Blossom Yixing pot, both with square shapes, and one tall Yixing with an elongated spout and top so the steam could cool and fall back into the tea as it steeped. There was one very old, classic Chinese clayware with a rotting bamboo handle. I was entranced. Gingerly, I moved the Chinese pots aside to find two Japanese pots—a Bodum Chambord teapot and an iron pot that looked positively ancient, the crosshatching on the sides almost worn away.

There were English pots in various sizes; porcelain and cast-iron pots with iron handles that rotated across the tops. In the front corner near the door were a dozen tea filters in different shapes and sizes, including a woven bamboo filter that crumbled when I touched it. The cabinet smelled like Katie, though from long ago, the scent muted by time.

I wasn't sure what I felt about Katie loving tea as much as I did. It was the first time I thought about vamps liking anything besides the taste of blood or alcohol. Vamps went by lots of names, individually and collectively: vampire, vampyre, sanguivore, damphyr, damphire, calmae, fledgling, elder, Mithran, childe, kindred, anarch, caitiff, and members of the camarilla, among others. I had studied what little *reliable* info was available about so-called sane vamps, and so far as I was concerned, they were all bloodsucking psychos. It wasn't easy seeing them in another light, and Katie's loss of control when she scented me hadn't helped.

I chose an English eight-cup pot and a filter to match and rinsed them both at the tap. While the water heated and my stomach growled, I found a bedroom suite on the ground floor at the front, showered and dried off, and slung a soft chenille robe, hanging on the bathroom door, around my shoulders. I brushed out my hair and tied it out of the way by flipping it into a knot. I could braid it later.

After dumping my meager belongings on the bed in a heap, I stored my toiletries in the bathroom, my clothes on hangers and wire racks in the closet, and my special wooden box on the top shelf of the closet. The box was only four by four by two inches, give or take, composed of inlaid olive wood from a tree outside Jerusalem. It held charms that had cost me mucho buckos, and were my ace in the hole for killing rogues. The box itself was charmed with a spell to make it hard to see. Not an invisibility charm, but a disguise spell, what my witch-friend Molly called an obfuscation spell. Molly likes big words.

I folded down the sheets and put two vamp-killers—

specially designed knives with a line of silver near the edge—on the bedside table. Vamps couldn't move around in the daytime, but that didn't mean that their human servants couldn't attack. If the rogue had one, or more, he might be sane enough to send them after me. A little silver poisoning if he drank after I cut one might make him easier to kill later.

As satisfied with security as I could be without replacing the doors and windows, I took a tour of the house. It was beautiful, something out of a magazine. It had hardwood floors, the boards twelve inches wide, maybe local cypress; intricately carved, white-painted molding at ceiling and floor; wainscoting in one room, which might have been intended as a dining room; walls painted soft, muted colors—latte, off-white, taupe. Charming antique tables and hand-carved chairs mixed in with comfy modern furniture, and sofas and a leather recliner completed the eclectic look. The AC came on as I explored, blowing up the bed skirt, chilling my skin. Fans turned overhead in each of the twelve-foot-high-ceilinged rooms, redistributing the air. A lot nicer than my minuscule one-room apartment under the eaves of an old house near Asheville.

Back in the kitchen, I turned off the fire under the singing kettle and poured the nearly boiling water over tea leaves in the filter in the porcelain pot. While it steeped, I made oatmeal the way my housemother at the children's home had taught me. Bring slightly salted water to a boil, add whole grain rolled oats—never the instant or quick kind—in equal proportion, and stir until heated through. Maybe a minute. Maybe less depending on my hunger. Dump it in a bowl, add sugar and milk. Eat. With properly prepared tea.

I'm a tea snob. My sensei had introduced me to teas and teaware when I was a teenager and I had made a study of tea after hours, after he had bruised and beaten me into a pulp and somehow along the way, taught me how to fight like a man.

I'd been up twenty-six hours and was exhausted, but I was more hungry than tired, so I ate fast, putting away three bowls of oatmeal. My belly bulged, satisfied, though I got a sleepy wisp of Beast's disgust and an image of a deer eating grass. Ignoring it, I carried the mug with me to the table and tightened the chenille robe. It was clean, and I figured whoever had prepared the house for me had left it. Or maybe the previous tenant had forgotten it when he moved out. He. Yeah. The house smelled of male most recently, over the other scents of the ages.

I sipped and relaxed, my feet in the chair across the table, the robe closed chest to shins. The table was old, maybe an antique, though I hadn't studied antiques. Maybe next year. Or maybe I'd start languages next year; I wanted to learn French, Spanish, and Cantonese—Cantonese because of tea, of course. When I finished the tea—eight cups, four mugs—I rinsed everything and placed pot, kettle, and stoneware on a drying cloth. I tossed the robe at the foot of the bed and crawled between the soft, lightly scented sheets.

Before I slept I called Molly, holding the cell close to my ear.

"Big Cat!" she answered.

"Morning, Mol," I mumbled, feeling sleep pull at me. "How's the kits?"

"Kits? You're still talking like Beast. You hunted last night." When I mumbled a vague yes, she said, "Catch anything?"

"The rogue smells weird. Beast thinks it's dying."

"Vamps don't die. Don't eat that, Evan," she said to her son, without missing a beat. "Crayons look pretty but taste bad. Angie, take the crayons away from him. Thank you. Vamps don't die," she repeated to me.

I closed my eyes, sleep so close it paralyzed my limbs, the world darkening. "I know. Weird, huh. You and your witch sisters figure out yet why Christian symbols kill vamps?"

"Not a clue, but the whole family's looking. Interesting research."

"Night, Mol."

"Night, Big Cat."

I woke at two in the afternoon to the sound of someone knocking. I rolled out of bed, feeling stiff, and pulled the robe on. I was still holding the cell phone and tucked it in the robe pocket. Barefoot, I padded to the front door and looked out through a clear pane in its stained-glass window. On the front stoop was the pretty boy, the Joe. Interesting.

He was standing at an angle so he could view the street and keep the door in sight. The too-cool, all-black look was gone. He was wearing well-worn five-button jeans and a tee so white it had to be brand-new, with scuffed, worn, stained, once-brown leather sandals. The sunglasses were still wrapped around his face. His nose had been broken once. A small scar across his collarbone disappeared into the shirt. On one bicep, I saw the fringes of a tattoo. I couldn't see much, but it was a good quality tat, something dark with globes of red, like drops of blood, the ink bright and rich. An Oriental job, maybe. He hadn't shaved, but the gnarly look suited him. I'd known kayakers—paddlers, river rats—who sported the look almost as well.

As if he sensed me, the Joe turned his head and removed his glasses. Black eyes looked at me through a tiny clear pane. The Joe didn't appear to be armed. He had come to the front door in plain sight of anyone who happened by. I hadn't heard the bike and smelled no fresh exhaust. He'd walked? He was alone. So I opened the door. Heat rolled in, sticky and heavy with moisture. "Morning," I said.

He smiled. It was a really good smile, full lips moving wider before parting, to show white teeth, not perfectly straight, but uneven on the bottom. Something about the canted teeth pressing against his lower lip was unexpectedly appealing. His eyes traveled from my face down my body and back up in leisurely appreciation. "Actually, it's afternoon," he said.

I nodded and my hair fell forward, knotted in a half bun, bead free. I had forgotten to take the stone and plastic beads out before I shifted. Dang. Now I'd have to round them up out of the dirt. "So it is," I said.

"You weren't here last night." When I didn't answer, he said, "I knocked. Walked around. The bike was in the back, I could see it through the gate. But there were no lights on, no sound or indication of movement. You weren't here."

It wasn't a question so I didn't answer; it wasn't quite an accusation, but it was close. This Joe was paying entirely too much attention to me and I had to wonder why. I was pretty sure he hadn't fallen in love with me at first sight when I motored by him yesterday. I let a small smile start and he went on, a hint of amusement now in his eyes.

"When I checked with Tom, he said you had disabled all Katie's security cameras. In eight minutes flat." He knew Troll. More interesting. I quirked a brow, his amusement grew, and he said, "Tom said you gave him a nickname, but he wouldn't tell me what."

"You got a point, waking me from my nap?" I asked.

"Yeah. Let's go for a late lunch. You can call Tom for an intro. Fair warning, though. He'll tell you I'm trouble."

I rested a hip against the door and considered. Whoever he was, he knew Troll, which made him a local boy; I needed someone with local contacts and connections, and it wasn't too early in the investigation to start cultivating sources. With his looks and cocky attitude, I pegged him for a bad boy with associations in all the wrong places, making him perfect for the job. And even bad boys have to eat. "What do you have in mind?"

"Crawfish, hush puppies, beer. Salads if you want 'em," he added, but sounding as if salads were an afterthought. Something he included because girls liked them.

"I've never had crawfish."

"So?" He drew out the word, waiting.

"You got a name?"

"Rick LaFleur."

"Walking or bikes?"

"Walk. I'll show you the Quarter. Or part of it."

I'd seen the Quarter last night, but I nodded anyway. "I'll get dressed." I pushed the door and the Joe's hand caught it, holding it open two inches. I could see more of the tat, four points just above the bloody globes. And another tat on the other shoulder. Black and gray.

"You're not going to ask me in?"

"Nope."

"Kinda blunt, aren't you. Fine. How long?"

"Ten minutes, tops." Rick's brows went up in disbelief. This time when I pushed the door, he didn't try to hold it. He musta wanted to keep his fingers.

I dialed Katie's Ladies, and when a sleepy-sounding female answered, I asked for Tom. Like Rick promised, Troll labeled him trouble, but then offered more. Rick LaFleur was his nephew, a good kid gone bad. Went to Tulane, got a degree, then went to work for a scumbag as muscle for hire. When his new boss went to jail for tax fraud, Rick started doing odd jobs: unofficial security, protection gigs, strong-arm stuff, and some low-level security jobs for the vampire community, Katie especially. He knew people. He had skills usually cultivated by thugs and thieves. Perfect for my needs. Troll suggested I stay away from Rick. I told him I'd take his recommendation under advisement.

Hanging up, I brushed my teeth and hair and dressed in yesterday's jeans, a tank top, and my one pair of sandals in four minutes. No weapons. Not in broad daylight. Not in heat like this. I slashed on a swish of lipstick. Red. War paint, of a sort.

I opened the door and pulled it closed behind me, locking it. Standing on the empty stoop, I saw Rick across the street. His bike was in the shade of a low tree and he was chaining it to the trunk. He stood in surprise, tossed his keys and caught them, tucked them in a pocket. I couldn't see his eyes behind the lenses, but I was pretty sure he was looking me over again.

I pulled my hair back and tied it in a ponytail. The ends hung lower than my hips, curling, kinking in the humidity. I had straight black hair. No curl. Not ever. Not even after I brushed the braids out. Until now. The day was wet and hot. Hotter than I'd ever felt it. And it wasn't even full summer.

My stomach growled. I pulled on sunglasses and stepped into the street, meeting him halfway. "Rick, your great-uncle said you were full of unrealized potential and info," I said.

He quirked a half grin, amused by my blunt manner. "A blight on the family name," he agreed. "And you're Jane Yellowrock. The out-of-town talent."

"You want to chat, let's do it somewhere with air-conditioning and beer."

Rick laughed, flashing the sexy little tooth, and gestured to the sidewalk in an exaggerated bow, like a carnival barker. He smelled good—heat, male sweat, and the faintest touch of scent, like Ivory soap. I resisted the desire to sniff the side of his neck and up behind his ear, but could do nothing about the hungers rising in me, pushing against my skin like a pelt. Beast's hunger, Beast's nature. I sighed. Beast wanted me to mate. She was getting pretty insistent about it, kinda like a mother wanting her daughter to settle down, get married, and have babies. A mother image with fangs and claws. This full moon, when Beast was closer to the surface, and harder to control? Was gonna be a bitch.

It was too soon to pump him for information, so we chatted about the weather, bikes, and music on the five-block walk—the Joe mentioned that, among other things, he played saxophone in a few local bands. It was casual conversation of the get-to-know-you variety, and we ended up in a dive near the river, one long narrow room with a bar on the right and red leather upholstered booths on the left. I'd have wondered at Joe's choice except the place was packed with everything from city blue-collar employees in work boots, to men and women in suits. Banker types. Maybe a few musicians. I smelled grass on some. And in the far corner sat three cops. I'd learned that if cops liked an eatery, the food was good.

The cement floor had once been painted red, the paint worn off except in the corners; the walls were a sun-faded and moisture-streaked midnight. The bar was chipped Formica, black with sparkles in it, and a darkened mirror ran the length of the wall behind the bar. Dirty glass shelves in front of the mirror were stocked with a jillion bottles of liquor; some were dust covered, with curling labels. A fine set of cooking knives, with green stone inlaid handles and wicked-sharp blades, lay in an open, velvet-lined tray, gleaming in the overhead lights.

There was no music, which, as I had discovered last night, was odd for the Quarter. But here, people talked. A dozen conversations wove through the air with the scent of food. The dive smelled heavenly of beer steam, grease, and seafood so fresh it still smelled of salt and sea.

The black man behind the counter wore a crisp white jacket, a tall chef's hat, and a smile. He patted the bar in front of the only two empty round seats and slid over little plastic bowls of hot sauce, ketchup, and tartar sauce. The Joe—Rick—and I sat in the indicated spots. The cook never said a word, just started dishing up food into red plastic baskets lined with newspaper to soak up the grease. He shoved baskets of hot onion rings, hush puppies, and round fried balls the size of golf balls at us; it smelled like heaven.

I tossed a scalding hush puppy into my mouth and bit down, sucking in air to cool my burning mouth. I groaned with delight. "This is good," I said through spiced, fried corn bread and scalding lips. "Better'n good. Wonderful." The man behind the counter set two mugs in front of us, again without asking, full of amber, frothy beer. I drank fast to cool my mouth and tried the onion rings. They too were fried, with beer-batter crust, and they crunched like God Himself had made them in His own kitchen. Lastly I tried the unknown fried balls and bit through the crust into highly spiced, ground hog meat and rice.

"Boudin, dat is, right dere," the cook said. "Good, yes?"

"I'm in love," I said to the cook as I chewed. "If you aren't married, please consider this a proposal."

He smiled, his face creasing into deep, dark chasms, exposing the biggest white teeth I'd ever seen in a human. "Your gal, I like her, I do, Ricky-bo," he said, in what I assumed was a Cajun accent. He glanced at me, a twinkle in his eyes. "But you bes' tell her 'bout my Marlene. I don' like it when a new customer end up bleedin' on my clean, purty floor."

Rick, a half grin on his face, was sitting with both elbows on the bar, a hush puppy in one hand and his beer mug in the other. He slanted his eyes at me. "Marlene is his wife. Two hundred fifty pounds of jealous, dangerous woman."

"And beautiful," the man said. "Don' forget beautiful, you."

"Slap-dead gorgeous," Rick agreed. "Like molten lava on the dance floor. Makes men moan just watching her. But she carries a fourteen-inch knife strapped to her thigh. In a garter."

"Jealous," the cook said again, sliding a steel mesh basket into a vat of hot fat, his chef's hat canted to one side. "Deadly, she be, yeah."

"Killed a woman in here last year," Rick said. He pointed at the floor three feet away. "Woman tried to flirt with him. Died right there."

Finally realizing I was being teased, I tossed another onion ring into my mouth and said as I crunched, "Buried her out back, I'm guessing? Under a full moon? Chants and drums?"

"Under a tree," the man said, laughing. "Marlene done fount her a nice stone from de funeral home. It say, 'Here lay fool woman done been messin' wid my man.'" He dried off a hand and held it over the bar. "Antoine."

"Jane," I said, wiping grease off my fingers.

"Antoine never forgets a face or a customer," Rick said.

"And he knows everything there is to know about this town."

"Handy," I said. I took his hand. It was big, long fingered, and smooth, and when I gripped it, the world seemed to slow down. Like a big bike after a long ride, energies pumping hotly, ready to roll, but puttering down to nearly nothing. Silence when the motor stops, silence almost as loud as the engine, thrumming and cavernous. Antoine stared at me. I stared at him.

His palm tingled with power, prickly and keen, like static electricity running just beneath his skin. Witchy power, like Molly's, yet different in a way I could immediately discern. His pupils widened, his lips parted. Something passed between us. A moment of . . . something. *Crap. What is this?* I seldom felt Beast in my thoughts unless I was in danger, but she was suddenly alert, hunkered, belly down, claws pricking my soul with warning.

Antoine's grip tightened. "Very please' to meet you, I am, Miss Jane," he said formally.

The prickly power traveled up my arm, questing. Beast coughed, the sound a warning deep in my mind. Antoine tilted his head in surprise, as if he'd heard her. "Likewise, Mr. Antoine," I lied, my lips tingly, almost painful, as I resisted the questing power. It slid around my puny attempt to block it. Beast reached out a paw and placed it on the energy that was rising within me. Pressed down on the current. And stopped the sensation.

"Likewise," I repeated. He released my hand, breaking the . . . whatever it was. The world crashed in, loud, boisterous. I took an onion ring and ate it, but the taste was now unpleasant, metallic, faintly bitter. I gulped beer. The odd taste washed away with the yeasty, peaty ale.

"Come anytime," Antoine said. I looked back up, meeting his eyes. They seemed to be saying something more than his words. "We have at night de music and dancing, sometime."

"Spills out in the street," Rick said. "If you like to dance."

I liked to dance. But maybe not here.

Except for the moments when he gripped my hand, Antoine had been working while chatting. He placed a bucket, like a gardening bucket, on the bar between Rick and me.

Beer- and sea-flavored steam curled up, hot with pepper and spices. Rick reached, drew out a crawfish, its red shell curled. I was pretty sure the crustacean had been tossed alive into boiling beer.

I looked at Antoine, seeing nothing of the power that had tried to search through me. I had never felt anything like that before, and the man's genial face seemed to imply that nothing had happened. If he could play innocent, I could certainly play stupid. But I wondered what he had picked up about Beast as he held my hand. Thoughtful, I ate another hush puppy. Rick had brought me here. He had wanted Antoine to read me. I tried to decide if that ticked me off.

Rick met my eyes in the dim mirror, holding up a four-inch-long crawfish as if in demonstration. His face held a hint of laughter and a warmth that claimed he was interested in me, if it was real. It had been some time since I'd seen that particular look in a man's eyes. Maybe since I met Jack when I went into the security business. Not many men wanted to date a girl who could toss them into a corner and stomp them into the dirt. I didn't need protecting and men seemed to sense that. It bothered a lot of them.

And . . . while I hadn't been a nun, I hadn't taken the dating world by storm either. I had friends who juggled several men, in and out of bed, at a time, but I was a one-man kinda woman. So far. And that man had been and gone a long time ago. I decided not to get mad about the reading. Not just yet, anyway.

To get the proper crawfish-eating protocol, I watched Rick as he broke the shell apart across the body, just above the tail, and pulled out the flesh. He ate the mouthful of seafood and then saluted me with the two pieces of mudbug shell. "Suck de head," he said, like someone else might have said, "Cheers," and he sucked the head part. I heard a liquid slurping. Rick smacked his lips and took another crawfish. I shrugged and broke apart the shellfish as he had, ate the meat, which turned out to be spicy with hot peppers, garlic, and onion, and beery. Good. Really good. Then I sucked the head as Rick had, and the spices exploded in my mouth.

He laughed at whatever was on my face, and said, "I forgot to tell you. The spices seem to concentrate in the head cavity."

"No kidding," I managed, half strangling on the potent stuff. "You forgot."

Antoine laughed with Rick. "Dis boy been coming here for twenty year. He always done forget."

CHAPTER 4

You scare the pants offa me

After lunch, my belly distended and my instincts about Antoine squashed beneath gourmand satisfaction, Rick and I walked along the river on a concrete boardwalk. A musician, sweating in the heat, swayed slowly in a patch of shade, playing a baritone saxophone. The jazz notes were low and rolling as the nearby Mississippi, the tune soulful and plaintive. I tossed a five in the open sax case at his feet and we stood to listen. After the melody, we moved on, the musician offering us a nod and starting another tune, the deep notes following us down the walk.

The air was hot and wet and my shirt stuck to my skin like it was glued on, my jeans damp with heat; yet it was an oddly comforting feeling, like a pelt after a swim and a lazy hour in the sun. I wasn't good at social interaction; in fact, I totally sucked at it, but the presence of Rick made the afternoon feel sociable, companionable—a good-looking guy, a good meal . . . But work was work, and I figured it was an appropriate time to see if Rick LaFleur was going to be helpful in my investigation, or just a distraction. I wanted to use his local knowledge and contacts, and that superseded any interest in him in a nonbusiness way. Or so I told myself.

Trying for a light tone, I said, "So, bad boy, blight on the family name. Want to tell me why you came to my house and introduced me to Antoine's delicacies? I'm guessing it wasn't because you saw me on the street and fell head over heels in love at first sight."

He glanced at me through the dark lenses once, and I could almost feel him thinking things through. When he stuck his thumbs into his jeans pockets, I figured he had come to a conclusion. He slanted a look at me over the tops of his glasses, his head tilted down, eyes tilted up, considering. It was a well-rehearsed gesture and it set off my play-dar. The Joe was a player. The realization was surprisingly disappointing.

"I asked you to lunch to see if we could work together." He pursed his lips, considering his words. "But something about you bothers me."

I allowed a smile to start, letting him see a hint of derision in it, but not enough to decide if I was deriding him, or myself.

"I got to tell you, lady, you scare the pants offa me and I don't know why. And you scared Antoine. I saw it in his eyes." He pushed his glasses back in place, hiding his expression. "*Nothing* scares Antoine."

I kept my light tone. "Your pants are still on. Antoine's still alive. I'm unarmed. I haven't killed and eaten anyone. Around here." I let my smile twist a bit and added, "Yet." Rick chuckled. "So why am I scary?" I finished.

"I wish I knew. You witchy?"

"Not a witch," I said, "no."

"Didn't think so. You don't "—he considered and discarded several words—"you don't *feel* like that. But lady, you're not human." It wasn't a question. It was more in the nature of an accusation. And it hit too close to the truth.

I turned on my heel and headed back downriver. "Thanks for the invitation and for the introduction to Antoine." I didn't thank him for the lunch because I had paid for my own.

"Hey, hey, hey. Don't run away mad."

I turned around, walking backward down the concrete boardwalk, and pulled off my glasses so he could see my eyes. "I'm *not* running away. And I'm not mad. I'm just not the kinda gal who likes to play games. You watched my house last night, smoking a cigar, hiding on the stoop across the street." His brows rose and he pulled off his glasses too. Which was only polite and made me see him in a slightly kinder manner. Only slightly. "You make semiaccusations and dance around questions, but you don't ask, you just prod and poke to see what I'll do. You take me to a friend who just happens to have some kinda witch magic and get him to *read* me"—I let some of the anger I felt about that show—"which just ticks me off. So, you see, I'm not mad. I just got better things to do with my time."

"And that right there"—he raised an index finger as if making a point—"is what scares me about you." When I stopped and cocked a brow, hands on my hips, sweating in the heat, he said, "Any other woman would have spent the next ten minutes trying to convince me she wasn't mad. Even if she was. You? You just tell me off. While you walk away. Calm and cool as all get-out. And lady, gals don't usually just walk away from me."

My smile twisted hard and I started walking again, backward, aware of a couple sitting on a bench in the sweaty heat, close enough to hear us had they not been necking like teenagers. Not that I cared. "Macho pride?" I asked, louder, over the distance.

"Fact."

I figured that was true. Women likely flocked to him, hovering like hummingbirds. I had noticed the glances he got at Antoine's, even from the lady cop, interested, willing. He was pretty and smooth. But I preferred up-front to a smooth player. Any day.

"I'm not most women," I said, louder, to cover the distance now separating us.

"I know that. You kill rogue vamps for a living. Took down an entire blood-family, you and a witch and a cop. And the cop died." I stopped walking backward. The couple looked up at the word "died" and focused on me. Blinked. Went back to business.

Rick started walking toward me, lowering his voice. "You and the witch walked out, you half dead, with that scar on your neck. But back then it was four inches wide, red and ridged, brand-new. I've seen the video. But you didn't have it when you went into the mine. I asked people who knew you."

Damn Internet. A college kid, camping in the mountains, had spotted Molly and me coming out of the mine, into the dawn light, both blood covered, me carrying Brax,

Paul Braxton, over my shoulder. Or what was left of him. A young rogue vamp had killed him.

Rick moved toward me, his steps measured, careful, as if he were approaching a wild animal. I tensed and took another step back before stopping. He slowed. Deliberately, I relaxed my fists, took a calming breath, knowing Beast was awake. She always woke when I faced any kind of threat, and I could feel her staring out through my eyes, intense and tightly gathered, ready for danger. I took a slow breath, not wanting to bring her to a killing alertness. But she had gone deadly quiet. Rick stopped directly in front of me, his eyes steady and calm. Studying me. Beast studied him back.

The camper kid had taken a short video with his digital camera when he saw two blood-saturated females walk out of the mine. He had zoomed in on my face, my peculiar amber-colored eyes seeming to glow, an effect that had been blamed on the golden sunrise. What else could it be, right? But it was Beast. And I knew she was staring through my eyes right now.

When word went out that the rogue vamp's entire blood-family had been taken down at the mine, the videographer had realized he had a moneymaker and posted the footage on YouTube. And Molly and I were famous. Yippee.

His voice a murmured burr, Rick said, "After only six months, that four-inch-wide scar is nearly gone." His finger lifted and I watched it rise to me, not a threat, not really. Yet I tensed. He traced the scar above my collarbone, thin white lines with thinner crosshatching, evidence of claws and vamp teeth, his finger slow and delicate, as if he traced the wing feathers of a wild bird. "It travels," he said, stepping so close I could smell the musk of the man, "more than halfway around your neck."

He smelled wonderful. Sweaty, slightly beery, spicy, and . . . meaty. And very male. Beast was very definitely interested. But suddenly no longer in defensive mode. Heat shivered in my belly, clamping down hard.

"Something tried to rip out your throat," he said, his fingers feather light on my skin. "Tried to suck you dry. And nearly succeeded. And you healed from it. Fast."

I stepped back, lifting and setting down each foot, staying centered, balanced. Beast rose in me, gathered. I was on the edge—the edge of what, I wasn't certain—but something in me wanted to nip, growl, and swat the man around. Either wound him or run. So he would chase me. "Molly healed me in the cave," I said, sticking to our lie. "She performed—"

"Not on the full moon she didn't. Your friend Molly is an okay moon witch, but her gift is as an earth witch, herbs and growing things. And dead things, which is why she went in after the blood-family with you and Paul Braxton. I did my research. She can sense dead things. Like vamps asleep in the day." He shook his head, still moving slowly, his eyes boring into mine. Holding me still with his gaze. *Dominant behavior. Mating behavior.* Beast liked.

"No," he said. I felt a spike of shock, as if he had heard my thoughts. But he continued, his words measured and deliberate. "She didn't heal you. Not underground, surrounded by a buncha true-dead vamps." Yeah, this Joe had done his homework. He was *dangerous*.

I felt the move before I registered the tension in his shoulders, his hand forming a claw. To take my neck in his fist. I blocked. Right arm up. Across my body. Fist moving clockwise. My forearm slammed his arm away. One quick step to his side. My foot behind his right leg. I pushed. As he went down, I finished the move. A hard slam to his solar plexus. Maybe a full second of action. His breath whooshed out with a grunt. Pain blanched him, then flushed him.

I walked away. My heart rate hadn't even sped up.

When I looked back, Rick was rolling to his knees, holding his middle, moving as if he hurt, as if he couldn't yet catch his breath. No. Not Rick. Not a man with a name. The Joe.

He stared after me. And he laughed. The laughter hurt; I could see the pain in his face. But he laughed. *Fun*, Beast thought at me. I curled my lips. "Not really," I murmured. "Ten bucks says he won't be back."

Jane can't kill more-than-five bucks. But I can. Beast shared a memory of feasting on a buck, points of his rack standing within her vision. The buck had been two hundred pounds, eighty pounds bigger than she. His blood was hot, his flesh so full of flavor it made the juices in my mouth run.

"Show-off," I murmured to Beast. To myself. We both walked on, sharing the only kind of humor Beast and I could. Blood-sport humor.

Rick's bike was gone when I tooled out of the side garden, braids streaming out behind me, beads clicking, my head sweltering in the helmet, motor rumbling with a heavy, powerful purr. My bike is a Bitsa. Bitsa this and bitsa that. Mostly parts from two 1950 Harley-Davidson FL pan/shovel bikes, modified, not restored to showroom perfection. The bike is dark teal with an iridescent, metal-flake, pearl sheen; it has black shadows of mountain lion forelegs along the gas tank, rising from the seat, between my legs, curved claws extended as if reaching to grab the handles and take over. And in certain light, one can see minuscule flecks of ruby blood streaking the claws. It's a custom, one-of-a-kind job: the paint color, the artwork, and the bike itself.

Hunting for transportation after my last, very profitable job, had been much like hunting for food, and Beast, who seldom entered my conscious thoughts except when danger threatened, wakened when I started looking six months ago, and hung around for the entire search. My Beast had very specific opinions about vehicles. She had refused to let me buy a car or truck, and had simply spat when I showed her a minivan suitable for stakeouts. But the first time she saw the bikes, rusting and busted in a junkyard in Charlotte, North Carolina, she had approved.

Jacob, the Harley master mechanic who had worked as an engine/chassis builder in a Charlotte NASCAR shop for ten years, was more a Zen Harley priest than a mechanic. He'd not so much rebuilt Bitsa as resurrected her into the perfection only a master mechanic could envision. She was still a basic pan/shovel on the outside, but with modern updates, like a dependable, low-maintenance, quiet-running Mikuni HSR42 carburetor and hydraulic lifters; she was a dream bike. We'd had only one argument over Bitsa. Jacob had wanted to install an electronic ignition, but keys are for wimps. Bitsa had an old-fashioned kick start and always would.

We rolled down the street, the roar of the engine claiming our territory as much as Beast's scream would announce and claim hers. Her scream, not a roar. African lions roar, panthers don't. Cougar, puma, panther, catamount, screamer, devil cat, silver lion, mountain lion, and North American black panther, all refer to one beast—the *Puma concolor*—once the widest-ranging mammal on the North

American continent, and one of the three largest modern-day predators other than man. As fierce as they are, pumas can't roar. They scream, hack, growl, purr, yowl, spit, and make low-pitched hisses, and the young make loud, chirping whistles to call their mothers, but they can't roar. Beast considers the gift of roaring highly overrated and likely to draw in the white hunter and his guns. Silent and deadly is better, with screams to frighten prey. She didn't need more. But she liked the roar of the bike. Go figure.

She would likely stay quiescent—she sleeps nearly sixteen hours a day—as shopping, though predatory, wasn't bloody enough to arouse her hunting instincts. I needed cooler clothes to survive this heat and humidity. The temps had reached mid-nineties, with hotter weather called for later in the week. I also needed to meet the butcher who would deliver my protein needs. To meet the ten-day bonus, Beast and I might be shifting every day, a round-trip ticket, making meat imperative. Five to ten pounds of fresh meat and a half box of oatmeal a day, and that was just to restore from two shifts. If I had to fight or run, I'd need a lot more calories.

As we powered out of the Quarter, accelerating down Charles Avenue, it started raining. From a clear blue sky. I sighed. My hair was gonna look awful.

I arranged an account with the butcher to deliver steak whenever I called in an order, and on the way home spotted a Wal-Mart, where I bought a swimsuit, lightweight cargo pants, shorts, tank tops, and a pair of neon-hued flip-flops. A mile distant, I passed a strip mall with a florist, a small Church of Christ, and a little storefront with calf-length skirts displayed in the window. Intrigued, I stopped the bike, unhelmeted, and went inside.

The skirts were patchwork. Not like something a sixty-year-old hippie would wear, but dainty, flared, delicate confections made of tiny, two-by-four-inch patches of gauze or silk or cotton in vibrant colors. Each one was color coordinated, all blues or teals or reds, and some were embroidered. I lifted a patterned gauze skirt in sea blue and purple and shook it gently. The hem flipped, flirty and cute. I didn't do cute well, but I liked this. The elastic waist would allow it to ride low on my hips if I wanted it to, or higher, on my waist.

"That would look totally rad on you."

I glanced at the teenaged girl who was sitting behind the counter with a paperback book in her hand. "Yeah?"

"Yeah. But you gotta see it with this shirt." She slid from a stool, taking a foot off her height, making her just over five feet, and walked to a shelf, pulling a shirt out. It was a peasant top with a drawstring neckline, made of the same sea blue material, but this time partnered with a paler purple fabric. "And this," she said, holding a purple and teal stone necklace. "Amethyst and chatkalite. Totally cool with these sandals." She lifted a pair of purple sandals from the front window, with straps for dancing.

I looked at the freckled girl, grinning. "I suck at putting outfits together and you did it in less than a minute."

"It's a gift," she agreed. "Try 'em on. You want I should pick out another one for you?"

I turned the tags over and winced as I looked around the small store. "It'll break my budget to leave this store with another one."

"And it'll break your heart not to," she said sagely. "I'll find you something just as cute but cheaper. Go on." She flapped a hand at me and I went. I tried on clothes for nearly an hour, a huge record for me. I left the store with two pairs of shoes, two skirts, three tops to mix and match, and the necklace. Six outfits. How could I say no?

Back at the freebie house, the clothes went into the closet with the rest of my meager gear. I travel light, just what will fit into the saddlebags, and the things I can't live without that get mailed to my new address each time I move, like my tea. The weapons in the closet took up more room than the clothes. A traveling vamp killer has to make do.

I cleaned up and changed into my only other pair of jeans and my Lucchese boots. I had an appointment for dinner at Katie's. I studied the papers in the envelope Troll had given me, including the info on New Orleans' vamps, and read over the fine print in the contract, making sure the clause about collateral damage I had insisted upon in our Internet negotiations was still there. If I found that the rogue vamp was being given safe haven and I had to kill one or more vamps to get to him, I didn't want reprisals. The special clause guaranteed me protection. It was present.

There was also a confidentiality clause stating that I

wouldn't share with the media or anyone else anything I learned about the vampires, their servants, or their households on pain of a slow and grisly death. Not that I planned on going on national TV with an exposé of the vampy and fangy, but it did bring me up short. Even knowing that the clause made perfect sense from their standpoint, the "slow and grisly death" line was pretty gruesome.

Near the bottom, there was a welcome line about needing to hire local contacts and a budget to pay sources who might not talk otherwise. From the way I read it, it looked like the council was willing to cover such expenses, pending Katie's approval. Sweet.

In the vamp info folder, I found a toll-road sticker for my bike and a list of New Orleans' seven vampire clans, digital photos of the head vamps, and a breakdown of the vampire power structure. It was similar to a parliamentarian government, with heads of clans sitting on the executive council, and elder vamps sitting on an expanded council. The council made decisions on finances, kept the peace with humans, worked with human law enforcement, and enforced its own laws on its members, including holding down the number of scions, blood-servants, and blood-slaves that one vamp clan might have. Interesting info, but not real useful when tracking one nutso whacked-out vamp that the council hadn't killed off or even managed to identify.

I signed the contract, input into my cell phone the contact numbers Katie had included, and jumped the brick fence. I didn't want the blasted Joe to know where I was. He was back in his hidey-hole, watching my yard, smoking another cigar. Making me wonder who he was working for, keeping an eye on me . . . Well, not for the rogue vamp. They were too mentally unstable to keep someone under thrall for extended periods of time. And the Joe—not Rick, just no-name Joe—hadn't smelled of vamp. But Katie for sure had other enemies. I didn't even have to ask. Vamps always had enemies, and the older the vamp, the more enemies. Living and dead.

I presented myself at Katie's back door at seven p.m. on the nose. Troll opened the door and stood there, staring at me, blocking my way in. I feigned nonchalance, while wishing I had come armed, and said, "Evening. I'm supposed to interview the girls."

"Join them for dinner. Not interview."

"You say tomato, I say interview. But I'll be nice. No broken arms or blood."

I coulda sworn Troll wanted to smile. He pushed open the door, but still kept it blocked with his arm and body. "You disabled all Katie's security devices."

"Yep. Contractual agreement." I slapped the contract on Troll's chest. "No spying on the help. I'm sure she just forgot to have the cameras removed."

"You found 'em all. Fast." He took the contract, but didn't step aside.

I touched my nose and quoted the short salesgirl. "It's a gift." I added, "I can smell security devices." Which was a total lie. But I could scent out where a human had spent a lot of time in an odd place. Like over the mantel, in the closet, in the kitchen, installing the bugs. "Time for my question. Why did Rick LaFleur show up at my place today?"

Troll tilted his head, thinking. I could see things happening behind his secretive brown eyes, but his body language gave nothing away. Maybe working with a vamp teaches you to keep everything inside. "Rick wanted the job hunting the rogue."

Okay. That was no surprise. "You ticked off that I got the job and not him?"

"I told Katie to hire you. Rick's good but not good enough to take on a rogue. My family knows it and asked me to keep him out. Which I did. You tell him that and I'll gut you like a pig."

"Thanks for the warning. Any chance he's working for Katie's opposition?"

"No chance in hell."

"So he's watching my place because he finds me irresistible?"

Troll's eyes went wide, surprised.

"Yeah. That was my feeling." I tucked my hands in my jeans pockets and wondered how much longer Troll was going to make me stand in the heat and chat. Cool, air-conditioned air flowed out around us and dissipated fast while I started to sweat. I could feel the silver cross under my shirt, the only thing I wore that could be considered a weapon, gathering moisture. Even my scalp was sweating. "He wants to work with me on the rogue deal," I said, "and

I'm interested in someone with local contacts if he's legit. And if the council covers the expense."

"I'll talk to Katie," Troll said, shaking his head. "How do you like your steak? Baked potato with the works? Salad?" He finally stepped aside and let me in, shut the door behind me, and locked it.

"Light a match under the meat, and if it's still mooing I won't be insulted, anything full of fat on the potato, and salad is for cows. Cola, with caffeine, no alcohol." I walked into the house, waiting for him to make a move. He didn't. He just pointed to the right and said, "Katie will leave you alone with them for an hour. The girls gather for dinner in the common room."

"Okay. And Troll?" He waited. "When I jumped the fence, I noticed that someone installed a security camera recently on Katie's side of the fence, pointed at her house. Within the last month. The scratch is still fresh. They came in from my side of the fence."

Troll cursed. He disappeared down a darkened hallway.

CHAPTER 5

It was wicked sharp

I'm sure television had cemented my ideas about what a hooker—a working girl—was like. Crass, hard-eyed, crude, probably diseased. And my Christian children's home upbringing had pounded the image in. Katie's ladies blew all that away in five minutes. They were seated in elegant chairs in a formal dining room, around a dark, carved-wood table, sleepy eyed and attired in brocade robes with tasseled belts, their hair in silken waves, their skin perfumed and oiled. They all looked and smelled healthy. Though with a distinct aura of vamp clinging to them.

There were six girls, and a seventh met me in the hallway as I entered. Three girls were Caucasian: a blonde, a crimson-haired beauty with emerald eyes, and a white-skinned, black-haired girl who caught my attention with the witchy energies around her. Three of the girls were dark skinned—one with skin so black it looked blue in the candlelight, one South Asian who looked twelve, and one with coffee-and-milk skin, hazel green eyes, and kinky blond hair. The seventh was different. She jingled as she took her seat, pierced, tattooed, and dangling rings from eyebrows, lips, nose, ears, navel, and nipples. She was wearing low-rise velvet harem pants and a peekaboo bra, so I wasn't guessing. And she wore a braided leather whip over one shoulder. The whip looked so supple it likely left no marks on human skin.

"I'm Christie," she said. "You looking for work? 'Cause Katie already has a full house."

Before I could answer, the walls vibrated as if electricity quivered through them. And a vampire screamed. The sound shivered, ear-piercing, like nothing in nature and nothing man had made. So high-pitched it came closest to sounding like a police siren. It was the sound they made when they died.

Beast flashed into me and I whirled, raced down the hallway, faster than a human could follow. I raced past Troll, opened the door, and slid into the room where I had been interviewed. Katie stood there, fully vamped out, claws extended, canines a good two inches long, pupils black and huge in bloodred eyes. The stench of wormwood filled the room.

Cripes. Beast slid to a halt. Troll pushed me aside and stood in front. The doorway behind filled with lovely ladies.

"Go back to dinner," Troll murmured softly, a measured monotone. Katie's face flashed to him. She raised her claws and hissed, animalistic. Beast understood. *Fear. Killing frenzy*. I got a single image of Beast attacking a doe. And her fawns. Raging, terrified, *hungry*. I backed out the door and closed it, standing with the girls in the dim hallway, surrounded by their perfumes and whispery clothes.

"I've never seen her like that," one whispered.

"I have. Tom can handle her." But there was a trace of uncertainty in her voice.

I said, "Let's go back to the dining room. She can smell us out here."

"How do you know?" Christie asked, close on my left.

I looked at her, my vision adjusted to the low light. Her eyes were wide and she cradled the whip in both hands, so tightly her knuckles were bloodless. I couldn't exactly reply, "Because *Beast* can smell *her*." I settled on a shooing motion and took a step in that direction, knowing that herd mentality would make them follow. Beast had once informed me that humans were hunters only by luck and because they had opposable thumbs. Otherwise they were prey. And not very tasty at that. I had been too scared of the inference to question her further. I really didn't want to know if I/we had eaten humans. Really, really didn't.

Back in the dining room, a black woman, distant relation to Methuselah, shuffled in wearing a floor-length black dress, a starched white apron, and loose house shoes, her sparse gray hair in a bun. She was pushing a cart laden with salad bowls. Without speaking further, Katie's ladies filed around the table and sat. I took one of three empty places, in the middle, not at the foot or head of the table. "Thank you," I lied, when a salad bowl settled on the spotless white tablecloth in front of me. I didn't have anything against salads—especially when they came smothered in bacon dressing—I just didn't crave them.

"You are most welcome," she said, her soft voice accented, but with what native language I didn't know. She placed a wineglass near the right side of my plate, and a water glass on a coaster to protect the dark wood beneath the cloth. I took one look at all the silverware and felt a faint panic. At the children's home I used a knife, fork, and spoon. Drank milk. Prayed over my food. Washed dishes. Since then, I had eaten with fingers over the kitchen sink or with claws in the grass and not thought much about it.

I watched the girls as they each lifted a silver—cripes, real silver—fork and started eating salad with oil and vinegar dressing. No bacon. As a guest, I was gonna havta eat it too. It had been weeks since I remembered to bless a meal, which brought on a fit of guilt, and, though it probably made me a bad guest in a vamp's home, I closed my eyes for thanks before selecting a similar short-tined fork and eating. As I chewed, I took in the room. Paintings hung in gilt frames, all portraits of Katie in various stages of undress. Heavy brown and black striped drapes covered windows on the far wall, tied in place with big tassels and fancy ropes. A thick, modern-looking rug in the same shades was beneath the table, black silky fringe on two ends.

When the salad was gone, I said, "Katie wants me to talk to you girls about the—"

Katie appeared in the doorway. Didn't move into view, simply appeared. Vamp fast. Beast threw back my head and shoved my chair from the table with a squeal. Katie's shaking hands braced on the jamb to either side of the door as if to hold her up. Her hair hung down in a snarl. Blood coated her lips and chin. "Jane. Come," she said, breathless.

Her eyes looked human, and her canines were snapped

back into the roof of her mouth, but she smelled of fear and fresh blood. Beast bristled. Not knowing what else to do, I followed Katie to the office, holding Beast down with an effort of will; she hated tagging along to another predator's den. As I followed, the vamp turned on the sconce, brightening the hallway with a touch of human color. But the scent of blood was growing stronger. Beast fought to get free and my lips curled to expose killing teeth I didn't yet have. Katie didn't glance my way.

In the office, the scent of blood and meat was so strong my stomach knotted. Contrary to books and movies, humans can't smell fresh blood, only old and decomposing blood, but Beast can. She gathered herself and growled, low in my throat. Troll sprawled on the leather love seat, blood clotted on his throat and T-shirt, his outer shirt ripped open. His skin was grayish blue, his eyes rolled back in his bald head. His chest rose with a shallow breath. Beast settled to her haunches in my mind, waiting to see what I'd do.

"I hurt him," Katie said, her voice astonished. "I . . . I took too much." She looked at me with empty eyes, the eyes of a child who had made a grave mistake and didn't know how to fix it. I relaxed my fingers, which had formed into fighting claws, and crossed the room, keeping Katie in sight. Kneeling, I checked Troll's pulse. Thready and weak, way too fast. His skin was cold and ashen, shocky. I inspected his neck. The punctures were neatly constricted closed. At least he wasn't losing any more blood. I adjusted his head slightly to open his airway, hoping Katie hadn't broken his neck while feeding, hoping I hadn't just paralyzed him.

Among the courses I had taken since I graduated from high school had been an emergency medical technician class, but I didn't have supplies to help him. I traveled too light. "He needs a transfusion," I said, "and fluids. Call 911."

"No." Still moving on the edge of vamp speed, she knelt, the motion graceful and wilting, and lay the back of her hand on Troll's cheek. The gesture looked tender and caring, in stark contrast to her refusing her employee medical attention.

"Why not?" I said, keeping my tone steady.

"They will arrest me." She looked at me across Troll's body, distressed and helpless. *Yeah. Right.* "I have supplies," she said. "I know you are capable of inserting an intravenous needle. You studied medicine. Rachael and he share a blood type. She can donate."

Katie had clearly studied my Web site well, and had discovered that I was a certified emergency medical technician. I sat back on my heels, though Beast sent me an image of vulnerability, a cat with belly exposed. When I could speak without a challenge, which could stimulate a vamp on edge, I said, "Are you out of your freaking mind?" Okay. Not challenge-less, but better than what I wanted to say. "I'm not gonna start an IV and give somebody blood. If I gave the wrong type I could kill him. Not gonna happen." I stood and looked down at Katie, at the desperation in her eyes.

"Do you know what happens to vampires in jail?" she asked. "We are chained in a dark room, without blood, and left to rot."

"That's just an Internet myth." At least I hoped it was. Laws for equal rights and legal protection of supernats was not something Congress was eager to push through. Most of their constituents hadn't exactly laid out the welcome mat to the vamps and witches when they'd been revealed a few decades back. Troll moaned, ashy, his breathing shallow. His carotid pulse fluttered like a dying bird. "Call your doctor," I bargained, beginning to feel desperate.

"He is too far away. If you will not help with the transfusion," Katie said, "then at least start intravenous fluids." She stood and went to the bar.

I swiveled so my back was never turned to her, and watched as she opened a door on the bar to reveal a well-stocked medical supply cabinet. *Well, looky there. How handy,* I thought, feeling sarcasm ripple through me. This wasn't the first time Katie had needed to treat a wound. Who woulda thunk it. I wondered how close to the killing edge Katie was. Lore claimed that vamps who started making blood mistakes late in life sometimes went feral, like the rogue I was hunting. Interesting. In a maybe-deadly kinda way. Beast didn't like this. And neither did I.

Still keeping Katie away from my back, I checked the expiration dates on the saline and the sterile needles and went to work. I tied on a tourniquet and found a vein, inserted an eighteen-gauge needle. It was a large-bore needle, suitable for giving blood, and had to hurt, but Troll didn't even flinch. I attached the line of fluids to the Jelco valve and turned on the saline, open all the way. Katie watched as I squeezed the bag to force fluid into Troll's system faster. "He needs a doctor," I said, hearing the near snarl in my voice.

"Will you make the call?" she asked, plaintive.

"Why don't you?"

"I don't know how," she said. I looked up in surprise. Katie handed me a cell phone. "I know the correct number is in the phone book inside that but I do not know how to use it. And I do not wish to leave him, to go . . . back and find the number."

Back. *To her lair*, I thought, deciding it must be too far away to make the trip easily. Yet she was here, on site, before the sun set. That gave me pause, though I didn't let her see me react. I punched a few buttons on the phone and found the address book.

"Ishmael Goldstein," she said.

I scrolled down, found the name, and punched SEND. The number rang on the other end and I relayed the message to the man who answered. When he questioned who I was, I gave Katie the phone and then had to show her how to hold it to her ear. She confirmed what I had said and I hung up. "You don't know how to use a cell phone?" I asked.

Katie shrugged elegantly, her eyes on Troll. "Things change so quickly. There was a time when only fashions changed, not how one lived. Now, to live requires constant adaptation. I do not like it." She looked at me, and some of the helplessness fell away. Her voice strengthened and her shoulders went back. "I have a telephone. But not like Tom's. He handles all matters of an electronic nature for me. It is his job. A matter of employment."

"So I see." I kept my voice neutral. If she heard a trace of snideness in my tone, she chose not to react. "You want to tell me why you went feral on me?"

Katie placed a long-fingered hand on her throat. "When I woke I knew something was wrong, but I couldn't place it. And then Leo contacted me." From my research, I knew Leo was Leonard Pellissier, the head of the vamp council in New Orleans. "He told me that Ming never woke. Her human servant entered her lair. . . ." Katie stopped to breathe, but vamps didn't need much air except to talk. That alone would have told me she was upset, even without seeing Troll near death. "She was missing. There was much blood in her crypt. Hers, by the scent." She looked at me. "Leo is on the way here."

On the heels of her statement, the doorbell rang. I figured with Troll a little under the weather, it fell to me to open the door and provide security. I gave Katie the saline and showed her how to squeeze the bag. With her occupied, I went through Troll's pockets looking for weapons. I found a specially designed, steel, twelve-inch-long, single-bladed, silver-edged vamp-killer. With a rogue on the loose it made sense for Katie's bodyguard to carry one. I had a few myself.

Troll had it strapped to his thigh with an opening in his pocket that allowed him to slide a hand in and withdraw the knife. Without getting too friendly, I unstrapped the sheath and strapped it on my own leg. His .45 I carried, safety off, finger on the trigger, from the office into the foyer. On the way, I opened the closet door where I had previously deposited my weapons and retrieved the stake I had left in the corner. It was always smart to have a stake handy when meeting a vamp on unfamiliar territory. I tucked the stake in my waistband and hoped I didn't hurt myself with it. It was wicked sharp.

There was no peephole in the door—no weak spot for someone to shoot through—but I spotted a modified highboy; its hinged top opened to reveal a series of monitor screens, part of the house's security system. There were a half dozen camera screens—most of them showing unoccupied bedrooms—and one was a small screen displaying the front stoop. Early night had fallen and the door lights had come on, revealing two men, a well-groomed guy wearing a dark suit, and a larger, broad-shouldered bruiser. Leo Pellissier and his right-hand man, blood-servant, and muscle. I held the gun out of sight, pulled the small silver cross from around my neck, took a deep breath, centered my footing, and opened the door. The muscle, seeing an unfamiliar face and the suddenly glowing cross, drew a knife and attacked.

I sidestepped fast and stuck out a foot. He tripped. Oldest trick in the book.

I was on him before he hit the floor. Riding him down. Troll's .45 rammed against his spine at the base of his skull. We hit. Bounced. My heart pounded. Beast growled.

Faster than thought, the vamp's weight fell on me. His hands encircled my throat. Tangled in my braids. He hissed. Fangs extended with a soft snap. They brushed the side of my neck, a predator's killing bite.

I rammed back my head. Connected, skull to something softer. Heard an *oof* of expelled breath. The pressure on my throat lessened. I slapped the cross on the back of the vamp's hand.

He howled. Fell away. I rolled, pulling the guard with me, until we lay on the floor, the gun at his neck, his body on top of, and protecting, mine. The reek of human sweat and vamp pheromones bathed the air. This one smelled of anise and old paper, maybe papyrus, and ink made of leaves and berries.

"I'll shoot your blood-servant if you move again," I said, my voice pitched low and cold. Leo paused, that inhuman, vampy shift from combat to utter stillness that was so startling. "If you listen, I'll let him live," I bargained. The stillness went deeper. I felt the servant gather himself and I clawed my hand around his throat, fingernails digging into his windpipe. I shoved the muzzle hard under his ear. "If you resist, I'll rip out your throat, then behead your master. Pick and choose." A shocked silence filled the foyer. Slowly, he went limp. "Wise move.

"Leonard Pellissier." I focused on the dark form, silhouetted by the streetlight flooding the open doorway. "I'm Katie's out-of-town talent," I said, using the Joe's phrase. "The tracker and hired gun the council contracted to take out the rogue. I don't want to kill either of you, but I will if I have to. The blood you smell was not spilled by me. I am not your enemy." Well, not right now, but nobody was taking notes. "Back. Off."

He backed. I tightened my grip on the bruiser. "You gonna play nice?" I felt him swallow under the pressure of my hand.

When he spoke it came out in a whistle from the pressure I had on his windpipe. "Yes." I heard truth in his tone, smelled it on his body, along with Leo's scent of ownership, the smell of vamp. I released my hold. He rolled to his feet and I followed him upright, keeping him between Leo and me. He reached around and shut the outer door. When he moved to face me, in front of and slightly to the side of Leo, I switched the safety on the gun. I was lucky it hadn't gone off while we rolled around on the floor. It was stupid to wrestle while holding a gun, even while facing down a vamp. Not that I could have figured out a better way. I had been between a rock and a fanged place.

"You don't smell human. What are you?" Leo said. Trying out his vamp voice on me, smooth and honeyed, and promising me a really good roll in the hay.

"Stop that," I said. "It doesn't work on me."

"She growled, boss," the bruiser said. "When she took me down."

"I heard her. What are you?"

"None of your business," I said.

"Whose blood do I smell?" Leo asked.

"Katie—" I stopped, not knowing what to say. Admitting that Katie had made a mistake by taking too much blood was on a par with saying an adult human had pooped his pants or eaten his own boogers. Really gross or stupid. Accidentally killing prey was a young vamp error, not something an ancient vamp did. Ever. And not the kind of thing a good employee said about her employer. The silence stretched, and Leo's brow went up. Just one. Waiting.

"I was forced to reprimand a member of my staff." Katie stood in the hallway, wearing a dressing gown that shimmered like silk. She was clearly naked beneath it, the thin fabric blood free and molding to her thighs. Not what she had been wearing. "May I ask that your blood-servant assist with the transfusion?" she asked. "It is not my intent to lose him."

I understood immediately. It was okay to nearly kill someone as discipline, but not by accident. Feudal attitudes, something the vamps had left over from, well, from feudal times. I understood it, but I didn't have to like it.

Leo glanced at his servant and the man looked reluctantly from me to him before he nodded. It was clear he didn't like the idea of leaving me alone with his boss, but he was willing if Leo gave the go-ahead. Leo inclined his head. Regal, giving permission. Bruiser rolled his head on his shoulders, and I heard two cracks as his spine realigned itself. He gave me a hard look, promising to kill me slowly if I acted out again, and went down the hallway, his booted feet silent on the wood and carpets. Predator silent.

"Your new guardian used a cross on me," Leo said, holding out his left hand. A livid burn, blistered and seeping, marked his hand, in the shape of the cross. Silver. I wanted to grin but that seemed impolitic. Katie moved to him and knelt at his feet.

"Humble apologies, my master," she murmured, as her blond hair fell forward, hiding her features. "May I be allowed to offer healing, or do you wish to chastise her yourself?"

Crap. I tensed. Leo lifted one corner of his mouth at my faint motion and speared me with his eyes. I stared back, though I didn't meet his gaze. Black eyes, coffee-and-milk skin, dark hair falling in soft waves to his shoulders. French lineage, maybe. Aristocratic and elegant. His photos lied. In them he looked ordinary. In person the vamp was drop-dead gorgeous. The drop-dead part would have been funny if I didn't feel like an insect about to be stepped on.

His smile widened, as if he read every thought in my head, from gorgeous to squashed. "If she dishonors me again," he said, "I will kill her, rogue vampire to be contained or no." He held his injured hand to Katie. She did something behind the curtain of her hair and I smelled vamp blood. A moment later, she stood and raised her bleeding wrist to Leo. He took it in one hand and pulled her to him, the motion exposing the side of her body as the robe fell open. The whites of his eyes bled red; the pupils expanded black as he vamped out. He put her wrist to his mouth, bit, and closed his lips around the wound. And he sucked. But his eyes were on me.

I felt the pull of his mouth as if he drank from my wrist. Heat blossomed in my belly. Beast rumbled a growl I just barely controlled. Leo chuckled deep in his throat, drinking. I couldn't help myself. I slid my fingers around the hilt of the vamp-killer. Those red-as-blood, black-as-death eyes followed the motion. And then looked into my own eyes. I resisted everything I saw there. Everything he made me want. *Son of a freaking sea lion.* This guy was good. Powerful as the devil himself. I looked away, at the floor, knowing he saw it as weakness.

I felt the cross grow warm and tucked the silver icon in my back pocket, hoping the glow didn't attract Leo's attention. No one knew why vamps reacted to Christian symbols and the symbols to them, and I didn't figure that now was the time to ask.

Moments later, Leo pushed Katie away. He raised his left hand, inspected the mostly healed skin, and wiped the blood smear from the corner of his mouth. And licked it. He was laughing at me. I could see it in his eyes. He was also testing to see if the sight of a vamp drinking would shock, repel, or excite me. Beast was interested, from a strictly predator standpoint, but that wasn't the emotional reaction Leo was watching for.

Katie knotted the belt of her robe, her eyes glittering behind the veil of her hair. "You may go," she said softly to me. "Report back before sunrise. You may speak to the girls then."

I was dismissed. And Katie was ticked off. I nodded once and backed down the hallway. In the office, the bruiser was attaching an archaic-looking, Y-shaped tubing from a girl to Troll. The right blood type was the redheaded girl with emerald eyes, Rachael. From her place on the couch, recumbent, she stared at me, expressionless. The bruiser followed her gaze.

I put Troll's weapons on the huge desk, noting that the center part was darkly tanned leather, worn and distressed. "Troll will need these," I said. "Tell him thanks."

"Troll?"

I tried to smile and found my mouth didn't want to. "Tom." I pointed to his patient. His expression altered with amusement and he pointed at himself. "You're Bruiser," I said.

"I have a name," he said. "I'm George Dumas."

I looked him over. Six-four, weight lifter, but not to bulging excess; rather, he was slender and toned, brown eyes and hair. Clean-looking with a sculpted nose, long and sort of bony. I had a thing about noses and his was primo. Not that I would tell him. "So what," I said, not sure why I was being rude except that I didn't want to express an interest in someone who might become an enemy. His eyes widened at the insult.

I left the room and took the narrow hallway to the back

door, the one that led to the garden. As I pulled the door closed behind me, I heard the doorbell ringing. Probably the first of Katie's Ladies' party customers. Not something I wanted to see.

I went back over the wall and got ready to shift. Time to hunt.

CHAPTER 6

Paranoid sometimes pays off

I groomed cow blood from face and paws, studying night. In mountains, moon was bright, different light but same shape. Edges sharp. Hungry moon. Not hunting moon, not round and full. There, stars were so many even Jane couldn't count them. Here, surrounded by *man*, moon was dull, stars few. Stars hid near man. Man and his false light.

Clean of cold beef blood, I breathed in stink of human blood and vampire spittle on cloth she left under plant bowl. Dead humans and *it*. The sick thing. *Mad one*. Short, fast sniffs drew scent deep inside. And . . . found something new. Not noticed before. Opened mouth, extended tongue, hard, lips back. Pulling scent across roof of mouth. *Yessssss.*

Plant pot rocked. Predator hackles rose. Placing paw on pot, batted it. Pot rolled. Scattered plant, roots, soil. *Alive*? Motion like porcupine. Not good eating. Pain. Careful of spines, batted again. It rolled. *Injured!*

Crouched. Unsheathed claws. Swatted. Hard. Pot-animal rolled to bench, hit, broke. *Kill!* Bounded up. Landed crushing weight on pot. Gripped broken body in claws. Soil spilled out from split like blood. Injured prey again pot, now broken. Sniffed, smelling man-blood on base. Smell of mad one. And faint odor of . . . other. Scent not in memory, not exactly. But also familiar. I rumbled deep. Spat.

Hunt. Command from deep inside. She was impatient. Shoved her down. Silent.

I flexed shoulders and leaped to fence top. Paused. Landed on other side. Crept to side of neighbor-den, beneath bushes. Into night. Circled block to front of Katie's. Mad one, rogue vamp, had been here. Heartbeats ago. Fresh/rotten scent overlay Leo's and Bruiser's. It tracked them. Waited in doorway, across street. I counted—two doors down. Watching, hiding in shadows. Rancid reek of excitement, mixed pheromones. Complex odors.

Vamp form of adrenaline, she thought. Knew about adrenaline. Tough meat if slow kill, or long chase. Better eating to lie in wait, drop on prey. Fast killing strike. But sometimes fun to chase, play with food. Difficult to choose. Tender meat or fun.

Scent called. Strange smell that almost was. Sick thing moved on. Keeping to shadows, its excitement potent. *Hunting*. Cars passed. Followed when shadows fell again, nose low. Smelled prey-scent beneath mad one's footsteps. Human female, walking. Sex-smells, many partners. She was unmated, searching. Loneliness was forceful, buried in scent.

I remembered true mating, before she came. Before we became Beast. Her surprise stirred, deep inside. Memories of *before times* were buried deep, beneath *after times* with her. Shocked her. She struggled. I batted away thoughts like plant pot. Useless. Later. *Hunt*.

More-than-five blocks later, smelled fresh blood. Crouched in shadow of alley wall. Crept forward, paw, paw, paw into darkness, belly hairs dragging across dirty stone of man-road. Mad one crouched in man-light. Wrinkled. Dry. Rotted. Stink of rich new blood. Human. Eating sounds. Mad one ate without regard for thief-of-food. Gray light and blackness formed over it. It seemed to *shift*. To *change*. Wrinkles faded. Rot smell died.

I hunched close to road. Padded close. Within range. Gathered all power in. Weight balanced. Silent. Sprang. Through air. Long tail revolving for stability. Forelegs reaching. Unsheathing claws. Lips back. Mouth open. Killing teeth bared.

It looked up. Glimpse of face, pale in dim light. And was gone. Gone. *Fast*.

Shock flooded through. Overshot place where mad one was, and now was not. Passed through empty air. Retracted claws. Lifted paws to break fall. Crashed hard into brick wall. Weight on one pad, bending into it. Body whipping. Hard slam. Bruising shoulder. Ramming hip. Drop to ground, eyes searching.

Strange sound. Look up. *There.* On ledge, one, two stories. Too high to leap. *It* clung to window ledge. Looking down. Laughing. I growled, spat. It jumped. High, to rooftop, running. Not hiding escape. I raised head. Screamed frustration. Echoed. Wild.

Get away, she thought. *Get away and shift back. White men with guns.* Image was memory, one we shared. White men hunting big cat.

Her thoughts came to fore. She was expert in man-world. For now, we shared control. Raced to alley opening. Down block. Into shadows. Creeping around tall, blocky truck. *Hummer.* Siren sounds. Police. Near kill.

Sped through dark, avoided human prey-groups. One witch family, celebrating, power leaking in sparkles. Almost back to Katie's. Sick scent suddenly overlapped. *Fresh.*

Hunched, nose low. Mad one came back this way. She went silent. I bent, took over. Drawing short steady drafts, air and scent, tongue extended to taste/smell. Looked at sky. Sunrise far off. Crouched. Followed, silent in night. I am good hunter.

Mad one crossed bridge over big river. Bridge full of cars, light. No shadows to slink across. I climbed high on steel. Truck drew near below, spitting clouds of poison. Pulled paws close. Timed passage like running prey. Leaped.

Claws and paws hit, scrambled. Metal scratched beneath. Crouched, catching balance. Like riding buffalo, rocking, claws scrabbling, instinct seeking flesh.

On far side of big river, city thinned, smells changed. Less death: sour river water, dead fish, alcohol, exhaust. More prey: domestic and feral cat, many dogs. Big rats—nutria. She had studied. Twenty-pound rats. Good to eat? Birds—prey and predator. Owls hunting. Bats. Squirrel, small mouthful. Mosquitoes, too small to catch. Swamp. Spill-waters emptying into lakes around New Orleans. Still-water stretched ahead. Sharp, pointed moon reflected on top.

Truck slowed. I jumped, landed. Drank water full of plant stuff and crawly things. House squatted in dark, down short road, just ahead, man-light in windows like predator eyes. No other houses near. Moved on bent legs, tail tucked close, following scent, to house, warded with power. Not witchy power. She came alert. Remembering. *The People*, she thought.

Her kind. Cherokee. I pushed her down. *My hunt.* Followed scent of mad one around property. Domesticated cat, dog-scent. Pets inside, with humans. In back, in trees, was low, wood hut. *Sweat lodge*, she thought, her excitement high. *An elder lives here. I remember!*

Inside, I put paw on her mind, demanding silence. Padded to lodge. Ground rank with mad one. Scent followed path, into woods. Well-used path. Lair near? Or it hunted elder.

No! she thought. Vision of kits, helpless. *To be protected*, she demanded. *Such is an elder.* I forced her down, deep, silent. She struggled. Swiped at her with inside claws, scoring her mind. This is *hunting*. She fell silent, angry, worried.

Tracked mad one into woods, pines, firs, oak, maple, sweet gum. Soil heavy with rotten stench. Elder's dogs had fed it, two dog bodies decaying in brush. This was hunting ground.

I moved slowly, tail held straight behind. Remembering speed of mad one. Didn't move like sick prey. Moved like wind, unseen. Fast. I stopped often, scenting air. Circled back, sniffing, into trees. No fire had cleaned forest; underbrush was thick. Path only way. Trap? Mad one would understand traps.

Trees opened into clearing, floor of pine needles. Hunched down, waiting. Nothing moved. Slowly, I circled open space. Found nothing, no out-moving path, no trace of scent leaving. Carefully moved into clearing. Soil rank with its scent, heavy with reek of old blood. Liver-eater rot. It hadn't left. Yet was not here. Puzzling. A game and hunt for her, for Jane.

I looked at sky. Little night left. I/we were far from new den, from rock she marked to find place. Far from food that did not have to be stalked. Much dead cow in cold place in den.

Refrigerator, she thought at me. *In the freebie house.*

Turning, I padded back down path.

Near dawn I stopped at edge of city, in safe place, full

of shadows. Garden near house where family slept. One snored. Jane awoke, clamored to be alpha. If I did not shift, Beast would *be* all day; she would not. But bad in this hunt. I/we slid beneath plant. Crouched. Let her come. I/we shifted. Gray place like half-dark of cave swallowed me. Light and dark, lightning in storm-torn sky. Bones slid, popped. Pain cut through like a thousand knives.

Hissed. Was gone.

I lay, naked and filthy on the ground, panting, trembling like I'd been struck by lightning. A spider crawled across my foot and I shook it off. The gray place of the shift had seemed to last longer than usual this time. I had no idea what really happened when I shifted, though I had seen a digital video of it, taken by Molly not long ago, and I didn't really disappear into some other realm. I just glowed like light and shadow, like lightning in a storm cloud. I figured it might be something like quantum mechanics or physics, my cells actually moving around but not going anywhere. Something like that. It wasn't like I had anyone to ask. When I got my breath, I rolled to all fours and to my feet.

I needed calories, fast, but first I needed clothes. I pulled off the pack and unrolled my clothes. Carrying them so tightly rolled meant they were always horribly wrinkled, but it was better than going naked. I slid into jeans and tee and strapped the pack, now containing only money, cell phone, keys, and weapons—a stake, a cross, and my derringer—to my waist and slipped on the thin-soled shoes. No bra, no undies. But covered. I wrapped my long hair in a knot, out of the way. At least it always shifted back untangled. Squaring my shoulders, I moved into the dawn, out from the eaves of a house. I had no idea where I was on a map, but my cat senses said I needed to head northeast. And I needed food. My stomach growled loudly.

In the early light, I spotted a convenience store and bought a candy bar for the calories, a Coke for the caffeine energy punch, and a new tube of lipstick. I took them to the bathroom, where I cleaned up, washing my face and arms, scrubbing beneath my nails. I'd need to call a cab, and no self-respecting cabbie would stop for someone who looked as if she slept in her clothes under a bridge abutment. As soon as I was more presentable, I went back to the cashier, paid for a second candy bar and put on my best I-partied-all-night, world-weary look.

"Can you tell me where I am?"

He laughed. He was maybe eighteen, pimply chin, greasy hair, and smelled of weed and last night's beer. "You're near Lapalco Boulevard."

"I just came from woods, a swamp, and a lake that way." I pointed. "What's there?"

He laughed again, thinking me too much a party girl to remember where and with whom I'd spent the night. Which was what I wanted him to believe. His leer was a pain, but I could live with it. "Jean Lafitte National Historical Park? Maybe Lake Catouatchie? There's several lakes out that-away."

I held up a five. "This is yours if you call me cab. Someone I can trust to get me back into the Quarter."

He leaned over the counter, resting his weight on an elbow. "I'm off in a couple hours. I can take you."

I smiled, looked him over as if interested, and shook my head. "Tempting, but I got to be at work in an hour. I need fast as well as trustworthy."

He sighed and pulled a cell phone. "You ought to reconsider. Jobs are a dime a dozen. Good fun is a lot harder to come by, and we could have some *fun*." I shook my head again, this time adding a rueful, regretful smile, and he punched in a number. The person who answered said, "Bluebird Cab," so I relaxed. I might be a bit paranoid but paranoid sometimes pays off.

He pressed the phone to his ear, cutting off the sound. "It's Nelson. I'm at work, but there's this chick who needs a cab into the Quarter." He looked at me. "You got cash? It's gonna cost you."

I held up a ten and a twenty. "After that I'm tapped out till payday," I lied. Too much cash might make me a mark. I didn't want to start my day having to break someone's arm.

"She's got money. Sure." He hung up. "Five minutes. My cousin Rinaldo. He's okay. Married with five kids. Works third shift *and* drives a cab to keep 'em all fed. I tried to explain to him about birth control, but he ain't the brightest bulb, you know what I mean?" He was trying to make a joke, and laughed as if he was really funny.

I smiled and nodded. "Thanks. I appreciate it."

He took a card from his pocket and passed it to me. "Call me next time you want to party. I got access to some stuff. You know?"

"Thanks," I said, pointing to the card. "Put Rinaldo's number on back. Never know when I'll need a cab in the morning." When he was done, I tucked the card in my pack and walked out the door. Minutes later, Rinaldo pulled up in a yellow cab with a large bluebird painted on the forward doors. He looked me over, waved me closer, and unlocked the doors with an automatic click. I climbed in back and gave him my address. "And I need breakfast. Drive through a fast-food place and I'll treat us both."

Rinaldo studied me in the rearview and said, "Yo."

I took that as a yes and lay my head back. I was exhausted.

The Joe was sitting on my front stoop when I got out of the cab. I had made arrangements with Rinaldo to pick me up in the mornings wherever I happened to find myself. Making nice with a cabdriver was always smart. I had learned the hard way that getting home on my own wasn't always easy or even feasible. And the places where I shifted back to human weren't places a cabbie would come unless you were a regular. Thinking I was the party girl my tired face and red lipstick proclaimed, he told me to be careful, call him anytime, and sped off.

I looked at the Joe and sighed. I needed a shower and a pot of tea and my bed. Not this.

"You want to tell me where you were last night?" he demanded.

"No. I don't. Get away from my door." When he frowned, I crossed my arms and jangled my keys. "You're not my daddy, my lover, or my boss. Where I was is none of your business. I'm not in the mood for this. I'm tired and I need a shower and I'll bust your chops if I have to. *Move*."

"I got questions." He eased to the side and I opened the front door. He stepped in after me, fast enough that I couldn't have shut the door on him without shoving him back first.

I sighed again as he followed me to the kitchen where I turned on the kettle. "Fine. But I'm getting a shower first. You can wait."

I closed my bedroom door and stripped, climbing into the hot shower for a personal grooming session. I didn't have much body hair, courtesy of my Cherokee blood, but what I had came back in every time I shifted, as if I had never shaved. Shifting every night made it a pain.

When I was pretty sure the kettle had been whistling for a long time, I turned off the water, pulled on a ratty T-shirt and shorts and went back to the kitchen, my wet hair soaking through the thin cloth down my back. He was at my kitchen table, sprawled out like he owned the place, his sunglasses near his left hand and his eyes on my legs as I walked to the kettle.

"I took it off the fire and poured it over the leaves," he said.

Surprised, I lifted the plastic lid of the tea strainer and sniffed. I had left a strong Madagascar Vanilla Sunday Blend in the strainer, sitting in the teapot, waiting. And now it was ready. "Thanks," I said, and poured it into a twelve-ounce mug, added a dollop of sugar, and stirred. "Want some?"

"I'm good." He seemed a little less demanding than on the stoop, and after a good wash I was feeling a little more magnanimous. But I had a feeling this conversation was about to get either very physical or very full of lies. I wasn't in the mood for either.

I had eaten six Egg McMuffins and downed three Cokes, so I wasn't hungry this morning. Which was probably a good thing. When humans saw me eat, they tended to get bug-eyed at the quantity. Rinaldo had assumed I had the munchies from drug use. I hadn't told him any different.

I sat across from the Joe and sipped, thinking. I wanted to say I owed him no explanations, but he was a local, with contacts I didn't have. I could humor him. A little. "Okay. You're here. I've had my shower. I have my tea. I'm listening."

"Where were you last night?" When I shook my head, he said, "How'd you get out of here without me seeing you?" I shook my head again, letting a smile start, and he narrowed his eyes at me. "How did you spot the camera looking into Katie's backyard?"

Oh, yeah. The camera. If he had been hoping to do Katie's security and he missed a camera that I found, that could only make him look bad. "That, I'll tell you." I let my smile spread and lowered my eyes to the tea. "I'm good." I sipped.

He huffed, a belligerent laugh, and let the silence grow, his eyes on me like a weight. But, in the game of waiting contests and which predator will blink first, he broke. His hostility melted in a plosive puff of breath and a faint stench of frustration. "Fine. You got ways of doing things I don't. You got the job; I didn't. But a girl was killed last night. By the rogue."

"I know. I saw him."

The Joe—Rick, he did have a name—sat up, gathering himself. I put down my mug, freeing my hands, and waited to see what he would do. He was wearing a T-shirt again this morning and, as his biceps bunched, the bottoms of the tats were more visible than yesterday. Definitely claws on the left arm. Something dark and fuzzy on the right arm and shoulder. I wanted to see them, but figured if I asked him to take off his shirt, he might get the wrong idea. I was so tired, I grinned without thinking.

"It isn't funny," he said, his voice low and dangerous. "I knew her."

I held up a hand, palm out, fingers splayed to show I meant no offence, and shook my head. He settled slightly and I picked up my mug again. "I'm sorry for your loss. If it makes you feel better, I wasn't smiling about the girl."

"You saw him kill her?"

"No. I was tracking him." Which was the truth, except Rick would naturally think I was following by sight, not by smell. Here was where our conversation would devolve into lies, partial lies, and total lies, and where I would get tripped up if I made a mistake. "He went around a corner and I paused too long, thinking he might have seen me. He got her before I could react. He's fast. He went up the wall when he spotted me." I watched Rick's face. He was studying mine. "Straight up. I'd always thought that thing about vamps being able to fly or climb walls was myth."

Rick shook his head. "Only the old ones can climb like that. The real old ones."

"And you know that how?"

"I know Katie. I asked."

And she just answered? I remembered Beast's first foray into the Quarter. The smell of vamps everywhere. There were a *lot* of real old ones. "I followed from the street as he ran across the rooftops." Also truth, well, sorta. I finished off the tea and stood to pour another cup, but kept my body at an angle and Rick in my peripheral vision.

"Nobody saw you," he said. "Cops were on the scene almost instantly."

It sounded like an accusation again. I shrugged. He was persistent and curious. Persistent and curious people often stick their noses into things they shouldn't, and this guy looked like a prime candidate for that particular trouble. I needed to point his nose into directions useful to me, keep him where I could see him, use him, and distract him away from things I wouldn't share. "I need backup on this and I got a budget. You want the job?"

"Yes. And I want to know how you get out of here without me seeing you."

I glanced back at him. Time for another lie. "You know the saddlebags on my bike?" I turned back to the tea. "Like that."

He sat back, amazement crossing his face. "You know a witch who can make an invisibility charm?"

Invisibility charms were legend, not reality, so far as I knew, but enough people claimed they existed to merit the lie being taken for truth. "Not quite. But sorta. She calls it an obfuscation charm." I added more sugar and stirred, keeping my face turned away. I didn't lie well and I knew it. "You won't see me come or go unless I'm in the mood to let you."

He stood and came close, leaning on the counter, facing me, a little inside my personal space. "What'll I be doing if I work for you?"

I took a breath to answer and felt it stop, felt my ribs freeze in motion. I inhaled slowly then, drawing in the air. The scent. His scent. I leaned in and pulled the air near Rick through my nostrils, feeling him tense when my face passed close to his neck. I pivoted, standing behind him, leaning in. His hands fisted in shock but I couldn't stop. I opened my mouth and pulled back my lips, pulling in his scent.

It was familiar. One of the smells on the cloth Beast used to track the rogue. *This scent.* A woman's perfume, a woman's body, so faint on the vamp I had hardly noted it. The Joe—Rick—wore the same scent the rogue carried.

They had been with the same woman. With, as in *with*. How could anyone, even a human, bear to be with a sick, rotting rogue? Yet I didn't smell rogue on Rick, only the woman. So why not? Why hadn't she carried rogue stink back and forth between the two men?

I clamped down on my reaction and stepped to the table. When I set the mug on it, my fingers trembled. I made a fist to hide it. I needed privacy to analyze all this. "Today, nothing," I said, picking up the conversation as if nothing had happened. "Tonight, I'll give you some addresses to track down, owner, renter, property owners nearby, that sorta thing."

"What the hell was that?" he asked.

I shook my head, letting the shorter hairs around my face fall forward. Hiding again. "Nothing. Now get outta here. I need a nap." Suppressing my trembling, I walked to the door and opened it. Held it wide.

Rick stood by the table for a moment. I was afraid he might demand an answer, maybe a lot of them. I knew what I must have looked like, sniffing him like an animal. I was afraid I'd say something to alert him to what I was or what I discovered. I couldn't look him in the eyes.

He slid his sunglasses on and walked to the door. And outside. I closed the door behind him and rested my weight on it. Whoever the Joe had slept with last night or this morning, sometime recently, she was sleeping with the rogue vamp too. How could she stand the reek of rot? And why wasn't it on her too?

CHAPTER 7

Fly it

I needed Mol's help. I dialed her cell and listened to the rings, leaving a succinct message when I got routed to voice mail. "It's me. Call. And check the wards again." I pressed the END button and curled up on my bed with the cell on the other pillow, knowing Mol would call me when she finally checked the messages.

Like most witches, Molly was forgetful. She even occasionally forgot to check her house wards, the ones that protected her home from casual observation by the federal government's newly established Psychometry Law Enforcement Division, the so-called PsyLED. It was a branch of Homeland Security, and the PsyOffs—PsyLED officers—were still gathering info on the nation's supernats. So far, Molly's kids were off the grid. Keeping her home and property from leaking magical energy was the key to keeping them safe.

Desperately sleepy, my limbs feeling weighted with lead, I closed my eyes.

I woke at three p.m. to the sound of knocking on the front door. My bedroom was L-shaped, with the short side on the front of the house. I peeked through the window and saw a marked cop car parked in the street, a man in uniform and a woman in a jacket and khakis on the stoop. I looked in the mirror and frowned at myself. I looked ratty, not the way the out-of-town talent, the hired gun the council had contracted to take down the rogue, should look. If this was Katie's liaison with the New Orleans police department, then I was going to make a really bad first impression. If Rick had gone to the cops about my seeing the rogue, then I was going to make a worse impression. And I hadn't washed the blood from my steak meals out of the grass in the backyard. *Stupid. Crap.*

One of them knocked again, less politely this time. I walked to the foyer, slapped the locks off, and opened the door, holding on to the door and jamb, arms stretched up high. I yawned widely and studied them through slit eyes and a strand of snarled hair. The guy was looking at my legs and the patch of belly showing between tee and shorts when I yawned. He was mid-forties and smelled of Cajun spices and aftershave. Lots of aftershave. I wrinkled my nose. The woman was younger, a little stout, bobbed hair. A lapel name badge said she was Jodi Richoux. Yep. Katie's liaison. I finished the yawn and said, sounding grumpy, "Yeah?"

She made a face at me. "Jane Yellowrock?"

"That's me. And you're Katie's pal at NOPD. Come on in." I pushed the door wide and walked to the kitchen, deliberately scratching at my armpit. I didn't like cops but I did enjoy messing with them. Much like the way Beast liked playing with her food before she killed it. There was a certain kind of challenge to the cat and mouse. "I'm making tea," I said, over my shoulder. "I don't have any coffee or donuts for y'all."

"I understand that you eat a lot of steak," Jodi said.

And the game begins. I grinned and shoved my hair back from my face. "I'm a carnivore. Veggies are for sissies." I filled the kettle while the two surveyed the kitchen. "You been talking to my butcher, I take it."

"Him. A few other people."

"Have a seat," I said.

"Mind if I look around," the guy said, "stretch my legs?"

Pointedly, I looked at his name badge. "Yes, Officer Herbert, I do mind. Have a seat or take a hike." I pointed at a chair and back to the door.

"And why do you mind?" Jodi asked. "Do you have something to hide?"

"Not especially. I just don't see any reason to let him paw through my undies without a warrant. Bring me a warrant and you can rattle around all you want. Just know that my landlady had the place wired with cameras. Not much privacy if cameras are rolling twenty-four/seven." All entirely the truth. Katie had indeed had the place wired. The cameras were simply not rolling anymore. And that part I didn't share. Life was so much easier without actual lies to remember. The cops looked at one another, startled. I could almost see them rearrange their tactics. I pointed again at the kitchen chairs. "Sit."

"Abear," he said, sitting next to the chair I had pointed to.

"Say what?" I put the kettle on the stove and turned on the fire.

"My name. It's pronounced Abear. The French pronunciation."

I thought about saying, "Big whup," but didn't. No point in stirring the pot just yet. When I didn't respond, except to open a bag of cookies and slide it on the table for them, Jodi asked, "Where were you last night?" She wasn't sitting. Jodi was standing at the corner of the table, back a little, so she could see both of us but not get in the way. Interesting position.

"All over." I leaned into the corner of the cabinets, the counter at my hips, and crossed my arms, putting one foot on the cabinet behind me, as if propping myself up. The fact that the position gave me leverage to leap was not incidental. "I was up and down the street in front of Katie's Ladies on Dauphine, down St. Louis Street to Royal. I wove around a lot after that."

"A girl was killed on Barracks Street last night. It's come to our attention that you might know something about it," Jodi said.

Well, well, well. Rick had been talking. Was he a source? "Something," I agreed, making it sound like it wasn't much.

"You want to tell us about it?" Implied was the threat that if I didn't want to talk here and now, we could go to the department. Where I could cool my heels for a few days in lockup.

I kept my voice unemotional when I answered. "I was hired to track down the rogue vamp. I followed him there. I was too late to stop him. He had drained and was eating the girl when I arrived. So when he booked, I tailed him."

"Where did he go?" she asked, her voice tight, her eyes focused tightly on my face.

"Over the rooftops, mostly, and across the river, where I lost him."

"You should have called us," she snarled.

"My cell was dead." Now that was an outright lie, but I wasn't going to admit that I had paws and couldn't dial. Nor was I going to say that I wouldn't have called anyway.

"How did you track him?" she asked. They were both listening with the kind of intensity cops saved for child rapists and serial killers. And cop killers.

"Line of sight and with a little witch amulet. Tracks vamps. One of a kind and expensive as all get-out." Lie number two. I couldn't afford to go much higher and keep my story straight.

"So, you saw him. Got a description of the guy?" Herbert/Abear said.

"Middle height, slender, long dark hair, hooked nose. It was dark and he was fast. That's all I got. Not enough to work with an artist," I added, to keep me out of NOPD HQ.

"I want to see this amulet."

My cell phone rang from the bedroom. "Excuse me." I grabbed the phone and returned to the kitchen doorway where I could keep an eye on them. The number displayed was Molly's.

"Witchy woman!"

"Hey, Big Cat. What's up?"

"Good timing on the call. I got two cops in my kitchen. They wanna know about the tracking amulet you gave me. The one for whacked-out vamps, not the one for humans."

"There's no such thing."

"Fly it."

Molly laughed. When a spell didn't work, she made paper airplanes out of the scratch pages and flew them across the room to entertain her kids. "Did you have a blood trace to work with?"

"Big-time," I said.

"Put me on with them."

I blanked the screen and handed the phone to Jodi. Saved by the bell.

I ate a cookie and listened to the cop chat with Mol.

Molly likes cops even less than I do, having had to register as a witch with the local law, but she'd had mostly redneck, hillbilly types as role models. I had met some nifty cops in my time and some were okay. Some, however, were on ego trips, had authority issues, or were chauvinist pigs. Herbert was an ass. I was withholding judgment on Jodi.

The lady cop handed my cell back and I said into it, "Thanks, Mol. I'll call back later."

"You having problems down there in the steamy South?" she asked.

"It's interesting."

"So, maybe I'll come visit sooner than we planned. Kill that rogue so it's safe." She laughed and cut the connection. I hit END and set the phone on the counter.

"So. May I see the amulet that tracked the vampire? And a demonstration?"

"No and no. Goes back to that warrant thing. Bring me a piece of paper and I'll share. Till then, no way."

"Why don't you like cops, Miss Yellowrock?" Herbert asked.

"I like some cops just fine. But I don't like all cops just like I don't like all dry cleaners or all street sweepers or all nurses. The job is fine, but it doesn't necessarily attract the best people. You want to go have a beer, maybe take in a movie, I might find you're charming as hell and the salt of the earth. So far, right now, I'm not too terribly impressed."

"She's glib," he said to Jodi, sounding mean and malicious. His face had twisted as I spoke and now he looked a little on the cruel side too.

"Shut up," Jodi said to him.

I laughed. "What you really want to know is how I found the rogue when you couldn't and why the vamp council hired me when they had enough money to hire the French Foreign Legion. Then you want me to promise to bring you anything I find out, including any interesting facts or info on my boss and her cronies, the vamp council."

Jodi opened her mouth, then closed it on whatever she had been about to say. Her eyes had sharpened, however. I grinned at her. Ate another cookie. Let the silence build in the kitchen. After a few minutes, Jodi said, "What are you?"

I hadn't expected that. It was one thing for the supernatural community to know I wasn't human. It was something else entirely for mundane law enforcement to know; cops might tell PsyLED. I held myself still when I wanted to spring across the table, claws slashing. Beast was awake and listening. Beast was of a mind to *gut them and ask questions while they die*. I held her down. After a pause a fraction too long, I put a thoughtful, agreeable tone in my voice and said, "I'm the best rogue-vamp tracker on the East Coast."

So. Who squealed? The only ones who knew I wasn't human were Katie, Troll, Bruiser, and Leo. I bit into another cookie and talked around the crumbs. Back to being rude, crude, and deliberately disagreeable. Back to giving the cops something to think about other than my more subtle reactions. "I don't have an aversion to sunlight or silver, I like garlic and old Bela Lugosi movies, and I attend church. I can't do spells and my witch pals tell me I'm not one of them. So I guess that makes me human, though that often puts me in bad company.

"I'm licensed to carry in most of the southeast states, and could get a waiver in the rest of the states." I swallowed and went on. "I have a hundred-percent track record. Most recently, I took down seven of seven in a raving-mad, young-rogue blood-family. I'm proficient, though unrated, in street fighting and swordplay, and I'm a good marksman. All that you can get off my Web site. I'm guessing you want to know something not on the site."

I raised my brows and let my most insolent grin start. "I'm straight. I wear size seven shoes. I like steak. Oh, wait, you know that already. I like to dance, and this verbal boogie with you two makes me think I'll go dancing tonight." I shrugged.

"One thing you left out." Jodi flashed a small black case at me, about the size of a pack of cards. It had a dial on it, like a Geiger counter, and the needle was pointing a little over halfway along the face, at sixty-two. The sight of it chilled me to the bone. *Crap. Crap, crap, crap.* Beast raised her lips and showed her teeth in threat. I smiled and ate another cookie. "Why you set off my psy-meter," Jodi said.

Sixty-two was halfway between a vamp at midnight and a moon witch on the full moon. Pretty dang powerful. I had wondered what I would read. Psy-meters, or psychometers, had been written up years ago in policemag.com. They were expensive, and, according to the magazine, only used by federally funded law enforcement agencies like the FBI, the CIA, and PsyLED. I had figured I would never see one, but here was a psy-meter in little old New Orleans. Lucky me.

"I hang around witches," I said, my tone nonchalant. "I have some powerful witch amulets. Molly washed my clothes before I left Asheville." I shrugged, lifting one shoulder, and ate another cookie though the crumbs stuck in my throat. "Pick one. I don't really care."

"We don't much like witches in New Orleans," Herbert said.

"Why not? They did their best to steer Katrina and Rita and Ivan back into the gulf," I said. The cop's face twisted in prejudice and hatred. *Ahhh.* I'd found his hot button and the reason he was brought to visit me. Beast could smell the adrenaline bead into Herbert's sweat. This guy was a serious witch hater. Which ticked me off.

"Not their fault that one coven didn't have the power to send major storms packing," I said, flicking crumbs off my T-shirt onto the floor. "Mother Nature's bigger than any one family. But they did get Katrina to drop from a category five to a cat-three at landfall. You gotta give them credit for that."

He stood, placing his hands on his gun butt and his nightstick. "Don't gotta do nothing."

"You gotta be a dickhead," I said, mildly. "No help for it."

He started around the table. I grinned at him. Beast nearly purred. *Fun . . .* I saw an image of her playing with an injured rabbit and let my grin widen. But I carefully didn't move from the corner. Jodi said nothing, watching us speculatively. Yeah. She'd picked her position.

"We don't like witches in N'awlins, no better'n we like vamps," Herbert said, moving in on me slowly. He hooked a chair with his foot and slung it aside with a screech of wood. Beast watched him through my eyes. *Fun . . .* She gathered herself. I held her still. "Vamps, who killed a dozen cops and ate 'em like they were meat. And you're working for the cop killers."

When he was two feet away, Jodi grabbed his arm and said sharply, "Jim. Go wait outside, please."

"Yeah," I said, pushing things and unable to help myself. "No one knows if the cameras in the walls also have audio or if they're straight video. You might just appear on YouTube making an ass outta yourself, and spouting off something NOPD would consider seriously anti-PC. The vamps bring a lot of tourist money in. I bet no one wants to annoy the moneymakers."

"The vamp council can kiss my—"

"Jim! Outside. Now."

He jerked away and stomped to the front door. He slammed it on the way out. I laughed and felt a bit guilty all at once. Though Beast was having fun, I didn't particularly like the fact that I enjoyed baiting the law. It wasn't smart or safe.

"You're not going to help us, are you?" Jodi asked, her voice so soft that it might not have carried to the imaginary audio pickups.

"I'm going to kill the rogue who's killing your cops, your hookers, and your tourists. Sounds like help to me."

"Are you really human?" she asked again, her voice soft with real curiosity.

"I already addressed that question."

"Your papers claim you're twenty-nine, but you act like a fifteen-year-old kid half the time and a fifty-year-old grandmother the other half. You carry yourself like a street fighter, you set off my psy-meter, which means you're leaking power, carrying power of some kind, or generating power, and you deliberately taunt a cop when you might need us."

"You brought him here to see what I would do when he got stupid," I guessed, but making it like a statement. Jodi had the grace to blush. I huffed a laugh. "Good cop/bad cop works only in the movies. I have your cell number, Jodi. I'll call if I need backup. I'll call if I need information. And I'll call if there's anything that NOPD needs to know."

"Why didn't you just offer that right up front?"

"Why didn't you just ask for it right up front?"

Jodi stared at me, uncertainty in her eyes. I said nothing. She said nothing. After a good minute of that, she heaved a breath and turned to the door. "Thank you for your time."

Silent, I followed her to the door and locked it after her. When they pulled away, I walked to the bedroom and threw myself onto the bed. Could I be any more stupid? Could I?

Beast purred in happiness. *Fun . . .*

I wished that Molly would call. On the heels of the thought, the phone rang. I rolled over, yawned at the ceiling, and answered. Molly's number showed on the readout. "How'd you do that? You're a witch, not a psychic."

"I didn't," she said. "Angie told me." We were both quiet for a moment at that one. The girl was scary strong. When Angie came into her power, she had been terrified, magic rushing out of her in a maelstrom, destroying the trailer they lived in at the time. When I rode up, it was to see the metal roof peel back as if with a can opener. Not knowing what was going on, I raced inside, right into the magic. And I shifted. It scared the pants offa Big Evan, who hadn't known what I was. Molly can keep a secret.

Evan and Molly had been trying to bind the girl's power, to keep it controlled until Angie was older and could handle it. Power, oddly similar to the gray place I saw when I shifted, was blowing through, ripping at everything. Angie was screaming. It was crazy. Beast, unafraid, had padded right up to the child and curled around her. Purring. Angie had gripped Beast's ears and pelt and hung on, screaming. Which had left Molly and Evan free to work. Without asking, I knew Molly was remembering too. Into the silence I asked, "Let me talk to her?"

Angie's little voice said, "Aunt Jane? You got my doll yet?"

A lump grew in my throat. It often did when I talked to Angie. Beast had adopted her like a kit, and so both parts of me loved her. "Not yet, darlin'. But soon."

"Okay. I love you."

The lump in my throat spasmed painfully. "I love you too." *Kit. Cub*, Beast murmured, sleepy and longing. When Molly came back on, I said, "So. You want to come visit me here in the hot, muggy, Deep South."

"You kill that rogue and we'll come. Evan's talking about finally adding on to the house after six months of dithering. I am *not* going to live in a house open to the elements, with carpenters and bricklayers traipsing through." Unsaid was the fact that the house would remain unwarded during the construction. "Later, Big Cat," she said. "And stop messing with the cops. Angie said you were playing with them." The connection ended.

Too wired to go back to sleep, I dropped over at Katie's Ladies, knowing it was too early for the girls to be up, but worried about Troll. The woman who had served dinner last night answered the door and peered up at me over her bifocals.

She waved me in and I followed as she tottered back to the dining room, her long black skirts swishing. "This way," she said over her shoulder. "I am having a lovely little Assam black. Would you join me?"

"Assam black" meant tea. "I'd love a cup," I said, meaning it. I needed caffeine.

"Sugar? Milk?"

"Sugar," I said, remembering the tea cabinet at the freebie house. Had this woman been part of Katie's love of tea? Maybe served it to her when Katie lived in the house?

I asked, "What do I call you?"

The small smile widened as she sat near a teapot wrapped in a cozy. "I am Amorette. The girls call me Miz A." She waved to a place, indicating I should sit.

"Thank you, Miz A."

I took the chair she indicated and accepted the delicate china cup, saucer, and a silver teaspoon. And a cloth napkin. I had a feeling Miz A did everything with old-world formality, but wondered how she dealt with the silver-kills-vamps problem. Gold tableware maybe? "Thanks," I said, sipping. It was smooth, dark, rich, and wonderful. I told her so as she settled in next to me, a tiny pixie of a woman with skeletal fingers.

"I'm so happy you like it." She twinkled at me over her cup rim. "This single-estate Assam is my current favorite. Most young people prefer coffee." She grimaced. "Tea is underappreciated in today's world."

"I'm a tea drinker. I have a nice Assam at home, and a single-estate Kenyan, a Millma. I'll bring some leaves over if you like."

"That sounds lovely. Please do," she said. She passed me a serving tray with delicate cucumber sandwiches and crackers with cream cheese, smoked salmon, and something pickled and strong on top. Maybe capers. I ate two and accepted a second cup of tea before I asked about Troll, remembering to use his proper name.

Miz A sighed. "Tom is alive, weak, and healing, asleep upstairs, the dear man. It was a near thing, I fear. And poor little Katherine would have been devastated to lose him. They have been together for over seventy years, you know."

I nearly spluttered the tea at the "poor little Katherine" and the "seventy years" comments, but was saved when one of the girls wandered in, wearing a moss green silk robe and fuzzy pink slippers. It was Tia, the girl with the coffee-and-milk skin, hazel green eyes, and kinky blond hair of her mixed-race parentage. "Morning, Miz A. Got any coffee?" she asked, her eyes half closed.

Miz A looked at me, her eyes saying, *See? Coffee, not tea. Such a shame.* "Coffee is in the kitchen."

Moments later, Tia joined us at the table and downed half a mug of scalding coffee in seconds. "Ahhhh. God, I'm beat. I need a vacation." She opened her eyes wide as if stretching her lids, yawned, and said, "Maybe Rio. Maybe Carlos will take me."

The way she said it made me realize that Tia was an innocent, even if she was one of Katie's ladies, an innocent because she wasn't the brightest bulb in the chandelier. She looked at me and seemed to wake up for the first time today. "You're the hired vampire killer. Don't kill Carlos, okay?"

"Ummm," I said, not knowing how to reply.

"Carlos is not a rogue," Miz A said. "He is safe from retribution. Did you have a nice time last night, dear?"

Tia reached for a cucumber sandwich. "Carlos is a dream. Mr. Leo and Miss Katie say I can be a blood-servant soon, if they get the right offer."

"*Offer?*" I said, hearing the edge in my tone.

Miz A patted my hand. "I will explain. Tia," she said to the girl, "take your coffee and snack upstairs, yes? Miss Jane and I must speak privately."

"Oh." Tia nodded sagely, her ringlets bobbing. "Business. I gotcha." She gathered up a handful of sandwiches and made her way out of the room. The girl glided like a dancer, her big fuzzy slippers sliding on the wood floor. At the door she turned and said, "Thank you for not killing Carlos." Before I could formulate a reply, she was gone.

"Offer?" I repeated. "Slavery was abolished a long time ago."

Miz A nodded and topped off my tea. As she poured, she said, "It seems Tia's parents were unaware of that. They were selling their twelve-year-old daughter out of the trunk of their car." At my hissed breath, Miz A nodded, her wrinkled face looking grim as she placed another salmon cracker on my plate. "My Katie heard about the girl's . . . situation. She put an end to it, but it was too late for her proper development. She had been badly scarred, emotionally. Katie has spent a great deal of time and money rehabilitating Tia, and trying to find the right protector for her." Miz A looked up at me, her black eyes suddenly snapping. "She cannot live alone and she is too sexually aware and vulnerable to simply be set free on the city's streets. She would end up used, homeless, and destitute. A husband might eventually desert her. A vampire master will provide for and protect her for as long as she lives. She needs only the proper arrangement."

I had no idea how to respond to that so I ate my pretty little sandwich and didn't say a word. When I could get away, I thanked Miz A for the tea and snack, jumped the fence, and fired up Bitsa, needing to blow the vamp webs out of my head. What can you say to logic built upon pragmatism and compassion? But it gave me the willies.

I tooled around the Quarter on Bitsa, sniffing things out, finding places where vamps frequented, but not discovering more fresh rogue trace—or maybe rotten rogue trace is the right phrase—even though I motored along last night's route. Finding my way into the Lake Catouatchie area—which is mostly swamp and infested with mosquitoes, and which Beast had entered off-road along the sick vamp's trail—wasn't fun. But I finally caught the distant scent of rogue and tracked it. I ended up on a dead-end, crushed-shell street in the middle of nowhere.

I slowed my bike at the dead end and stopped, putting my feet down, the motor rumbling softly beneath me like a big cat's purr. The house was small, probably built in the 1950s: a gray, asbestos-shingled house of maybe twelve hundred square feet, with the screened porch I vaguely remembered seeing in the back. It was well kept, with fresh-painted charcoal trim, a new roof, and a garden that smelled of herbs in the midday heat.

In human form, something called to me from the house. Distant memories, things clouded in smoke and fear and blood. And the sound of ceremonial drums. The power of The People. *Tsalagiyi.* Cherokee, to the white man. Cold prickles raced along my skin. *Tsalagiyi* was a Cherokee word. I remembered it.

A sweathouse was out back. An elder of The People lived here. And the rogue had hunted here, close, too close. Stalking him? Her? I shivered in the heat, hope and fear crawling through the sweat beading on my skin.

Not quite sure what I intended, I turned off the bike and set the kickstand. Propped the helmet on the seat. I walked up the crushed-shell drive, shells crunching under my feet. In the Carolinas, roads and driveways were coated with gravel when unpaved, and stone was mixed in with asphalt when paving was used. Not much stone in the delta; they used what was handy. Shells. Dim-witted thoughts, my mind steering away from the fact that I was walking up the drive to an elder's house. I took the steps to the porch, noting only then that the house was on brick pylons, raising it up above hurricane flood line. I pushed the bell. It dinged inside.

I stood in the heat. Waiting. Sweating. Flies and bees buzzing around, the distantly remembered scent of sage and rosemary hanging on the air. And no one came. *This is stupid.*

I pushed the bell once more as I turned away and was startled when the door opened. I don't know what I had expected, but the slender, black-haired woman in jeans and a silk tank wasn't it. She didn't speak. She just looked at me. My shivers worsened. Time did one of those weird rocking things where the earth seems to move.

"*Gi yv ha,*" she said, and held open the door.

Come in. . . . She had said, *Come in.* And I understood her words.

CHAPTER 8

A warrior woman

I sat at her table and she smiled down at me as she handed me a partially frozen Coke, the old-fashioned bottle crusted with ice, ice crystals gathered in the top. The woman was spare and muscular, but older than my first thought. Maybe mid-fifties, maybe older, but not a strand of gray traced through her black hair. Her eyes were full of life, laughter and, oddly, compassion. I took the Coke and drank, and when she offered a plate of cookies still warm from the oven, my shivers dissipated along with my sense of trepidation. How can you stay worried when someone gives you warm chocolate chip cookies? Beast's hyperalert state was still with me, however, hunched deep within, silent and watchful.

"My name is Aggie One Feather." She paused. "*Egini Agayvlge i*, in the speech of The People."

"I'm Jane Yellowrock. Jane"—I took a breath—"*Dalonige'i*."

Aggie sat across from me, holding her own Coke. "You know some of the speech." Her voice was soft, melodious, the gentle voice of dreams and nightmares both.

"I don't remember much of the old words," I said, my voice and English grating by comparison. I lowered my volume and tried to find the melody and rhythm of the old speech. "When I hear it, maybe it will come back to me."

"How may I help you?" she asked, the question similar to the traditional words of the shaman.

Shamans were tribal helpers, there to assist, free of charge, any who asked, whether for healing ceremonies, counsel, or more practical help. I remembered this. *I remembered.* I looked at my icy hands on the frozen Coke. I had no idea what I was going to say until the words fell from my mouth. "Are there old tales about a creature called a liver-eater?"

"Yes. Several. Why do you ask?"

Shock slithered through me, snakelike. "Because I was hired by a representative of the vamp council to hunt down whatever is killing and eating tourists and cops. I followed it. And according to a very good source, what I saw last night was a liver-eater." Beast coughed with amusement in the deeps of my mind at the idea of being "a very good source."

Aggie stiffened. The skin around her eyes tightened, the fine wrinkles at the corners of her eyes deepening. "Why do you think this?"

Because I smelled it? Because I followed it here in cat form? Rather than reply, I said, "The thing I saw looks like a vampire, smells like something rotten, and hunts in the woods and swamp behind your house. I followed it here." *Ah, crap. Yep. That came out of my mouth.*

Aggie sat back. "Ahhh," she breathed, sounding relieved. "I read about the rogue vampire in the newspaper." She tilted her head, watching me. I tried to interpret her body language and expressions, but they were too swift, too ephemeral. "Why would it come here?"

"It was interested in your sweathouse. It circled it several times."

"You saw this creature?"

I paused, remembering the scene in the alley, the form bent over the girl's body. "Yes."

Aggie watched me as myriad thoughts, speculations, and conclusions raced behind her eyes. I had a bad feeling that I shouldn't have come here. "What clan are you?" she asked.

The question was unexpected, but the answer was there, instantly, for the first time in more years than I could accurately remember. Surprised, I said, "My father was *ani gilogi,* Panther Clan." I caught a fleeting image: a mountain lion pelt and a man's face. *My father . . .* An image of shadows on upright logs followed it. I couldn't tell what the shadows meant, but I knew it was something bad. I said, "My mother was *ani sahoni*, Blue Holly Clan."

My shivers worsened and I let go of the frozen bottle, clenching my cold fingers. Other images, senseless fragments of memories, stabbed me. A shadowed cave wall, a vision of snow, a memory of freezing cold. A fire in the center of a wooden longhouse. Drums, softly beating, a four-beat rhythm, the first beat strong. And the smell of sage, sweet-grass, and something harsh like tobacco burning. Beast gathered herself, but not to leap. To watch. To stalk. She had said my past was hidden in the depths of my mind. Now it seemed as if the past was pushing to the surface, like a spring from far underground. Would I finally remember the years I had forgotten? Was I going to remember who and what I was? Breathless, I asked, "You?"

"My mother is *ani waya*, Wolf Clan, Eastern Cherokee, and my father was Wild Potato Clan, *ani godigewi*, Western Cherokee."

Which could be a problem, my unreliable memory told me. Long ago, before the white man gathered us up and sent us into the snow along the trail west, there had been bad feeling between some families of Wolf Clan and Panther Clan. Remembrance of insult and blood feud was often generations long among the Cherokee. Had the conflict been resolved? Clans passed through the matriarchal line, so perhaps the bad blood had been worked through. My memories shouted that there was a problem, but it was all fractured and shattered.

"My great-grandfather was Panther Clan," she added, as if acknowledging something important. And perhaps it was significant. Tribal relationships were valued by the elders. I remembered that, in the mishmash of my past.

The sound of drums still echoed in the back of my mind, insistent, and the reverberations brought fear. I would dream about this. And it wouldn't be good.

"What are your parents' names?" she asked.

"I don't remember. I was found in the woods near the Old Nation. I was hoping . . ." Impossible hope burbled up with memories, the need of all orphans, to discover their blood kin.

"You hoped I could tell you?" she guessed. "Send you to your clan, your people?" I nodded. "I will help if I can.

If you are of The People," she said gently. "But from your eyes, I see that you are not full-blooded Cherokee. What are you?" Aggie asked.

I stood so quickly her eyes didn't follow. She tensed. Half rose. I forced myself to stop, hands high on the jambs in the doorway of her kitchen as if hung, suspended over a fire, from deer antlers thrust through the flesh of my back. *Where did* that *image come from?*

Aggie flattened her hands on the table, her palms hugging the surface. She relaxed one joint at a time, slowly. I turned to the kitchen, hands out as if balancing, and remembered to breathe. Beast restrained herself, gathered tight, close to the surface. Claws flexed. Ready.

"Forgive me," Aggie said, controlled, subdued, motionless as the air before winter snows. "I didn't wish, didn't intend, to cause you pain."

"Why did you ask me what I am?" The words were half growled, and I saw her flinch, the reaction minuscule. Everybody was asking me that these days.

Aggie shrugged, a slight lifting of narrow shoulders. "Your eyes proclaim you are part white. And I see something in you, a shadow of something . . . old." She pointed to my stomach, between my ribs. "There. Like two souls in one flesh. They do not battle, but live in uneasy harmony." When I said nothing, when the moment stretched into discomfort even for a shaman, she blew out a breath and took a cookie, ate it. Visibly gathered herself and her thoughts. "To answer your first question, the liver-eater is a skinwalker."

Breath caught in my throat, hot and burning. I don't know what she saw on my face, but she paused again and waited as if she thought I might speak. I looked Cherokee. Had spoken a Cherokee word. In the years in the children's home, I had read Cherokee tribal history, mostly through the old writings of James Mooney, hoping that I would find something that correlated with my splintered past, but nothing I read had sounded like what I was. I found my breath, shook my head, and gestured for her to continue.

"It is also called skinchanger. There are several tribal stories about liver-eater. In one, she is female. In her human form, she is usually a grandmother and so is respected and trusted for many years. But when she is aged, and the greed for youth and power overtake her, she seeks to replace what she has lost and temptation leads her into the practice of evil. She changes her skin for another human's. This is the blackest of magic.

"Our stories tell us that when she gives over to evil, the skinwalker has one long fingernail that she can insert into a child and remove the liver." When I still said nothing, Aggie went on. "Another skinwalker is *Callanu Ayiliski*, the Raven, Moker. He likes to steal hearts." Her eyes studied me, missing nothing.

"The liver-eater is usually referred to as a skinwalker who has gone mad. Skinwalkers can be a nasty bunch," she said. "However, in distant times, before the white man came, with his lusts to always have more, before the Spaniards in metal helmets came to enslave us, skinwalkers were the protectors of The People, keeping our ancestors safe from evil and evil magic. Only when they became old, and after the white man came, did many turn from protection to darker tasks and black magic." Her voice fell silent.

Aggie watched me, her body loose, tranquil, her eyes seeing more than I wanted her to. "Some call liver-eater Spear Finger. *U'tlun'ta*." She pronounced it like *hut luna*, which was a different pronunciation from the word in my distant memory, but it was a word I remembered from the legends in Mooney's books. Aggie smiled. "I see that you know of Spear Finger."

I nodded. "Is there any chance the liver-eater is a vampire instead of a skinwalker?"

"No. Vampires are foreign. They came with the Spaniards, the first white men."

I nodded slowly, though it didn't make much sense. Deep in the house, I heard the soft turning of fan blades, the sound of the motor driving it a steady hum. The refrigerator ticked, popped, and an automatic ice maker dumped ice cubes with a clatter. I moved back to the table and sat in the chair. "The words between an elder or shaman, and a seeker in pain, are protected, aren't they?" I asked. "Like discussions between a psychologist and patient?"

Aggie inclined her head. "Somewhat. If you tell me you are going to kill someone, I will put the needs of The People, and even the white man, before yours. But if you come for counsel, I will help as I may, and retain your confidence."

She tilted her head, like a bird studying the ground from a tree, amusement playing at her lips. "You aren't going to kill anyone, are you?"

"Yes. I am." She twitched, a faint movement of shoulder blades, and her amusement slid away. "I'm going to kill the thing I followed here. It's an old rogue vampire, a male. I'm sure of it. But my source . . . my source says it's a liver-eater, not a vampire."

After a moment, Aggie said, "Skinwalkers, before they turned to evil, were of The People. They lived among us from the earliest times as protectors, as warriors, sharing our history." Aggie shrugged. "When the white man came, much was lost, much changed. I have heard it said: The skinwalkers shared the blood of The People. The liver-eaters stole it."

Beast's focus sharpened. *Blood*. And the strange scents caught in the bit of fabric that carried the rogue's saliva and the blood of his victims, and the stink of rot. Beast went still, as if she understood, but if she did, she didn't explain it to me. I needed to get back to the house and take another sniff of the bloody cloth.

But suddenly Aggie was talkative, her placid eyes intent, her mouth turned up in a smile. "My favorite story of the crone liver-eater is about *Chickelili*," she said, "whose name means Truth Teller. *Chickelili* is a little snowbird, and the only one who tells the truth about the crone. Since *Chickelili* is little, nondescript, and has a small voice, her words are drowned out by the jays and crows, until a little boy listens and warns the parents that the killer of children is near. The message of the story is that the small voice is sometimes more important than loud ones."

I stared at her, not knowing what her words might mean, but knowing that an elder seldom spoke unless there was great truth in the story, truth that was pertinent to the current situation. Little voices? I flashed on Katie's ladies sitting at the dinner table.

"This creature you saw near the sweathouse. Does it have a long fingernail?"

I thought back to the vision of it in the alley, the prostitute's body cradled in his arms. Then the brief glimpse as it lunged up the wall. "No. I didn't see one."

"Could you see its energies?" she asked.

"Gray light, black motes. I smelled them on the wind," I said, and felt instantly foolish.

Aggie nodded. "Yes. I see that. You are a tracker of evil. A warrior woman, like the great ones of the far past." I felt a blush start at the praise, and shifted uncomfortably on the hard wooden chair. "I will set wards and burn smudge sticks at dusk," she said, "to cleanse the taint of any evil that may be nearby. And my mother and I will watch in the night."

"Your mother?" I asked, surprised.

"My mother is only seventy-four, and is still vibrant. My grandmother passed last year."

Things clicked in my mind. "Her bones are buried in the back? Near the sweathouse."

The same things clicked in Aggie's mind and the animation drained from her face, showing me a clearer picture of her age. "You think this creature, this rogue vampire you hunt, is after the bones of my ancestors," she said, her voice so low it was like grass in the wind. "Or after one of us to have power over the bones of my family and the magic in them."

It made sense, and unknown knowledge fell into place in my mind; it made a lot more sense than anything Beast was thinking. "Having the bones of an elder who shares a bloodline buried nearby helps boost a shaman's power, yes?" I said. Aggie nodded once, a jerky motion, full of fear. More gently, I said, "If the thing I'm chasing is a vampire, and if he turned one of you, could he call upon the ancestors, the *mach e i a ellow*, to give him strength?"

Aggie whispered, "Perhaps. It depends on what he knows. What magic he has."

"He's old," I said. "Very, very old. Several hundred years, I'd guess. How many generations of ancestors are buried out back?"

Aggie dropped her eyes to her hands; she laced her fingers on the tabletop. "My grandmother, her mother and father, and my great-great-grandmother, who slipped away from the Removal—the Trail of Tears—and settled here." If I reacted to the mention of the Trail of Tears, Aggie didn't see it, her eyes downcast. "The bones of my sister, who died when a child. My uncle and his wife, who was a white woman but who joined us when she married. My grandmother's brother, much older than she. Seven of the blood of The People, and one who joined us."

"That's a lot of powerful bones in one place," I said.

"I'll let the dogs loose tonight, to guard the yard," Aggie said.

"Aggie," I said gently. "It killed two of your dogs already."

She closed her eyes, as if to block out the truth. But when she opened them again, they burned with fury. Low and fierce, she said, "I'll kill it." Her hands clenched on the table, small and dark and fragile, but with a terrible underlying strength of purpose. "If it comes here, I'll kill it." She took a breath that seemed to ache as she drew it in. "Do you have a cell phone number?"

I pulled a card out of my T-shirt pocket and placed it on the table between us. Aggie took it up and rubbed it gently, as if feeling the texture of the paper, but I knew she was feeling my energies stored in it. "You have decided to keep your true nature from me?" she asked.

"I'm sorry." I bowed my head deeply as I had seen my father do so long ago. *My father!* The memory of his face rose in my mind, nose sharp and cutting. I blinked back tears at the new/old memory. As formally as I could, I said, "I give thanks for your help. I'll provide protection as I'm able. For now, may I know who owns the property behind the house and into the woods and swamp?"

"The property borders on the Jean Lafitte National Historical Park, so the government owns most of it. I'm not sure who owns the rest, though there is privately held land dotted all around here, like my family's land."

Park land. Crap. That meant the rogue vamp had acres and acres to roam, and no one to stop him. Except for me. And this stern, delicate shaman. "Thank you for your time," I said.

"I offer my counsel and the use of the sweathouse. If you go into battle ill prepared, you fight to lose. I sense it has been some time since you went to water. Purification and smudging will help you, center you, let you find what you seek."

Some time. Yeah, you could say that. The weight of decades pressed onto me, heavy and fraught with pain. "I may take you up on that," I said.

Aggie pursed her lips. "You're lying to me. You have no intention of taking me up on anything. Why not?" She cocked her head, little bird fashion. "Is it the same reason why you won't tell me about yourself?"

I backed to the door, my eyes on hers, my most disarming smile firmly in place. This woman was way too smart for me to hang around any longer. "Thank you, Grandmother, for your help and counsel."

She made a sound I hadn't heard in years, but which was instantly familiar. Sort of a snort, a pshaw, and a single syllable of negation. It was very much a sound tied to The People, as "*alors*" is tied to the French, and "cool" is tied to generations of Americans. "*Dalonige'i*," she said, and I stopped at the sound of my name. "It isn't a traditional name. It means more than yellow rock, you know." When I lifted my brows in question, she said, "It also means gold—one reason why the Nation was stolen from the Cherokee, why The People were set on the Trail of Tears, so the white man could dig *dalonige'i* from the earth of the Appalachian Mountains."

This time I didn't react to the words, but I knew she still saw more than I wanted anyone to see. "My thanks," I said again. And I backed out her front door onto her stoop, into the heat and bright sun.

I kick-started my bike and took off for home. As I rode, I considered what I had learned, not about myself—that was for later reflection—but about the thing I chased. Beast was wrong. It wasn't a liver-eater—I had seen it and it had no long fingernail. It was a vamp. A seriously whacked-out, flesh-eating, rotten-smelling vamp to be sure, but a vamp. A vamp gone way bad. An old, mad, rotting rogue.

Though my nose wasn't as good as Beast's, I still had better olfactory senses than any human. Standing in my backyard, I held the bit of cloth to my nose and breathed in, parsing the pheromones and proteins that made up the four distinct scents, three of them human and heavy with fear, alive when their blood was spilled. Perhaps Beast's memory helped, but I could actually partition the human scents into one female and two male humans. And beneath it all was the scent of the thing I was chasing. I drew in its chemical signature. Vamp. Definitely vamp. Weird vamp, rotting vamp, but vamp. I shuddered with relief, allowing myself a small moment to relax at the certainty. Whatever it was, it wasn't a skinwalker gone bad.

Returning to the bit of cloth, I isolated the differing chemicals in it, finally detecting the faintest tang of the woman the rogue had been with. Caught the smell of sex. And something even fainter, that I hadn't placed. Or perhaps hadn't remembered. I breathed in again. Shivered. Breathed in yet again, this time through open mouth, tongue extended. Chill bumps rose on my skin. My breath stopped. *The scent of The People.* I sat down heavily, landing unsteadily on the steps to the back porch. *Is the rogue vamp I'm hunting . . . Cherokee?*

One hand on the top, supporting my weight, I jumped the brick wall over to Katie's at just after five, over at the spot where the security camera had once been secreted. As I jumped, pivoting my weight on one arm, I took a quick look. No camera. There was a small scar on the brick. Since it was gone, and I therefore wouldn't give away what I was doing to whoever had put it there, I gripped the top of the wall and let my body swing against the brick, in a rappelling stance. I sniffed the site and was surprised at the commingled scents I found.

On top, fresh and bright, was the smell of the Joe. Rick LaFleur. He had removed the camera, likely at Troll's command. Beneath the Joe's scent, however, was another, fainter scent, and the weird thing was, I recognized it. The camera had been placed by Bruiser, the muscle who worked with Leo Pellissier, the head of the vamp council in New Orleans.

Why would Leo feel it necessary to keep an eye on Katie? It smacked of nasty politics in the council. Big surprise there. I pushed off from the wall and landed softly. Turned to the house and was surprised to see Troll standing in the open back door. He made a snorting sound, his gaze measuring the wall. He was holding himself up with both hands on the door, his skin the pallor of old parchment, yellowed and brittle, especially the dull dome of his bald head.

I stuck my hands in my jeans pockets and strolled over, trying to look like every human could drop from a fifteen-foot wall without injury. "You look like death warmed over," I said.

"Anybody ever tell you that phrase is insulting to the members of a vampire's household?" His rough voice sounded even more scratchy than usual, dry as stone dust.

I laughed, feeling a bit mean, not liking myself for it. "No, but I'll try to remember that. You get enough blood from last night's *donation*?" And that was why I was angry. A vampire nearly killed someone I was sorta starting to like, and he wasn't ticked off, so I had to be, right?

"Not enough from Rachael. But Katie allowed me a small drink from her wrist."

I didn't react, though anger and disgust pinged through me. *Yuckers*. Troll stepped aside and I walked in. "You still look awful," I said.

"I'll survive," he said. "But you're in trouble."

"Yeah?" I felt my hackles rise and wanted to growl. "With who?"

"Katie had to go out last night to feed, to make up for the blood loss. Between what that bastard Leo took, and what she gave back to me—before she fed—she was depleted. She won't be up early tonight, and she won't be feeling too well when she does rise. So if you have anything to tell her, you might want to run it by me first."

Confused, I said, "And all this has to do with someone being mad at me?"

He said, pointedly, "Katie told you to be here by dawn to report. You didn't show."

Crap. I remembered that, *now*. "At sunrise I was on the other side of the river, the Jean Lafitte park, on the trail of the rogue vamp. Unlike Katie, I can't turn into a bat and fly home."

Troll chuckled, the sound oddly sad. "Don't let Katie hear you say stuff like that. She hates the myth that vampires turn into bats. In fact, with the exception of a few fiction writers who happened to get it right, she's pretty pissed at everything the media has portrayed about her kind." He turned on lights as he led me through the house. "So. Bat talk aside, you want to tell me what you discovered?" I filled him in, succinct to the point of brevity, with no mention of Beast, of course. He said, "Huh," when I finished, and pointed to the dining room. I figured I was dismissed and went in.

The girls were gathered around the table again, all of

them looking sleepy eyed and a bit wan. Especially Rachael, who was lounging back in her chair. There was a bandage on the inside of her elbow at the antecubital vein. Dark circled beneath her eyes and she was sipping something neon green through a straw in a crystal glass. It looked and smelled like Gatorade. Not the sort of drink that belonged at the formal table with all the silver, china, and crystal. I'd never understand the rich and dead or their servants.

Miz A appeared, her wrinkled face seeming more creased but smiling in welcome. I resisted kissing her cheek as if she were an old auntie, which was a weird impulse and could get me slapped, or worse, and said, "I don't guess I could have the meal I didn't get last night?"

A smile repositioned the wrinkles all over her face. "Tonight's steak is bourbon pepper, but you may order it served rare if you like."

"I like. And if it's not asking too much, I'd also like a baked potato and iced tea. No wine." She nodded.

When she left the room, tottering on legs that seemed weak beneath the long skirts, I looked over the "girls." I needed to find a way to get them to open up to me. Sorta like I had once needed to get a house full of twelve-year-old girls to open up to me, when I was first sent to the children's home. I wondered if bonding would be any easier now that I was twenty-nine—according to my totally fictitious though totally legal birth certificate—and spoke English.

Tia smiled sweetly if a bit sleepily at me and ate something green from a salad plate. The silk robe was gone. Tonight she wore a silk lace bustier that shoved her boobs up proudly, an opal necklace nestling in her cleavage.

My gaze settled on Christie, who was wearing about fifty tiny braids—a lot like the way I often wore my hair—and a face full of silver in her eyebrows, nose, ears, even around her collarbone. The silver rings had chains running through them, connecting her nostrils to her ears and points between, all dangling little bells. Bells everywhere, even up under her peekaboo bra, which had the cups sealed with latches tonight. Thank God. The girl, who couldn't be more than twenty, was wearing a dog collar with wicked-looking spikes. Christie shook her braids back when she took a bite of salad, and the bells tinkled.

To fit in, I tasted the salad, mixed greens with lots of

spices in the dressing. Something bacon-y, which I instantly loved. "Christie," I said, chewing, "I like the bells."

She raised the mismatched rings in each brow, considering. "Lucky you."

I laughed. Nope. It wasn't going to be easier now that I was grown. I hadn't fit in then, with a bunch of orphaned or semiorphaned girls, and I wouldn't fit in now with a bunch of . . . girls. "Christie, you and Rachael. Tell me what you know about the vamps in this town. Especially the council."

The girls looked at each other and at me. "Not much about the politics," Christie said.

"Does Leo visit any of you? For . . ." I didn't know how to phrase it and I just stopped.

Christie laughed, the sound taunting. "For blood? Sex? Or maybe combo entertainment, fun and games and dinner afterward?"

I managed to keep a blush under control. "Yeah." I stuffed in another bite of greens and broke off a piece of roll. It was flaky and sweet and left traces of butter on my fingers.

"We all get a visit from Leo when we first come here," Rachael said, her vivid eyes on me and her voice toneless. "He gets first try. He calls it the dark right of kings."

I had heard of the divine right of kings, where a monarch had the right to deflower any virgin or use any woman he fancied, often on the night before her wedding. It was archaic rape, similar to the slave owner visiting his slave in her cabin, or having her brought to him. No way to say no. Rape in any form had always brought out the—I half smiled at the thought—the Beast in me. Rachael looked at Christie when I smiled. I didn't need Beast's nose to tell me Leo scared the crap out of Rachael. Leo Pellissier was shooting to the top of my list of people I didn't like. I needed to interview the bloodsucker. My grin twisted in grim satisfaction. "I need to talk to old Leo, but since I burned him with a silver cross yesterday, I doubt he'll be agreeable."

Rachael looked at me, nervous laughter burbling in her chest. "You burned him? And he didn't kill you?"

"He thought about it. Katie healed him. If she hadn't, I might've had to stake him."

The table went silent. No one moved. Every eye was on me. This sort of thing had happened occasionally when I was in the home, when I said something that came out weird. I looked at the little witch, her white skin and jet-black hair contrasting in the candlelight. This girl had touched me on some level the first time I saw her. I had felt a subtle connection, which had to be a mistake, didn't it? But it was there, nonetheless, and my voice was softer when I said, "Bliss, right? What did Leo say when he . . ." The correct word eluded me.

"You have trouble with this, don't you," she said. It wasn't mocking. The tone was gentle, almost pitying. "With what we do, I mean."

I almost said, "You could be with a coven learning how to do witch stuff," but I caught myself. Just in case she didn't know what she was. "Where are you from?"

Bliss lifted a shoulder, and I realized she was wearing a silky gauze top that laced across the front like an old-timey corset if it had been put on backward. Her small breasts were pushed up and fully visible through the cloth, a necklace dangling between them. Suddenly I felt like a voyeur. "I was raised in foster care, so that means I'm from everywhere and nowhere."

So that meant she might not know she was a witch. Katie knew, didn't she? Couldn't vamps smell witch? I'd have to ask. "I have trouble with it, yeah." I looked around the table, making eye contact. We had finished our salads, and I didn't have to be told that the meal was more silent than usual. Without even volunteering that I'm a predator, I make people wary.

"Any of you have an idea who the rogue vamp is? Maybe someone's been acting different? Maybe something weird about one of Katie's vamp customers? She has vamp customers, right?" They all nodded, and from the force of it, I gathered that Katie had a *lot* of vamp customers. "A vamp acting weirder than usual? Even someone who smells different?"

"They all smell weird," Bliss said.

"No, they don't," a dark-skinned woman said. "But you'd have to define weird in totally different ways to cover some of Katie's clients." I was pretty sure her name was Najla.

"How do they smell?" I asked.

The other girls looked at Bliss. She said, "Like old leaves. Sometimes mold. If they haven't bathed in a while they can smell like old blood. You know. Like a woman in her period. I have a really good sense of smell," she insisted.

I'll bet you do. I could tell this had been a sore point with the others. "Do any of them smell sick? Infected?"

"No." Bliss glanced around the table. "I know you think I'm crazy, but *they all smell.*"

Before any of them could reply, I said, "Najla, right?" to the dark-skinned girl. She had an on-again, off-again accent that I couldn't place, but then accents weren't my strength. Like Bliss, I was better at scents. "Let's talk weird. First, where are you from? Wait," I said as the girls laughed and Najla narrowed her eyes at me. "That didn't come out right. What I meant was, I want to hear about weird and vamps, but first, I'd like to know where you're from."

"None 'a your business," she said.

"Katie says it is," Miz A said as she shuffled back into the room. She was pushing a cart that smelled of spices, charcoal, and meat. Beast rumbled appreciatively. "Anything she wants to know, you tell her."

Najla tossed her head. "My parents and I emigrated here from Mozambique when I was four." I rotated my fingers, giving her a little tell-me-more gesture, and she said, "From a place called Namaponda. You might find it on a map. If the map was big enough."

"And your parents?"

"Dead." When I waited, she grudgingly said, "Car crash when I was fifteen. Katie took me in. Don't look at me like that. I was turning tricks on the street to buy food. She brought me in, made me finish high school before she would let me work. Tried to send me to college. But I was good at making men happy." Whatever she saw on my face made her bristle. "I want to retire before I'm forty. What other job can you name where a girl fresh out of high school can pull down two hundred K a year and retire in less than twenty years? Name me one."

"Modeling. Acting. Music business." Grudgingly I added, "If you're lucky."

Najla nodded emphatically. "I never had a lucky day in my life except the day Katie found me. I got close onto a mil in stocks and bonds and gold. I'll have two mil, easy, in five more years, with compounding interest and dividends, assuming the market goes where I think it will."

I was shocked. Two million for turning tricks? Najla laughed. "I can see it now. You think a girl should work hard and retire at sixty-five. That's bullshit."

Miz A slapped Najla on the shoulder as she set a plate in front of her. "Miss Katie don' allow dirty talk at the table."

Najla rubbed her shoulder. "Sorry," she mumbled. Miz A put a plate in front of me. The steak hung off at ten o'clock and four o'clock and leaked bloody juices into the trough of the china and onto a larger plate beneath. The potato was stuffed with all sorts of goodies, including bacon and sour cream. I smiled, my mouth watering. "Thank you. This looks wonderful."

"Nearly two pound of Black Angus, yeah. Tom say you like meat."

"Tom is my hero. So are you. So is the cook."

Miz A chuckled and finished serving the girls. I had enough etiquette training to know I had to wait until we were all served before I dug in. And enough self-restraint to resist Beast, who woke up at the scent and wanted me to eat the meat with my hands. "You may eat," Miz A said. I watched and picked up the proper fork and the serrated knife. And cut into the steak.

When I put the first bite into my mouth I groaned. The girls all looked at me. "Sorry," I said as I chewed. "This is the best piece of meat I ever put in my mouth." Which made the girls break up and dig into their own meals, laughter reflecting off the walls like tinkling silver.

Inadvertently, I might have just made friends. Bordello humor. Who'd a thunk it?

CHAPTER 9

I really love rock and roll

I learned little that was useful over dinner, at least not about the rogue. If I ever needed to tie up a lover and whip him, however, I had plenty of info. I think the girls just liked to see me blush.

Katie hadn't arrived by the time I finished my meal, so I left without seeing her. However, on the way out, I took a circuitous route, openly scoping out the place, and found Troll in her office. He was leaning over that ancient desk, bent over papers, his laptop turned so I couldn't see the screen. That seemed significant, so I pulled on Beast's stalking attributes and stepped into the room, silent as the predator Katie had called me.

Troll turned as I approached, which gave credence to the old legend that when a vamp willingly shares blood, some of its speed and extra-keen senses get passed along. Faster than I could focus, Troll hit a key and the screen went blank, but the man himself smiled, a welcoming expression that surprised me.

I said, "I see you removed the camera from the back fence. Any reason why Leo Pellissier would spy on Katie?"

He frowned. "Leo didn't put up that camera. He couldn't. Spying is against the Vampira Carta."

I laughed, a sharp cough of sound. "The what?"

"The Vampira Carta." He lounged back and I spotted the .45 on his other side, within reach. Troll was antsy or scared or something worse. I guessed that getting one's body drained of blood could do that to a guy. "What do you know of vampire history?" he asked.

"Frankly, except for finding new ways to kill them, vamps don't interest me much."

The easy humor left his face. "In Katie's presence you use the term 'vampire' or the more proper term, 'Mithrans.' 'Vamp' is insulting."

I sat on the arm of a chair, a position that allowed me to see the doorway in my peripheral vision and Troll full on. It also gave me leverage to launch myself in any direction without a change of balance. Troll grinned at my choice as if he'd had a mental bet on it. Considering that I hadn't seen this chair before, and that I suddenly scented Katie on the air, maybe the bet was more than mental. I wondered if she was in the foyer watching on the security screens. I said, "Mithrans. As in the mystery of Mithras in ancient Roman lore?" Troll looked impressed until I said, "The whole thing is on Wikipedia, you know. Anyone can look it up. Not that the vamps and the Mithrans have been linked absolutely. Unless you just did. I might have to update the site." I was joking, but Troll didn't seem to catch that.

He glanced at his laptop in irritation and I grinned. The real world was catching up with the vamps. Mithrans. Whatever. They couldn't like it. However, more than half of what was available about vamps in books and online was bogus, fiction, or wishful thinking, sometimes a mixture of all three. And nowhere was there an explanation of why vamps were affected by Christian symbols. It was my personal quest to find out about that, not that I'd had any luck.

"Leo's muscle planted the camera," I said. "Bet on it."

Troll sat back in his chair, bemused but not disagreeing, obviously wanting to ask how I knew with such certainty. I changed the topic to see what happened. "I'm going dancing tonight," I said. "Where in the Quarter do you recommend?"

"Dancing?" He couldn't quite keep the startled tone out of his voice.

"Great way for a gal to smell out any problems in the city." Literally. "The rogue chased down and ate a working girl last night. I'm up for seeing if it comes after me."

"You couldn't pass for a working girl in your dreams."

I grinned. "I clean up good. I'll drop by on my way out. Maybe you'll think of a place."

Back at the freebie house, I streaked on dark red lipstick and wrapped my braided hair up in a turban with Beast's travel pack in the folds. I strapped three crosses around my waist so they dangled inside my skirt, hung one around my neck in plain sight, and strapped a short-bladed vamp-killer to my inner thigh, not where a dancing partner would find it unless we were doing the tango and got *real* friendly. I put two full-sized stakes into my turban and two hand-made, silver-tipped, collapsible travel stakes into specially sewn pockets in my undies. The purple and teal skirt rode low on my hip bones and the peasant top rode low on my breasts, the tie open, a skin-toned jog bra beneath. Sexy, but showing nothing. The skirt whispered around my calves with each step.

I swished on a little bronzer to brighten my natural skin tone, drew on some sparkly gold eyeliner, and slipped into the new dancing shoes. In the mirror, I tested the movement of my skirt in a little *maya* hip move that looked like sex. Satisfied, I snapped off the bath light, made sure the house was secure, and closed down the laptop, standing in the dark house, thinking.

I had spent an hour in an online search into the mythos of the American Indian skinwalker, coming away with a confusing battery of images and legends. There was nothing that sounded like me, not exactly. Certainly nothing sane or free from evil.

The doorbell rang, interrupting. The house was dark and I moved through it by memory and the illumination of outside streetlights through the windows to the front door. I smelled the cigar before I saw him. The Joe. Rick. I threw the locks and opened the door, swished my skirts forward, saying, "Well. Looky what the cat dragged in." I couldn't resist the taunt. Rick's eyes bulged at the sight of me. I was afraid I'd have to catch them and stuff them back in the sockets. I chuckled and said, "Thanks for the compliment. Lemme guess. Troll sent you over."

"And me," a soft voice said from the street.

I looked over the speechless Rick's shoulder and spotted

his companion. She wore a short flared skirt and T-shirt, dancing shoes, flashy jewelry, and lots of makeup. "Bliss?"

"Miss Katie sent me. She said I could help?" She looked uncertain. "She gave me a week's wages to miss work." She started to say something else and stopped. The scent of fear was faintly bitter on her skin. I had no idea why Katie had sent her to me but I didn't like it.

"It should be safe enough tonight, Bliss," I said. "All I'm looking for is a really stinky vamp. He should smell sorta . . . decomposing."

"A rotting vamp?" She put a hand on her hip, rings flashing and bangles clanging. "You're kidding me, right?"

"Nope. And Bliss. I'm not prying, but what do you know about your birth parents?"

"Nothing. Why?"

"It doesn't matter." Bliss was more than a rogue vamp lure and vamp sniffer-outer. She was also Katie's eyes.

Before we left, I wrote down the address of the Cherokee elder for Rick and asked him to track down the owners of all property within three miles in any direction. It was a lot of land, and the research would keep him occupied and out of my hair, doing stuff I hated. Then I locked my door and left with the two, Rick's cigar leaving a trail on the air even a human could follow.

Three abreast, we walked through the Quarter, taking our time in the heat, heading for Bourbon Street. We were passed by tuxedo-clad waiters on the way to work, couples out for a romantic night, small groups of men looking for a good time in strip joints, and a few vamps out trolling for an early dinner or maybe just a snack to hold them over till later.

I spotted a group of young witches glamoured to look like older women, and I wondered what they were doing and why they needed a disguise. Bliss watched the group, her face tight with concentration, and I wondered what she saw. I wondered a lot of things and I had very few answers. She and Rick chatted as we walked, and I felt their eyes settle on me often, their curiosity like a blanket held around me. But I had nothing to say, and let my silence build.

The air was hot, muggy, and heavy, as if it carried extra weight, as if lightning and tomorrow's rain infused it, waiting. I perspired in a smooth, all-over sheen and my new skirt brushed my legs and thighs with each step, the moist air swirling around me as I walked. The amethyst and chatkalite necklace and my gold nugget lay together around my neck, the stones warm. The voices and people we passed were relaxed and slow. The ambiance was heated, as if dance had already found me, as if I had slid into the rhythms and steps and was already mellow. I breathed in, sorting out the various scents.

The smell of seafood, spices, hot grease, and people filled the air. Food and liquor, exhaust and perfume, vamps and witches, drunks and fear, sex and desperation, and the scent of water. Everywhere, I was surrounded by water, the power of the Mississippi, the nearby lakes, the not-too-distant reek of swamp. The overlay of coffee with chicory, the way they brewed it here. The scent combinations were heady.

The streetlights hid as much as they revealed, like an ageing exotic dancer hiding behind fans or party balloons. Music poured from bars and restaurants, rich with jazz licks and dripping with soul. Together, it brought Beast close to the surface. I could feel her breath in the forefront of my mind, hear her heartbeat. Her pelt moved against my skin as if ready to break through.

There were a few cops on foot, their presence meant to bring a measure of security to the tourists. But the officers were nervous, each with a hand resting on gun butt, faces and eyes hyperalert, radios transmitting information to them in a steady stream. They were all twitchy.

Besides weapons and Kevlar vests, NOPD cops carried GPS tracker devices. Each had a built-in "officer panic alarm," activated by pressing a button. If a cop pressed it, an alarm went out to dispatch, transmitting the officer's GPS location, calling for all officers to respond. And it made an awful racket, an ear-piercing *whoopwhoopwhoop*.

The devices hadn't helped the cops the rogue had killed. Had they not carried them that night? Or was the rogue so good at mind games that he took them all over before they could press a single button?

Cruising every street were media vans, local affiliates of CBS, NBC, ABC, a FOX News van with a picture of Greta Van Susteren painted on the side, even a local cable van.

The reporters were looking for local color and anything they could get on the killer of cops and prostitutes—each hoping for an exclusive they could parlay into bigger ratings and increased personal fame.

Cops and reporters notwithstanding, the streets were less crowded than I expected, far more empty than the first night Beast hunted. The word about the killer vamp had done a number on the crowds. I had never been in the French Quarter on a Saturday night, but I had a feeling the bar and restaurant traffic was down. Not good. I had mental images of armed men taking to the streets in packs, searching for the rogue. Killing any unlucky, handy vamp.

Our walk ended up at the Royal Mojo Blues Company. The smell of fried food and beer and the sound of live music blasted its way into the street, the house band rocking. The RMBC had an outside dining area, a bar, food that smelled hot off the grill, and a dance floor. And the people not on the streets? They were inside. The place was packed. My feet were tapping before I reached the door. After a preliminary sniff to rule out the presence of rogue, I headed to the dance floor, losing Bliss and Rick in the crowd.

A black woman with the voice of an angel blasted a foot-stomping seventies piece by Linda Ronstadt. She was backed up by five other musicians on drums, keyboard, bass, and guitars. A selection of wind instruments rested in a rack.

Conversations merged into a background roar, with Beast picking up a few words here and there: flirting, business complaints, a drug deal taking place sotto voce between two patrons near the bar. No vamp discussions. And the only vamp scent in the joint didn't smell fresh, though it was familiar. Couples and singles were on the floor, so dancing alone wouldn't make me stand out. I flowed onto the floor, into the crowd. Into the heat and swirling smoke and started to move. I opened with a corkscrew and shifted into a *maya*. One of the courses I took between children's home/high school/teenaged misery and the freedom of RL—real life—was a year of belly dance classes. The best thing about belly dancing was the freestyle moves it added to my repertoire. On a dance floor? I smoke.

I attracted the attention of a half dozen women and they joined me on the dance floor, all of us dancing together, making a space for ourselves and crowding out the couples, at least for the moment. Men left the bar and stood in a line, watching, beer bottles in hand. The women with me shouted and hollered. Beast woke up and purred, pumping energy into the dance.

By the third number I was dancing in front of the band, buffeted by the bass speakers, sweating and dancing my heart out. It had been too long. I really love rock and roll, and the band was good, currently sounding more like Sting than Sting himself.

Three bars into a jazzed-up version of "Moon over Bourbon Street," I caught the eye of the horn player, just joining the band. Dang if it wasn't my Joe. Rick. Holding my gaze, he picked up a sax, made a few adjustments. I'd paid no attention to his clothes when he picked me up at the door, but he was wearing a black tee, the fabric so thin it was almost translucent beneath the stage lights, and jeans so tight they molded to his body like the skin of a lover. Oh, my.

He moved to the front of the stage, a bad-boy smile on his mouth and his black hair falling forward in an Elvis curl. He took the mouthpiece between his lips in a move so sensuous it sent shivers down my spine. He started to play. For me. His fingers danced up the keys, and the mellow sound curled around me like a loving hand. So what could I do but dance for him? I moved into the camel walk—figure-eight hips—and added in a few small belly circles and belly drops. It was a come-hither song so I did a come-hither dance.

The number wasn't the three-minute, fifty-second-plus version of "Moon Over Bourbon Street" once released to radio stations. It was the live version, the male lead's voice so perfect for the lyrics it tore the heart right out of the entire dance floor. The horn added just the right pathos to a song dedicated to the life of a vampire. Empty floor space filled up fast. Sweat trickled down my spine and I undulated to the beat, a catlike move all my own. The lead singer was crooning, "The brim of my hat hides the eye of a beast," when I heard Bliss's scream.

Muffled. Panicked.

I dropped my arms. Whirled. Tore from the floor. Dove around dancers faster than they could see. Weaving fast.

Following the sound as it trailed away. Past the bar. Into the dark.

Ladies' room. I blasted through the door. Slamming it back on its hinges. Two sets of feet in one booth, one female, one male. Vamp smell. *Blood.*

Time dilated. Slowed. Took on the texture of oiled wood, grained and patterned.

Beast rose. I ripped a stake from my turban with my right hand. Tore the large silver cross from the leather thong around my neck. Yanked the stall door open, breaking the hasp.

The vamp, wearing T-shirt and jeans, whirled. Snarled. Fangs bloodied. Bliss dropped from his arms. A slow-motion fall, like a doll, to the floor. His left hand went down, as if to catch her back to him. Her blood stained his shirt. Stained her clothes. Pumped weakly from her throat. She was pale as death.

Beast screamed in fury. I reversed the stake and lunged. Right-handed, the vamp caught my right wrist. *Not the mad one we hunt,* Beast warned. *Young. Very young.*

Very young meant lack of control. Rogue of a different kind. I rammed my left forearm, powered by all my body weight, into the back of his elbow. Into the joint. His arm bent across his body. Bones snapped as the joint broke inward. He roared.

His grip fell away from my right wrist. I continued my forward motion. Slapped the cross onto the side of his neck. He screamed. Skin smoked. His left arm sliced up, vamp nails slashing. I jumped back. The cross ripped away. Blisters wept blood. The vamp reached for his neck. Giving me the opening I needed.

I reversed my right hand. Caught his injured wrist. Pulled him off balance. Toward me. Out of the stall. Away from Bliss. I twisted my body. Pulling. Stepping back. Stuck out a leg. He fell across my thigh. Hit the floor. I shoved the stake against his back. Over his heart. Thrusting deep, into his flesh. He screamed and twisted. Ripped the stake out of his flesh with the motion. Faster than I could follow, he was gone.

Time fell inward, speeding fast. The music and voices and the smell of blood crashed into me. Two bouncers filled the doorway. Still moving Beast fast, I stood straight and palmed the stake back into the turban. The silver cross on its broken thong I was stuck with. I raised both palms in the universal gesture of "I'm weaponless; please don't shoot me." Letting them see the cross, dangling. They paused at the sight of a girl, surprise in their faces. They were clearly expecting something or someone else. Odd.

I said, "A vamp just attacked a girl. She's in trouble." I pointed over my shoulder. When they hesitated, I said, "She's bleeding bad," and slid between them, into the crowd that was gathering. There was nothing I could do for Bliss that the bouncers couldn't. But I could track the vamp. *Young. Very young,* Beast had thought. Young enough that he hadn't learned how to use his voice and seduction to get a meal. Young enough to be attacking girls. And not the vamp scent I had recognized when I entered.

The young vamp should have been under the power of his master, not allowed into public until he had learned control. Which sometimes took long years when they were chained to the basement wall in their master's house. Why was he free if he couldn't be trusted? Either he got away, like a zoo animal over the fence, or he was an accident.

He had to be stopped.

I breathed in, finding the scent of the vamp on the air, Bliss's blood on his clothes, bright as a signpost. He was leaving an easy trail and I had a scent marker on me, in my turban. I dove through the screaming crowd and outside.

CHAPTER 10

Semper fi

I trailed the young vamp while half unwrapping my turban to retrieve Beast's travel pack. I strapped it around my waist with the extra crosses now hanging out, before re-wrapping the turban. The vamp was moving fast through the near-empty streets, showing a familiarity with the alleys and narrow passageways. He was leaving a trail so strong that I didn't need to shift to follow it.

From the travel pack, I pulled my cell phone and speed-dialed number five, the head of the vamp council. Not that I wanted to be talking to Leo Pellissier, but as council head, he had to be informed about the attack of a human by an uncontrolled vamp. The Bruiser answered.

"This is Jane Yellowrock," I said softly, so my voice didn't carry on the still night air. "Let me speak to Leo. Vamp council business."

"It'll have to go through me first," Bruiser said. "Mr. Pellissier's policy. Sorry." He didn't sound sorry.

I dodged into yet another alley. The scent of the Mississippi was fading, the slightly sour scent of Lake Pontchartrain growing. I had left the Quarter, heading north. I could smell slum close by. "Fine. I'm on the trail of a young, unmastered vamp who just attacked a female in a bar bathroom. I'm about to finish what I started in the bar and shove a stake in him. This is the obligatory notification of a vamp hunter to the blood-master of the city."

"Mr. Pellissier and I are on the way. Give me the location," Bruiser said. I spotted a street sign, its pole bent in two as if a car had hit it and no one had repaired the damage. I had no idea which of the two streets I was on so I just gave Bruiser both names. "When you reach the corner, whichever direction you're coming from, follow the sharp-pointed, two-night moon."

Bruiser said, "Say what?"

I was speaking Beast-talk. I shook my head to clear it. "Follow the moon."

Moon different every night. Never same, Beast thought at me. I ignored her. "I've gone two blocks. I'm getting close to his nest."

"And how do we know that?" he asked.

I could smell him everywhere now. Couldn't tell Bruiser that. "Gotta go," I whispered. I hit the END button, the MUTE button to kill any ring, and closed the phone, tucking it back into the travel pack. I melted into a shadow, a vacant house's wall at my back.

Beast's and my skills and strengths are different. Usually, Beast found a lair; I came back by daylight, when vamps' activity level was inhibited, going in human form for the kill. Her tracking skills were better than mine. My fighting skills were better than hers—only because I had hands to grip a stake and cross, as she often assured me.

No vamp had ever considered Beast's spoor a threat, so I didn't mind leaving her scent on vamp territory. But I was leaving human spoor on the vamp's terrain. *He* could hunt *me* now, if he wanted. Follow me home. Unless I killed him, true-dead.

I stopped and shook out my arms, stretched my neck. Wished I was wearing boots. And clothes that covered more skin. Jeans. Leather. My mail collar. *Crap.* I was dressed all wrong. I unstrapped the vamp-killer and its sheath from beneath my skirts, reached between my legs and pulled the back hem of my skirt up and tucked it into my waistband in front, making trousers. The vamp-killer I strapped back over the fabric, on the outside of my thigh, the strap holding the skirt hem in place. Uncontrolled young vamps had one thing on their minds. Dinner. Though some preferred other sites to feed from, this vamp was a neck sucker, so the extra crosses went around my neck in plain sight. I was hoping the crosses would deter him for a single, crucial instant if he attacked me and went to feed.

I adjusted the two full-length stakes in my turban—one tacky with vamp blood—and tucked the collapsible ones into my jog bra. Holding the vamp-killer in my right hand and the cross in my left, I moved into shadow, following the scent.

The broken and pocked street had no streetlights; shattered glass littered the roadbed; spent cartridges had fallen here and there. Large housing units were dotted close together, chockablock, along the road. Some of the individual apartments had glass in the windows. Most of those had bars over the glass. Unpainted wood trim. No trees, no grass, stripped cars on blocks. The stench of mold was everywhere, maybe left over from Katrina—worse in the empty units that were damaged in the hurricane and never repaired. Not in this part of town. The smell of an old fire came from ahead. A house fire. Nothing else smelled quite so bad.

Music blasted from almost every occupied dwelling, a mismatched cacophony of bass and drums. Lights poured into the night. The smell of fried food. Humans. And everywhere the vamp. It had been here a while. Had hunted a while.

I stopped, nostrils flaring. I swiveled to the left. I smelled another vamp. *Its mate,* Beast thought. *It has made itself a female*. A stick snapped to my right. A faint rustle came from the left. The scent of female vamp shifted with the sound.

"Oh, crap," I breathed. They had me surrounded, one to each side. *They* were hunting *me*.

I could take down one vamp alone. I had done it before. But not two attacking together. And like an idiot, I had given chase without proper equipment.

A door in one of the units just ahead opened and three young men left the light, stepping into the dark, closing the door and the music behind them. Black men, lightly clothed. Heavily armed. I smelled sweat and steel and gun oil and ammo and beer and marijuana. "You out there?" one called. "Lady huntin' a vamp?"

"Mr. Leo said we was to come out and *assist* you," another said. I heard the sound of steel hitting flesh, a kind of come-get-it taunt.

"What's my name?" I asked. And quickly slipped through the shadows into the protection of an empty porch, away from where I had spoken. The position put the men and the male vamp in front of me, the female behind.

"Jane. Jane something stupid."

I chuckled. "If you're the center of the clock, and my voice is six o'clock, then we got a young male vamp at one and an even younger female coming up along seven, behind me. You know what 'young' means?"

"Wild. Bloody," another one said. There was a tremor in his voice.

"You think you three can take the male?"

"We can do it," the first one said.

"What you got?" I hated to ask, knowing that the vamps could hear anything I could. They were that close. But I needed to know what kind of weaponry my helpers had. I heard a faint crackle and knew the male vamp had turned his attention to my new pals.

"Crosses. Holy water from Father John. Concentrated garlic oil from Sister Selieah. She a voodoo root doctor."

"We all got vamp-killers," the first one said. "And I got a shotgun."

"Aim away from me, how 'bout it." Before they could laugh, I said, "Yours is here."

The female was rustling grass nearby. I bent my knees and moved toward the sound, away from the three men. Behind me now, the male vamp attacked the men. The shotgun roared. A vamp and a human screamed. Silent, I rounded the house. A thump sounded from somewhere close, but I couldn't place it in the aftermath of the shotgun blast. Dull moonlight lit a dry yard, dead grass in the corners and along the foundation, a fence mostly gone, wood planks still standing here and there. Something white and rusted in the dirt. A washing machine? Otherwise, the yard was empty.

A whisper of sound alerted me. Air displaced. Drawing on Beast's reflexes, I ducked. Whirled the stake up. A weight crashed into me, driving me down. The stake caught her side, too low. Fangs latched on to my forearm, biting into muscle as I hit ground. My left arm and the cross were pinned beneath me. We rolled. She was feral. Gnawing on my arm. Agony like fire. My blood splattered over me, hot and tangy. Her eyes were vamped, bloody and black, crimson and darker than night as they caught the faint light.

Beast rose in me. I could shift now if I had to, but it was harder, pain like death itself, without the ritual. I held her off, but took the strength and speed she shared.

My turban fell, bounced, fell apart. The stake went with it. My braids tumbled around me, tangling. I undulated, a dance move. Brought up the cross and slapped it onto her chest. Steam and crackling of burned vamp flesh misted the air. She didn't notice, gulping my blood with desperate hunger. I released the now-glowing cross, leaving it in her skin. She ground down with her teeth. Pain sizzled into me like lightning. Hand useless, I dropped the knife.

She settled, sitting on my torso, sucking my arm. A parasite/predator/nonhuman *thing*. My skin crawled. I slid my left hand into my jog bra and pulled out a stake. Awkwardly slapped it open. She didn't react. Too busy feeding. I rammed the stake into her side. She stiffened. If she had been even a few days older, she would have rolled away. I adjusted the angle of the stake and shoved it in. Hard. She gasped. Released my right arm, her fangs clicking back, snakelike.

Her eyes focused on me. The vamp eyes bled away into human white. Just for an instant. "What . . . ?" she said. Slowly, the life eased from her eyes. Her vamp-black pupils contracted to human size. In the night, I couldn't see the color of her irises, except that they were pale. Gray, maybe. In a café au lait face that had once been beautiful.

Without a sound, without a human exhalation, in a silence that always left me nonplussed, the vamp died. She fell toward me. Using the momentum of her fall, I pushed her to the side and rolled from beneath her, to my knees and to my feet. Crap. She had bled all over my new shirt. Beast hacked a laugh deep in my heart.

I looked at my savaged arm and tried to make a fist. Three of my fingers wouldn't close. Tendon damage. It didn't hurt as badly as it should, which meant nerve damage too, though blood wasn't pulsing from the wound. She'd injected enough vamp saliva to spasm most of the arteries and veins closed. I turned my arm over, inspecting it, still breathing hard. A human would require major surgery and months of rehab to recover from such an injury. As soon as I could shift, I would be healed. But I had to live long enough to get to someplace safe.

Unlike in fiction, real-world vamp saliva doesn't cause clotting. It causes a spasm of the artery or vein, sealing it tight around vamp teeth, and when the teeth are removed, the same spasm seals the wound shut, so it can clot and heal. The same effect happens on the skin, a localized spasm sealing a flesh wound so tight it's no larger than a pimple. Well, unless the victim has been chewed by a newbie. Of course, vamp predators' evolution didn't require that the prey of the young ones stay alive for long.

But the pain was growing. I had to get out of here and shift. I found my turban and unwound it onto the bare ground, clumsily refolding it into a pressure bandage.

"Need help with that?"

I stiffened. Palmed the stake that had rolled away from the turban.

"It's okay, Jane with the weird last name. I'm cool."

He was behind me. A scuff let me know another one was back at the battle scene. I breathed in the night air. The male vamp was dead. I smelled human blood as well. And human feces. One of them had crapped his pants in fear or in death.

Afraid that Beast had bled into my eyes, I kept my face turned away, forcing her down sufficiently for me to appear completely human, but keeping her close enough to the surface to use her reflexes. I listened for the slightest sound. "You're cool?" I said, my tone asking for clarification. "You mean you won't jump me?"

"Right." A flashlight came on with a sliding click. The beam hit me, landing on my injured arm. The man cursed. He crossed the space between us. "You hurt anywhere else?"

"No," I said, closing my eyes against the glare when it hit me in the face.

"Here. Hold the flash." He knelt, set a weapon on the dirt at his side, and closed my good left fingers around the flashlight, aiming the beam on the wound. It looked a lot worse in the light. I swallowed, heart rate tripping, breath too fast. He was older than I thought, and when he folded my turban into a passable field dressing and tied the bandage with the right amount of pressure, I upped his age again.

"Medic?" I asked.

He glanced at me above the flash. "Marine. Two tours in Afghan, one in Iraq. You learn to do all sorts of shit when you're in the line of fire." His tone was bitter and his smile was full of shadows and mockery, from the night and the military. "Thought I'd be safe when I came home to the United States of America." He made the country sound worse than a war zone. "Instead, I find my hood is fulla bloodsucking vamps, and I got to go back to war just to keep my family safe."

"You got it, though?" I said, turning it into a question at the last moment. "The vamp."

"Staked, belly opened, head a few feet to the side of where it used to sit. True-dead." He paused, then added, "I knew the kid. Fifteen when I left for my first tour."

Not knowing what else to say, I said, "I'm sorry."

He snorted softly in laughter and shook his head as if to say, *Life sucks*. "Yeah. Kinda gripes my ass too."

"You lose any men tonight?" I asked, craning my neck back. I could see only lumps at this distance, in the uncertain light.

"One hurt. Mr. Pellissier can fix him." He took up his weapon, rose, and held a hand down to me. "Can you stand?" I took a breath, steadying myself, and nodded. I took his hand and let him pull me to my feet. "Nice dress." He ran the flashlight up and down me. My skirt had loosed from the makeshift trousers. "You always hunt vamp in a dress and party shoes?"

I couldn't help my laugh. "No. Tonight was a surprise. I usually hunt in better garb." *Pelt*, Beast thought. *And claws.* He still held my good hand, so I increased the pressure, turning it into greeting. "Jane Yellowrock. The girl you just saved from being dinner." Which he had. I might have killed two vamps alone, but not without serious injury. Caught up in the bar fight and the chase, I had miscalculated tonight. A rookie's mistake. I was ticked off at myself.

"Indian name?" he asked. I nodded as he shook my hand, holding it a bit longer than necessary. "Derek Lee. Nice to meet you, Injun Princess. Mr. Leo say you hunt vamp for a living. Kinda strange to hear that from the city's head bloodsucker." He dropped my hand and looked around at the night. A soldier's alertness. I followed his gaze along the street.

Even with the gunshots, no one had come out to see what was happening. Or maybe because of the gunshots. But the music had faded away and the night had gone silent. I was surprised not to hear sirens. "No cops?" I asked.

"Not after dark," he said, the bitterness back in his tone. "They'll respond in daylight if there's enough of them available and if they're in the mood to look for trouble and knock heads. But they stay away after dark." I had nothing to say to that. "You think we got 'em all?" Derek asked, changing the subject.

"I don't know for sure. But the smell of blood usually draws out any in hiding. Especially the young ones." I cradled my arm to my waist. Adrenaline faded; I was hurting. Throbbing. Bad. "I haven't decapitated the girl," I said. "You want to do the honors?" I picked my vamp-killer up from the dirt and handed it to him hilt first. I could have done it myself. I had done it before. But this was his turf. His true-kill, if he wanted it.

He took the hilt, reached into a pocket with his other hand, pulling out a small, vibrating cell phone. Glancing at the display, he flipped it open. "Mr. Pellissier." He sounded exactly like a Marine reporting to headquarters. Beast perked up, listening. Derek strolled away, but not far enough to give him privacy. Unlike a human, I could hear both sides of the conversation.

"Two encom down," he said softly. "One of my men wounded and needing assistance, life threatening if he doesn't get to a hospital or get an infusion from one of you, sir."

I understood that Leo or one of his family could and would heal the injured man. Interesting. I knew vamp blood could heal, but had never seen it happen, the vamp-on-vamp scene between Katie and Leo notwithstanding. I heard Leo say, "And Miss Yellowrock?"

"The girl's injured. It's non–life threatening but she's lost blood and use of one arm, sir. She needs a surgeon or one of you. She took one vampire down single-handedly. She's a good soldier, sir." I felt like I was being recommended for a medal, which might make me one of Derek's men. Funny idea.

"Keep the girl there. I wish to speak with her."

"Yes, sir. How far out are you, sir?" Derek asked.

"Ten minutes." The connection ended and Derek put the phone in his pocket. He looked at me. I sat down heavily on a curb, trying to look weak, light-headed. Not difficult under the circumstances. I put a hand to my head and then to my wounded arm.

Derek said, "You okay?"

"Not really," I said. "I feel kinda sick to my stomach. I think I might throw up." Beast sent me an image of a big cat with her tail flipping, amused.

"Normal reaction. Combat hits some guys that way. Just take a break. I'll finish off your vamp for you."

"Thank you," I said, sounding frail and feminine. Beast hacked a cough and gathered herself for flight. Right. I would not sit here waiting for Leo, no matter what he'd ordered. Moments later Derek walked back, his booted feet agile, his tread soft on the dry ground. He handed my knife back. Though he had cleaned it, I could smell vamp blood on the silver, corrosive, like sulfur and nitric acid or something equally caustic. I hadn't paid much attention to chemistry in school. Now I wish I had. If I ever went to college, I wanted a Chemistry 101 class.

I sheathed the knife. "Thank you." When he didn't answer, I tilted my head up and studied his face. It was hard, closed. "You knew her, too, didn't you?"

He nodded once, the action crisp as a weapon snapping shut. "Jerome's sister." He bit off the words. "She was twelve. I saw her last Saturday." I heard a car engine in the distance. "Seven days . . ." His voice trailed off. "Seven damn days. And she's a vamp." He looked into the distance. "The other one we took down, he made her?" I nodded. "So who made him?"

"I don't know. I couldn't—" *Smell another vamp on him.* Right. I substituted for that, "Leo might be able to tell."

"I'm goin' after whatever made him." The words were low and hard: a *vow*. I had heard a few in my time, and knew the tone. His eyes were bleak. "No matter what Mr. Pellissier say."

Well. That was interesting. I'd love to dissect the relationship between the Marine and the vamp leader, but I wanted out of here before Leo got close. I didn't want to be beholden to the city's head bloodsucker for healing my wound, and I didn't want him to know that I could heal from something this bad on my own. And I wanted to take the girl vamp's head; my blood was on her mouth, and I wasn't keen on Leo smelling my blood for reasons that had everything to do with his dark right of kings. I had no intention of making myself look *interesting* to him. I shifted my feet under me, prepared for the moment when Derek's head was turned. I needed only a second, but I hesitated. "Just a suggestion," I said, gesturing at my clothes. "Vamp hunting's dangerous. Dress the part."

Derek laughed shortly under his breath. "I'd take you with me if I could. But I can't wait till you're a hundred percent."

I accepted the compliment with a small nod. "Leo has my number if you need anything. And hey. If there's a bounty on these two, it's yours."

He accepted and turned. The car engine was growing closer. A powerful motor, finely tuned, sounding heavy on the night air, as if the vehicle it powered was massive. I pushed my feet under me and stood, let myself sway in the night. Derek caught my good hand to steady me. The pain from the other arm pounded through my veins. Beast had better resistance to pain; I drew on her reserves. But I knew my arm was bad. Real bad. "Thank you," I said. "For coming out here tonight. I'd be dead, or close to it, if you had stayed inside where it's safe."

"Ooh rah," he said, and shrugged.

"Semper fi," I said, wondering how many medals he had in his junk drawer.

He laughed, the sound derisive and harsh.

CHAPTER 11

We sa . . . Bobcat

I still didn't know for sure what Leo was driving because I was three blocks away by the time he pulled down the street. The vehicle lights were high off the ground. I figured it was a Hummer. The older, heavier, military model, not the newer, lighter, better mileage version.

I slipped away, taking the girl's head with me, carrying it by its soft curls. I'd dunk it in a nearby pond or swamp to remove my blood, and leave it where Leo could return it to her family for proper burial. Vamp spit had kept my pain down, but was wearing off. Walking hurt.

Cradling my injured arm at my waist, I was out of the hood pretty quickly, but I stuck to the shadows, dangling the head. I figured even the most jaded and cynical inhabitant might report a bloody girl in a party dress carrying a severed head by its hair.

Two things about New Orleans: There is always water nearby, and the very rich live within walking distance of the very poor. In less than a mile, I found a fenced yard with the scent of koi pond. I scanned the area, didn't spot any cameras, didn't smell any dogs on the other side, and hopped the fence. Not trusting my quick scan, I knelt in the heavy shrubbery and surveyed the place. The pond was huge, complete with a miniature waterfall and green plants. The house beyond it was a monster, with arches and lots of screened porch space. It was dark, soundless. I figured it was near two in the morning, so any inhabitants were sleeping.

Concealed behind an elephant-ear plant, I set the head to the side and untied my bandage so I could scoop pond water over my arm, washing off the blood. It was dried and cracking, and had started to burn. I don't know what pH vamp blood is, but it has to be acidic. More chemistry. Maybe a class in Vamp Physiology 101 would be better.

When I had washed off most of the blood, I stripped and rinsed my dance clothes, wrung them out, and put them back on wet. It didn't help the pain, but being clean—well, more clean—helped me in some way I couldn't have explained. The clothes were cool on my skin and smelled sorta fishy. Beast was hungry and informed me she wasn't averse to fish for dinner. "Later," I murmured, keeping an eye on the house as I dunked the head into the pool. Dried blood, fresh blood, and bits of vamp floated free. Attracted by the smell or maybe by all my movement, koi swam close and watched, golden, pink, black-and-white, in tabby cat–blotched patterns. One nibbled on a bit of vamp flesh and spat it out in a puff of water. "Smart fishy," I murmured. I hoped vamp blood wasn't toxic to oversized goldfish.

When the head was as clean as I could get it without bleach and a stiff brush, I turned it in the water and studied it. She was a light-skinned black girl, delicate of bone structure, with loose curls. Her gray eyes stared at me from the water, still wearing the confusion of death. I reached between her lips and eased her vamp teeth down from the roof of her mouth. They were hinged, like a snake's, the bony structure growing in behind her human teeth. I let them contract back. With her dead, the motion was slow, as if the small joints were frozen. Rigor mortis, vamp style, maybe. As I studied the head in the pool of water, the surface stilled, reflecting back the security lights. Reflecting back my face beside hers. Cheekbones prominent, hair a riot of braids falling over my shoulders. Yellow eyes next to the gray ones.

I didn't know her name, only that she was Jerome's sister. And that she had been twelve. I had just killed a twelve-year-old killer. Did that make it okay? Worse than an adult killer?

If I had waited, would Leo have been able to trap her, chain her in his basement, or the New Orleans equivalent, until she developed self- and appetite control? If I hadn't gone behind the abandoned house, would she have waited, hiding while her maker was killed? Would she have not attacked me? Crap. I hated morning-after regrets of any kind, especially the ones that arrived before morning. I didn't know what to feel. Sorrow. Shame. Something.

Beast was silent. She felt no shame, didn't understand the emotion, considering it a waste of time. Reaching into the still water, scattering my reflection, I closed the vamp's eyes.

I stood, still hidden by the huge leaves, and spotted a towel draped over a chair, on a short deck. I stole the towel, wrapping the head, awkward because of my arm. Which was now hurting like a misery—a pounding, pulsing pain that, even with Beast's help, was making me nauseous. I rewrapped the turban around my wounds and loped to the fence, tossed the head over, grabbed the fence top with my good hand, and pulled myself after it. Feeling exhaustion in every muscle, breathing too hard for the exertion, I headed home.

If the U.S. Congress ever passed laws giving vamps complete civil rights, making them something more than monsters, I would have to find another way to make a living. I could go to jail for staking them. Beast showed me a vision of the children's home I lived in for six years. Beast's idea of jail. I'd have to show her a real prison someday. Or a zoo. Beast hissed at me.

I made it back to the freebie house by four, and hit REDIAL while standing on the porch, calling Leo's number again as I unlocked the door. I heard a soft tone from inside just as the smell of vamp hit me. And Bruiser. Beast came alert. Leo Pellissier, head of the NOVC, and his muscle, were in my living room. In the dark. Crap. Crap, crap, *crap*.

The tone came again. I swung open the door. Located their positions by scent. Leo was immobile to my right, Bruiser to my left. I said, "How you doin', Leo, Bruiser? You planning on jumping me when I walk in, or is this a social call?"

I heard a click and the phone didn't ring again. There was a sigh in the dark, from Leo, breathing for effect. "Come in, Jane Yellowrock."

It wasn't exactly a command, but Beast and I weren't in the mood to let a vamp take a dominant position in any kinda way. "You asking or telling?"

After a moment, Leo said, "Please."

I figured that was the best I was gonna get, so I took a breath, pushed the pain down somewhere deep inside, and gripped the head in the towel. It would make a squishy but effective weapon if needed. I stepped inside and turned on the light. Leo was sitting in a yellow floral chair in the living room to the right, elegant legs stretched out and crossed at the ankles, fingers steepled over his chest. No weapon. A suit and tie. Silk shirt. Bruiser was standing in my bedroom doorway, equally weaponless, unless I counted his body as a weapon, which I did.

"You been going through my undies?" I asked. Bruiser's mouth twitched. " 'Cause all I got with me are the travel undies. The leather, silk, and lace stuff is all in the mountains."

"You got leather undies?" Bruiser asked, intrigued. The guy wasn't here to kill me just yet. He was too relaxed. He crossed his arms over his chest. Nice arms, well-defined pecs and biceps, and the forearms of a man on a very lean diet. Slender, muscular.

I smiled, showing teeth. "Nope." I held up the bloody towel and indicated it with a minuscule movement of my injured hand. Which hurt like a mother. Bruiser's arms came free fast. "No weapon," I assured him. To Leo I said, "I think this is what you want."

I knew he could smell what I carried. Leo nodded, the gesture imperious; Bruiser relaxed. I lobbed the wrapped head at Leo. The towel fell free in midair. Leo caught the head, watery blood showering over him. The towel landed in a bloody heap on the hardwood. Leo was holding the vamp's head upside down. Showing great restraint, he raised an eyebrow. I grinned.

"You took the head with you. Why?" he asked, conversational, civilized, a bit . . . droll. Yeah. Droll. The guy was having fun. You coulda blown me away with a feather.

Seeing as how he was sitting in my house, and surely could smell my blood from where he sat, the decision to make off with the head and wash it up to remove traces of my blood on it turned out to be wasted. And not one I wanted to defend. Part of the reason I applied for the New Orleans' job was a vague hope that an old vamp might know what I was, but being sucked on wasn't part of my plan. I shrugged, the defense of a recalcitrant teen.

Leo held the head to the side. It was dripping. "George. Would you be so kind."

George paused. Maybe it was the first time his boss asked him to take a severed head. "There's dishes in the kitchen, Bruiser," I said. "I'm sure Katie wouldn't mind, long as you bring it back all squeaky clean." Bruiser and his boss shared a look that probably had all sorts of meanings, and the henchman went to do his master's bidding. Maybe I should call Bruiser "Igor". I didn't say it, but I couldn't help the grin. My sense of humor is going to be my death.

"You are bleeding," Leo said. His pupils went vamp black. My grin disappeared. Leo Pellissier was probably as good at sniffing out stuff as Beast. He pulled the air into his lungs through his predator nose, little sniffs, like he was at a wine tasting. Which he was, to a vamp. I had an image of glasses of fresh blood and a bunch of vamps sitting around sampling. Or maybe just passing around humans, comparing vintages. *Warped. I'm warped.* The whites of his eyes bled crimson. *And I am so in trouble.*

"You went after a young vampire all alone," he said, his voice silky. "You cost me the use of a good man as he heals and the temporary use of another as he goes after the maker of the male, bent upon revenge. I am not pleased."

"You let a young, uncontrolled vamp into your place of business," I said. Leo's brows went up a half notch, as if surprised I knew he owned the place. I hadn't till now. But it had been his scent there, and I figured if he had been there enough times to leave his vampy fragrance on the furniture, then he probably owned the joint. Some of the red in his eyes bled away, but I wasn't about to relax. Bruiser was taking a bit too long in the kitchen and he wasn't making enough noise to still be searching for a container.

"The Royal Mojo Blues Company used to have a reputation as a safe place in the city that made vamps famous and sexy," I said. "Tonight, a young rogue had a fast, forced meal there. I followed him to his lair. I hadn't intended to take him down, but I injured him in the women's room with a stake. With a wood wound, I knew he'd need blood fast to heal." I was explaining myself. Which I hated. I stopped.

Bruiser entered before the silence could stretch on too long, and set a plastic bowl on the floor and the head in the bowl. It was a perfect fit. I wanted to laugh, and I knew it was because of pain and blood loss. I had to shift soon or I'd be too bad off to meditate; I had to be calm for the ritual. I soooo didn't want to shift without it.

"You are bleeding," Leo said again.

"Yeah. So would you and Bruiser here take a hike? I need some Band-Aids and aspirin."

"You are a pert and prickly child. George."

I hadn't realized it, but Bruiser had eased to his feet and beside me. At the sound of his name, his arms encircled me. Heart rocketing into my throat, I lunged the other way. His fingers clamped down on my wounded arm. I hit my knees. Gagging.

Pain surged through me, waters of agony tiding up my arm, into my belly, pooling and writhing like snakes in a swamp. Black closed in around my vision. For a long moment I couldn't find a breath. Gorge rose in my throat, and I swallowed it back. I was *not* gonna hurl in front of the head of the vamp council. Beast clawed her way up, a hairsbreadth from a shift.

George let go of my arm. Pain did a little shake and slide before it settled down a few notches into what was only a throbbing agony. My ribs heaved, the belated breath its own kind of pain. Beast hesitated, uncertain, waiting. When my vision cleared, I was lying on Katie's floral couch, my injured arm being bathed in icy water by George. Leo stood behind him, his suit coat and tie off, rolling up his sleeves.

"Oh, crap," I said, my voice full of gravel and bigger rocks, grinding over one another. I cleared my throat and tried again. "I'm too old for a spanking and not quite up to defending myself from a butt whupping. Can we do this another time?"

Leo smiled, the grim expression pulling the flesh of his cheeks tight to his bones. He was an elegant man, his silk shirt catching the light and hinting at the olive-toned flesh beneath. His butt was cupped by the tailored pants like a second skin. He was beautiful. Really beautiful.

He knelt by my side with that fluid vamp grace. "Thank you," he said, quietly amused. At which point I realized that I had spoken at least some part of my musings about his butt aloud. If I hadn't been in so much pain, I might have squirmed at the thought. "You are some species of supernatural," he said, his tone conveying that vamp look-into-my-eyes thing they do when they want to mesmerize prey. "But what kind?" His words slid along my flesh like feathers and silk and heated sex, and I trembled slightly. But I didn't answer.

He took my arm from George and inspected it carefully. Pain pounded through me like Cherokee drums. I looked at the wound for the first time in direct light and felt an electric shock quiver through me. The muscles and tendons of my lower arm were shredded like so much raw, pulled meat. My heart sped up. My breath rate increased. Small pools of blood welled from the flesh with my reaction, glistening. Leo's eyes were still crimson, pupils vamp black. But instead of attacking the blood meal, he looked from my arm to my face. Into my eyes.

My heart rate steadied. My breath hitched and stuttered. For a moment, staring into his eyes, I smelled sage and rosemary on the night wind. Saw shadows dancing against cliff walls. And then the images were gone, the living room of Katie's house and Leo's cologne and his slightly spicy, vampy scent in its place.

The vampire blinked and broke the gaze, and I wondered for an instant if he had seen the dancing images. He placed his face along my arm and breathed slowly in, his head tilting on his neck, tendons standing out. He had tied his lovely mane back, a black satin ribbon curling over his shoulder with a tendril of hair. I wanted to touch it, and to keep from reaching out, I curled the fingers of my good hand under until the nails pressed painfully into my palm. I tucked the hand beneath me, between my side and the couch cushion.

"Tell me about yourself," he murmured, tone steely. The breath of his command touched my open wound. It was a balm on the awful pain. The thrumming subsided slightly, a piquant numbness in its place. "Tell me." And the bad thing was that I wanted to. I really wanted to. This guy was good.

To keep from spilling all my secrets, I murmured, "A Christian." I felt the shock strike through him, loosening the bonds he was trying to lace into me. I laughed, a bit of

Beast in the tone. "I'll tell you what I am if you tell me how the vamps came to be."

"Impertinent," he murmured. "Brazen." There was a warmth in his gaze that hadn't been there a moment past. "Cheeky, even." A secretive smile touched his lips, a smile that was almost, but not quite, human. His head followed the length of my arm up to the elbow as he breathed in my scent. And higher, close to my neck. So close.

His breath exhaled against my face, smelling peppery and slightly of almonds, an odd combination that should have been unpleasant or jarring, but wasn't. Heat pooled in my belly, conflicting with the pain. "Bold," he said, his voice dropping low, "rude." I laughed, the sound more Beast than me. His pupils widened a fraction more. "But you smell so good," he finished.

He turned his head, his chiseled nose sharp as a stone axe in the lamplight behind him. He bit his lip; a drop of blood eased out, sliding down his chin. He placed his bloody mouth on my arm. The pain receded like a wave drawn back from shore. I gasped, breath hissing in through my lips as if he'd kissed me. He met my eyes and smiled, his mouth curling against my flesh. He sucked gently on my arm, lapped at torn flesh, his tongue laving, our blood mingling in my wounds. The pain vanished fully and I shivered hard at the loss, my muscles easing.

Vamp saliva really is an analgesic, I thought. I relaxed against the upholstered couch. My belly warmed. Fluttered. I sighed, the sound uneven. Leo chuckled against my skin, the vibrations of laughter pulsing through my arm like blood.

He pulled away a fraction of an inch, his lips parted, revealing long, slender canines, white as bleached bone. He placed his teeth on his bottom lip and bit down again. Blood welled in his mouth. And he bit into my wrist at the damaged vein. I gasped and jerked my arm back, but he held on tight. He wasn't feeding on my blood. He was forcing his blood into me.

The sound of drums returned. Shadows danced on stone walls. Tunics and leggings, fringed and beaded cloth and deer hide, cotton dresses swaying. Sage and wormwood, rosemary and mint filled the air. Sweetgrass smoke billowed around me. Shadows closed over, dancing. Dancing. Cedar and sage burned, the aromatic smoke rising like dreams. Diaphanous, gossamer as butterfly silk, the smoke touched me. Drums beat into my veins. The night wrapped around me like the hand of God. And I fell into sleep. A deep, deep sleep. Dream and memory, both ancient, came together, melded like an alloy into one.

Slowly, I dragged my eyes open, my lids sluggish and heavy. Drums . . . Drums . . . I raised my head. Shadows danced, grotesque and monstrous on stone. Stone everywhere, flickering from campfire flames.

Night. Darkest night. I looked up, searching for the moon, the stars. And saw only the curve of the world above me, stone on stone, melting down like the white man's candles. Pooling, dripping, melting stone.

Underground. The caves . . . Caves? The thought, alien here, vanished.

My father's face, half lit by flame, half shadowed, as black as death, loomed over me. "*Edoda*," I whispered. *Father . . .* His eyes were yellow, like mine. Not the black of The People, the *chelokay,* an alien thought whispered, but the yellow eyes of *u'tlun'ta,* the skinwalker.

Edoda smiled and I breathed in his pride with the herbed smoke—stern, yet full of laughter. An old woman appeared beside him in the night, her face crosshatched with life and age. Her skin pulled down in long droops and stretched up in sharp lines. And her eyes—yellow eyes like mine—were lively and full of tenderness. "*A s dig a*," she murmured. *Baby . . .*

I breathed in a new scent, burning, sweet, choking. The drums took on depth and power. The beat reaching into my blood, into my flesh, melding my heartbeat with it. Taking me over.

"*We sa*," my father whispered. *Bobcat . . .*

Time passed. The drumbeat mellowed. *Edoda* sat close, his flesh hot in the chill air. The old woman, his mother, *u ni li si,* grandmother of many children, sat beside him, her fingers tapping on a skin-head drum. The echoes of her fingertips on the skin beat through me, vibrating deep. Touching sinew, bone, and marrow.

"*A da nv do*," she crooned. *Great Spirit . . .*

"Follow the drum," *Edoda* said.

I looked at the cave wall, at the shadows dancing there,

swaying with exhaustion. The beat of the drum filled me, slow and sonorous, echoing through the cave.

Warmth settled onto me. Fur tickled me. On the wall of dancing shadows, I saw myself as the cat rested on me, ears pointed, tufts curling out. Pelt brushed my sides. My legs. *We sa* . . . bobcat. My face. The overlay of cat face, above my own. Settling onto me, a cured skin.

A necklace of claws, bones, fierce teeth—*Edoda* settled it over my head onto my shoulders. "Reach inside," *Edoda* murmured. "Breathe inside. Into *we sa,* into the snake within." The snake in the skin of the cat . . . Magic tingled along my sides, into my fingers as I slid down, inside the bobcat pelt. Dreaming. Floating in grayness.

Drunken, drugged, a distant voice thought. Mild surprise merged with the drumbeat. I saw the snake resting below the surface, encapsulated in every cell of the hunter cat. In its teeth and bones, in the dried bits of its hardened marrow. A snake, holding all that *we sa* was. The awareness of where the cat and I differed. Where we were the same. And how easy it would be to *shift* from my shape, into the bobcat. So simple. With understanding came purpose and desire. Clarity. The *longing* to shift into the snake within *we sa*. The desire to *become* bobcat.

My first beast. My first *shift*. I let go. I melted, as the stone melted in the cavern above. Taking the shape of bobcat. Pain radiated out, like spokes of the white man's wheels. Yet distant, caught up in the drums, and so, not quite a part of me. The shadows on the stone merged and glittered, gray and dark and light. All color bled out of the night. And I *was* bobcat.

The world was grayer, duller to my eyes. But when I took my first breath as *we sa*, the scents exploded inside me, heavily textured and layered, yet distinct. Smoke, sweat, bad teeth, bear fat, white man's whiskey, blood, herbs. Hunger tugged at me.

I tilted my head and looked at my father, my pointed ears and tufts of curling ear hair moving shadows on the stone. *Edoda*, beside me, had shifted as well. The beast he had chosen was *tlvdatsi*, mountain panther. Killing eyes met mine, round pupils in amber irises. Marauder claws flexed and stretched on the earth. I hunched, making myself small in fear.

Beneath the smells of fire, dancers, and the cat, my father's scent was all but lost. All but. Not quite. I breathed him in, *Edoda* caught beneath the pelt of the shift.

My father was there, clinging to humanity as he looked out at the world through the eyes of predator death. Purring, he nudged me, forcing me to my feet, four legs offering better balance than two. I followed him through the no-longer-so-dark cave, into the night.

Scents and sounds were volatile, intense, so full of power they felt like knife wounds. Air touched my pelt, telling me everything about the world around me. The direction of the wind. The moisture content in the air. The nearness of storm clouds. The season of the year. The last rain was still wet in the dirt beneath my padding paws. I heard the running feet of rodents, an owl overhead in a tree, two does up the ridge, chewing. The owl lifted wings. Night birds hunted and called. Every sense was powerful and concentrated. I flexed out my claws, smaller versions of *Edoda's*, but no less dangerous to my own prey.

Edoda, tlvdatsi, led me into the rhododendron thicket, trunks writhing from bare earth, leaves forming a canopy less than the height of a man above, teaching me to hunt. I followed, watching, scenting, hearing, learning how to bring down a rabbit. My own prey sat still as stone in the brush. Until a fear-crazed rush. I leaped. My claws sank deep, teeth ripping into the back of its neck. I gave the small prey a single shake, breaking its spine. *Edoda* teaching me to kill and to eat. The feel-taste-scent of blood and food, the crunch of bone and hot meat.

The night closed in with the taste. All scent wisped away. I lay on the couch in my freebie house, eyes closed. I remembered. I knew. I knew what I was, from the very beginning. When I appeared out of the forest I wasn't the twelve-year-old girl the white authorities had thought I was. I was far . . . far older. And I had spent a much longer time in Beast's skin than I had thought.

I shivered. I opened my eyes. To meet the vamped-out gaze of a far greater predator, canines exposed, lips drawn back in a slight snarl.

CHAPTER 12

Naked vamps. And the food was naked too

I should have been alarmed. Terrified. Instead, I stretched and sighed. My pain was gone. I flexed my fist, inspected my arm, watching the play of whole muscles beneath unblemished skin. I tugged gently, suggesting by the action that Leo release me. Not fighting him, not jerking free, none of the motions that prey might make. I knew better than to fight myself free from a predator. *Attack or play dead if one wanted to stay alive.* Edoda's *lessons. Returned to me. A gift of this predator. This killer.* So, gently, calmly, I pulled my arm free of his grip. And Leo Pellissier slowly began to seep back into his own eyes.

I smiled at him. And saw surprise swim into his gaze.

"Thank you," I said, knowing I thanked him more for the return of a memory than for healing. I reached slowly toward him with my healed arm, fingers brushing the skin of his neck. He breathed out with the touch. I curled the tendril of his hair around my fingers, my tendons restored, healed, the motion pain free.

When his eyes were not human but no longer fully vampy, he turned his face into my palm and rested his cheek against my fingers, his black hair caught between hand and face. "What are you?" he asked, wonder in his voice. When I didn't answer, he whispered, "Your blood tastes of oak and cedar and the winter wind. Tastes wild, like the world once was. Come to my bed," he breathed on my hand. "Tonight."

I watched, knowing he was using his vamp voice on me, but not minding so very much. Not right now. He kissed my palm, his hair still tangled in my fingers, his lips cool, but soft. His eyes took mine, his gaze velvet lined but powerful, like a gilded cell. "Come to my bed."

"No," I murmured. "Not gonna happen."

Slowly, he took my wrist in his chilled hand and pulled me from his hair, bending my arm and draping it across my body. He pressed my hand there, his cold, dead hand on my living warmth. His eyes searched mine. "Tell me what manner of supernatural you are," he asked. "You are not were, I think. You are something I never tasted. Never heard told of."

I let a faint smile steal over me. "Again," I said, knowing I was risking whatever harmony currently existed between the head of the vamp council and me, "I'll share my secrets with you, if you'll tell me where the vamps came from. Originally. The very first vamp."

He seemed to consider my bargain. "Why do you wish to know this?" he asked.

I settled into the couch, feeling rested and lethargic and vaguely happy, as if I'd downed a single chilled beer on a hot afternoon. "Because all supernaturals fear something. According to the mythos, weres, if they still exist, fear the moon, the planet Venus, and the goddess Diana, the huntress. A witch I know fears dark things that go bump in the night, demons and evil spirits and fickle djinns. And vamps fear the cross," I said. "Not the Star of David, not the symbols of Mohammed, not the sight of a happy Buddha, no matter how strong a believer's faith or how certain his devotion. But the symbols of Christianity all vamps fear, even if wielded by a nonbeliever. So it isn't faith that gives the symbols power. Theologians disagree about why. So I'll trade. Tell me why vamps fear everything about the Church."

"Our curse is different from the weres' ancient curse, and different again from the elvish curse—and curses are what made us all." Pain shadowed Leo's face.

Elves? Crap. There are elves? *And . . . weres. His words claimed that weres were real.*

"No," he said. He stood, fluid and sinuous, more graceful than a dancer. "You ask too much." He looked around the room. Squared his shoulders as if they carried a burden. "George, I'm ready to leave."

Bruiser rose from a chair at the table, the chair legs scraping on the wood floor, and crossed the room. Without glancing my way, he lifted and shook out a suit coat, the silk lining gleaming softly as he held it. Leo Pellissier unrolled his shirtsleeves and shrugged the jacket on. "Have the car brought around," he said.

George flipped open a cell phone and punched a button. A moment later, he said, "Car," and flipped the phone closed. Succinct, was our Bruiser.

Leo looked at me from his full height as I lay on the couch, unconcerned by the disparity in our positions, knowing, without understanding why, that I was safe, though my soft underbelly was exposed to his dominant position, his claws and teeth. Leo's eyes burned into me, unvamped, human looking, yet still forceful, piercing, as if he would cut through the layers of my soul and uncover the secrets at the heart of me.

He said, "I heard drums. Smelled smoke. And there was this . . . mountain lion? Sitting beside you? But it didn't kill you." In a seeming non sequitur, he said, "They say you were raised by wolves."

I let a smile fill my eyes. "No wolves."

His head tilted slightly to the side as he studied me. As he considered whatever it was that he had picked up from my memory. "The cat. It wasn't you."

He was getting close. Beast stirred, uneasy. I let my smile widen, as if I found his statement even funnier than the news accounts that I was raised by wolves. "No," I said. "It wasn't me." *It was my father. It was a memory of my own lost past. And this, this* vampire, *gave it back.* "Thank you," I said again, offering no enlightenment.

"Healing is one responsibility of the elders among us. A . . ." He paused, his gaze turning inward, far away, as if caught still in my memories. Or his own? He seemed to shake himself mentally and looked at me, his black eyes faintly mocking. "A *duty* to those who *serve* us."

"I *work* for you," I said, feeling a bit smug, "for a price." I eased my elbows under me and lifted my body to a half-sitting, half-reclining angle. "I'm not your servant. In fact, because you're paying me to do something I want to do anyway, it seems like you're more the servant than I am."

Leo laughed, real humor crinkling the skin at his eyes. "Pert. Rude."

I acknowledged the accusations with a nod.

"In that case," he said, "I am happy to oblige." He studied me a moment longer. "I wish you to attend a soiree tomorrow night." He held up a hand at the derision and denial that spurted up from inside me. "Most of the vampires in the city will be there. It will be a rare opportunity for you to see them all in one place. We seldom gather in such large numbers."

I watched his face, and if he had ulterior motives in issuing the invitation, I couldn't spot them. "I own exactly one little black dress. One."

"I'm certain it will be fine," he said without expression. "Wear your hair down. No one will notice the dress."

I laughed, sputtering with surprise.

"George will pick you up at midnight." He glanced at his bodyguard and blood-servant. "We're late. I hear the car."

George nodded and stepped to the front door. I heard the lock click and the door opened on well-oiled hinges. And Leo Pellissier and his henchman were gone, leaving behind the scent of pepper and almonds, anise and papyrus, ink made of leaves and berries, and the warm scent of his blood and mine intertwined.

There was still time to shift and let Beast roam the night, but for once, the animal in my soul was silent, quiescent. I lay on the couch in the silent house, half napping, taking a moment I seldom allowed myself, to relax. Near six a.m. I found the energy to pull myself from the couch and move into the bedroom. I stripped and soaked my party clothes in a few capfuls of Woolite while I showered, letting hot water scrub the scents and blood off of me.

I was spending a lot of time in the shower these days, but I had to rewash my hair to get the vamp blood out, combing the long length before braiding it into a single French braid. When I was clean, partially groomed for church in a few hours, still oddly relaxed, I wrapped up in the robe and checked the new outfit. Amazingly, all the vamp blood and my blood had soaked out. Pleased that I hadn't thrown away good money, I left the clothes hanging, dripping in the shower stall, and crawled into bed. I lay there, hearing the echoing plink of water, studying my healed arm as my body relaxed into the mattress.

Leo Pellissier had healed me with vamp blood and saliva. Pretty icky in some regards. In others . . . ? One of the reasons I accepted this job, other than the fact that council-sanctioned vamp-hunting gigs were few and far between, was the half hope, half fear that one of the older vamps might recognize my scent and tell me that they had met my kind before. Leo, who had to be centuries old—older than Katie, if vamp hierarchy made any kind of age-dominant sense—had no idea what I was. As far as I could tell, he didn't know that skinwalkers existed. But weres and elves . . . He indicated they both were *real*, existing somewhere.

I pulled the covers over me as the air conditioner came on with a low hum, blowing chilled air into the house. The sheets were softer than any I owned. Probably high-thread-count Egyptian cotton or something. I usually slept on polyester pulled over a lumpy old mattress, but I could get used to these. I made a fist again, feeling the pull of tendon and muscle. The healed flesh over the injury was pale and pinkish against my coppery skin. The young rogue had left slashes in the periphery of the wound, around my arm, like the tines of a bracelet. It was a wound like any wild animal with fangs might have left. Not unlike Beast might have left on the arm of someone she attacked.

Beast stirred. *Not a vampire*. She spat the thought, repulsed in the same way she would have been at the taste of rotten meat. *Me and you. Us. More than skinwalker, more than* u'tlun'ta. We *are Beast.* She fell silent, brooding. Not quite sure what Beast meant about us being more than a skinwalker—and Beast not being in the mood to enlighten me—I turned off the bedside light and tucked my arm under the covers.

Lying curled in bed, I let my mind wander through what I knew of myself, or guessed of myself, what Aggie had told me, what Leo had revealed, and what I had discovered online, letting my thoughts drift, knowing that, once I relaxed, seemingly unrelated facts often connected. The most important? I smiled in the dark to *finally* remember, to *finally know*, that I was definitely Cherokee. I was from a line of skinwalkers, with a father and grandmother who'd had eyes like mine. The memory proved that not all skinwalkers were evil, despite the legends and stories.

In Western American Indian tradition, primarily Hopi and Navajo, the skinwalker practiced the art of the curse, lured into the murky study of dark arts to control and destroy. The skinwalker practitioner may have begun his studies with the intent to do good, but always gave in to the desire to take the skin of a human, perhaps to obtain a younger body. He became a murderer and went mad. That walker was depicted as a black witch.

In Southeastern Indian lore, primarily Cherokee, the skinwalker had originated as a protector of The People. But in more modern stories, maybe after the white man came, the skinwalker myths changed, and the skinwalker became the liver-eater, the evil version of the skinwalker, sort of like Luke Skywalker going over to the dark side. But the thing I had seen in the alley had smelled vampy, a vampire underneath the odor of rot. Not skinwalker.

And as for me . . . I am a skinwalker. I had lived for a long time, decades longer than the normal panther's or the normal human's life span. I had shifted into cat shape as a child, at some point in my life, probably a point of great danger, and had not gone back except to find the human shape and regenerate. That's what skinwalkers did. We regenerated back to our remembered age each time we shifted, giving ourselves a longer life span. Leo had given me back much memory of the forgotten times.

The shadow of a bush outside the window moved on the far wall as a wet wind blew. In the distance, I heard the fall of raindrops growing harder, faster as they approached, pushed by storm winds. Limbs swept window screens with a *scritch, scritch* sound. Thunder rumbled.

Under the covers, I opened and tightened my fist again. Released it. A drowsy thought came to me on the edge of sleep. Why did Leo refer to the men tonight as "his," as in "cost me the temporary use of one good man . . ."? With the rain falling in torrents, pelting the street and roof and windows with furious force, I fell asleep.

I woke to a blue sky and rain-wet streets, bells tolling in the distance. Half asleep, I rolled from bed. It occurred to me that I had killed a young rogue vamp and given away the bounty. I was nuts.

While a kettle sizzled on the stove top, I dressed in jeans and my best T-shirt, pulled on my boots, and rolled the unused skirt up in Beast's travel pack, hoping it didn't wrinkle too badly. I drank down a pot of tea and ate oatmeal as I read the paper, the *New Orleans Times-Picayune*. Weird name for a paper anywhere but here. Here it was perfect.

The headlines proclaimed that a local politician had been caught leaving a hotel with a transvestite. The mayor and his wife posed for pictures with the governor and his wife. The Obamas were being featured at an event in France. New Orleans musicians were raising money for rebuilding more Katrina-ruined houses. The weather for the next few days was going to be hot, hotter, and hottest. And wet. Big surprise there—not. The vamp deaths hadn't made the news. Sad commentary when nothing that happens in the hood makes the news. Or maybe Leo had quashed the story. Who knew.

At ten thirty I helmeted up, left the house, and kickstarted the bike for an early morning ride through the city. I wasn't Catholic, so I wouldn't be attending services in the Quarter's big cathedral. I had never fit in with a big, fancy church. But the little storefront church next to the dress shop had looked promising.

I parked the bike in the shade of a flowering tree, its branches arching over and down to provide shade. I stuffed my leather jacket in a saddlebag, pulled the skirt over my jeans, and shimmied them off. Rolling them up, I stuffed them in beside the jacket and removed my worn Bible, which hadn't come out since I got to New Orleans. Guilt pricked at me but I squashed it.

Though the boots looked a bit odd with the skirt in the reflection of the storefront windows, the skirt hadn't wrinkled, and it was better than jeans. Some churches were picky about their congregation's wardrobe. I had no intention of offending, even if I didn't like the service well enough to return.

The congregation was singing when I slipped in, late, and took a seat on the back row. There were no musical instruments, which was weird, but the congregation sang hymns I knew in four-part harmony, and with the exception of two loud, off-key voices, it was pretty. Before the sermon, they served the Lord's Supper, which I hadn't had in a while.

I was letting the cracker soften in my mouth, when something seemed to heat in the back of my mind, and I saw a glimpse of Leo Pellissier's face in my memory. But the thought, whatever it was, was gone faster than I could grab it.

The sermon was about church doctrine, not exactly a rabble-rousing, heartwarming, or hell and damnation sermon, nothing to get the spiritual juices flowing. But not bad. And the people were nice, most finding me after the sermon and introducing themselves in a confusing blend of faces, names, and scents. The preacher was an earnest man who could have passed for twelve, with a scraggly attempt at a moustache, but he was probably older. Had to be. It was okay. I might return next week. If I was still here.

There was a ladies' room off the front entrance, where I pulled on the jeans again. I expected the churchgoers to look askance when I emerged in biker gear, but they just smiled harder, if that was possible, showing teeth to prove they wanted me back. No matter what kind of fool motorcycle-gangbanger I might be.

In the parking lot, I chatted about my bike with a few teenagers and an elder who wandered over to make sure I wasn't selling crack to the kiddies. Bitsa's a cutie-pie and the boys were entranced. For that matter, so was the elder, though he tried to act all stern. When I caught the eye of an impatient parent, I shooed away the boys and geared up. Waving in the remaining churchgoers' general direction, I pulled into traffic.

In the packet of papers that came with my contract were the addresses for each of the clan blood-masters. Not their hidden sleeping places, not their lairs, but their public addresses where they entertained, where their mail was sent, and their IRS refunds, and their bills, though it brought a smile to my face to imagine a vamp opening an IRS refund or a Visa bill.

I wanted to drive by as many as I could. *Sniff out their dens*, in Beast-think. Four blood-masters lived in the Garden District: Mearkanis, Arceneau, Rousseau, and Desmarais. The other masters were farther out, with Leo living the most distant. St. Martin, Laurent, and Bouvier were somewhere in between. The "saint" part of St. Martin was a surprise, but then, what I knew about sane vamps was, well, nothing, until now. I was learning stuff I'd never have believed only a month earlier. Sane vamps were a whole different order of business from rogues.

I motored down St. Charles Avenue and entered the Garden District on Third Street. I zipped up and down the blocks, locating the houses, taking time to park the bike and walk down the street in front of and behind each house, sniffing for rogue, trying not to be too obvious.

Vamp security was good. I was riding past the third house on my list, the address of Clan Arceneau's blood-master, looking for a place to park the bike for a walk-around, when a security guy stepped outside. He was lean, narrow-waisted, broad-shouldered, and made no attempt to hide the holstered megagun he carried. He wore khakis, a red T-shirt, and a tough attitude that looked military, along with wraparound sunglasses, which looked pretty stupid in the shadows.

I figured, what the heck, I might as well push the boundaries. I gunned Bitsa through the open, six-foot-tall, black-painted, wrought-iron gate, the twisted bars in a fleur-de-lis and pike-head pattern at the top, and braked at the back bumper of a black Lexus parked in the narrow drive. I killed the engine. Kicked the stand and unhelmeted. The guard watched me the whole time, walking out onto the porch, hands at his sides, ready to pull the big ugly gun if he needed to.

Beast awoke at the possible threat and thought at me, *Holstered gun, like sheathed claws. No match for us.* And, *Other one at door.* I heard footsteps and knew a second guard had come to the door as backup. If there were only two guards, that left the rest of the house vulnerable.

I smiled at Big-Gun, pulling in the scents of the yard. Chemical fertilizers, traces of yappy-dog and house-cat urine and stool, weed killer, dried cow manure, exhaust, rubber tires, rain, oil on the streets. Big-Gun didn't smile back, but he must have decided I was harmless because he put both hands on his waist. "Lost?" he asked. He sounded almost friendly. But then I guess you can sound friendly when you're carrying a small cannon under your arm.

"Nope. I'm looking for Clan Arceneau."

Slicker than lightning, he drew his weapon. He had clearly been drinking vamp blood, to be so fast. Beast tensed. I stared down the barrel of the cannon. "I'm Jane Yellowrock, the hired gun looking for the rogue vamp. You got a minute? For a nice, friendly visit?"

"Depends. You got ID?" When I nodded, he said, "Real slow. Two fingers. Unzip the jacket. When I'm satisfied, you drop the jacket and turn in a circle. *Then* you can pull an ID."

With two fingers, I pulled down the zipper on the jacket, held out one side and then the other, showing that I was not wearing a holster. At his nod, I slid the jacket off and laid it over the leather seat. Holding my arms out, I did a slow pirouette, keeping an eye on the gun. I was certain that Beast could move faster than he could fire, but it wasn't something I wanted to test.

I stopped when I faced front again and set my smile back in place. Being in the gun's sights, it had slipped. "ID?" I asked. He nodded. Still using two fingers, I lifted the jacket and revealed the inner pockets. I pointed to one and slid my fingers inside and back out, the ID between them. At his gesture, I flipped it to the concrete pathway and stepped back. He studied it from the safety of nearly six feet in height before backing toward the house.

"Bring the jacket. You'll be searched at the door. Thoroughly." He grinned. He was going to enjoy it too. I could accept a little groping or I could leave. Not much in the way of other choices. But . . . this was a chance to see inside.

"I can live with a search," I said, pulling off my sunglasses so he could see my eyes. "But if it turns to groping, I'll bust your balls." Beast rose in me like a wraith. Big-Gun started to laugh, but it disappeared fast, his eyes watching me like I was a bomb about to go off.

"Yeah. Guests in the house," he said. Which made no sense to me, but seemed to mean something to him. And then I saw his ear wire. The guys were wired into the system.

Big-Gun looked like an instinct kinda guy, the kind who listened to his gut, followed it, and his gut was telling him I was trouble. But his eyes couldn't see much reason for the reaction, except for the Beast look I had thrown him. Uncomfortable, he kept his eyes on me, as if he thought I might pounce without warning.

To placate him, I smiled sweetly to show I was just a little old thing, female and weak. He wasn't buying it. I had always wondered what Beast looked like to others. I had tried to see the effect by studying myself in a mirror, but it just didn't look like that big of a deal to me.

Beast huffed at the thought. *Looks like death. Big claws. Big teeth.*

Big-Gun waved me in. I picked up the jacket, still with two fingers, and led the way. Inside was another guy, who took my jacket, indicated I was to stand against the wall for the search, and who looked like Big-Gun. Exactly like Big-Gun, except he was wearing a navy blue T-shirt. "Twins?" I asked, putting palms on the wall as I tried to see over my shoulder. They both pulled off glasses and grinned while I did the back-and-forth to compare. "Huh," I said.

Big-Gun-Red-Shirt did a professional, nongroping search, while Big-Gun-Blue-Shirt went through my jacket pockets. I just smiled when his brows rose at some of the stuff he found, announcing them aloud to the house system. "Four crosses. Small New Testament. Keys, seven of them, two that look like storage unit keys, one safe-deposit key. Three house keys, a gate key, all on a Leo horoscope key chain. One small, pearl-handled folding knife with silvered blade. Velcro tourniquet." He sent me an interested look. "Tourniquet?" he said again.

I shrugged. "What can I say? Be prepared." I quoted a Boy Scouts motto.

"Small flashlight," he went on. "What looks like a tooth. Cuff bracelet, silver."

"Hey," I said, delighted. "I thought I lost that. Gimme." When he placed the ornate silver cuff in my hand, I slid it on my arm and admired the gleam. The twins rolled eyes at the girly reaction, but it had the effect of calming Big-Gun-Red-Shirt down from his Beast-induced state of readiness. "Tooth." I held out the same hand. It was a tooth from the same panther that comprised my fetish necklace, carried around for emergency shift, when I didn't have time to do it the easy way, with meditation, in a gold nugget–marked rock garden. He put it in my hand and I tucked it in my jeans pocket. "So. Can we talk?"

"Sure. Brandon," Big-Gun-Red said, pointing at his own

chest. "The ugly one is Brian." They both laughed as if at an old joke. "Staff quarters are this way."

Brian behind me, Brandon led me through the three-story house, which was larger and deeper than I would have thought from the outside. Maybe forty-six feet across the front, and twice that deep, the house took up most of the small lot, with kitchen and added-on staff quarters on the back of the lower story. Which was nice, because the walk through the central hallway allowed me to see the layout.

There was a wide staircase in the foyer, leading up into darkness, carpeted with an Oriental rug in shades of blue and gray and black. The dining room and parlor were on opposite sides of the foyer, with hand-carved cherrywood table and chairs and loads of china showing through glass doors of built-in cabinetry in one room, and antique, upholstered furniture, statues, and objets d'art in the other. Our feet made no sound on the carpeted hallway floor. Gilt-framed paintings hung on the right wall in the wide hall, and a mural graced the left.

A few doors were closed to either side. From the scent of coffee and tea, I identified a butler's pantry that separated the dining room from the expanded kitchen. I got a glimpse of an old-fashioned music room behind the parlor, and smelled mold that was peculiar to old books in the room behind it. But the rooms on the left at the back of the house were for the servants, including security. Brandon opened each as we passed.

There were six bunks in one room, five neatly made, one with a body under the covers, snoring. I smelled blood on him, but as he was still breathing, I figured he was a human blood-slave of the clan and said nothing. I didn't have to like it, but I wasn't here to rescue junkies.

Lockers were on one wall of the bunk room, a laundry on the other. A unisex bathroom was on one side of the hallway, a big storage closet across from it, and a tiny cubical marked SECURITY. Inside was a security console with six monitors, each flipping back and forth with different camera angles, viewing the house and grounds from multiple positions. One showed the street. They had seen me coming. They grinned at me, and I grinned back. "Nice setup."

"It works," Brian said. "Plus we had heard from the Rousseau and Desmarais security teams that a female biker was in the District. We talk." I nodded, impressed. "Want sweet tea?" he asked, indicating a break room with minikitchen, table, chairs, sofas, recliners, and TV.

"That would be nice," I said, on my best children's home manners. I took a seat at the table while he got out glasses and poured tea, and Brandon went back to the security console, glass in hand. He was close enough to participate in the conversation, sipping, his chair at an angle, one eye on the screens, one on me. "Mind a few questions?" I asked, trying for girly and innocent, but not really fooling either twin, even after the silver bracelet incident.

"As long as they aren't about the security precautions or systems of the clans, you can ask anything you want," Brian said. The brothers had mellow voices with a strong Deep South accent, one I had heard only in Louisiana, spoken as if they talked through a mouthful of melting praline candy.

"Ask away," Brandon said.

So I did. We drank cold sweet tea, which tasted fresh brewed, from good quality loose tea, not the tea dust called fannings in grocery store–quality tea bags. I asked about any recent changes in any vamps they knew—feeding changes, habitat changes, scent changes. The twins were an integral part of the vamp security community, which, I discovered, was a growing and lucrative business in cities with a city blood-master and vamps who were out of the closet. Not all of them were, even now with the improving vamp-human relations.

They volunteered info about social relationships, which clans were feuding, which vamps were entering and exiting affairs of the heart, which clans and individual vamps were having financial trouble, or gambling, or building too many blood-servant relationships, or too few, their habits, feeding times, and the emerging human donor systems that allowed vamps to feed without forming blood relationships. This new change bothered them the most.

I studied them as we talked, and my impression of their military backgrounds was reinforced. These guys were smart, and something suggested they were older than they looked. More like Vietnam War military. Or maybe even World War II. It was clear from their carefully controlled physical motions that they fed on vamp blood often enough to be fast. Not quite vamp fast, maybe not even Beast fast, but faster than any regular human.

I wanted to ask about it but that seemed rude. Like, "So, tell me. How often do you suck vamp?" No way to ask directly and still be polite, so I asked, "These human donor systems. Who sets them up?"

While Brian was pouring more tea, Brandon said, "We don't know. It's an Internet thing, like a call-girl site, but for blood donors. Blood for cash. If a vamp needs blood for an evening, he can message the site with contact info, city, cell phone, credit card, and restaurant or hotel where they want to meet. They're in four cities in the United States: New Orleans, New York, San Fran, and LA. But it's spreading. We hear that a new branch is opening in Nashville."

"We're trying to get a handle on who's behind it," Brian said. "Unfortunately, there's nothing illegal in blood for money. Winos have been selling plasma for decades. And it's great for vamps who want an occasional safe, fresh-meat snack, but as a permanent lifestyle it isn't good for the vamp community."

"Why's that?"

"Because the blood-slave and blood-servant relationships are special. They give vampires stability," Brian said. "Emotional, as well as personal and clan security."

Brandon stood and scooted his chair so he could reposition and still see both the screens and me. He straddled the chair, resting his arms across the back. When he spoke again, it was the voice a master sergeant might have used instructing soldiers or grunts, a clipped and well-thought-out spiel, almost rehearsed. I suddenly had to wonder if the brothers had been watching for me, to tell me this. Since any reliable info on vamps was hard to come by I had to wonder why.

"Vampires," he said, "are volatile at the best of times. The younger they are, the more high-strung, hot-tempered, impulsive, unpredictable, and capricious they are. Almost erratic."

"And violent," I said. "Let's not forget violent."

He went on as if I hadn't spoken. "They need good, steady, strong human servants to provide emotional balance and a ready supply of safe, clean blood. Servants who aren't easily riled to help them navigate the human legal, financial, and social systems. Which is why the blood-slave and blood-servant relationships were put into the Vampira Carta. You know of it?"

I nodded. Troll had mentioned it.

"According to the oldest of us—Correen, who lives here with Clan Arceneau—without this stability, vampires go rogue faster. They need the long-term, lifelong bonding that takes place with the slave and servant relationship. They *need* it. They need us."

"Is that what Correen thinks happened with this rogue I'm after? He lost his blood-servant?"

"She thinks it's possible."

I tapped my fingernails on the glass, little tinks of sound as I thought. "What's the difference between slave and servant?"

"Time, money, and monogamy," Brian said. "A blood-servant is a paid employee who offers work and blood meals in return for a salary, security, improved health, expanded life span, and other benefits resulting from a few sips of vampire blood a month. If the relationship works, then a servant is adopted into the vampire's family, becomes part of the financial, emotional, and legal running of it, just like an adopted child would be, but with the benefits not dropped when he or she reaches majority. Servants are too important, too difficult to replace, to let grow old, unhealthy, or slow. Of course, getting out of the relationship is problematic from our end too."

"We're hooked on the blood," Brandon offered, "and on the relationship, which is . . . intense." The brothers shared a quick look that said the type of intense was sexual, but was also something else. Something I hadn't penetrated yet.

"A blood-slave is a blood-junkie, but one who doesn't have a permanent master," Brian said. "Slaves are passed around between masters, usually only inside a family, but not always, and without a contract or the security offered in the longer-term relationship. They're used for food, fed on several times a month, and might be offered a small salary and an occasional blood sip in return. But slaves do it for the high they get when they're fed on, not the relationship."

I rubbed my head, more as an excuse to think than to relieve tension. I had known there was a difference between blood-slaves and blood-servants but the particulars weren't easy to discover. And I was certain that I didn't have the full picture now. I hadn't gained much new info from this conversation, but I had discovered, over the years, that I would eventually use and expand on what I learned. "Thanks," I said. "I'll think about all this. Okay if I call you with questions?"

"Not guaranteeing we'll answer, but you can always ask," Brandon said.

I dropped my hand and stood, stretching. "Okay. So on that note, how about two favors. First, call the other security people and tell them I'm riding around, learning the lay of the land. Ask them not to shoot me if I bike up to their doors." I grinned to show I was only half jesting. "And . . . tell me. How old are you guys?"

Brian laughed. Brandon sighed, looked at his watch, and handed his brother a five-dollar bill, saying, "We have a standing bet. You asked within the first hour. So I lose."

"And?" I asked.

The twins exchanged a look, the kind that only those who have worked closely together for years, like old married couples, or twins, share, the kind that says so much more than words. Brandon said, "We were born in 1822."

I stared. "Crap. You're *old* farts." The brothers laughed, at which point I realized I had spoken aloud. I smiled weakly as they showed me down the hall toward the door, while offering assurances that they would pave the way for me with the other security personnel.

I thought I was done, until I passed the hallway mural. I stopped midstep, midword, midthought. The nighttime pastoral scene was of vamps having a candlelit picnic. Naked vamps. And the food was naked too—alive and human. I couldn't help my blush when I saw Brandon and Brian were part of the scene, and that they were depicted as being very well endowed. Very, very well endowed. My blush made the brothers laugh, one of those manly he-men laughs that said they were, indeed, well endowed, and that they thought blushing was cute.

Beast is not *cute*, she thought at me. I took a steadying breath and said, "I recognize you two, and Leo, and Katie." My blush deepened. "But who are the rest of the . . . um . . . vamps and . . . um . . ."

Brandon took pity on my stumbling and stepped to the mural, pointing. "Arceneau, our blood-master, Grégoire"—he indicated a blond man who looked like he was fifteen when he was turned, like a child beside the lithe and muscular twins—"currently traveling in Europe. Ming of Mearkanis"—he pointed—"now believed to be true-dead, and her blood-servants Benjamin and Riccard. Rousseau and his favorites, Elena and Isabel. Desmarais with his Joseph, Alene, and Louis. Laurent with her Elisabeth and Freeman." The phraseology had taken an old-fashioned cant, and I wondered if the mural took them down memory lane, bringing out archaic wording.

Brian took up the instruction. "St. Martin, and his blood-servant at the time, Renée. And Bouvier with his favorite, *Ka Nvsita*." I reacted with shock. The girl in the painting had long, braided black hair, coppery skin, and lost, lonely eyes that seemed to have a familiar amber tint, much like my own. Her name was Cherokee for dogwood.

Anger rose in me, hot as burning heartwood. "Is she still alive?" I asked, swallowing my anger, to burn in my stomach with sour, acidic fire. I forced my hands to unclench.

"No," Brandon said. "She died in the twenties. She was a good kid. Her father sold her to Adan Bouvier when she was eleven, back in, what was it?" he asked his brother.

"Maybe 1803 or '04? She was mature when we came to servitude," Brian said.

Her father sold her. Like chattel. The vampires hadn't made my tribeswoman a slave; her own father had. I remembered then that selling their own, like cattle, was once the way of The People. I nodded and moved on down the hall and out of the house into the fresh air before I tried to kill a twin. "Thank you for the tea and the information," I said when I had myself under control, standing on the porch. "I may call with questions."

"And we may answer," Brian said.

"Or we may not," Brandon said.

I forced a smile on my face, slid into my jacket, strapped on the helmet, kick-started the bike, and got away.

I spent the rest of the afternoon meeting and greeting the blood-servants who worked security in other clan blood-family houses in the Garden District. After sunset, I motored back home, taking my time through the District and the Quarter. Sunday in the city that parties forever was laid-back. Tourists and citizens went to church, mass, or brunch and then visited museums, strolled along the river, shopped, or had dinner at a quiet restaurant. The Quarter's bookstores, cafés, and small shops did big business. Then came nap time, nearly officially sanctioned nap time in the European style.

At night, the public went back out and started it all over again, the wealthy sitting in elegant restaurants and the penny-pinching back in the cafés. Music played on every street corner. Magic acts and comedy acts spilled into the street along with jazz and blues and every other form of American, African, Island, and European music. Despite the rogue, despite the media vans patrolling the Quarter, and despite having to travel by taxi rather than risk the dangers of walking the balmy streets, people were having fun.

I would join them in a skinny minute, but I had a command appearance at a party full of vamps. I was not looking forward to it at all.

CHAPTER 13

You may call upon me

I checked myself out in the closet mirror, halfway disgusted at the prospect of spending time at a vamp party when I could be tracking down the rogue, and halfway scared to death—and not only at the thought of being surrounded by vamps. My one little black dress was V-necked, thigh-length microfiber that could be scrunched into a travel pack and never show wrinkles. The dress had a built-in bra, was skintight across my chest, plunged enough to make a man look twice, and had narrow straps, and the skirt moved well for dancing. The skirt fabric was cut into various-sized squares that hung point down from the asymmetrical waist and fluttered around my legs. In three-inch heels, my legs looked like they went on forever. I did a little dance step and the squares flipped up higher here and there, showing more skin.

I adjusted the length of the chain until the gold nugget hung a half inch above the neckline, between my breasts. Put on earrings, the old-fashioned kind that held on with screws or little hinged bobs. I had my ears pierced when I was a teen and wore earrings like all the other girls. But the first time I shifted, after I was free and out on my own, my lobes came back healed. I tucked the panther tooth the twins had discovered into the specially made pouch in my undies—the one that usually held a collapsed stake.

I don't own or travel with much makeup. I brushed on a bit of blusher, lined my eyes in black, and added a swish of mascara. Buffed my nails, all twenty of them. Put on three shades of red lipstick before I settled on one. I'd never be beautiful. But I was . . . interesting.

I wondered if any of the vamps would know what I was by my scent. And if I should wear a vamp-killer strapped to my thigh. Just in case. Reluctantly, I decided against a weapon, though I hid a small silver cross in a minuscule bag that also held keys, ID, one credit card, a twenty-dollar bill, and the lipstick. It went on a narrow strap over my head and a shoulder.

I almost left my hair down—it was a nearly four-foot-long veil that hung below the hem of the dress—but at the last minute, as headlights lit my front door, car engine idling, I braided it halfway and clipped a clasp in. I opened the door before he knocked.

Bruiser stood there, dressed in a classic tuxedo, a simple crimson cummerbund, his hair slicked back to reveal a widow's peak and sexy little mole next to his hairline. "Wow," I said before I could stop myself.

He chuckled, pleased, and looked me over, not hiding his perusal of my legs. "Wow yourself. You clean up nice for a vampire-hunting motorcycle mama."

"Thanks," I said, shutting and locking the door behind me. A chauffeur stood beside the open door of a black, slightly stretched Lincoln limo. It could hold six passengers on two bench seats, but there were only the two of us. A privacy partition was up between the driver and the back. Bruiser indicated I should slide in first, and he waited, watching my legs—Bruiser was a leg man, for sure. He slid in beside me and the door closed. The car pulled from the curb and into the night. The suspension was so good the car felt like it floated, and the leather seats were so soft they could have been glove leather, cradling me like a baby. A girl could get used to this.

"I'm guessing you aren't wearing weapons," Bruiser said dryly, still looking me over. "I was supposed to search you, but I see no place for stakes, knives, or guns."

I couldn't help it; I had to toy with him. It was something I had picked up from Beast—a desire to play with my prey. I slanted him a look from the corner of my eye and said, "I own vamp-killer sheaths I can strap to my inner thighs."

"Yeah?" he said, his eyes on my legs and the little skirt.

Bruiser was looking at me the way a woman liked a man to look at her. Appreciation without condescension or objectifying. It was nice. It had been a long time for me, and never by a man who looked so good in a tux, slender, lithe, and elegant. A mental image popped up, of Rick LaFleur in a tux, and nearly made me salivate. I pushed the vision away. "Are you wearing them now?" he asked.

I just smiled, figuring when we arrived I'd either have to lift my skirt or be frisked. And I wondered how I'd react to either.

Bruiser settled back and offered me champagne. I refused. With my metabolism, alcohol filtered out of my system quickly, but I was also unused to it and didn't want to show up at the party sloshed. As we rode, Bruiser pointed out hotels and businesses that catered to vamps, and private homes of the rich and fangy. I nodded a lot and said little, keeping pace with landmarks and street signs as we headed out of the French Quarter, in case I needed to get back alone.

Bruiser asked what drew me to my line of work. I mumbled something about the security business leading to other things. He asked about my dress. I answered with where I bought it—Ross Dress for Less. He chuckled so I didn't volunteer what it cost, which was twenty bucks on sale. I wanted to squirm. It was the kind of small talk I hated. Eventually I fired the same questions back to him, except the one about the dress, of course. "Where is this party?" I asked during an extended conversational lull.

"The Pellissier clan home. Its purpose is to welcome Leo's two newest blood-family members into public life. It should be interesting for you."

"New vamps?" My curiosity went up a couple of notches, and so did my interest. "New as in, 'This is the first time they've been unchained from the basement'?"

Bruiser raised a brow, amused at my deliberate gaucherie, and I suddenly felt better about the conversational footing. "You would do well not to refer to them as 'vamps,' and Leo is not the kind of sire who keeps his scions chained. But yes, this is the first time they will move among humans in a social situation. You've had a chance to study the folder Katie gave you, with photos of the clan blood-masters?"

I nodded, and he produced a similar slim folder from

the side pocket of the car and opened it to reveal three photographs. "The woman is Amitee Marchand," he said of an exquisite woman, black haired and dark eyed, with skin like alabaster and a swan neck that looked like it belonged on a ballerina. "Her brother, Fernand." He pointed at the photo of a dark-haired man. I could see the family resemblance, though the woman looked elegant and her brother just looked jaded. "Miss Marchand is the intended bride of Leo's son, Immanuel," he said, pointing at a digital photograph of a vamp.

The information and the vamp's Christian name were arresting. I pushed myself into an angle on the seat so I could see the photos better. Leo's son, whatever that meant, had short, ash blond hair and chiseled bone structure. His smile was infectious, even from a photo. "Not trying to be catty," I said, "but son like his blood-son, and bride like Bride of Frankenstein?"

Bruiser chuckled. "Immanuel is Leo's biological son, turned when he reached his majority some years ago."

Which could have been years meaning decades or centuries. The young-looking man had little of Leo about him, except for the shape of his jaw and nose, and I never would have caught the resemblance. "I didn't know vamps could breed at all," I said, intrigued. "I figured sperm and eggs died when vamps were brought over."

Bruiser had an agenda and didn't reply to my nosy statement. "Immanuel met the bride in Europe and the marriage was arranged. And please don't use phrases like "Bride of Frankenstein" at the party. I'd rather not have to duel over your insult."

I wasn't sure if he was serious or not, and I had a metal image of Bruiser with a fencing foil or pistols at twenty paces. "I'm just yanking your chain," I said. "Arranged marriage?"

"Things are done differently in vampire families as old and influential as the Pellissiers. The Marchand family has served as blood-servants to Clan Rochefort, in the south of France, for two centuries. The joining of the two families creates business opportunities for Clan Pellissier and strengthens the blood and commercial connections that they currently share."

"So, if the girl is part of Clan Rochefort, why didn't *they* bring her over?" I asked, trying to gain as much information as I could while I had a willing source. And trying to ignore the fact that I was as fascinated as any vamp-fangirl.

"Leo wanted to bring both of the young people over himself, so that Immanuel and Amitee could share in a mind bond later, if they so wished. We're nearly here." He lowered the privacy partition and gave the driver instructions.

I'd have to ask about the mind-bond thing. Along with vamp reproduction. Ick.

Leo's house stood on a bend of the Mississippi River, the water purling softly in the night. It was at the end of a well-paved but little-used road, no houses within sight. The house was built on high ground, the hillock rounded and smooth and clearly artificial, some twenty feet above sea level, higher than anything around it. Curling-limbed live oaks arched over the long drive, standing like sentinels on guard in the night.

The white-painted, two-story brick house was a mixed architectural style all its own, with dormers in the tall slate roof, and gables at each corner with turret rooms, or whatever they were called, on the third floor. Light poured through the windows, black shutters at each, two shutters hanging open at an angle, proving they were working devices, not just for show. Stained-glass windows were here and there, shades of crimson and scarlet and cerise pouring into the dark.

Porches wrapped around both stories, interrupted by the turret things. Lights hidden in the foliage threw a soft white glow on the outside walls while others lit the drive and walks. It was a house originally built in the nineteenth century, one that screamed it had been constructed by slave labor. Slave labor probably kept it looking nice even now, all painted and pristine, but by willing blood-slaves, not by humans bought and transported wearing chains.

Limos moved toward us and turned in behind us, headlights glimmering on the drive. An old man stood at the bottom of a staircase to gesture at the house, as if the guests couldn't figure out where to go once they arrived. When we pulled to a stop, he opened the car door and said, "Good evening, ma'am, George. Mr. Pellissier is waiting for you and the young lady to arrive."

There were probably a dozen steps to the front door. I flashed a lot of leg going up and could tell that Bruiser was enjoying every moment. At the top of the stairs, a woman in sensible shoes and tux skirt with apron offered us champagne, and this time I took a glass to have something to do with my hands. Which were clammy with apprehension.

I had never been to a party as froufrou as this, and I already hated it—designer party clothes, party social manners, and party people milling around chatting. Give me a beer keg, a radio blasting country music, and a bunch of security experts discussing guns, edged weapons, and Harleys and I was fine. This was agony.

At the door I said to Bruiser, "You forgot to search me."

"I'm saving that for later," he said with a half grin. "Much later."

Oh boy. I gulped the champagne. Bruiser chuckled and watched me look the place over.

Inside, the foyer was as big as the living room in the freebie house, floored in white marble, with a mosaic heraldic emblem in front of the door in black, white, gray, and maroon marble, depicting a griffin with drops of blood spraying from his claws, a battle-axe, shield, and banner. A real stone fountain splashed near the crest, beside tables loaded with fruit, cheese, and hot and cold meats: a whole salmon; a roasted piglet with an apple in its mouth; various fried meats; boudin in heaps instead of fried into balls, piled in a heated serving tray; sauces, crackers, and the overwhelming scents of spices and food and vamps. Lots of vamps.

Beast rose, seeing through my eyes, making me breathe deeper, faster, taking in the scents, the world a textured smorgasbord of fragrances, smells tangled as a tapestry, bright as a painting. I counted ten vamps standing in one group. Dozens in smaller groups. *Crap.* There had to be fifty of them, all well fed and moving human slow. All wearing designer gowns and tuxedos, any one of which cost more than everything I owned. Beast went all twitchy. So did I.

Bruiser stood to my side, watching me watch them. I knew I was giving away all sorts of things about me. And I couldn't stop. I had never been in a room with so many vamps—sane or not—or so much money. I focused on the house and the scents I could parse. Vamp scent of old parchment, dried herbs, subtle perfumes, traces of fresh blood from recent feedings. And an underlying reek of entitlement. I didn't smell the rogue. And no one instantly turned to me, pointed, and shouted, "Skinwalker!" I felt a faint disappointment even as relief washed over me.

There were two sets of stairs, one on each side of the huge foyer, curving up and around to a small space at the top, like a stage, with another hallway extending back. Rooms opened up to either side. On the ground floor, the foyer stepped down to a formal reception room beneath the upper floor, with furniture done in shades of charcoal, gray, and soft whites. It wasn't bland, however; touches of color were everywhere from the paintings lining the walls to the pillows on the couches. Rugs in every shade were scattered all over the marble floors, their placement looking haphazard, but they had to be carefully positioned, didn't they? Or did vamps not fall?

I had a mental image of Leo's feet flying up in front of him as he landed in a thumping tumble, fanging his lip. Beast's soft laugh escaped me, breathless. Bruiser raised his brows in puzzlement. I didn't enlighten him. We moved on inside. Maybe ten feet from the front door.

As we passed a group of vamps in formal wear, one black-clad blond woman turned and sniffed the air in my wake. Faster than I could follow, all the others followed suit. Eyes began bleeding black. Fangs snapped down. I stopped. Whipped around to confront them, my back to the wall. Beast rose in my eyes. For a single moment we faced each other. Me wearing heels. No weapons. *Crap*. My heart rate sped up. Beast poured speed into me, her pelt rising and rippling beneath my skin, her claws flexing in my fingertips. The vamps each took a single measured tread toward me. Spreading out. Ringing me. Crap, crap, *crap!*

Bruiser stepped to my side. Placed a proprietary hand on my spine. "The rogue hunter," he said. At his touch and the words, they stopped. I stopped. Beast went still, but so close to the surface I could feel her killing claws burning in my fingertips as if I were already shifting.

As if the vamps shared a single thought, their fangs snapped back in place. The pheromones of alarm in the air reduced. I remembered how to breathe but it hurt, as if my lungs had dried out and lost elasticity. I forced my clawed hands to relax. The blonde looked me up and down, slowly, as if committing me to memory. Cataloguing me. The way a cattle baron might remember and catalogue his herd. "Dominique," she said, her voice heavily laced with French. "Acting head of Clan Arceneau. You may call upon me." Moving human slow, she turned her back. The others followed suit.

"Crap," I whispered. *"You may call upon me?"* Was that a command? Like hell I'd call on her. Bruiser took my arm, pointed to the food, and murmured, "I'll be right back; try not to get killed."

"Good idea," I said, breathless, trying to shake off the fear and adrenaline. "Why didn't I think of that?" He stepped away, gliding almost as smoothly as a vamp. Music started up and I spotted a trio of human musicians with stringed instruments in the corner beneath a huge portrait of a king in robes and crown, slender hunting dogs at his feet. The musicians were playing something classical and vaguely whiny. Not good dance music. I wanted to giggle at the thought. A hysterical, terrified giggle.

Keeping my back to a wall when possible, and my eyes on the vamp groups, I raided the meat table, adding a wedge of cheese and a strawberry just for kicks, and tried to figure out what to do next. What did one do to celebrate not being eaten? Maybe I could go up to all the vamps present and ask if they knew any rogues. A single adrenaline-laced giggle burbled up, like a terrified *heeee*, and the waiter behind the meat tray looked at me oddly. I stuffed a hunk of piglet in my mouth and said around it, "Low blood sugar," to explain the laughter. He set an icing-covered pastry on my plate by way of reply.

Still shaky, I took myself and my overloaded plate on a house tour. Unlike the homes I visited on my Garden District excursion, here I was an invited guest. I figured that meant I could roam where I wanted. It might not help me kill a rogue vamp, but it might help with future searches and vamp contracts to know how the fanged and moneyed lived.

To the right of the reception area was a restaurant-sized kitchen. Inside there were two chefs in white hats and at least a dozen waiters coming and going. The pantry and linen rooms were behind the kitchen with a hallway leading to the backyard and a five-car garage not visible from the front. It was full of fancy cars: the limo that brought us here; an old, boxy Mercedes; a 1950-something Chevy, fully restored; an old Ford from the early days of the automobile—maybe a Model T? I didn't know my old cars. But Leo had a Porsche Boxster in old-blood maroon, which made me smile. It was the Porsche that finally made me relax. That and the protein. I had never tasted pig this good.

Behind the foyer was a short hallway and a locked door, the room seeming to take up a lot of space. Leo's personal quarters? Several fresh human blood scents wafted under the sill and Beast's hackles rose at the smell, but there was no fear mixed in the blood. Curious, I stood in a shadow and watched for a while.

Shortly, two vamps, a man and a woman, left the room, reeking of fresh blood and sex. They didn't lock the door or catch my scent, didn't turn my way. I stepped up, caught the door before it closed, and peeked in. It was a suite with a huge bed, couches, chaise lounges, a studio-sized TV screen, and several humans in various stages of undress. Two were cuddled up with a female vamp who was feeding from them, one at a time. I got it. This was the blood bar. Where vamps came for hors d'oeuvres. And now I knew what to call the donors. Blood-junkies. Yuck.

I let the door close without making a scene because none of the humans was chained, showed signs of physical abuse—if I didn't count multiple fang marks—or looked drugged. Well, drugged beyond the blood bliss they experienced when fed upon by a suitably mature vamp. I moved on. Fast. Back to the reception room and a fresh plate of piglet and salmon. This time I added a cracker and three grapes and meandered on.

A female vamp, walking alone, slowed when she scented me. She smiled, an attempt at humanness, intended to disarm. It worked. I stopped, curious. Waiting. When I didn't speak, she leaned in, too close, way inside my personal space. I tensed, but her fangs stayed back, out of sight, and she didn't try to bite me. She only sniffed my neck. So I didn't react. Much.

She stepped back and tilted her head. "I am Bettina, blood-master of Clan Rousseau." I nodded, but couldn't think of a thing to say. Cat got my tongue. The titter tried to rise yet again. Rousseau was a beautiful woman, with mixed-race heritage, mostly African and European. "They tell me that the rogue hunter is here tonight, as a guest of Pellissier. Are you she?"

When I nodded, she walked around me, a dance step, like a cat walks, one foot carefully placed at a time. She breathed in as she moved. Taking my scent. "You smell so . . . good. Will you call me when this . . . unpleasantness . . . is over?" She stopped in front of me, looking up into my eyes. "I wish to know you better."

There was something in her eyes that said the "know you better" part was in the biblical sense. Lucky me. I swallowed. A smile started in her eyes. And they landed on my throat.

"Bettina. Pellissier wishes to speak with you."

We both turned to the small, rotund human at her side. I had no idea how long he had stood there, but the look on his face said it had been long enough. "Please visit," she said, extending a card that hadn't been in her hand a moment past. And she followed the man away.

"Okaaaay," I murmured to the walls. "Next time I'll wear a whole bottle of perfume."

To the left of the foyer and food was a bar, three waiters serving real liquor, wine, and beer, not blood. I took a second glass of champagne and continued my tour. Behind the bar, a short hallway led to a music room with some stringed instruments and a grand piano. Probably priceless. I wondered who played, and figured it might be Leo. He looked like the type. As the thought entered my mind, a half dozen vamps walked in the room and a male vamp sat at the piano. He began to play, pounding the keys in something martial, the notes rising to the ceiling and spilling out into the hallway, deliberately overpowering the strings in the reception room. The other vamps laughed at the sophomoric prank and one ran to peek around the corner at the human musicians. I guess they thought it was funny. I left.

Through a connecting doorway, I found an empty, two-storied library filled with books, leather furniture, and a first-class sound system playing a soft salsa, which is not the way a salsa is meant to be listened to. I shut the door to the music room, impressed when the pounding piano was muted out. Really good soundproofing in the house: You could kill someone and not have to worry about the screams. I hunted around until I found the sound system controls in a recessed console and upped the volume. Alone, I ate piglet and salmon while my feet danced and I studied the titles on the walls. Some were in English, some were French, Spanish, and maybe Latin. And there were a few that looked Greek. *Leo can read Greek?*

Inside a glass case were twenty-four fired-clay, metal, and carved-wood tablets on display stands, clearly ancient and valuable. I couldn't resist looking over their security and waved at the high-tech minicameras focused on them. Pretty good, if the cameras were monitored. When the door opened a scant twelve seconds later, and Bruiser entered, I patted myself on the back. "Not bad," I said, toasting him with my glass. Which was nearly empty.

"I think you've had enough," he said with an amused smile, as he stole away the glass and the empty plate. "Mr. Pellissier wants to see you."

"Yeah?" I took the dishes back and set them on the console. "Do you salsa?"

"Not in years," he said.

"It's been a while for me too," I said, turning and taking his hands, ignoring Beast's amusement at the double entendre. I placed one of his hands on my hip and kept the other, tapped my foot, and moved into a fast forward step, forcing him into a back step. To give him credit, he followed my lead. And then he took over. Firmly. Salsa is a three-step-pause-three-step dance—a reinvention of the mambo from the original rumba, and it *moves*.

Bruiser took me into a side step, dropped his arm down, up into a J, leading me into two simple turns, and instantly into a double turn as we found our rhythm. After that, things got sweaty. The man could *dance*. It was half seduction, half contest, as if he offered me his bed while testing my footing, my reflexes, and my ability to respond to his vamp-enhanced speed all at once. Our gazes locked, his brown eyes holding mine as I followed his lead. Seduction pheromones, his and mine, filled the air. I wanted to run my fingers through his dark hair and maybe touch the little mole. With my tongue.

The music swelled. Fast. Fast, fast, fast, Beast in control of my reflexes, which told Bruiser all kinds of things about me. I didn't care. The volume rose, dropped, went from fast-paced to slow. I missed a step, only because I was unfamiliar with his lead, not because I didn't know the move. Bruiser's eyes held mine as his hand slid along my side, over my hip. He took my waist and jerked me close at the finale, a tango move I hadn't tried since class.

The music fell silent. We stood in perfect position, chest to chest, breathing hard. A single clap followed in the stillness. Another. Bruiser broke contact, stepping back faster than the dance. My hands were left empty, in the air. I turned to the doorway.

Leo stood there. The door closed behind him. His eyes were on Bruiser. Something crackled in the air between them. Challenge. Anger. Beast growled. Both vamp and man turned to me. Feeling Beast just beneath my skin, pelt moving in anticipation, I laughed, the sound cruel, a bit wild. "Bruiser is good. Are you better?" I/we challenged the predator.

Emotion thrummed through the room: anger, disputation, confrontation, alpha pheromones. The smell of violence baited. For a moment I thought that whatever was between the two males would boil over, but Leo broke, taking a single breath, and the scents evolved from censure, to startlement, to curiosity, to . . . eagerness as his eyes studied me. An anticipation as strong as Beast's rose on the air. All Leo's. From Bruiser, I felt a trace of sentiment, perhaps disappointment, but overshadowed by his master's impatience.

The next track started, a mellow, sex-laden rumba. The rumba is a slower, more formal dance than the salsa, and Leo moved to me, his body already in the dance, his feet in the slow-quick-quick-quick steps of the dance. He took my hands and placed one on his shoulder, starting with an eighth turn of the box step. When the music rose, he pursued it into a quarter-turn box, faster, and then a series of turns and dips, drawing me closer with each measure until only a hint of space separated us. He led me into a difficult cucaracha step, not one I had practiced except with my instructor, but Leo's lead was flawless, beating Raul hands down, his body balanced so perfectly it was poetry to follow. We finished the set with a fast, twisting pretzel of a turn and a dip, my body bent back over his thigh, his body over mine, his eyes bearing down into mine in a classic predator-prey posture.

Beast reared up hard, fast, shoving him back. Growling. The sound was lost in the applause. Gazes fastened to one another, we stared, breath heaving. I was vaguely aware of vamps in the doorway, clapping. Cheering. And then Leo vamped out.

His eyes bled crimson, pupils widening to vampy black. His fangs snapped down. And he growled back at Beast. The crowd in the doorway fell silent, that scary vamp-silence that always presaged violence. Bruiser pushed between us, took Leo's hand, and mine, and led us forward, hands raised like actors on a stage. Weirdly, totally unexpectedly, Leo and I broke gazes, allowing Bruiser the upper hand. He bent forward, pulling us into a deep bow.

"Mithrans, I present Leo Pellissier and his . . . human . . . dance partner, Jane Yellowrock." The pauses at "human" were infinitesimal, but present. The applause started again, uncertain, then growing stronger, more assured, as they believed the growls had been part of a performance. Smiling impeccably, Bruiser led us to the doorway and the accolades of the vamps.

I slipped away from my host shortly thereafter and made a quick round of the second story, searching for and not finding a staircase to the attic or third story. Not once did I scent rogue. I did catch a hint of the woman the rogue and Rick were sleeping with, and later, one of the underlying taints the rogue carried in his blood, but they were lost in the press of guests.

I knew Leo wanted to talk to me, but after the dance and the way he looked at me, like I was a tasty treat, I wanted to avoid that. Totally. So I kept a wary eye as I hunted through the house, turning down a hallway or slipping into an empty room when I spotted him, smelled him, or heard his voice. He wasn't stalking me, exactly, but a frustrated reek pervaded his scent, and I figured I was part of it. But I was able to keep away, and Beast was having a good time helping.

When a bell sounded over the house intercom and sound system, I figured it was time for the presentation of the guests. Curious, I hid behind a marble statue on a matching marble stand over the foyer and watched. Leo stood with his back to the front door, facing the crowd, who gathered vamp fast or drugged-blood-junkie slow, and smiled at them all, the genial host.

"I thank you all for gathering," he said, a slight accent on the word "gathering," "in Clan Pellissier for this celebration. Our clans may no longer expand as they once did, held to lower numbers by Vampira Carta, U.S. law, and social convention. So when a new Mithran is added to us, it is a blessing. And when two are given over to us to fulfill a contract of marriage and clan binding, it is a significant event." He flashed a brilliant smile, all human-looking teeth. "Tonight I present to my honored guests my future daughter-in-law and her brother, Amitee and Fernand Marchand, and the bride's future husband"—he paused, drawing it out, as if in expectation of some huge event—"my son and scion and heir, Immanuel Pellissier."

There was startled silence; then the crowd reacted, half in exultation, half in buzzing, whispered dismay. It took me a moment to realize why. Until now, Leo hadn't named a clan heir. Clearly some of the vamps in the place didn't like his choice. Despite myself, I took note of who wasn't pleased and wasn't afraid to demonstrate it. The most obviously ticked off was a swarthy-skinned vamp I thought might be Rafael Torrez, heir to Clan Mearkanis—blood-master once Ming was declared true-dead. A number of other vamps were looking his way to gauge his reaction.

Violence and dominance pheromones swirled in the room and Leo looked up, his genial smile still in place. But when he spoke, there was a steel edge to his voice that hadn't been there an instant gone, though he didn't look Torrez' way. "And as *my guests*, partaking in the *hospitality* of *my house*, I trust you will abide by all conventions and protocols in welcoming new Mithrans and my clan heir."

It took a moment, but Torrez visibly controlled himself and plastered a false smile on his face. He pushed to the front of the crowd, where he took Amitee's hand and kissed it, murmuring something I missed. With the kiss, the entire room seemed to relax, and I figured that whatever was afoot in vamp politics, like whatever Leo had going on in the human population of the hood, was going to take a backseat to the celebration.

I got a look at the new vamps. They weren't uncontrolled,

ready to vamp out and drain the humans; they looked elegant, sophisticated, and rich. So I avoided them like the plague. But I did get a good look at Leo's son, who appeared genial, urbane, and approachable. However, when I got close, he turned fast, eyes going vampy, sniffing and searching the crowd, so I ducked my head and slipped away. No point in spoiling the engagement if he came on to the little nonhuman in the room for a quick snack. I haunted the back hallways instead.

Near four, after avoiding Leo and Bruiser in a cat and mouse game of "hunt the girl," I slipped outside and called Bluebird Cab. Rinaldo, off from his third-shift job on Sunday night, picked me up half an hour later, full of startled questions now that his regular passenger had come up in the world. I said something about an invitation I hadn't realized would be so vampy, and how happy I was to get out of there—all true—then sat silent in the backseat, holding myself separate from Beast and her demands. And for once, I didn't beg for a trip through a fast-food joint.

There were violent undercurrents in the vamp social fabric, riptides of political unrest, problems I hadn't known existed. It was the kind of thing that cop Jodi Richoux would want me to tell her, and that I was prohibited from sharing on pain of that slow and grisly death, as spelled out in my contract. And . . . I had created friction between Bruiser and his boss. I was still beating myself up about both problems when I went to sleep near dawn, without shifting, yet again.

Monday in New Orleans is laid-back. Not as relaxed as Fridays, but close, though without the dedicated party expectation of the day before the weekend. I elected to stroll, but with purpose, revisiting all the places I had been and places Beast had shown an interest in.

Wearing my light cargo pants, a tank top, and flip-flops, I tied two crosses around my waist and stuffed a stake in my undies and two in my hair, just in case, though I didn't really think I'd be out long enough to lose the protection of daylight. I added sunglasses. Dressed like a local, I strolled, sniffed, and window-shopped.

I don't wear much jewelry, as a hurried shift will leave it broken in the dust, along with torn and mangled clothes, but when I spotted a silver and stone ring and a nugget-style necklace in the window of a narrow storefront, I couldn't help myself. I went inside and when I came out, I was wearing the set, along with the gold chain and nugget I seldom took off. The new necklace was made of Baltic amber, warm, yellow, fifty-million-year-old tree resin that brought out the amber of my eyes. The nuggets were as big as pecans and looked really good with the gold nugget. The silver setting of the ring was styled like cat's claws holding the stone. It was destiny. The set looked really classy against my burnt orange T-shirt, and though I remembered girls from my youth saying I shouldn't mix gold and silver, they weren't here to tease me.

Back on the streets, I strolled, but I wasn't rambling for the ambiance, I was hunting the rogue, tracing the path Beast had taken on her first tracking expedition. My nose is better than most humans for reasons I'm not entirely certain about, but I put it down to the number of years I spent in cat form. I had thought the memories of that time and my early life were gone, never to be recovered, but since Aggie and Leo had brought some back, in startling, three-dimensional, five-sense clarity, perhaps there were others, deeply buried. Really deeply buried.

Three blocks from the river, I spotted Antoine down the block from the hole-in-the-wall eatery Rick had taken me to. The Cajun was wearing a T-shirt, baggy shorts, rope sandals, and dreadlocks in a thick ponytail knotted at his nape with rope. The hair threw me off for a moment, as it had been hidden under his big white chef's hat before. He didn't see me, so I stepped into a recessed door and watched. He was in a hurry, heading away from the river.

Antoine took a direct route, striding hard and fast. A man with purpose. So I followed. Hands in pockets, I ambled up the street, around corners, keeping back, lazy and innocent but moving Beast fast when no one was looking, shadowing him in the tourist crowd. He ducked into a side door of the Royal Mojo Blues Company. "Well, well, well," I murmured to myself. Did I follow? Not sure, and content to just watch, I sat at the tiny table of an outdoor café, ordered beignets—French donuts—and a hot chai despite the heat, studying the RMBC, lazing and calling it work. Nothing much was happening, but I liked the mélange of scents on the wind.

I wasn't far from the kill zone where the rogue had taken down the cops. That could be coincidence—the Quarter was small, after all—and Beast had noted a lot of vamp activity, but I didn't know what to make of Antoine's destination. While I people watched, I sweated and rested in the slow, heated breeze, eating three beignets, which left a dusting of powdered sugar on my shirt. Three more people entered the RMBC, two men and a woman in a long skirt and lots of dangling jewelry. Unlike Antoine, all went in through the front door, though the restaurant wasn't open, a CLOSED sign in the front window. I was getting interested. I caught the eye of the waiter and held up a ten, which I left on the table for the bill and a comfortable tip.

Antoine had entered at the side, near the outdoor seating, so I hopped the gate and followed through that door, which swung on silent hinges. Not breaking and entering exactly, but trespassing for sure. Inside, the heat, which I had somehow forgotten as I sat and sipped tea, was shut out, the air colder than the inside of a refrigerator. Chill bumps rose on my arms as I stood in the blackness and let my eyes adjust.

The restaurant and dance hall smelled of old smoke, old beer, cleansers, a mixture of human and vamp scents, urine and sweat, fried grease, fish, beef, spices and peppers, and minty toothpaste, the scent dissipating as I waited. I followed the faint prickle of power on the air, Antoine's power, familiar from the way it made my fingers tingle, as if the pads itched.

I followed the power signature through the club as easily as a scent, leading me to the back. I could still smell Bliss' blood, and an aromatic whiff of vamp blood, from the aborted staking, and another witch scent, a spicy and tantalizing perfume buried beneath the power signature. The scent perfectly fit the woman in the long skirt and jewelry.

A door opened. The muted sound of a car engine passed, placing it at the front of the building. "Marceline? Anna? Y'all here yet?" It was the Joe. Rick. Which was just one coincidence too many. Or was it? Beast woke and rumbled quietly in my mind. I breathed in, sorting scents as well as I could in this form. Several vamps, including Leo, scores of humans, cigarette smoke. But no particular scent jumped up and screamed logic to me. Rick was getting closer. I had a feeling that if I just stayed put and asked what was going on, I'd be hustled off, so I looked for a hiding place. Nothing. No closets, no cupboards. I peered into the dark overhead. The ceiling was about fifteen feet above me, painted black, along with the exposed ductwork, wires, and fixtures. Beast liked the big duct, and I got an image of a huge tree limb on which to lie in wait for unwary prey. I could probably make the top of the duct if I jumped from the bar.

Beast fast, I raced from the shadows and leaped to the bar top. Crouched on the balls of both feet and the knuckles of one hand. Scanned the room. And spotted a small ledge behind the bar. I gauged the distance, jumped, and caught the ledge with one hand. Swung toward the mirror. Why do all bars go for mirrors? So unhappy drunks can watch themselves cry? So drinkers on the prowl can look for likely sex partners? My fingers slipped and Beast swatted me mentally. My toe touched the mirror and I pushed off, using the swing to get my other hand on the ledge and lever my body up, the new ring cutting into my palm and finger.

The ledge was eighteen inches wide, painted white to reflect tiny lights, which were off. Dust bunnies swirled around me, some big enough to be dust hippos. Beast sent an image of a rabbit the size of a small car. *Good eating.* I grinned and swiveled into a comfortable seat shadowed by, instead of on top of, the duct. From my vantage, I could see almost everything: tables, a curtained area behind the band's stage, a long rack of individual keys behind a sign over the cash register. And Rick, walking into the room. The remembered stink of old cigar clung to him, and I wrinkled my nose. Fresh cigar smell is one thing. Old cigar is another thing entirely.

"In here," Antoine said, emerging from the back. Not from the hallway to the restrooms, but from the far corner, an opening I had missed in the dark of night and not visible from the shadows of the side door or over the bar. "Ricky-bo," he said as the men shook hands.

The front door opened again; Rick turned. A woman entered, a shawl around her head and shoulders despite the heat. The two exchanged a look as she folded the shawl. Her scent reached me and I tensed. It was the woman who slept with the rogue vamp. Surprisingly, she looked familiar, but

I couldn't place her. Had I passed her on the street? Not at Sunday church service, surely, not with her understated elegance. This woman would have stood out—blond, elegant, blue eyes and peaches-and-cream skin, silk and linen and delicate shoes, probably Italian. Big diamonds and gold at her ears and on her ring finger, along with a wedding band. Married. To Rick? Surprising jealously zinged through me. On its heels came the certainty that she was married to someone else, not Rick. The jealousy faded, but not my discomfort that it had emerged in the first place. Rick was too devious for my tastes. Too sly. Too . . . something. Which was why Beast liked him. All these thoughts in the time it took me to take a breath.

"Anna," Antoine said, his Cajun accent thickening as the power he wore like a second skin gathered and tightened about him. "Good, you come. To back." Antoine locked the front door and skirted through the shadows to lock the side door. The three disappeared into the gloom down a short hallway. A door opened. Voices filtered out. The door closed. The place was well built—hurricane proof—and soundproofed. I couldn't make out anything.

I considered jumping down and eavesdropping, but from the way the sounds had echoed when they entered the room, there might be no exit from the back. I didn't want to be caught trespassing, listening at the door. I dropped down, landing lightly on the bar along with a scattering of dust bunnies, which I swept to the floor on my way to the keys. Silently I thanked the nice person who had carefully labeled each, and I made off with one of three for the side door. I hoped no one would notice it was gone.

It was only after I was out on the street, the stolen key in my pocket, that I considered the possible presence of cameras in the restaurant. Cameras that could have seen me leap to the ledge. Not a totally human move. I dismissed the worry that followed. The meeting in the Royal Mojo Blues Company was secret. Unlikely that cameras would be active to catch the attendees arriving or leaving. I was pretty sure I was safe.

I was halfway home when I remembered where I had seen Anna. In the *Times-Picayune*. Anna was the mayor's wife. Now, that was an interesting situation. Rick and the mayor and the rogue all with the same woman. How in heck did she stand the rogue's stink?

CHAPTER 14

Beast was born

By dusk, I made it back to my freebie house, stripped off jewelry and sweaty, dusty clothes, and took four steaks and the necklace of panther claws into the yard. Though it was only marginally night, I shifted.

Hungry. Ate dead cow. Stretched. High on sun-warmed stone, plopped on side, face on rock, whiskers tickling. Purring, as sunset painted sky many purples. Rain sprinkled on warm stone, damping pelt. Scents strong in shower. Mold, river, fish, cow blood, dogs, cats. *Prey.*

Mouse came out to play, leaving tracks in mud. I softened breath. Watched it dart among stones. Eyes slit, lazy, content. Had eaten or would play with mouse. But hunting soon. Foolish to waste strength on mouse. No matter how fun.

Full dark fell. Rain was constant and sluggish. A distant bell tolled. Time passed. Stirred, stretched again, pulling joints, muscles, shaking off rain. Studied garden. Prowled it. Marked it. *My den.* Leaped to wall, slipped into shadow. Padded along alleys and side streets, full of smells. Jumped over tall gates keeping humans out, pets in. Kept to shadows, following her scent back. Food/alcohol/mating place open. Club. Different music makers filled night with sound. Crowd smaller. Humans smelled lonely again.

Slow, steady rain returned, keeping humans indoors. Prowled walls of building, finding dark place on side street. Cars parked. Sniffed out big one, owned by vamp. Leo.

She commanded me, *Hunt. Now*. Huffed but rounded building at swift trot. When street empty, crept near front door. Made self small in shadow, tail tight, feet together, close. Pulled in scents, mouth open, lips pulled back. Found Anna's and Rick's trail, covered by many others, washed by rain. But I am good hunter. Could tell they had left within short time of each other, taking same route. Rick's trail overlay Anna's. Perused her. *Prey*. Followed down Royal Street, away from club. Trail scents overlapping. *Rick stalking Anna*. Hunched low, creeping, keeping to shadows. Cars passed, moving slow. Hid from each. Following. Hunting.

Found their scent hanging on air. Mixed with smell of sex, sweat, chocolate, wine. Above. On ledge. *A private balcony with an open door*—her thoughts. *A hotel, an expensive one.* Room beside theirs contained only faint people scents. Empty. Dark. Doors closed.

Single leap over balcony railing, tail spinning for balance. Table, two chairs took up floor. Dropped between them, bumping table. Pot rattled, rolled for edge. Rose fast. Caught in front paws, held still. Released pot, which settled. Crouching in dark, I/we listened.

"You have to go soon?" Rick asked, his voice lazy.

"Why? You miss me already?"

"Always." Lies in tone of words. Human lips made smacking sounds. Kissing.

Silly thing, kissing. Licking better. But the sound made Jane sad. Angry. I hacked softly. *Take him.* Hunt *him*. She fell silent.

Bed creaked. Scents of sex spilled into night: sweat, semen, hot breath, scent of flowers. Chemicals of Anna-human perfume, stink of detergent, fabric softeners. Also, faint, was part of mad one's scent and blood. Anna-human had been blood meal to it recently, after it fed enough to hide rot scent from human nose. Though Anna-human water-washed, I still smelled it, hidden under chemicals.

Ahhh, Jane thought, excited. *It only smells of decay when it's hungry. That's one reason the scent signature is so complex. Why didn't I figure that out?*

Jane not Beast. Not good hunter. I made quiet sound—*sheeeeghhh*—inhaling, pulling air over tongue, over scent sacs in roof of mouth. Anna-woman not fertile. Yet mated. Confusing humans. Strange. Scent of mad one was also strange. Had new, different parts. Still mad one but not. Confusing as humans mating out of season. Sound and smell of sex ended.

She thought, *Soooo. It eats flesh to hide whatever is happening to it that makes it stink like rot? But why is it rotting? You said it was sick. . . .*

"I still don't understand why you want to talk to him," Anna-human said.

"Business, baby. A deal big enough to take you away from him." Smell of lies on words. "You heard what my friends said today. We *need* to know about those land purchases."

She sighed, pouting. "I'll try to get you in to see him."

Another lie. More kissing sounds. Stinks on wind. Sex without mating is always lies. Humans cannot smell lies. Sad.

"I'd better go. It's a long drive into the country," she said. "Unless you have energy for . . ." More kissing. Low laughter. Smell of sex rising.

Deep within, Jane went silent. Retreating. Beast thought of mouse in garden. Should have stayed. Played with it. Small snack, fresh and frightened. Better than this.

Low moaning, laughter, whispers on air.

She was angry. I growled, soft. *I/we should hunt, kill man. Kill mate who was not.* Some, in past, crossed into my territory, giving signal to mate. Appearing again, again, yet only teasing. Memory of claws raking rump of one. Blood welling in hide as he flipped. Dashed from my hunting land. I huffed in remembered satisfaction. She smiled, amused, less sad.

Mating took long. Far longer than any beast's. When it was over, Anna-human left bed. Showered off scent. Rick didn't shower. Carried her scent on him. They left room. I listened, tracking them as they moved through hotel. A car pulled away from parking garage, her scent on it. Rick walked on street, passing beneath. Gone. I leaped to walkway below balcony. Followed, Jane's interest rising. He walked two blocks, turned down side street.

His bike rested in small lot. I crouched tight beside wall and small porch, watching, listening. Rick stood, half in shadow, half in light from tall pole. He held out piece of paper. Sleepy human hidden in dark reached out. Took it. Money. "Thanks, man," Rick said.

"Anytime, Ricky-bo. You get lucky?" Sex in question, leering. Hidden human stood, a lighter shadow on night.

"Don't I always?" Pride and amusement in question.

"Details, man. I want details."

"Not this time, Paco." Rick grinned, his teeth white. "Maybe next time."

"Come on, man. At least tell me if it was that high yaller gal. You say she put you down like a fighter pro. I didn't figure you'd get lucky with her anytime soon."

"Not her." Man-grin in tone. "But I'm working it. Part of the game, my man. Part of the chase. But the girl's not high yellow. She's Cherokee, I think."

"Yeah? I hear them Injun gals is hot after it."

"We'll see."

Curled my lips, showing teeth. *Jane* not *part of game.*

Rick bumped fists with Paco, dropped helmet over head, and straddled bike. Started it with turn of key. Over growl of machine, he said, "Later, my man." Wheeled bike around, over uneven pavement into street. Bike's roar grew louder. Turned north. Hunter instinct gave destination. He headed toward her house. Her den. *Go home!* she commanded. *Fast!*

I leaped, whirled in midair. Threw self backward, into run. Raced through shadows and light. Streets empty. Dawn was close. I took unknown paths, following air currents moving through Quarter. Heart raced. Breath hot. Body hot.

Big cats are fast. But in summer, only for short time. Better chases in winter, breath billowing, ice on whiskers. Here is always summer. Water splashed from puddles, rank with gasoline and urine. Tongue lolled, breath hard and hoarse, wet sounding.

Smells flew by like wind: humans, dogs, cats, an opossum heavy with young. Food, spices, peppers, rotting garbage, stink from storm drains—warm, wet, full of dead things. Wanted to explore. Slink into dark. She refused. Heat built up inside. Breath like fire.

Near Katie's I sprinted. Bike puttered slowly closer. Slower as he entered my/our territory. Too close. Whipped down narrow passage. Leaped. Landed atop brick wall, running on narrow ledge, like limb but flat. Birds squawked, fluttered, panicked in night. Bike died.

Not dead. She had explained. Not dead. But not alive. Stopped.

Dropped over wall. Landed on big rock. Breath heaving. Hot. Too hot. *Too hot.* Rick rang bell. Knocked, sound loud through empty house. Must shift. *Must* shift. *Now.* Rick at gate. Opened lock. Light in his hand. *Where did he get the key?* Her worry.

My territory. Mine. Pulled back lips to show killing teeth. Saw again paw swatting teasing male, drawing blood. Chasing teasing male from my den. *Mine.* Wanted to attack, but she held back. *No. Wait. Watch.* Panting, I dropped into shadow between rock and wall, curled tight, trying to stifle hot breath. Need water. Much water. Fountain tinkled softly. Teasing with need. As male cat had teased. Hated teasing.

Light played over garden, back, forth, up, down. Boots crunched earth. He moved broken pot, spilling earth, soft sounds of pot, of soil sliding out like insides of dead meal. He paused. Squatted down. I raised head to see; nose and ears not enough.

He was bent over, leg-sitting, torso high. Shining beam of light over place where I ate. Rain washed blood away? Should have . . . He touched ground. Put fingers in light. Watery blood on them. She tensed, watching. Rick wiped hand on dirt, stood, looking at garden. I dropped low. Light and footsteps moved away. He left, locking gate after.

Raced to fountain and drank, drank, drank. Found her form in memory and shifted.

Heat steamed off my naked body in the warm, wet night air. The muscles in my thighs and calves cramped where I crouched on the boulder. Sweat broke out on me in huge puddles, pooling, rivulets running down my spine and between my breasts. Through my hair, tangling the strands. Nausea and hunger warred in my belly, cramping there as well.

A pain gripped my middle and I retched. Startled, I threw up the heated water I had just drank. That had never happened before. I was too hot. I had seldom run for so long in Beast's form, and I was having trouble throwing off the heat. I could trot or walk for long distances, but a dead run was for the final killing sprint, when claws and teeth locked down on the hindquarters and leg tendons of escaping big prey, prey marked from a botched ambush, when dropping down from a high limb or ledge went wrong. Sprinting was for killing. Not for running city streets.

I forced myself to stand, pulled the travel pack from around my neck; it had slid during the run, choking. Unsteady, sweat slick on my skin, I made my way to the house and inside. Instantly I smelled another intruder, gone now; his scent hanging on the air was several hours old. Bruiser had paid me a visit. Dang, I was getting popular. I stumbled to the shower, tossed the now dry clothes outside the shower door and turned on the cold water, or as cold as water ever got in this heated swamp of a place. I stood under the spray, letting it wash away the stink of sweat and the gasoline I had splashed through, draining away the sick feeling. It took a long time. Longer than I expected. The shower pounded down and I drank the spray to rehydrate. Rubbed my cramping calves, one foot at a time on the corner seat. I shuddered with reaction.

No wonder the big cats native to this region were so much smaller than their Appalachian cousins had been. Heat dissipation was hard with a larger body mass. When I was finally cool, I dried off and walked to the kitchen where I ate two Snickers while cooking a big, eight-cup pot of oatmeal. I ate every bite standing up at the stove, naked and trembling and shoveling it in.

I shouldn't have forced Beast, not made her run so long and hard. But then I'd have missed seeing the Joe search my garden. I had to find out who had given him a gate key. And take it from him. And teach him a lesson about invading my home.

My territory, Beast rumbled angrily. *My den.*

"Yeah. I agree totally," I said between bites. "My territory." No matter how temporary.

When hunger was sated enough for me to think, I twisted my hair out of the way, into a knot and long, wet ponytail, and walked through the house, scenting. Bruiser had entered from the side porch. Another interloper to deal with. Just how many keys to my freebie house and garden were there? Had Katie given them out like candy?

Bruiser had made his way through the house slowly, pausing at each of the places where I had discovered cameras. I knelt and sniffed at each; he hadn't touched anything. Even in human form I was pretty sure his scent wasn't on the wires or the cables. He just paused in each spot, as if studying the destruction. In the bath, he had touched the clothes hanging in the shower, still damp at the time, his scent on them stronger, as if he had inspected them for bloodstains.

His MO changed in my bedroom. He stayed by each camera longer, maybe looking around, studying, taking it in. His scent was on the handles. He had opened each drawer, looked in the closet. Touched my clothes, squeezing pockets and hems with a thoroughness that wasn't carnal—it was a professional search. I got a chair and checked the box on the top shelf. I placed a finger on it, feeling the faint buzzing that indicated the obfuscation spell was still activated. He hadn't touched it. But I couldn't say the same thing about my weapons. They had been handled.

I carried the Benelli M4 Super 90 shotgun to the bed and checked it for tampering. This model M4 had been designated by the military as a Joint Service Combat Shotgun. Its steel components had a matte black, phosphated, corrosion-resistant finish; the aluminum parts were matte and hard anodized; the finish reduced the weapon's visibility during night operations. The shotgun is considered by many experts to be nearly idiotproof. It requires little or no maintenance, operates in all climates and weather conditions, can be dumped in a lake or pond and left there for a long time and not corrode. It can fire twenty-five thousand rounds of standard ammunition without needing to have any major parts replaced. I had studied long and hard before investing in the weapon.

The Benelli, a smoothbore, magazine-fed, semiauto shotgun, is designed around the autoregulating gas-operated—ARGO—firing system, with dual gas cylinders, gas pistons, and action rods for increased reliability. Locking the barrel is achieved by a rotating bolt with two lugs. It can fire 2.75- and 3-inch shells of differing power levels without any operator adjustments and in any combination, and can be adjusted or fieldstripped without tools. It's perfect for close-in fighting in low-light operations. It's a totally cool weapon. Mostly, though, I just liked the fact that it was idiotproof.

The weapon was loaded for vamp with hand-packed silver-fléchette rounds made by a pal in the mountains. Fléchettes were like tiny knives, which, when fired, spread out in a widening, circular pattern, entering the target with lacerating, deadly force. The fact that each fléchette was composed of sterling silver decreased their penetrating power but made them poisonous to vamps, even without a direct hit. There was no way a vamp could cut all of them out of his body before he bled out or the silver spread through his system. I opened the cock, inspected each round with eye and nose. Bruiser hadn't messed with the weapon except to see what I carried.

Other than camera hunting, I hadn't been to the second story. Still naked, I followed Bruiser up there, from room to room, all four of the antique-decorated bedrooms, closets, and both baths. He was faster here. A lot faster, as if he knew I was seldom upstairs. Which was a little odd. He might *guess* I stayed downstairs, but how could he *know*?

Back downstairs, he spent a lot of time in the kitchen, especially looking in the refrigerator. Most of the original beef was gone, leaving only a few good quality sirloin steaks.

It took me some time to work through the emotional pheromones in the traces he left, but I finally settled on two. Disgust and curiosity were in his scent in equal parts. Now, why did the henchman of the head of the vamp council need to know about disabled cameras in my house? And look in my closet and drawers? My refrigerator? Had Leo sent him? If so, why?

The memory of the cave dream returned, bright and shocking in its intensity. For a moment, I was in the cave, breathing herbed smoke, shadow figures dancing on the walls. I jerked back to the now, putting out a hand for balance.

Exhausted, feeling violated at the intrusion into my home and garden, I walked from door to door, checking the locks—what little good that would do me with all the keys floating around. After that, with dawn graying the sky, I crawled into bed and was asleep instantly.

The dream came at me, slow, predatory. Slipped up, padding close, a vision of a pregnant moon, big, round, full of light, glistening on snow, reflecting back from icicles hanging from tree limbs. Stars in the sky were cold, less bright than on sickle moon nights. I was cat, but not Beast. Was myself but not quite, in the odd way of dreams. I scented the darkness, whiskers trembling, smelling the forest, alive beneath the snow but heavy with winter's long slumber.

I sat, unmoving, short, stubby tail tucked close, staring over a pristine expanse of meadow left by white man's fire. Pangs tore at me, hunger gripping my belly. I had hunted, had caught a rabbit days ago. Now I waited, watching for movement on snow. I had to eat or I would die.

The wind changed, lifting my fur. The frozen scent of meat came on the air. Blood. A kill, not mine, lay beneath snow. Close. Hunger clawed at my belly. I stood, opened my mouth, and pulled in scents as *Edoda* had taught me. Big-Cat scent was merged with the blood scent. Fear cut into hunger, fear of Big Cat. Panther. *Tlvdatsi*. Hope shot through me. *Tlvdatsi. Edoda*. I huffed hard. No. Edoda *is dead*. His blood scent was a cruel memory.

Grief brought the awareness that I was dreaming. An awareness that pushed me up and out of the dream, making me an observer. *This is new*, I thought. *Not a dream. A memory*. Excitement built along my nerves. In the dream/memory, I sniffed deeply; *flehmen behavior,* another part of me thought, sleepily. *Jacobsen's organ, necessary for all creatures who use olfactory and pheromonal communication methods*.

This was a different cat scent, dangerous to bobcat—to *we sa*. To *me*. But the Big Cat was gone. It had hidden its kill. I crept across the snow, pausing often to crouch and to listen. To scent the wind. Gone. Big Cat had abandoned its prey.

The scent of blood grew, frozen beneath the snow. Hunger clawed at me as if alive, demanding, *eat, eat, eat*. The kill was shoved beneath the lip of a white and yellow rock, quartz white as snow, veined with the white man's gold. The blood scent reached up through the snow. I unsheathed my claws and batted snow away, moon-touched fluffs flying in the dark night.

A frozen deer carcass was revealed and I tore into it with claws and sharp teeth. Eating, desperate. Blood melting and smearing across my cold fur and paws and jaws. Hunger stopped tearing into me, satisfied. And still I ate. Gorging.

Weight slammed me into carcass. Claws tore into my shoulders. *Big Cat.* I tried to run. My pelt ripped in her claws. The smell of my blood was hot in the night. *Tlvdatsi* screamed. Pawed me over, exposing my belly. I raised my paws, claws extended, ripping into her face. The scent of cubs, born out of season, was strong on her. Her blood fell onto me. Her fangs tore into my belly. Ripping. My claws slashed deep into her. Our blood mingled, running together. The snake buried in the blood of *tlvdatsi* opened to me. Pain tore into my heart. My breath stopped. *I am dying.*

I sank into the snake of the *tlvdatsi*. Deep. Deep. I saw where we were similar. And different. I couldn't be Big Cat. I was too small. Darkness pushed inside me. Dying. One last clench of claw. Hopeless. Frantic.

I shivered into the snake. And stole the body of *tlvdatsi*. Not just the snake under her skin, to share her form. I took *her*. Stealing her body. *Stealing her soul.*

Light and cold and blood exploded through me. *Tlvdatsi* screamed in rage. Fighting me. Inside with me. *Nonono-nonononononono.*

I took *tlvdatsi.* Made her mine. I shoved my memory into her skin. With her.

I/we rolled across snow. Heaving breaths. The world shifted, shuddered, quaked. I fought her for control. And I/we rose up, hunger demanding. I/we ate from her kill. My kill. *Tlvdatsi* screamed and raged. *Eat, eat.* Belly aching with need. Then, *Kits. Kits. Kits.*

I stopped eating when I was full. Satisfied. And *big*. The Beast was crouched inside *tlvdatsi* with me. Watching. *Kits*, she demanded. Showed me the path, back to her/our den. Scents, landmarks, places marked to make it ours/hers, hers/ours. Followed near the trail, in the spoor of a wolf, hiding my tracks with his. Would have to kill the wolf soon. Danger to kits.

Kits made hunger cries, chirping whistles. Squealed low-pitched. I/we followed my beast scent to den, low cave in rock, opening wide enough to crawl through, into the dark of earth, into cave. Leaves had blown in. *Good den.* I/we touched, licked, smelled cubs. Very young. Breath full of milk, open mouths in dark. I/we settled with them, grooming paws. Cubs pulled at us, milk teeth uncomfortable yet soothing as they nursed. Language and history and memory fell away. Buried. Beast was born.

I woke with a shudder. I was drenched in sweat, my heart an uneven trip-hammer. "Crap. What was that?" But I knew. *I knew.* It was a memory of my own past. It was the memory of how Beast and I ended up inside me together. I had stolen her body. And ended up with her soul, inside, with me.

Deep within, I heard Beast's panting breaths. I tasted her anger, old and worn like a bone with nothing left inside or out, no marrow, no substance except memory.

"Dear God," I whispered. "What did I do?"

Neither God nor Beast answered me.

This was outside the life of a skinwalker. I knew that without knowing how I knew. I had done foulest evil. I had stolen the body of a living creature. Beast had called me liver-eater.

I rose from the tangled damp sheets and stripped the bed, made it up with fresh sheets, tossing the damp ones into the corner. Stinking with flop sweat, I took a shower, standing a long time under the water as if it could really clean me. Exhausted, I climbed back in bed and pulled the sheets and coverlet over me.

Black magic. I had done black magic.

CHAPTER 15

I was still buck naked

I woke at the sound of a scream. Scream on scream. Women. In terror. *Katie's*.

I was up and running before I came fully awake. Grabbing weapons and crosses from the closet. Slinging the shotgun free of its harness. I raced through the house and outside, into the half-light of predawn. Dropping crosses over my head, sticking stakes into my hair. I went over the wall without breaking stride, brick scraping my legs.

"Crap," I grunted. I was still buck naked. Time to worry about that later. If I lived.

Katie's back door was hanging open at an angle. Ripped from its hinges. I paused and took in the door; claw marks had scored the wood. The rogue's compound scent was smeared on the door, the rotten reek uppermost, rank in the air. If what I had figured out in the previous long night was true, it needed to feed. *Mad one. Liver-eater.* Beast bristled and I growled.

I had just checked the loads, but my hands flew through the motions anyway. Satisfied, I set the stock at my shoulder and moved into the house, placing each bare foot carefully before transferring my weight forward, my hair brushing my back with each step. My breath hurt in my lungs as I tried to breathe silently after the run, unable to draw in enough air; my heart tried to slow from sprinting speed, pounding an erratic rhythm.

The sconce lights were on, but muted, dimmed for the

night. I smelled blood, heard crying. Someone else gurgled with each breath, as if breathing underwater, or through a restricted airway. The blood and gurgling came from my right, the dining room, maybe.

An aborted scream tugged me the opposite direction. I took a hard breath, settling myself. Weapon muzzle leading, the butt tight to my shoulder, I moved left down the hallway. Silent, I stepped into Katie's office. For an instant that lasted forever, I took it in.

Blood was sprayed over the walls and ceiling in huge, glistening gouts. Troll was against the wall. A lamp burned, casting the room into jagged shadows, cutting his face into planes of light and dark, his bald pate shining with sweat. He was watching across the room, cheeks red, fisted hands at his sides. Muscles straining. He grunted with effort. Immobile. *Pinned*, Beast thought. Not breathing; trying to get free. His skin was both flushed and gray. Tears coursed down his face.

At the desk, across the destroyed room, the rogue vamp was bent, hunched. He held Katie to his mouth, his fangs buried in her stomach. Sucking. *Chewing*. His hair streamed forward, hiding his face. Black hair. Dark skin showing through, coppery. Like mine. His hands were clawed—not recurved, retractile claws for catching and bringing down prey, but bird claws, for grabbing prey on the fly.

A drop of blood fell from the ceiling. Slowly. Catching the dim light. Landing on my shoulder with a soft, cold plop. I took in a breath, so heavily scented with vamp blood and rogue it was choking.

Faster than thought, pictures of possibility overlay one another in my mind. Me firing. Katie taking some of the poisonous rounds. Me racing in to place the shotgun into his side. Him stopping me with his mind. Me slapping silver crosses all over him, to watch him bubble and burn. Him stopping me with his mind. Me racing in to stake him. Him stopping me with his mind. No good alternatives. I pulled a stake from my hair. Sprinted in. Time went sluggish.

The rogue looked up. Vampy eyes, black pupils the size of dimes in crimson, bloody orbs. He lifted his mouth from Katie. Blood spouted over his face. His tongue was black.

His mind reached out, black tingles of power stinging

along my skin. His mind gripped mine. Vampiric and frozen. *Stop*, he commanded.

Momentum fought his compulsion. I couldn't stop. Stumbled. Beast reared up. I/we screamed. Caught my balance two steps away. Still moving. The black electric power tightened on me, gripping. Time slowed, taking on texture, thickening to a heavy, oily consistency. Feeling as if I moved underwater, my muscles stretched. I turned the stake for an underarm thrust. A killing strike as I ran. One step.

Gore coated his mouth and chin and spilled down his clothes. Fancy clothes. A tuxedo. A second step. He laughed. The laughter splashed over me like warm honey. Congealing over me. *Stop.* . . . Blackness took me. Momentum still had me in its grip. His mind . . . closed over me.

But Beast had my soul. With a scream that tore through my brain and out my throat, Beast ripped me free of his control. I crashed into the rogue. The Benelli and my body slid between his and Katie's. She started to fall. The stake rose up on its arc from near my thigh. Lifting to slash up between us. Aimed into his belly and up, under his ribs. I caught a glimpse of his face. A man. Hawkish nose and chin. Lips pulled back from fangs on both upper and lower jaw. Not something I had ever seen before.

The air shivered. Cold. *Icy*. And the vamp was gone.

I fell forward, stumbling, catching myself with Beast's reflexes. Bent-kneed, body in a half crouch, I caught Katie across my thigh. I eased her to the floor. Whirled. Whipped my head, following the rogue's scent. His complex, compound scent changing. Beast sucked it in, over her/my tongue. *Changing . . . liver-eater rot. Something else . . . rogue/not-rogue.*

Troll's breath like a bellows, ragged and hoarse as he knelt beside me. "Katie," he said, his voice rising on the last syllable. He stopped, his hands hovering just above her, uncertain. Her dress had been ripped away, exposing small breasts with tiny pink nipples. A scar, brown and uniform, marked her upper arm. A fleur-de-lis. A *brand*, I realized. What the heck?

A hideous wound in her belly started at her rib cage and ended at the juts of her hip bones. Fangs had scored across her skin. A large portion of her torso on the right side was gone. Over the liver. It oozed. Katie had been eaten. "Katie," Troll whispered. Shock and horror froze him immobile, as he had been when the rogue held him at bay. Beast's hearing detected a faint thump.

"Her heart's still beating," I said, blood pumping once in her throat, up her carotid artery to her brain. "She's still . . . with us." Not quite alive. But not gone.

He gathered Katie in his arms, cradling her, pressing a hand over the gruesome hole in her stomach. Her blood covered him to the wrist. I handed him a pillow to press over her instead. He looked up from her, tears drying on his face. Visibly, he pulled himself together, the poise and self-control of an old soldier. "He busted all the phones. Disabled the security system. Get Leo." Then he looked at me. "You're naked."

"I noticed. Did you see him? Did you get a look at his face?"

"No. All I could see was a blur. Vamp mind games."

Get Leo, he had said. Not yet. I ran from the room, chasing the evolving scents of the rogue. Trying to understand. I had assumed the rogue's compound scent was like a human's, changing due to emotional stress, exercise, spices—or in this case, blood—eaten. But this was different. Its scent signature was actually changing, new scents evolving, wiping out others.

Nothing can change its basic, individual, singular, one-in-six-billion scent. We can wash until it's faint, cover it with chemicals so it's hard to distinguish, alter it with fear, illness, or age. But the basic, underlying scent, in its most elemental state, is unique, the distinct chemical reactions in the cells of one person, no matter how layered, masked, or compounded. But this guy's scent wasn't just compounding. It was altering. I followed it down the hall.

The crying, gurgling, and odor of fresh blood I had noted when I entered the house came strongly from the dining room. I put my back against the hall wall and checked behind me, swinging the weapon back and forth, up the hall and down. A sconce was broken. I stepped over shattered glass. My heart had stabilized with activity into a fast, hard rate, my breath deep and steady. The smell of my sweat was free from fear, marked by concentration and adrenaline.

The dining room was a shambles. The huge carved table was overturned, chairs tossed and broken. Blood was splattered across Katie's paintings. But the rogue had come and gone. I said softly, "Who's here? It's Jane Yellowrock."

A blond head came out from behind the table, hair streaked with gore. It was Indigo, blue eyes so wide that white showed all around. When she saw me, she scrambled to her feet, around the table, and into my side, bumping me hard. Trembling so forcefully even her skin quaked. She stank of fear.

"Help Miz A," she whispered, pointing. "She's bleeding bad." A stocking-clad foot stuck out from the overturned table, a house shoe hanging from gnarled toes.

"Is your room upstairs?" I asked, my voice dropping low. She nodded yes, her teeth chattering with reaction. "Go up. Lock yourself in." I pushed her gently toward the hallway. "Find a phone. Call Leo and tell him to get his ass over here. Then call 911. We need cops and ambulances." Maybe a SWAT team. Or the military.

Indigo looked from me to the hallway. Her breath stopped.

"If he's still here, he's downstairs," I said, barely controlling a frustrated growl. And I knew it was true. His scent on the air currents veered away from the stairs that led to the girls' quarters. My lips peeled back. "Go!"

I shoved her and jumped over the table, landing beside a skirt-and-apron-covered leg that was attached to the stockinged foot. Miz A was wedged between the table and the wall, her face purpled with bruises and so pale she looked drained. Blood pumped from her upper arm.

I lifted a linen napkin from the floor and tied a tourniquet above the wound, around her arm. I used a long splinter of broken chair to twist it tight, and saw with satisfaction that the blood stopped pumping. Another body was half beneath her in a tangle of chains and blood. Christie. And she wasn't breathing. I remembered the sound of gurgling.

I had no choice. I released the tourniquet. Blood flowed again, but more weakly this time. I stepped forward, my hip brushing the drapes away to reveal a slice of window and pale gray light. It was near dawn. Finally. Gently, in case she had suffered cervical spinal damage, I straightened Christie's head, opening her airway. The instant intake of air was reassuring, but if I let go of her head, it was going to flop back again, closing her airway. And Miz A's tourniquet wasn't going to tighten all by itself.

"I can do it."

I whipped the shotgun one-handed, animal fast, my finger on the trigger. It centered on Indigo's white face as she danced back, both hands in the air, surrendering. "It's just me!"

"I told you—"

"I have my cell." She held out a bright pink, multikeyed phone, and slid around the table and under my arm, slapping the cell into my hand as she took Christie's head, maintaining the airway. "It's Leo."

"You know how to keep a tourniquet tight?" I asked, pointing with the wireless.

I was gratified to see her handle the airway with a knee and the tourniquet with her hands. "Red Cross first aid course," she said. She was still pale and wide-eyed, but seemed calmer. Sometimes it helped with panic to have a job to do.

"Fine." I lifted a long splinter from the floor and set it beside her. "I reckon you know how to use a stake too." She wet her lips and nodded. Not that the rogue would let her. I remembered the cloying tug of his mind. Stopping me. But it might help her to feel a little safer.

I put the phone to my ear as I moved back toward the hallway. "Hang on," I said, then set the cell on an overturned chair. Once I was satisfied that the hallway was secure, I slung the weapon across my back and retook the phone.

"Okay. I know you can't do the bat thing, but if you want Katie to live to sunset, you better get here before she goes to sleep." Lore said that vamps who suffer total blood loss and can't feed before they sleep either wake up rogue or don't wake at all. I didn't think Katie could feed. She was too far gone for that. But maybe Leo could help her.

He hesitated an instant, as if checking the time. "I am close. Open the front door."

Weapon to my shoulder again, I sped to the front. Opened the door. Dull light splashed across the floor, filtering into the room. The security system was not in its console; it was splinters, the shattered security screens in the corner. A single red light flashed on and off.

From outside, I smelled the changing patterns of the rogue's scent. He was gone. I slung the shotgun on its strap to rest behind my back and pushed the crosses back as well. Better not threaten the vamp I had just called for help, no matter how innocent the mistake. I could use some clothes, however. I looked at the drapery over two narrow windows and considered pulling a Scarlett O'Hara, but before I could act, I felt a cold wind. It whirled past my body, carrying with it Leo Pellissier's scent.

"Shut the door," he said from the hallway. Breathing hard. The list of reasons why vamps breathe is short; I could now add "doing the hundred-yard dash" to it. Leo's usual papyrus scent was overlaid with a faint, scorched aroma, like browned steak with the juices trapped inside. I pushed the front door and it closed with a heavy thud, shutting out dawn light. I heard Leo move into Katie's office. Heard him curse. And the office door shut.

Sirens sounded in the distance. I ran to the dining room. "Indigo?" The girl looked up, her face tight with concentration. "Cops and paramedics are here. Leo is with Katie in her office. Anyone who goes in there is likely become supper. Understand?" Vamps are unpredictable at night. I had no idea how bad that might get in daylight, one injured, and the other away from his coffin. Or wherever the old ones slept.

Indigo nodded, biting her cheek as if to keep from saying anything. Or maybe to keep from screaming.

"I'm going to dress and go after the rogue. As far as the cops are concerned, I was never here. Okay?" When she looked uncertain, I said, "If I'm in a holding cell for questioning, I can't be chasing the rogue. I want to find his lair and stake his ass."

Her face cleared. "I never saw you." She looked at the wall and yelled to it, "Tia, it's safe. You can come out now!" A small, hidden door opened in the wall, about four feet off the floor. Tia's delicate face ducked down and out. "Get the door and bring the ambulance drivers in here," Indigo said. "Don't let them into Katie's office. Not for anything. And Jane is going after that thing. So we're not going to mention her. Okay?" Tia nodded with childlike certainty. Indigo was clearly at the top of the pecking order. "Go get the other girls out of hiding. Then open the front door, but only to the cops," Indigo added. She looked at me. And unexpectedly grinned. "You'd better get dressed or some cop is going to think you're one of us."

I looked down, nodded, and lifted the stake in my hand as good-bye. I skirted out of the house, avoiding the broken glass, blood and gore. As dawn traced pink and purple and golden streaks across the sky, I jumped the wall and headed home.

I showered off fast to get rid of the scent of Katie's blood and dressed for vamp hunting in jeans, leather, boots, silvered vamp-killers, crosses, a vial of holy water. Studded gloves and a collar made of sterling silver jump rings overlapping like chain mail, extra ammo, my Bible, and extra stakes went into the bike's saddlebags. Within ten minutes after I entered the house, I was helmeted, the Benelli strapped to my back. I kick-started the bike and whipped around the block, past Katie's front door, past the rolling, siren-screaming emergency vehicles. I picked up the rogue's changing scent, the face shield of the helmet shoved up, out of the way, sunglasses protecting my eyes.

How did he change his scent? If he changed it so easily, and I lost it on the wind, I might not find him again. For that matter, if he could change it totally, maybe I had been near him and not noticed. I wondered *why* it changed as well as *how*. Like, maybe it wasn't something he could consciously control. Like maybe Beast wasn't totally wrong about the liver-eater stuff. Maybe he *wasn't* just a rogue. Maybe he was something more.

Not only humans were being targeted by the rogue, and every rogue vamp in every case I knew of drank exclusively from humans; but here, at least one vamp had gone missing, the woman vamp whose disappearance had made Katie weep with grief. Ming. Then he went after Katie. Maybe there had been others. Or . . . maybe the rogue wasn't just crazy nuts; maybe he ate livers for a medical reason. Maybe his diet lacked something that human blood wasn't providing. Maybe he needed blood-rich vital organs like livers to stabilize him. And maybe vamp organs were better than human organs for that. Did that make him a liver-eater from legend? Crap, no. Part of his compound scent smelled like vamp. Ergo, he was a vamp.

The vision of the rogue flashed into my mind. *Eating* Katie. Like a wild animal tearing at prey, ripping into the organs. Upper and lower fangs. Beast was silent though I knew she was awake. And I knew she agreed. Beast ate that way, liver, heart, kidneys, lungs first. The most protein-, fat-, and mineral-rich parts *first*. So, he *wasn't* a vamp?

I finally had to admit it; I had no idea what I was hunting. I filled my nostrils with scents as the city came to life, stirring for morning business, school, jobs. I tracked the rogue as he all but flew through the streets, the sun chasing him. If I didn't lose his scent, I'd find where he slept today, maybe his main lair. And kill the bloody bastard. Collect my bonus. And get gone.

CHAPTER 16

Are crosses weapons?

The rogue's scent continued to change, growing hotter. I remembered the way Leo smelled when he flew through with the sun touching him—scorched meat tainting his usual peppery-almond-papyrus smell. In one way, the heating scent made the rogue easier to follow; in another it was harder. Breakfast smells of bacon and sausage sizzling were hitting the air too, obscuring the warm meat stink of the rogue. I wasn't as good at parsing smells with my human nose, but I breathed through my mouth gently as I rode, and found the vamp's scent evolving, like licorice, but more delicate. Maybe hazelnut.

And a hint of sweetgrass. At the thought, I slowed, breathing through my open mouth and nose, straining to find and separate it from the mix of city and river stink. Sweetgrass. One of the ceremonial herbs most loved by The People. I remembered the glimpse I had of his blood-covered face, eagle-sharp chin and nose. Yeah. *Tsalagiyi*: The thought burbled up from the dark of my mind. He could be a Cherokee turned by a vamp. I could be chasing someone like me.

I pulled onto the shoulder, stopped the bike, and put my boots to the pavement for balance. Closed my eyes. Smelled with everything I had in me, Beast alert and tense, her claws pricking my mind. Sweetgrass . . .

I pulled down the face shield of the helmet. Gunned the bike. Following.

The scent blasted at me under the edge of the shield, intensified, concentrated by speed as I wove through the streets, heading to the river, the same pathway taken when Beast tracked the rogue from the kill zone where he took down the prostitute. The exact same route. *Prey*, Beast whispered, picturing an animal track through the brush, low down, well worn. The liver-eater was using the same trail home.

Beast rose into my mind as we roared over the river, part of the I-90 snarl, taking the Greater New Orleans Bridge. The Mississippi was a huge sleeping snake, muddy brown and somnolent. And then, in the middle of the bridge, the rogue's scent disappeared. Just . . . totally disappeared. Traffic was growing heavier. The breeze across the river was strengthening. I didn't have much time to find it again.

Had I been in a car I would have been in trouble. Much more maneuverable, I wove from lane to lane, breaking traffic laws all over, to the far shore, still unable to pick up the scent. It took a while to get turned around as the road became the Westbank Expressway, snarled with traffic. In Beast form it hadn't been rush hour, and I had been riding on top of a truck.

I took the bridge back twice, searching up and down the road, scenting the few off-ramps and smaller turnoffs for any hint of the thing I chased. He could have dropped off the expressway onto the ground below at any point. Or, for that matter, off the bridge into the river. Beast sent me a mental picture of a mountain lion with her face to the ground.

"Air scenting is a waste of time," I agreed. I pulled the bike to the shoulder, stopped, put my boots down, and shoved back the face shield again. Yanked off my sunglasses. Disgusted.

Beast sent me another image, of a pile of poop. Then a third, of bark torn from a tree as if by claws or deer horns. And yet a fourth, of a big cat, hindquarters bent, forelegs stiff, depositing scent from anal scent glands onto a pile of leaves and sticks.

"Territory. You think I can find him by hunting his territory. Places he's marked as his. But people don't mark territory, and from what I've seen, neither do vamps."

And Beast sent me an image of Katie's Ladies. No sign

in the window, no neon, but a street number in brass on the door. I hadn't paid much attention to it. But I got the idea. Track the rogue vamp by things he does, has, and is, things that he doesn't even realize are markers. Gotcha. And I could start at Aggie One Feather's and the sweathouse out back. I strapped on my link-mail collar and my other protective equipment. Now I was loaded for vamp.

Aggie had to have heard the bike puttering down the road. It wasn't like I could hide the sound of the motor. I half expected her to be waiting at the door, but she wasn't. The house was silent when I rang the bell, except for the electronic hum of appliances and air conditioner, and the smell of cooked bacon. Twined with it all was the rotten stink of the rogue. Beast came alert, her mouth open in my mind, showing fangs. The rogue had come past the house, his skin probably smoking if the scorched smell was any indication, beating sunrise by seconds. The scorched stink made him a vamp. He was leaving mixed evidence everywhere, confusing.

He was fast, faster than anything I ever hunted. I wanted to ignore the protocol of asking permission and just race around back, following the scent. Eagerness gathered inside me, my heart beating hard. The rogue was *close*. The woods behind Aggie's house were not just hunting grounds. He did have a lair near here.

I heard footsteps inside. Aggie stepped back in shock when she opened the door, one hand out as if to ward off a blow. Maybe it was the Benelli slung over my back. Maybe it was my expression. "It's okay," I said.

She halted backpedaling and swallowed, one fist over her heart, recovering her poise. "What do you want?" she asked, her voice not quite steady. *What do you want?* Not *Come in*. She held the door with one hand, barring my way.

I shook my head. There was no time for the polite necessities of dealing with an elder. "The rogue vamp came through your yard. I need to—" I stopped myself, knowing I was botching this, and said instead, "*May I* hunt in the property behind your house?"

She looked me over and settled herself as I remembered the elders doing, a relaxing of the facial muscles and shoulders, one hand on the door, still holding me out, the other still curled in a loose fist on her chest, the gesture protective. A memory hovered in the back of my mind, foggy, hazy, an old, old woman making the same motions, the remembrance almost in reach for an instant, before it wisped away like smoke. *How long? How long ago was that a reality?*

Aggie searched my face, her hand now fluttering down like a bird to a branch. I restrained my impatience, riding it into submission, took a deep breath, and blew it out. I waited as she studied me. It seemed a long time, though it couldn't have been more than seconds.

At last, satisfied, she said, "Yes. You may hunt. But first, my mother wishes to meet with you." She pushed the door open and stood aside.

"I don't have time," I said, my frustration breaking free. "It *came by your house*."

"I know. My mother has had trouble sleeping since you told me about it hunting here. She was awake. Listening. She heard it. Felt its hunger. Its anger. We've been expecting you." She stood aside.

Irritated, but not knowing what else to do, I huffed a sigh and started to walk into her house. Aggie held up a hand, stopping me. "Please. Leave your weapons at the door."

I closed my eyes so she wouldn't see the flash of fury. I did *not* have time for this. Then I remembered. To bring weapons into the house of an elder was to bring insult and violence, no matter if the weapons were intended for someone else. Forcing out the words through my teeth, I said curtly, "Sorry." And though I was in a hurry, I *was* sorry. I didn't intend to insult Aggie One Feather. *Egini Agayvlge i*. But the rogue was so close. . . .

I unstrapped the Benelli and set it on the front porch. If someone came by and took it, I was out a *lot* of money. I placed the stakes beside it, and the vamp-killers. All three of them. As I divested myself of my weapons, something began to happen to me. My motions began to slow. My frustration began to dissipate, as if seeping out through my pores along with the perspiration of the heated day, or maybe as if the frustration clung to the steel, wood, and silver and fell away from my limbs as I set the weapons aside.

I took off the link collar. The leather gloves. Sitting on the floor of the porch, I removed my boots. I should have taken them off the last time I came. I looked up at Aggie from my perch on the cement. "Are crosses weapons?"

"Do you think they are?"

"Yeah." I pulled the crosses from my neck. Sock-footed, I stood and bowed my head, patient, waiting. "*Gi yv ha*," she said, her voice soft. *Come in.* I walked into the house and Aggie closed the door, shutting out the world. I followed her through the small house to a tiny back bedroom. Sunlight spilled out, bright, from yellow walls. A double-sized bed was covered by a handmade quilt, pieces of cloth in different patterns stitched to look like a tree, roots at the foot, branches reaching high to pillows. A dresser stood in the corner near a comfortable-looking chair, where a wizened woman sat in quarter view, facing the windows.

She was hunched over, her black hair braided and dangling over her left shoulder. Not a hint of gray marred the tresses. Her coppery skin was crosshatched with lines, furrowed by wind and sun and time, and she turned her head when I stood in the doorway, gesturing me in. Her eyes were bright black buttons. "*Gi yv ha*," she echoed her daughter, her voice the soft, whispered cadence of the very old ones, I recalled. "*Gi yv ha*." She pointed to a stool near her.

I sat on it, the position putting my face low enough so she could see me from her bent posture. "*Li si*," I said. *Grandmother*.

"My mother's name is *Ewi Tsagalili*. Eva Chicalelee," Aggie said from the door.

I remembered the story Aggie had told me about the little snowbird, *Chickelili*, whose soft voice wasn't heard when she warned about the danger of the liver-eater. "*Li si*," I said again, ducking my head.

"Pretty girl." She touched my cheek with cool fingers. Traced the line of my jaw. "No. Not a girl. My eyes fail. You are . . . old," the old woman said. My eyes flew to hers. Like her daughter, she saw too much. "Very old," she said.

I stared at my hands, clasped in my lap.

"You carry time beneath your skin. Memories out of reach."

"*V v*," I said. *Yes*, in the language of The People. Cold seemed to blow along my bones, the ice of blizzard, of frozen winter, remembered from long ago, from the cold of the long trek, the Removal, the Trail of Tears. I shivered once, my sock-covered toes curling. Remembering. *Cripes. I was there. . . .*

She took her hand away and the memories fell with it. "You should go to water," she said, speaking of the Cherokee healing ceremony that involved a ritual dunking in an icy stream.

"There is no time, *Li si*."

The old woman puffed a breath, a half huff of negation. "When your battle is over, you will come here." The proclamation wasn't so much a command as a prophecy. I shivered again, my flesh cold as stone. "We will smudge you. And my daughter will take you to water. Your memories will begin to find their way back to you."

"*V v*," I said.

"My daughter has called you warrior woman. Blood chases after you, rides you. You pounce on your enemy, like a big cat onto prey." I looked up fast and found her smiling, white dentures like perfect pearls in her mouth. "Go. Fight the enemy. And come back to us."

I left the house without speaking to Aggie, who had vanished from the doorway of her mother's room. Sitting in the sun on the heated porch, I pulled on my boots and strapped on my weapons. My fingers shook and the cold still filled my body, remembered cold from the hunger times. The sun warmed me only slowly. I closed my eyes and tilted my face to it, letting its rays touch me as the old woman's fingers had. Giving myself a moment, just a moment, to breathe. To remember.

The scent of the rogue was fading in the heat. I pushed to my feet and jogged around the house, scenting. The past could wait.

I followed the rogue's scent into the piney woods, along the nearly invisible path, tracking him into the forest. The soil was heavy with his scent, though with my human nose it lacked the full vibrancy of Beast's hunt. I passed the places where the elder's dogs had fed it, their bodies decaying, bones scattered on the damp ground. I smelled the carcasses of four cats, numerous opossums, rodents, and other animals. It hunted here often. And it was always hungry.

I moved slowly. I wasn't in danger from the rogue . . . providing he was indeed a rogue vamp. He couldn't stand sunlight. What else could he be? But if he had a human servant, he or she would be near, and human servants had no problem with sunlight. I stopped often and sniffed, rotten meat overlaying the odor of hazelnut and sweetgrass. I dropped to my knees, crawling, nose at the ground. No one was around to notice. The compound, complex scent contained a faded hint of tomatoes, sage, rosemary, and even fainter things I couldn't name. I circled back where I could push through the brush, and sniffed. Moved from the small path into the trees. It had been a long time since fire had come through, and the underbrush was too thick to go far.

Beast thought the path well trod. To my eyes it was little more than a ribbon of smooth earth. The path was the only way deeper into the woods. Trees and head-high brush closed in. Birdcalls went silent. The slow-moving breeze was saturated with pine sap smell. Mosquitoes found me, buzzing. Was I entering a trap? Beast hadn't found one, but I wasn't Beast.

The trees opened out into a clearing remembered from Beast's hunt. I hunched down, waiting. Nothing moved. As Beast had done, I circled the clearing, but found nothing, no other paths, no trace of scent leaving the woods. Carefully, testing for traps, I moved into the clearing. The soil was rank with the scent of the rogue, heavy with the reek of old blood. The evolving scent had come through here, as if several different beings used the place. Yet I was pretty sure they all were the same being, one undergoing a peculiar metamorphosis that affected his scent in a Dr. Jekyll and Mr. Hyde revolutionary way. Not a skinwalker. He didn't smell anything like me. Not a were, if such even existed. Elf? No. A vamp—a very sick, very wacky vamp.

After several minutes, I was satisfied that there was no trap hidden in the clearing. The liver-eater had come here. He hadn't left here. I scuffed at the ground. Starting on the periphery, at the edge of the piney woods, I stomped on it, around and around, moving in a spiral, ever tighter, toward the interior. In the center of the clearing, the sound of the earth changed.

It rang hollow. Something was buried beneath the ground.

Cave, Beast thought. She was still awake, though sleepy. *Its den. Its lair.*

"Yeah," I murmured. I squatted and brushed at pine

needles, but they were stuck, glued to a door, set into the ground. *Camouflage*. I rocked back, resting on one knee and toe and the other foot. The wood of the door was brown, the same shade of the pine needles, weathered and worn, unexceptional looking, with raised panels and a brass knob, the metal pitted and darkened from weather and sun. It was something a middle-class homeowner might use as a front door. Sweat ran down my back and pooled under the mail collar. My breath was steady but too fast.

I swung the Benelli forward and palmed a stake. Reached for the handle. Not knowing what I would do if it was locked. It wasn't. The door didn't open as if hinged, but slid back, revealing a hole about three feet wide and five feet deep. A round tunnel moved from the hole north, like a rabbit's burrow, but wider, big enough for a man to duck-walk. "Crap," I whispered. I was going to have to go inside.

The walls of the tunnel were damp, roots sticking through and dangling. Mold smell and the decay of a freshly opened grave wafted out. Footsteps had smoothed and hardened the floor of the tunnel just below the opening. Odd-shaped prints dug into the ground just beyond, where the rogue had dropped to knees and hands, the toes of boots poking the ground. I studied the floor, making out only one set of prints. All boots. All the same. If the rogue had a human servant, it wasn't here.

Eaten, Beast suggested.

I breathed in, sifting out scents: mold, pine roots rich with sap, water close by, wet earth, and something dead. Long dead. Just ahead. I dropped into the tunnel, landing with bent knees, Benelli at the ready, and knelt, letting my eyes adjust. As far as I could see, I was alone. I slung the shotgun back out of the way and palmed my favorite vamp-killer. Its blade was eighteen inches long, heavily silvered, the fuller deep to channel vamp blood away fast, and the hilt carved by Evan, Molly's husband, from elkhorn. It felt like silvered luck in my palm. This would be close-in work, if I found the thing I was hunting.

Crawling into the earth, into the dark, along the horizontal part of the tunnel, I spotted a satchel. I opened it, revealing clothing. The rogue's scents wafted out, the reek of the decay and the scent he had worn when he left Katie's. Scent of the insane and the sane, maybe. Boots were beneath the satchel on their sides. Knee boots, like English riding boots. Bare footprints moved along the tunnel. The rogue had stripped and gone ahead. Naked. How weird was that.

Just ahead, my eyes picked out something white against the gloom. A skull stared at me. Tissue still clung to the bones, wisps of red hair. Leg bones and ribs, no longer attached to feet or vertebrae, were scattered along the tunnel. I lifted the closest bone. A femur. Teeth had scored deeply into it, predator fangs, upper and lower. I was pretty sure I had found the rogue's human servant. I dropped the bone and crawled ahead. Into the dark.

The ground became wet; the roof sloped down. My jeans' knees began soaking up water. The tunnel ended abruptly, the ceiling dipping down sharply onto a cement pipe, a county water main. I looked in, to see black water with only a narrow space at the top for airflow. I snapped a root from the tunnel wall and stuck it into the pipe. It didn't touch bottom. I dropped it onto the surface of the water; the root was snatched away. Frustration brought a growl to my lips.

I eased through the tunnel, shuffling backward. The rogue had found the perfect daytime hiding place. An underground water main. Probably had dozens of potential exits. No way was I going diving. He might not need to breathe but I sure as heck did.

Back on the surface, I sat with my feet dangling into the pit and breathed shallowly. This was indeed a perfect daytime hiding place for a vamp: multiple exits, dark, the water system itself offering built-in escape routes. And if he did happen to come up here, where he left clothes, he'd catch my scent and be gone faster than I could react, even if I fired the Benelli the moment he broke the surface. I'd only get one shot, and if I didn't kill him instantly, he'd be all over me and I'd be dinner. No point in laying a trap. He could come out anywhere, and probably had clothes at every opening. I was betting he used this site often because of Aggie and her family.

I sighed, stood, and walked back to Bitsa, mud drying in the steamy heat.

CHAPTER 17

Stick a dollar in your garter?

I motored the bike across the bridge, taking the toll road back to Katie's. Mud dried on my jeans to a crusty stiffness. My hair uncoiled from its knot and ponytail, and strands whipped in the hot wind. My stomach growled in hunger the whole way.

Outside Katie's Ladies, the EMTs and ambulances were gone, but law enforcement types were still out in full force, blocking the street with cruisers, talking in small groups of uniformed men and a few women. Yellow crime-scene tape was stretched everywhere. I stopped the bike halfway down the block. I was carrying a perfectly legal weapon, out in public, not concealed. But the Benelli wasn't just a gun. It was a kick-ass gun. And a violent crime had just taken place. Cops would be itchy.

Bruiser was standing apart with a uniformed cop, Jim Herbert, and a woman in plain clothes—Jodi Richoux, Katie's contact at the New Orleans police department. Maybe Katie's friend, though I doubted it. She looked harried. Jimmy looked ticked off. No surprise.

But Bruiser. Bruiser's hands were on his hips, low-rise jeans tight across his butt, boot cut over brown hiking boots. T-shirt tucked in. No butt-dragging, sloppy look for this guy. Buff, muscles bulging, short brown hair. Remembering the twins, I wondered how old Bruiser was. My interest stirred, and I shoved away curiosity; it killed the cat. Feeling an interest in Leo's favorite wasn't smart, especially if the blood bond between them included sex.

I lifted a hand to catch his attention. He looked from me to the cops and raised his brow in question. I shook my head in a "No, I have no desire to talk to cops" gesture. I pointed to the back of Katie's, hopped my hand up and down, as if hopping a fence and dropping down at my house. He almost grinned and nodded fractionally. I wheeled the bike around and took the long way to avoid the cops. I figured Bruiser could find his own way. It wasn't like this was the first time he'd been there. *Or the second*, I thought sourly. I'd have to deal with the invasion of my home and privacy at some point. Maybe now. Beast half woke from sleepy purring. *Fun* . . .

I motored up to the house to find Bruiser at the front door, leaning against an iron support that held up the three-foot-deep balcony overhead. He held himself with the easy balance and readiness of the experienced martial artist, though as I pulled up, he crossed his arms and his muscles bulged. Very nice.

I pointed to the side gate, gave the bike a little gas, rolled over, and let myself in. Bruiser came after and I locked it. *Should have asked him to lock it*, I thought. I eased the bike into the garden and turned it off, removed the helmet, and shook out my hair. I hadn't taken the time to braid it before I left hunting, and I watched Bruiser's eyes follow as it fell. His scent changed, a minuscule shift. Bruiser liked long hair. A lot. "Want tea?" I asked.

"Coffee would be better," he said, returning his gaze to my face.

"I have tea."

He lifted one corner of his mouth and shrugged. "Tea it is then."

He followed me to the door and I paused. No time like the present. "Let yourself in. Like you did last time"—I stepped back, giving him access to the door and lock—"when you came to snoop at the cameras." He slanted a sharp look at me. I shrugged and added, to make sure he understood what I was saying, "And the time you came with your bloodsucking boss to wait for me in my dark house, hoping to pull some vamp crap and scare me."

He thought about that for a moment, as the day grew even hotter and brighter and the flowers in the garden began to wilt and droop. "You angry about that?" he asked, sounding honestly curious. When I didn't reply, he explained, "It's part of the job as Leo's security. You should understand that."

"And if he told you to kill a little old lady, would you do that too?"

He thought about that, amusement lurking at the corners of his mouth. He shrugged by tilting his head to the side. "If she needed killing."

He was serious. Ice shot through my veins. Beast crept forward. "And if she didn't?"

"Then Leo wouldn't want her killed."

I snorted. It was a Beast sound, originating at the back of my throat, full of nostril movement and derision. When that was all I did, Bruiser turned and pulled a ring of keys from a pocket, chose one, and opened my door. I thought about ripping them out of his hand and feeding them to him, but why bother? His bloodsucking boss would just get more. I liked that term. Bloodsucking boss. Bet Leo would hate it when I used it on him.

Inside, I unstrapped and lay the Benelli and my helmet on the kitchen table. Followed them with gloves, neck collar, and various weapons. The crosses. As I removed steel and stakes, mud crusted off my jeans and pattered to the floor in little *shush*es. I could smell my sweat.

Bruiser set one hip on the table and watched as I divested myself of weapons. His eyes were hooded, but that small smile still played over his lips. He said, "Am I supposed to stick a dollar in your garter when you're done?"

I laughed. I couldn't help it. And Bruiser grinned. I set the kettle on to heat, then spooned Nilgiri Tiger Hill leaves into the strainer and set it inside the open mouth of the yellow ceramic pot. The tea was robust enough to maybe suit a coffee drinker. And it wasn't so expensive that I'd care if I had to throw his out. I placed the teapot in the kitchen sink.

He took a chair, resting his forearms on the table. I noted that he instinctively took the seat to the side, so that window and front and side doors were within line of sight and the sun didn't blind him. I got out mugs, a plate, spoons, and sugar, and sat at the foot of the table to his right. Second-best seating from a security standpoint.

"You want to tell me what happened this morning?" he asked.

I started to say that I heard screaming, it woke me up, and I rushed over. But I doubted that a human could have heard the screaming. I said, "I keep weird hours. I was awake, in the back garden, when I heard screaming. I grabbed a few weapons and raced over."

"Naked."

"What?"

"The girls said you were naked when you came through the door. Shotgun in hand. Crosses. Stakes." A slow grin started. "Which had to be something to see." His brow went up a notch. "Half an hour before sunrise, you were in the backyard." Disbelief tainted the words, but so did something else. He added, softer, his smile widening, "*Naked.*"

"Meditating," I said, fighting the blush that wanted to rise at the way he said "naked." Like it was something wonderful, and he was sorry he had missed it. "On the rocks Katie got for me."

"I heard about the rocks."

"Did you inspect them too, while you were roaming around my house?"

"Not your house."

My den, Beast growled, but I kept it inside. "For the moment it is. What were you looking for? Or do you just have an unnatural affection for broken cameras?" The kettle started that low hiss it does before it whistles.

He looked mildly surprised at the camera comments. Or maybe he was just surprised at me in general. "Boss wanted to know the hunter hired by the council."

I scented the lie. It stank from his pores. And since we both knew that Leo, as head of the vamp council, had known exactly who I was before I was hired, the lie hid a secondary purpose. If I could figure it out. Silent, I considered his words. Remembering little things that had been said. Others that had not been said, but left hanging, unspoken.

I understood. *Son of a gun. Leo was getting the feed from Katie's security system.* Probably everything, not just the cameras in *this* house. So why hadn't he seen the rogue attack Katie this morning?

The whistle started low and rose in volume. While I thought, I stood and lifted the kettle off the flame, splashed boiling water over the teapot and into the strainer in its top, equalizing the temperature inside and out before filling the pot. I set it on the table, wrapping it in a tea cozy to keep it warm while it steeped. Bruiser's eyebrows went up at the domestic motions. "Do you cook too?" he asked, the tone teasing. " 'Cause any woman who does a weapon striptease, handles a Benelli like she knows how to use it, and can cook, pushes all my buttons."

"I don't cook," I said, smiling when Beast showed me a stack of raw steaks. Bruiser smiled back, thinking I was flirting. Casually, while he was relaxed, I said, "Does Katie know Leo has access to her entire security system?" Bruiser went still. *Gotcha.* I smiled and twisted the knife a bit deeper. "Leo put a camera in Katie's backyard. Makes sense for him to have access to all her security cameras, too." Making a mental leap, I added, "I bet he has video from the security of all the vamps in the city. Maybe audio, too." Bruiser's face went hard. I unfolded the tea cozy and slipped the strainer full of leaves from the pot, setting it on the plate. Carefully, I poured tea into both mugs. "Sugar? Milk?" I asked sweetly.

After a moment he said, "Sugar," the word clipped.

I put a heaping spoonful into each of our mugs and stirred both, the spoon making dull tinking sounds. Pushing his mug to him, I sat back with mine, letting the steam warm my face, the mug heat my fingers. "I'm not interested in vamp politics," I murmured, watching him through slit lids, "except where it impacts my life and pocketbook. But I have a job to do, so I want answers. With cameras in place, why didn't Leo know about the rogue vamp attack this morning until I called? And the attack on the Mearkanis master in her lair. Ming. Why didn't he know and stop it? Unless he hopes to gain something from the deaths." I took a chance and added, "Like worsening the schism developing in vamp politics. Like Leo's little pals in the hood, armed to the teeth to hunt vamps." Bruiser didn't twitch or anything, but I could have sworn the skin tightened around his eyes. "Is Leo mounting his own rogue hunt? And if so, why?"

After a moment, Bruiser raised the mug and sipped, a delaying tactic while he thought. He was annoyed at my questions, but his expression mutated into a that-wasn't-so-bad look at the taste of the tea. Finally, "I'll tell you that, if you tell me how you found the cameras so fast. You didn't even sweep for them," he said, meaning an electronic sweep. "You just went right to them. I know. I checked the digital footage when the system told us they had gone out."

I actually considered it, half wanting to see what he'd say when I told him I sniffed them out. But I had figured something out when he mentioned digital surveillance and a system sophisticated enough to send out notification when there were problems. I said, "No deal."

This was Leo's city, Leo's people. He treated them like a feudal lord would serfs, so I wasn't surprised he spied on them. And cameras in all the houses and lairs meant a huge system, one he checked only when there was a problem, trend, or power play. Probably not many vamps discovered the surveillance, unless they hired outside people—*young* outside people, independent security experts, not hundred-year-old human blood-servants—to look into safety measures. I had expected vamps to be mostly like Katie, lost in changing technology, but Leo seemed okay with modern devices, relying on them, which I figured was odd for an elder.

Then something hit me and left me feeling really stupid. "If Leo has video footage of Ming and Katie being attacked, then he knows who the rogue is. I want to see the footage."

Bruiser shook his head. "Not in Ming's lair. He didn't know where she slept. That's why it wasn't discovered until evening, when her human servant went to check on her." He sipped his tea, his eyes considering me over the rim. He set the mug on the table, turned it slightly in the fingers of both hands, as if making sure the handle was pointed just so. "Of the five vampires attacked, all were taken in their lairs. No footage. Katie was the only one taken in her place of business, and the rogue disabled her system before we got any footage."

Five vamps attacked? Crap. They didn't tell me that. "No video or pictures of him at all?" Bruiser shook his head, his eyes on me. "I saw him . . . when he attacked Katie."

Bruiser went still, much like a vamp did. Must be the long association.

"He's five-eleven in shoes. Long, straight black hair. Dark skin for a vamp." I could see Bruiser cataloguing the vamps he knew, his eyes moving from one of my eyes to the other, back and forth, as I spoke. "Hawkish nose. No facial hair. Coppery skin makes him South Asian or American Indian. I'm betting AmIn. When he's feeding, he has upper and lower fangs." Bruiser's eyes widened at the dual fang comment. "How many local vamps fit the description?" I asked. "And how many local vamps have disappeared in the last year or so? Beginning, say, a month before the first human victims turned up dead or disappeared?"

"Four vampires fit the description. Five if you count Mario Esposito. He's Italian, and shorter, but he's dark skinned. None of them went missing that I know of, no vampires except the five, and of the five known dead, two were fair-haired, one was Negro, and the others were of European background, with brown hair. But I'll ask around."

"I'd like the security dossiers on them all."

Bruiser smiled into his mug, a that'll-never-happen expression. He sipped once more, put the mug down, and stood, moving with grace suited to the dance floor or a dueling ring. I edged his age up from the fifty or sixty I had given him. "Thanks for the tea. It wasn't bad."

"You're welcome. The security dossiers?"

"I'll see what I can do." His tone said he wouldn't put much energy into it.

"Where'd you get the key? More of Leo's security precautions?"

"Yeah." He stuck his hands in his pockets, pursed his lips, and looked around, as if about to say something. Instead he moved to the front door. "Lock me out." And he was gone.

"That accomplished jack," I said to the empty house.

I swept up the dried mud, showered, and hit the sack. I was exhausted.

A ringing phone woke me. I fumbled until I found Beast's travel pack and unzipped it. The cell's battery was low, emitting a warning beep even as I answered. "Yeah?"

"They're sending Katie to ground tonight. You need to be in the cemetery before midnight."

"I need to what?" I stretched my lids, sleep-sand cracking at the corners. It was still daylight, and I heard laughter outside, tourists chatting. "Troll?" I said to the cell.

"Katie survived the attack," he said, his voice weary. "But Leo says she needs to go to ground. It's a healing ceremony. I don't know much about it. But all the Mithrans congregate at the cemetery and they . . ." His words trailed off. "They bury her."

"And getting buried heals her?" I said, striving for sarcasm, and having to settle for disgust. Vamps creep me out. "And I have to be there why . . . ?"

"They've been summoned to a gathering. The older vampires will be there, all in one place." I heard him lick his lips. Softer, he said, "Humans aren't allowed to attend, so you have to get there early and find a place to hide."

So I can do surveillance. Right. I checked the time on the cell and rolled to my feet. "My cell's dying. Send one of the girls with directions."

"Will do. And Jane? Get this guy." His voice broke, and I realized he was grieving for his bloodsucking boss. I had a quick memory, snapshot sharp, of Troll held against the wall by the rogue's will. "Take him out," he said.

"Sure," I said, uncomfortable with his emotion. How did you grieve for a piece of meat? "I'll get him." I plugged in the cell to charge it up and took a look at my hair. The snarl would not do for a funeral. And how was I supposed to hide from a big group of vamps who could scent-search as well as Beast? Big question and no answer. Not yet.

I spent the next few hours doing the scut work of the security and investigating business—records search and paperwork. I started out studying the boilerplate of contracts with blood-servants and the security dossiers of the five missing vamps that came by scooter messenger. Leo was willing to let me have access after all, not that there was much in them. The files had been well scoured of anything interesting beyond name, date and country of birth, and vamp bloodlines back to an original vamp sire. It was interesting to see the interconnected and twisted relationships all the way back to AD 700 in one case, but little was really useful. So far as I could tell, there was nothing linking the five missing vamps. I was wasting time.

I called the twins, Brian and Brandon, asking about anything they might have heard, which turned out to be nothing. The five vamps had just vanished from their secret lairs. They did invite me over anytime, sounding quite interested in seeing me, which did a lot for my ego, and they tendered an invitation to a party for the city's security-specialist blood-servants, to take place at a shooting range that served beer and pizza. Networking in the city of vamps.

Online, I discovered where land deeds and real estate records were kept, and that New Orleans records were not all in one centralized place. They were in lots of different places and in various states of integrity. I could have called Rick, but there were some hands-on security tasks I couldn't delegate, especially to a guy who seemed to have his own agenda. Before leaving the house, I looked up criminal records of the missing vamps. Nada. Zilch. Their financial records were no better and no worse than the ordinary human's. Some lived on savings and investments, and some lived on credit; some had been wealthy, and some hadn't. They still had nothing in common.

Tia came over in the middle of my search with the address and map to the vamp cemetery. She was sleepy and looked drugged, but it was vamp I smelled on her, not chemicals.

I cranked up Bitsa and rode to the Orleans Parish Civil District Court, and then to the Notarial Archive Office on Poydras Street to check records and look for recent land purchases, building permits, and similar activities that involved vamps. The Notarial Archive Office had been recently painted but smelled like mold and stagnant water to my sensitive nose—maybe remnants of Hurricane Katrina. There were a lot of records to go through, all the way back to the early eighteen hundreds, and what I found didn't seem to have anything to do with my hunt.

Clan St. Martin had published a book on Mithrans, due to be released in twelve months. They had used the proceeds from the sale of a horse farm near Springhill to finance it.

Clan Arceneau was cashing in city and parish public works bonds and investing in land.

The mayor's wife, Anna, had recently purchased fourteen parcels of swampland south and west of New Orleans.

Clan Bouvier was hurting for cash, if the recent sales of *their* land was any indication.

Nothing jumped out at me and said, "Here's where the bodies are buried, who the rogue is, and where he hides." More wasted time.

I did stumble upon the original deed to Clan Pellissier land, made to one Leonard Eugène Zacharie Pellissier, Marquis. I also discovered a deed to a graveyard that changed hands; it was the same cemetery I needed to visit tonight, privately held land, unlike human cemeteries in the area that were owned by churches or by the city. The deed to the vamp graveyard had been signed over in 1902, by Leo, to one Sabina Delgado y Aguilera. Not a vamp name I recognized, and not something I really needed to know. Altogether, a total waste of time.

I was on my way out of the building, late afternoon sunlight hitting me hard, when I ran—almost literally—into Rick LaFleur, on his way inside.

If he was surprised to see me he didn't show it, and dang if he didn't look good in jeans, T-shirt, and the same old sandals he'd worn once before. He stopped two steps below me, one knee bent, and pushed his sunglasses back on his head. "The vampire hunter," he said, a wry tone in his voice that I couldn't interpret.

"The Joe," I said, in the same tone. "You got that info I was looking for on land deeds?"

"Most of it. I'll bring it by. You had lunch?"

I squinted up at the sun, which was nearing the western horizon, and let a trace of amusement into my voice. "Several hours past."

He shrugged. "Hours of a musician. Come to the club tonight. I have a solo set." His lips turned up and his black eyes flashed in frank sexual interest. "You can dance for me again."

I felt my blood warm at the possibilities in his gaze. "I'll think about it," I said, walking past him to where Bitsa sat patiently in the shade. Feeling the heat of his gaze on my butt as I walked, my face warmed. "But I'm not much for being a notch on a guy's bedpost," I said over my shoulder. "I think a player like you has enough of those." I straddled my bike and helmeted up. "Let me know about the info." I cranked up Bitsa and motored off, Rick visible in the rearview until I was out of sight.

I had studied the map, committing it to memory, and by

sundown, I was naked, in the back garden. And Beast was ticked. Skinwalkers have the magic of sinking into the genetic structure of animals, sinking deep and changing form, from human to another, to match, exactly, the body of the other animal from the genetic structure up, copied from genetic material stored in bones, teeth, and skin of the dead.

I had been making shifts for eleven years and Beast had always hated it when I chose any shape but hers. Now, since the dream/memory of the making of Beast, I too was suddenly unhappy with the process. Itchy-uncomfortable. Okay, maybe guilty. The dream of the thievery had proved how Beast came to reside inside me, a theory I had never investigated, which made me a coward. To save my own life, I had stolen the body and soul of a living being. I knew, deep down, it was black magic—accidental, but no less dark for the lack of intent.

We—Beast and I—had learned to live together, to share her form and mine, but I was pretty sure she never forgave me for my sin of stealing her. The alliance was never easy, and when I chose another form to shift into, another animal, my fractured, doubled soul didn't survive the transition intact. Beast was buried so deeply I couldn't find her then, which meant I walked alone. When I shifted back to human, Beast always made me pay the price.

The price was even higher when I took a form that required a change of mass into something smaller or larger than Beast, because mass has to go, or come from, somewhere. The law of conservation of mass/matter held true, especially in skinwalker magic, so there was always the fear that I'd permanently lose all or part of myself or Beast when I shifted into a smaller body with a smaller brain, leaving so much behind. She hated it and always found a way to punish me.

As the sun cast golden spears across the sky, I sat on the topmost stone. It was warm, the heat comforting on my bare bottom, soothing. I opened the zipper bag containing my animal fetishes and pulled out a necklace. I set one of feathers and talons around my neck, and placed the gold nugget necklace on the boulder. It was too large for the form I chose.

I touched a talon. Closed my eyes. Relaxed. Listened to

the wind, the pull of the moon, larger than a sickle, growing toward fullness, on the horizon. I listened to the beat of my heart.

I slowed the functions of my body, letting my heart rate fall, my blood pressure drop, my muscles relax, as if I were going to sleep. Knees folded, arms at my sides in the humid air, I sat on the boulders. Nothing biological would work to steal mass from—even wood had its own RNA—but stone was clean, which was why I required it. Easy to steal mass from. Easy to deposit mass. When I was forced to risk it.

Mind slowing, I sank into the feathers and talons and beak strung on the necklace. Deep inside. My consciousness fell away, all but the location of this hunt. That I set into the lining of my skin, into the deepest parts of my brain, so I wouldn't lose it when I *shifted*, when I *changed*. I dropped lower. Deeper. Into the bottomless gray world within me. And began to chant, silently, *Mass to mass, stone to stone . . . mass to mass, stone to stone . . .*

The drums of memory beat a slow cadence. The smell of herbed woodsmoke came on the air. The night wind of The People's land brushed across my flesh. I sought the double helix of DNA, the inner snake lying inside the talons and feathers of the necklace. It was there, as always, deep in the cells, in the remains of soft tissue. I slipped into it, into the snake that rests in the depths of all beasts, the snake of DNA. I dropped within, like water flowing in a stream. Like snow falling, rolling down a mountainside. The gray place swarmed over me.

My breathing changed, heart rate sped. My last thought was of the animal I was to become. The Eurasian eagle owl, *Bubo bubo*. My bones slid, skin rippled. Mass shifted down, to the stone. To the rock beneath me with loud, cracking reports. Black motes of power danced along me, burning and pricking like arrows piercing deep. *Mass to mass, stone to stone.*

Pain like a knife slid between muscle and bone along my spine. Wings slid out along my shoulders, metamorphosing from arms. Golden feathers, tawny, brown, sprouted. My nostrils narrowed, drawing deep, filling smaller lungs. My heart raced, a heart meant to power flight. My talons clawed across the stone.

The night came alive—everything new, intense. My ears were bombarded by sounds from everywhere. The mouse on the ground. Unaware of danger. The movement of tree leaves a hundred yards away. Chicks cheeping. Bird nest. *Food.* The house settling.

Eyes meant for the night took in everything, seeing as clearly as if the sun still shone. Light and shadow stung my vision, bright, acute. Ugly human light. I gathered myself, spread my wings, and leaped from the boulder, out over the garden. Beating the air with a five-foot wingspan, the wings of an animal that had never lived on this continent. It had been long since I flew, but the memory was stored in the snake of the bird. I wobbled, stretched into flight, caught a rising thermal, let it carry me up with less effort than beating wings alone.

I looked down, reaching into the night, finding the gold nugget on the boulder, its place in the world. Identifying it amid the grid of streets in my owl memory. My human consciousness merged with the owl's, dispersed into the cells of the *Bubo bubo*.

Hunger ripped my belly. Below, a form moved, silent in the night, four paws padding, gray striped with white. I folded my wings tight, and dove. Talons reaching, I slammed into the prey. My forward-curving talons gripped, held. My beak tore into the back of its neck, through the vertebrae. I took down the feral cat. Sitting in the shadows, I ate, ripping bloody flesh with talons and beak until my belly was full. It was always like this after the change. *Hunger.* There was little left of the cat when I was done. Feet, bones, skull.

The memory of myself, buried under my skin, began to stir. *I like cats. . . .* My human self grieved. Then memory moved. A map. *Ahhh. The hunt. For one of* them. I drew in the night, sounds of shouting and gunfire in the distance, foul human smells and sounds and filth of their world. Motors and engines. Cat blood. I leaped into the air. Thermals were confusing in the city, rising and falling over buildings, stirred by unexpected drafts from the river. *The river.*

I banked and found it, sparkling and whitecapped in a rising breeze. *Rain soon.* The knowledge of weather was part of a raptor's native genetic snake. I rose on the leftover heat of day, soaring high. Below me, I found the highway, a ribbon laced with moving lights crossing the river. I followed it, away from the city, along the map stored beneath my skin and in the human part of me. To the place where vampires lay their true-dead and find their healing.

CHAPTER 18

We still search for absolution

From a thousand feet up, the moon silvering the night, stars shining like a million lights, the ecstasy of flight filled me. My heart beat powerfully. My wings spread wide, soaring. Air currents ruffled my flight feathers as I cruised, my belly full, joy singing in my veins.

My attention was caught by a large rat emerging from a swampy place far below. Good eating if I was hungry—good for feeding chicks. Near the wet ground, I spotted a small, whitewashed building at the end of a crushed-shell street. Curious, I half folded my wings and dropped six hundred feet. Spread them again, to circle.

Distant memories stirred. I was searching for this place. The building had no cross, but its walls were tall, its roof was vaulted, and a spiked steeple speared the sky. *Katie. Vampires.* Remembering, I dropped lower.

Narrow, arched windows were pointed at the apex—chapel windows of stained glass. But unlit. Dark. Vampire dark. The white building was made of ancient cement mixed with shells, and it glowed with the light of the moon though no lights lit the windows or the grounds.

The earth all around the chapel-that-was-not was studded with white marble crypts, family-sized mausoleums, shining in the moonlight. They studded the ground, little houses for the true-dead or the living undead. I circled down, seeing car lights drawing in from every direction. Yet here, in this ancient building, no lights burned.

I inspected it all with eyes built for the night and with hearing that missed nothing. As I dropped lower, soaring on the breeze, candlelight bloomed inside the nonchapel and brightened, shining, flickering through the arched windows, throwing muted hues of color onto the white shell walkway. The stained-glass windows were all in shades of blood—ruby, wine, burgundy, the pink of watered blood—bloody light spilling onto the ground.

A vampire stepped from the doorway, smoothing her dress. She was *old*. Her skin was the white of the full moon, her face grooved. She was dressed all in white, the toes of her shoes, her long dress, the nunlike wimple on her head, hiding her hair; her hands were pocketed beneath an apron like a vampire mother superior. A distant car purred. She stopped moving, the stillness of stone, a carved statue, fit for a graveyard. The sight of her brought me to myself.

She squared her shoulders and raised her chin as if she were going into battle, and I saw that she had black brows and a beaked nose. Mediterranean ethnicity, perhaps Greek. Not beautiful, but imposing and serene, as if she had made peace with herself and her world.

The car crunched down the shell-gravel lane. The smell of vampire rose on the air. I canted my flight feathers and dropped lower, silent on the wind, wings making no sound at all as I chose a tree to land. Tall. Dead. Branches white and stripped of bark. Close to the land where the vampires went to earth. Close enough for my owl ears to hear them speak. I stretched my wings full, spread my flight feathers, and raised my breast. Reached out with legs and talons. Back-winged to break my forward movement. Gripped the barkless branch. I was down. I shrugged my raptor shoulders and fluttered my flight feathers as balance and gravity took over. I settled on the deadwood, my wings folding tight against me.

The woman vampire turned as I landed, seeing me in the tree. I called, owl sound, lonely in the night. Not an owl of this place, but she wouldn't know the difference. After a moment, she turned away to the first limousine, watching as it rocked near and its tires ground to a halt.

Vampires slid from the long car, seven of them, all moving fast, at full vamp speed, all well fed, the smell of fresh blood on them. All wore black, somber suits and tailored gowns in summer wool or silk, shimmering in the night. They were dressed as if for a funeral or a party.

More cars moved up the drive as the first circled and headed out, lights passing, like birds in flight. Like a dance. Dozens of cars approached, some depositing one occupant, some many, until there were nearly a hundred vamps gathered under the young moon. Lastly came a hearse, white, gleaming pearlescent in the night. It bumped to a stop in the midst of the vampires.

Two males jumped out and raced to the rear of the hearse. They were human, ungraceful, slow moving, and one carried a roll of fat around his middle. No vampire ever managed extra weight, most living at near starvation, gaunt as a winter hunt. The vampires moved subtly closer, tightening a circle around the hearse. The humans' fear grew as they unloaded a white coffin. Near panic leached from their pores and tainted the night wind.

"You sure you can bury her without . . . ? Never mind," one said.

One of the vampires laughed, the sound sly and cruel, enjoying the terror that increased tenfold on its echo. The two humans rushed back and slammed the hearse doors. The locks clicked, though mechanical locks and glass windows gave them no protection at all. The mocking vampire laughed again. I saw him lick his lips, heard the smack of dead flesh.

The hearse roared and spat loose shell like gunshots as it pulled away. It fishtailed at the entry to the graveyard, tires shrieking as they caught on the pavement. The hearse roared all the way down the road. When it was gone, the old vampire, the one in the nun's wimple who had lit candles in the nonchapel, moved to the coffin and placed her hand atop it.

"Gather," she said, soft and compelling. I leaned from my branch, coercion pulling on my flesh and bones, urging me to come. It was a kind of vamp *calling*, full of enticement. "Gather and give the gift of blood," she said, "that our sister might be healed." Her words rose above the crowd, dancing on the air, full of beauty. Age made her voice potent, mellow. Her words chimed and rang inside my head, commanding and demanding. My talons danced on the old wood. Dark sparks of energy and magic soared through me. I spread my wings to fly to her.

"I challenge the right to blood ceremony," a man said.

Startled, I snapped my wings tight to my side.

The crowd shifted and sighed, as if expectation was satisfied. Those closest stepped away from the new speaker until he stood apart, opening a path from him to the pale coffin. He seemed amused at the way his kindred moved. The vamp was slender and willowy, even by vamp standards. Dark, delicate, but not effete, he walked through the space in the gathering the way a fencer might, feet placed with care and with a thought to balance. When he stood in front of the old woman he said, "Rafael Torrez, heir of Clan Mearkanis. Challenger."

"Sabina Delgado y Aguilera," the old vamp said, and I started. I had seen that name today. "Priestess of the sacred ground. You may speak to the challenge."

A dandy, he flicked at his cuff, a bit of lace gleaming silken in the night. "There is no requirement for any to offer blood. The injured was either foolish or weak. She offered her neck to an attacker. Prey should be allowed to die. Thus has always been our way."

There was a rustling in the crowd, murmurs of agreement. "I champion the fallen," a voice said. Leo moved through the crowd, equally graceful—who among them wasn't?—but with the grace of the bullfighter, strong and determined. I fluttered my long feathers in the still air, shaking off the last of the compulsion to gather.

"Leonard Eugène Zacharie Pellissier," he said. I figured they all knew who was who, so the speaking was formulaic, like a legal process, with proper names and titles required. "Blood-master of the city, blood-master of Clan Pellissier, these seven hundred years." Seven-hundred-year-old vamps were rare, to the best of my knowledge, and the priestess had to be older. A lot older. I hadn't seen her lineage in the hall of records.

He stopped in front of the priestess, Sabina. "The old ways are dead and gone. When the humans found us, revealed us, proved the ancient myths were true and blood hunters were among them, the old ways changed. The old ways died.

"We may no longer build blood-families as we did in the past, not and survive in the human world. And we are not so numerous today that we can allow the oldest among us to die true-death. As the world has moved on, so must the Mithrans evolve to survive."

"Pretty words. But my clan has suffered the death of our leader. As eldest, my blood is precious to my line," Rafael said, "and needful to cement my rule. Why should I give of my own blood to save a scion belonging to my *enemy*? Why should I help *you*?" The air crackled with animosity, and I half expected Rafael to bare fangs or draw a sword and attack.

"We must stand together to defeat the rogue," Leo said. "We may be enemies, Rafael, but the enemy of my enemy is my friend. We stand together against the humans who would destroy us. That part of the ancient ways must remain unchanged." Softly he added, "I would give my blood for you, if you were attacked by the rogue." The crowd breathed out, surprised.

"And because if we do not help," Sabina said, "it is possible Katherine Louisa Dupre, who is not yet true-dead, may heal on her own, and rise as a rogue herself. And may then infect others of us, as the old tales say." The congregation of vamps shifted position in what could have been a slow, complicated dance. Indecision was evident in their collective stance.

"That a rogue might infect another Mithran is a tale of old women and fools," Rafael scoffed. "It was myth before I was turned." He looked at a woman in a black silk evening dress, and she looked away. I cocked my head and gave a soft, twittering coo of surprise. *Dominique*, I remembered.

Sabina said, "*I* was myth before you were turned, Rafael. I have seen myth made reality. Now, in this time when light is thrown upon our *dark and tainted past*, an old rogue haunts the streets of our city, maddened in his *sin*." Her words slid away on a softly released breath.

"Taint," one of the gathered said.

"Sin," said another.

I wasn't sure what the words meant to them, but the tone was sorrowful, like the call of lonely birds in the night. I twittered again, and the priestess looked over at the tree where I sat. I stilled my voice and gripped the limb with my talons to still my movement.

Sabina turned back to the vamps and said, "As with other races who, at different times and places, sought to steal from God, our sin has cost us much. We must not allow it to destroy us before redemption comes." Again the crowd murmured. *Steal from God?* I thought. *How does a vamp steal from God?* "Rafael Torrez," Sabina said, "does your clan withdraw its challenge? Will you share blood with the dead?"

"Clan Mearkanis withdraws our challenge," he said, with ill grace. "But we will not soon again accept the call to gather."

"Are there other challengers?" When no one spoke up, the priestess said, "Acceptance is given. Open the casket."

The vamps moved in, closing slowly around the white coffin in a tight circle, obscuring my view, even from the height of the dead tree. The coffin hinges toned faintly, slowly. I heard a blade pulled from a sheath, saw a glint of steel in Sabina's hand, and smelled vamp blood, pungent and tart upon the downstroke. She said, "As eldest and priestess, I offer first blood to our fallen sister," and held her arm over the casket, blood flowing fast, dripping inside with a soft patter. The smell of vamp blood intensified. After a long moment, she held a cloth to her arm. A woman beside her tied a strip around the bandage to hold it in place. Taking up the blade again, she wiped it on a second cloth and looked at the gathering, waiting.

Leo rolled his sleeve to his elbow, his forearm out. "As blood-master to our fallen sister, I offer second blood." He accepted the slice of Sabina's blade. He stood over the coffin, letting his blood flow like an offering, but there was a challenge in his stance, and his eyes were on Rafael. Long minutes passed as he clenched and unclenched his fist, encouraging the blood flow. A human would have passed out cold. Only when the blood stopped flowing on its own did he accept a clean cloth from the priestess and step away.

"To show mercy, Clan Mearkanis offers blood to the fallen." Rafael took the blade from Sabina and sliced his own flesh. From the vamps' reactions, I gathered that the gesture was rude, but Sabina said nothing, letting him have his way. He returned the bloody blade and held his arm over the open coffin, his blood flowing. His blood ran nearly as long as Leo's had, and when his wound finally clotted over, he was reeling.

It looked to me like a vamp version of a pissing contest. *Men will be boys.*

A female offered Rafael a shoulder to support him. Beside him, a woman stepped up. She was elegant, but thin, almost emaciated. "As acting head of Clan Arceneau, I offer blood." She accepted the downstroke, drawing in a breath at the pain. She let her blood fall, only half the time Leo had bled, yet she was wavering on her feet. To my bird eyes, Dominique looked odd. Not quite certain how, but just . . . not quite normal, even for a vamp. She moved with less grace, perhaps. I watched as she was led to a bench on the grounds. And then I got it. She had already been bled tonight, probably by a vamp, one to whom she owed blood debt.

Blood-master of Clan St. Martin bled next, offering only a token splatter. His eyes swept the assembled as if daring them to comment on his paltry gift. Bad blood between St. Martin and Pellissier. Birds can't grin, but I felt the urge. After that, the heads of the other clans offered blood, some playing the vamp version of "keep up with the Joneses" by nearly draining themselves, others offering a more modest amount. I worked to recall the clan names and the order of importance, though such memory wasn't easy for my current brain.

Pellissier, Mearkanis, Arceneau, Rousseau, Desmarais, Laurent, St. Martin, Bouvier, some enemies, some not. The "saint" part of St. Martin was still a surprise, but then, what I knew about nonrogue vamps had just been trebled again. Maybe quadrupled.

After the clan heads declared themselves and bled, the lesser members approached the coffin, still according to clan as best I could tell, but the drama was over and the rest of the bloodletting was without theatrics. I figured Katie was likely swimming in blood. Ick. I looked at the moon and judged that the bloodletting took over two hours before Sabina called a halt by saying words I didn't understand, in French, or Latin, or Mandarin for all I knew.

The vampires closed around the open casket, standing

shoulder to shoulder. And they started to hum, a fluctuating harmony that sounded like a funeral dirge without words. After several bars, the priestess sang out and the congregation fell silent. "Ēlî ēlî lamâ švaqtanî."

Startled, I tilted forward, neck out, and nearly tottered from the limb. I fluttered my wings and danced back, my talons scraping on the loose bark. "Ēlî ēlî lamâ švaqtanî," she intoned again. The entire crowd sang back in minor-key harmony, "Ēlî ēlî lamâ švaqtanî. Ēlî ēlî lamâ švaqtanî." I stared, feeling cold in my bones, placing the words in my memory. The phrase was among the last words I would have expected to hear from a bunch of vampires. And they didn't go up in flames. Needing warmth, I fluffed and fluttered my feathers, twittering in fear.

I had heard the words at every Easter passion play from the time I was twelve to the time I left the children's home. I was pretty sure the phrase was among the last words uttered by Jesus on the cross, Aramaic for "My God, my God, why have you forsaken me?"

The vampires fell silent.

I stayed in my tree as the vamps interred Katie, shoving her coffin into an empty slot in a Clan Pellissier mausoleum. The harsh sound of metal on stone was grinding, and the thunk of the coffin settling in its niche echoed across the grounds. As the door to the crypt was closed, its iron grating sealed and locked, they seemed to take a collective breath, as if to free themselves from the vestiges of a trance. The formalities were clearly over.

Some of the vamps formed into smaller groups, to chat or plot or whatever vamps did at undead nonfunerals. Oddly, they talked about the stock market and the latest flare-up in the Middle East, like any well-educated group of humans. It was almost as disorienting as hearing them quote Jesus. Then, one by one, they called for their rides on cell phones, and the limo and fancy car procession reversed itself. First to arrive were last to leave. That pissing contest again.

When all the vamps were gone, I was ready to take wing back to my garden and shift into something with arms. But Sabina still stood, head down, white skirts fluttering in the breeze. She spoke without raising her voice, her tones heavy now with an accent I didn't recognize. "It has been many years since I heard the call of the *Bubo bubo*," she said. She looked up at the tree, her face bright in the scant moonlight. "I know not if you are real, or prophecy, or the mad imaginings of an old, old sinner." She shook her head slowly, her predator eyes on me. Though I was raptor, and afraid of little, I wanted to lift wings and fly far away. My flight feathers shivered and my taloned feet danced on the limb. "If you are prophecy, if you are the breath of God on my stained and darkened soul, then know this, and take my words back with you to paradise. We still seek forgiveness. We still search for absolution."

When I didn't move, she bowed her head and walked to the nonchapel, so graceful her skirts scarcely swayed. She shut and barred the door. I watched as she doused all lights but one, a single flame in the night. Silence settled on the graveyard. I lifted my wings and launched myself, swooping low over the grounds, seeking currents to gain altitude.

I banked and soared over the nonchapel, ready to fly home; then I heard the now familiar grating of a crypt opening. I canted once more over the cemetery, seeking with raptor eyes designed to spot the smallest prey, and with keen ears, half expecting to see or hear Katie. Instead, a man walked from a crypt, hunched and gaunt, and reeking of the grave. The rogue.

He closed the wood door to the crypt and pushed shut the wrought-iron gate protecting it, his movements uneven, almost human slow. His feet were bare and filthy, his hands sticklike, skeletal. His clothes were ratty and torn, ill fitting, not the same long coat and wool slacks he had left at the water's edge in the pit behind the shaman's house. His head was down, hair straggling over his face, obscuring it. But I knew him by his rotten stink, his gait, and the set of his bony shoulders. He didn't move like any vamp I knew. I soared silently past, so I could read the clan name on the mausoleum. St. Martin.

The rogue tripped and swayed across the grassy ground to the Clan Pellissier vault. He fell against the barred doors and gripped them with pale white hands, shaking them. The quiet rattle sounded loud and harsh in the silent night. His actions grew frantic, his fingers beating the locks, clawing past the iron bars into the door, his face pressed against the metal. He mewled piteously, like a small, hungry animal. I could hear him breathing, snuffling, as he smelled the mixed vamp blood, the aroma a rich blood scent on the wind, stronger than his rot.

He slammed his palms against the bars and pushed away with a final clang. Furious, he lurched to the nonchapel. I circled tighter, watching. His fingers brightened with heat and gray sparkles of power. An energy signature I recognized. I circled down fast, watching as claws grew on his fingers, hooked and curved, longer than Beast's. He was shape-shifting.

Crap. This thing wasn't a rogue vamp. It was a were. Or a skinwalker. Beast was right. This was indeed a liver-eater.

CHAPTER 19

I'm psychic

He stopped, drawing in his shoulders, breathing deeply, a wet, hacking sound, familiar from Beast. The liver-eater threw his face to the night sky. And he spotted me.

His face was no longer human but a blunted snout, long fangs curving from upper and lower jaws. He had gone furry, a tawny pelt covering his face and arms and down his neck. Jaw elongating, ears rising, pointing. Claws larger than Beast's by far. His shift stopped there, as if he had control enough to shift only partway. Or maybe he was stuck between forms. The stink of rot was gone, leaving the musky odor of male big cat.

Sabertooth, some part of me thought, stunned. Watching, I hesitated an instant. Missed an air current, an uprising thermal. The twisting air threw me off. I tumbled. My wings fluttered uselessly. I started to spin and reached out with wings and taloned feet, spreading myself, steadying my body in flight as the earth rose fast.

Below me, the sabertooth jumped, reaching high with a clawed hand. An impossible leap. I caught the air and rotated my shoulders, back-flapping hard. A cry escaped me, raptor anger. The rogue's claws scraped through my flight feathers. I flailed the air, gaining altitude, and screamed again. The rogue landed on all fours. The back of his coat ripped with a dry, rasping tear, golden fur spilling out, a long and ragged mane, his back striped. The stones of a nearby crypt exploded, breaking with a crack and rumble.

He was stealing mass. Stealing from stone. The front door of the nonchapel opened. Sabina stepped out.

I screamed at her to get back inside. But my throat and beak called only hoarse, cawing cries. The rogue roared, a sound not human. Turning from me, he raced toward the chapel.

I folded my wings. Dove at his nape. Hit with killing force. Slammed my beak into the base of his skull. A dull, echoing crack. Raked his scalp with talons. He stumbled, shook himself. I toppled to the side. Narrowly evaded his claws. Shoulders rotating, I shot back into the sky.

He leaped at the priestess. I dove, but I couldn't help. Not against this creature, not in this form, maybe not in human form. I hadn't understood, but Beast had known. No matter the evidence, this *wasn't* a rogue vampire. This was *liver-eater*, a creature of darkest legend. A creature of black magic.

From the air, my body diving, I saw Sabina pull something from behind her back. Raise it aloft. It was a wood cross. Held in gloved hands. Light blazed from the cross. The creature roared, jumped, shied. Rotated in midair. He screamed a big cat's pain, like a woman in travail. Landed facing away, a paw over his eyes. He raced away, his body shifting as he sprinted. He went four-footed, his clothes ripping away. A black-tipped mane writhed out. Another crypt exploded, stone shrapnel flying. *Sabertooth lion . . . afraid of a cross like a vampire.*

I back-flapped, reversing direction, my talons out, wings shoving against the air as if I pushed it away. On the nonchapel porch, Sabina dropped the cross and wrapped her arms across her middle, cradling herself. She moaned with pain, her eyes on me, pupils vamp black, her fangs fully extended. The reek of seared flesh and leather polluted the air.

She took a breath and shouted, "Prophecy!" Claws an inch long extended from the ends of burned suede gloves, constructed to leave the tips of her fingers exposed, like driving gloves or golf gloves, incongruous with the nunlike dress. I wanted to stay, to see that she was okay. Foolish desire for a vamp killer. Instead, I keened in anger and wheeled, following the black-magic skinwalker, who was repulsed by a cross.

He raced across the graveyard, between crypts and into the woods. I flew higher, found a current moving toward the river. Tracking him. There was no way for him to lose me, not in this form. My eyes could follow a mouse at a hundred yards.

He sprinted through the woods, looking often into the sky, at me. A mile later, he crossed a wide road, avoiding car headlights going both directions, running with vamp speed toward a well-lit area, a cul-de-sac where security lights shone, cars and trucks were parked in the street, and the small, square houses were dark. Air conditioners purred. A dog barked. Others took up the warning, a raucous chorus. One house had windows open, a television laugh track spilling into the dark, screen flickering. The rogue burst from the woods. Raced into the open. And dove through a half-open window into the house.

Through the window, I heard snarls, a choked cry. *He's killing someone.* Nearby dogs went wild, growling, barking, throwing themselves against chain-link fencing, metal clanking and twanging. I screamed a challenge. Dove. Swooped close. But I was in the air, in winged form. I couldn't help. And I couldn't shift back into human form—there was nothing to take mass from, and even if I could risk it, I had left too much of myself back at the garden.

A woman cried out, the sounds gurgling away. I screamed back, damning the sky and the air and the liver-eater. I heard thumps from the house, hollow, reverberating, and then the sound of water falling. A shower, water hitting tile, thudding into a body for a long time. Then there was nothing. The house fell silent. Focusing tightly, I circled higher, watching. Nothing moved. Nothing changed. Helpless, I soared, current to current. The air cooled. A storm raced in on the gulf. Far off, lightning flickered on the dome of the sky. Clouds dimmed the stars. Dawn was near. And still I flew.

A door slammed. A man walked from the house. But it wasn't the liver-eater. I folded my wings and plummeted close. This man was tall and redheaded, wearing jeans and a T-shirt and an unfamiliar scent. I caught an updraft, not sure what his presence meant. He got into a car. Cranked it up, and drove onto the adjoining street. I followed long enough to place where I was, where the house was, in my bird memory. Dawn was pinking the east sky.

If I met the sun in this form, I couldn't change back until sunset. Conflicted, struggling with myself, I wheeled and beat the air, back to the garden where I had left most of my mass. I made it just in time, alighting on the topmost stone, wings out, tail feathers wide. Talons on the rocks, scritching rough and rasping. I put a talon on the nugget. And thought about Jane Yellowrock. Human. Scarred. Female. Earthbound. *Mass to mass, stone to stone . . .*

I pulled the memory of her snake to the surface. I melted into it. Into her. Rock rumbled beneath me. Pain ratcheted along my bones and I gasped. Fell onto the breaking boulder. It split wide. Dumped me to the ground. Knocked out my breath. Jagged rocks tumbled over me.

Stunned and hurting, I lay on the ground, staring at the sky. I was woozy, not sure what had happened, remembering only that I had been *Bubo bubo*. Hadn't I? I looked down, proving to myself that I was human. Slowly, the memories came back to me. My stomach growled. I took up the gold nugget and placed the necklace over my head. A golden streak crossed from the east. A bird began to sing. A striped yellow cat walked along the fence between Katie's place and my garden, watching me.

The boulders in the back garden hadn't been so lucky. The top one had been reduced to rubble, its largest chunk less than half the size of the original, the smallest like pea gravel. I didn't like storing mass. I didn't understand how I did it, and I had the feeling it was dangerous. But so far, I had come back whole. Leaning against the stone, I touched the nugget.

When I turned eighteen and left the children's home, I headed to the mountains, following some innate imperative north and west. After motoring my bike up Wolf Mountain as far as the dirt road, then a trail, led, I found myself at Horseshoe Rock. I hiked down from it into the woods. At the bottom of a narrow ravine, I scuffed through dry leaves and found a quartz boulder, weather stained, canted down the gully. Through the center of it ran a vein of gold.

In the dark and the rain, I crawled inside a sleeping bag and slept near the boulder. And for the first time in six years, though I had no necklace, no marrow to find the snake within, I shifted. Into a big cat. Beast spoke to me like an old friend, long silenced. For weeks, I/we hunted, ate, visited old dens. Hid from humans. Searched for my/our progeny. All my kits were gone. All others of my kind were gone. I was the last one. Anywhere.

When I shifted back to human, I dug out a few nuggets of gold and tucked them into a pocket. I later had one strung on an adjustable, doubled gold chain, to carry it with me, while the rest went into a safe-deposit box for a rainy day. If I concentrated, I could sense the gold, no matter where I was, both the position of each nugget and the original vein in the boulder deep in the mountains. It gave me security, a sense of refuge. Of comfort.

Now, shaking, I hung the nugget necklace over my head and went inside. I made it to the stove as my cell rang. "Mol," I answered, "I'm okay."

"It's me, Aunt Jane," Angelina said, sniffling. "You scared me."

Stunned, I said, "Huh?"

"Don't be the bird no more, Aunt Jane. You coulda fell." She was crying.

I clutched the cell, my frozen heart melting. "Okay, Angie baby. No more bird."

"I love you," she murmured. "I gotta go. But Mommy says we're gonna come visit you." And the call ended.

After a two-quart pot of oatmeal, one of Beast's steaks grilled nearly rare—but not quite—under the oven broiler, and a whole pot of strong black tea, I felt more like myself, more or less, though I was emaciated and sick to my stomach, and was experiencing vertigo to the point that I held on to the cabinets or furniture when I walked. Angie was right. What I had done was dangerous. Really bad stupid.

Cold, unable to get warm even after steaming until the hot shower water cooled, I curled up under the covers with a pen and pad, and jotted down what I remembered about the night. The location of the chapel—not nonchapel, but chapel. It had contained a cross and a nun. Well, a priestess, but close enough. That made it a chapel, right? The half-remembered location of the house where the creature entered. Had he killed? The TV had been on. Had I mistaken a sound track for a real murder? Had the rogue-liver-eater gone to ground *under* the house? Questions, no answers, and a fractured, hazy memory.

My last coherent thought was of the priestess, holding aloft a wood cross, shining with light. Wood didn't do that, not even in the presence of evil, which is why I always carry silver crosses. Weird. Just plain weird. And weirder still—a vamp holding a cross. How did she survive it? Halfway through my recollections and questions, I fell asleep.

I woke up feeling warm and annoyed. Someone was pounding on my door with loud, impatient fists. I wasn't sure, but it may have been going on a long time. Couldn't people just let a girl sleep in? Stiff and sore, I rolled out of bed, trailing covers, found the borrowed robe, and slid it on. Through the glass I saw the Joe, Rick LaFleur.

"Crap." With ill grace, I opened the front door. "It better be freaking damn important."

He was wearing jeans, boots, and a cowboy hat that he pushed back by the brim, raising it enough to take me in from head to bare toes. A slow perusal that went from inventory to sensual in a heartbeat. His scent changed from business to sex.

A grin spread across his face. "Please tell me you're alone and lonely." When I glared, he raised a hand and reached toward me, moving slowly, as if he thought he might get slapped. Or taken down in the street and left bruised. He brushed a strand of hair back from my face, behind my ear.

Beast woke with a sudden lurch. And purred. She drew a breath and fought me for control. It was payback time for becoming *Bubo bubo*. I felt her claws in my belly. In the old wound across my chest, tightening. Rick's fingers trailed along my neck to the collar of my robe, a slow caress across my collarbone and down.

Mastering Beast, I caught his wrist before he got too friendly. "What do you want?" I snarled, holding his hand away from me. I was tickled pink that my voice showed only annoyance, not desire. But I had started to sweat behind my knees and along my spine. Beast wanted him. Badly.

"I came to see if you wanted to ride."

"Do what?" Images poured into my mind of big cats mating, snarling and drawing blood.

His grin stretched with a kind of sexual teasing I had

never mastered. "Horses," he said, drawing out the word as if I were an imbecile and he could see the images in my mind. "You didn't come to the club last night, so I came to see if you wanted to go horseback riding." I dropped his wrist. He let it fall, grin in place.

"I didn't sleep last night," I said. "What time is it?"

"It's four p.m., time to rise and shine, especially in the city that parties till dawn." He pushed his way inside and I let him, which had to be really dumb. Beast wanted to reach out and slide a hand across his butt as he entered, but I resisted. No freaking way. Her usual payback was less sexual, more in the nature of refusing to shift back when it was time. I think I preferred her stubborn streak to her sensual one.

Beast tightened her claws on me, tearing. It hurt and I gasped in pain. "Put on the kettle," I said. Spinning on one heel, I went to my room and shut the door. Firmly. Maybe a little more than firmly, but it made my point. I was not happy with Rick LaFleur. But he knew Anna, who had slept with the rogue—no, the liver-eater—when he smelled unstinky. And he had something going on with Antoine, which pricked my curiosity. I wanted to know what Rick knew, which meant I had to spend time with him, get to know him better, pick his brain, always assuming he had one. I needed to go check out the house the liver-eater-rogue had entered. But first—I needed food. A lot of food. I was unexpectedly ravenous.

I brushed my hair, braiding it halfway down my back, tying it off with some yarn I'd seen in a drawer. I dressed in jeans and a spaghetti-strap top. When I looked in the mirror I expected to see dark circles under my eyes, hollowed cheeks, pallid skin. But I looked pretty good, if a lot skinnier than yesterday. The oatmeal and steak for breakfast had helped, but my stomach was growling, and I knew I wasn't going anywhere until I had protein.

Still barefoot, I padded back to the kitchen and took a steak out of the fridge. Four left. I had to go shopping. But manners pounded into me in the children's home took precedence over my possible starvation, and I said, "Want a steak?"

"Sure. If you're having one. Rare. Still kicking."

Deep inside me, Beast rumbled approval. I flushed a bit

at her reaction and wished she'd go back to sleep and find another way to torture me.

Rick sprawled in the chair Bruiser liked, long legs spread, taking up a lot of space. Aware of his body language, of the way his eyes lingered on me, I took out a second steak, colas, and a package of baby spinach put there by Troll. "Hey," he said, "I got that info you wanted on the property owners out near Lake Catouatchie and the Jean Lafitte National Historical Park."

I nodded, and when I could speak casually, asked, "Did you hear anything about a murder over near Westwego? Out that way?"

"Nope. Why?" When I shook my head, he didn't press. "So. We going riding?"

"I'll think about it after lunch," I said, and lit the broiler.

I wasn't able to turn the conversation around to Anna. How did you ask a guy if he was sleeping with the mayor's wife, especially when you can't explain why you have an inkling that he is? So, after a steak, microwaved potato, spinach salad with bacon dressing, and some idle conversation, I said, "Much as I like the idea of horseback riding, I need to bike out to Westwego. Rain check?"

Rick was again sprawled in his chair, one arm draped over his middle, the other resting over the back of the chair nearest, a Coke can dangling in his fingers. He shrugged. "I got nothing to do. I'll ride out that way with you and we can stop and get supper on the way back. Make a date of it." His eyes sparkled. "I know me a good diner, serves the best oyster po'boys in the state. Fried up crackling crisp. It's not too far from Westwego."

I shouldn't take him with me, not when there might be a house full of dead bodies at the end of the ride. But instead of telling him no, I said, "Sure. Sounds like fun." And could have slapped myself. But pragmatism reared its head. If I did find dead bodies, I'd need to call the cops, and I'd need a good story. I could practice on Rick.

It was after five when we headed out of town, the sun still far above the horizon and glaring, the air hot and muggy, burning where it hit bare skin, making us sweat beneath the riding clothes. I would heal from road rash if I took a tumble, but rapid healing was not something I wanted to explain. So I wore jeans, boots, and leather jacket despite the heat. Rush hour traffic was snarled everywhere, but having bikes meant we could weave through stopped traffic. Not exactly legal, but no one had ever stopped me, and Rick didn't seem like the kind to wait patiently on hot asphalt, breathing exhaust fumes. He followed when I motored between stopped vehicles on 90 and across the bridge.

The traffic opened out on the other side of the Mississippi and I gunned the motor, Rick at my side. The world looked different from the road, and it took me a while to orient myself, but I eventually found my way to the exit that led through secondary and tertiary roads, and lastly to the crushed-shell drive of the vamp graveyard.

The drive was blocked by two hinged metal arms on solid stanchions, the arms connected by a chain and secured with a good lock. I slowed to make the transit around the stanchion on the left and gave the bike enough gas to coast along the curving drive, pulling off my helmet and looking the place over. It looked different from nighttime and twenty feet up. I didn't know what he was waiting for but Rick eventually followed me. I was walking between crypts, the sun broiling down on my bare head when he caught up, his Frye boots crunching shells as he jogged.

"You did see the No Trespassing signs, didn't you?" he said.

"Yeah." I spotted the Pellissier mausoleum and checked the locks on the barred door. They were top quality and still secure, which meant that Katie was safe, or as safe as an undead drowned in the mixed blood of a hundred vamps and buried in a casket in a vault can be. I swiveled, spotting the St. Martin crypt, and strode that way, peeling out of my leather jacket as I walked. Sweat was dribbling down my spine, under my arms, and pooling in my waistband as I circled the small building. The St. Martin crypt was made of white, dry-stacked marble blocks. Its door was centered on the front between elegant pillars; two windows were close together on the back, windows matching the pointed, arched style of the chapel's. The crypt had been badly damaged. A section of marble was missing from a corner, broken, as if it had been attacked with a mallet; I knew better. Stone shards were scattered around from the rogue's mass change.

Rick swore softly. "Damn kids." When I glanced at him,

he said, "Graveyard vandalism is rampant in this part of the state." I didn't bother to enlighten him.

The building was fourteen by twelve feet, with a stone statue on the peaked roof—a six-foot-tall winged soldier with a bronze sword and shield. Except for the weapons and wings folded to his sides, he was naked. And exceptionally well endowed. I shook my head, not smiling, but wanting to. A sculptor's vision of St. Martin? Or St. Martin's vision of an angel?

Rick caught up with me again. "You do know this place belongs to the vampires, don't you?" He sounded half amused, half speculative, as if he wondered how I found this place and why I was here, but didn't really want to ask.

"Yeah." I checked the locks and the vault's barred door. The locks were old and broken. The bars were freshly bent, with shiny metal showing along stress lines. "So?" I opened the barred gate door and pushed on the wooden one behind it. It opened with a soft groan.

"So, the gate had electronic sensors," he said. "They'll send someone to check on us."

I looked inside. "Good. They can clean this up."

"This" was the destruction of five of the six coffins. They had once rested in stacked stone biers, three high, and each individual bier had a small marble door at the foot end. The marble doors were busted and the coffins inside had been pulled out and slammed against the back wall, if the scars there were a clue. The casket contents were scattered everywhere. Contrary to pulp fiction, vamps don't blow away in ashes when they die unless they're burned, so the floor was littered with bones, scraps of ancient dress, boots, a few grinning skulls—one with black hair attached—some gold coins, glittering jewelry, and rotting casket stuffing.

I gestured inside. Rick bent around the side of the door and looked in. "Crap almighty. Who—shit! Who did this? What's that smell?" He backed quickly away, a hand over his mouth and nose.

I was already upwind. "Partly the dead and partly the rogue. I think he spent the day here yesterday." I calculated the distance from the edge of the woods. It was farther than it looked from the air. "I think he knew the vamps would put Katie to earth, and he hoped to get at the blood in her coffin."

"Blood in her coffin?"

I considered his expression and decided that I wasn't the only one who hadn't known what the ceremony last night involved. I wondered if any human knew. I also decided it was smarter not to know the answers to his question and smarter not to share the information I had discovered. "Katie's blood," I lied. "He didn't finish draining her." Which was the truth.

"Uh-huh."

I had to work on my lying. To keep from having to respond to his skepticism, I walked to the chapel. On the way, I passed the other crypt damaged by the rogue, stealing mass. It belonged to Clan Mearkanis, and the damage was greater, two square feet of stone blasted away.

I reached the chapel. The cross was still lying on the small porch, but no longer glowing or burning. I leaned over it, pulling off my sunglasses to get a better view. The wood was untouched, unscorched by the fire I had seen, and no fresh scent of smoke clung to it. It wasn't made from carved or cut wood; the crosspieces looked like large splinters ripped from a timber.

The cross looked old, blackened by time and usage. The four ends were smoothed, as if they had been slightly rounded off by sandpaper and oiled. Or slowly shaped from the repeated caresses of human hands. The two pieces were held together by twisted metal, the finish a green verdigris that had bled into the wood it touched. *Old*, I thought. *Old, old,* old.

Rick took the narrow steps and bent to pick up the cross. I reacted without thinking. Grabbed the waistband of his jeans. And yanked. He flew past me. Made a soft *oof* when he landed, tumbling, expelling air. I stood, blocking the porch, waiting for him to catch his breath. He groaned and cursed. "Why the hell did you do that?" he grunted. "What did I do this time?"

"You were about to touch the cross," I said. "It belongs to a vamp. She'd have smelled your scent on it. Not smart."

"Vamps don't own crosses," he said. He pushed his elbows under him and half sat, legs splayed, feet digging into the shells, making little troughs that ended in mounds at his heels. "Besides, a simple 'Hey you, stop' would have worked just fine. Anybody ever tell you that you tend to overreact?"

"Yeah. A few people. Some of them are dead," I said, letting my grin out. "I'm not."

Rick blew out a sound of disgust and rolled to his knees. "What do you press, anyway? You got arms like a gorilla." He made it to his feet and stood looking at me.

Press. As in bench press. I didn't like his expression. I had received similar looks when I did something a normal human couldn't, and I usually just made light of it. That worked, mostly because humans didn't want to recognize otherness, difference, or oddity. They would rather stuff the unusual into an acceptable niche, someplace comfortable, tucking a square peg into a round hole. It was easier for them and a lot less scary.

I had a feeling Rick LaFleur wouldn't accept my usual misdirection. There was a certain look in his eyes, harder and more speculative than I expected; not an average-Joe expression, but something else entirely. I couldn't come up with a single response, so I shrugged and walked to the dead tree. What you can't fight or explain away, you can sometimes ignore.

The tree was a dead sycamore, thin bark curling, exposing silvery wood beneath. The branch where I had sat was scored by raptor talons. A small feather rested on the ground, one of mine, and it felt really weird to see it. Had I lost part of me when I lost the feather? If I lost more of me, say if a leg were amputated while in animal form, what would I be missing when I shifted back? How much could I lose and still be me? I tucked the feather in my pocket.

Scanning the graveyard, I took in the layout, refamiliarizing myself with the clan crypts. I wasn't sure if I had missed it last night or forgotten it, but most of the mausoleums had statues on top. Each marble statue was male, winged, had a weapon and shield, and was naked. They could have been carved by the same sculptor, but the faces and bodies of each were different, all male, all beautiful. Angelic defenders of the demonic undead. Weird.

Rick walked up behind me and I studiously ignored him. I had seen enough, and I was ready to put some distance between the yank-Rick-off-the-porch episode and me. I flipped open my cell and dialed Bruiser as I headed back to the bikes. When he answered, I said, "You got alarms going off at the vamp graveyard?"

If I surprised him he didn't indicate it. "Yes. We have a team on the way."

"It's me and Rick LaFleur. Tell them not to shoot us if they get here before we leave. And tell them the rogue did a lot of damage to the St. Martin and Mearkanis crypts last night. I think he spent some time in St. Martin's, which means either he bypassed the security system, or he has access to it."

Bruiser cursed once, eloquently, and his voice dropped into a near snarl when he asked, "You have any more news for me?"

"No. I'm done. Wait. There's a cross on the chapel steps. Sabina dropped it, fighting off the rogue. Tell your guys how you want them to handle it."

"How do you know she dropped it? And how do you know about Sabina?" His tone was suspicious, the way a murder investigator's voice is suspicious when he finds a body and a bloody suspect standing over it. Holding the murder weapon.

I grinned and straddled my bike. "I'm psychic." I closed the phone and geared up, ignoring Rick as he followed my lead. I got the feeling that he didn't like playing follow the leader, but wasn't sure what to do about it. I also had the feeling that he was more than he let on. And I wasn't sure what I should do about that. Which made us even, in some strange kinda way.

I kick-started the bike, set my sunglasses in place, leaving the face shield up, out of the way, and wheeled down the drive. It was time to see the house the rogue dived into last night.

CHAPTER 20

Crap. I'm starting to like vamps

The house was at the end of Old Man's Beard Street. I smelled the blood and death through the open window from halfway down the road and it got stronger as I neared the house. The rogue-liver-eater had indeed killed here. I gunned the engine up the drive, next to the house, stopped, yanked off my helmet, and dialed Katie's pet NOPD investigator, Jodi Richoux. Rick pulled up next to me and killed his bike too.

"Jodi," I said when she answered. "This is Jane Yellowrock. I was following the rogue's tracks last night, and I got a house with open windows, one with damage consistent with a B and E. Place smells like dead meat."

"Hang on," she said, and I heard muffled conversation for a moment before she said, "Okay. Gimme the address."

"It's on Old Man's Beard Street, out Highway 90 not far from the Lapalco Boulevard exit, at the end of the cul-de-sac. You might want to send a team. And bring your psy-meter. I'd like to see what it reads."

"The team is on its way, and so am I. But give me one reason why I should share confidential information with you."

"Because the next time I find something interesting, you want me to call you and not the *New Orleans Times-Picayune*." I snapped the phone shut. I did so love toying with cops. Jodi would hate my guts, but she'd share. Of course, if she found the slightest reason to charge me with anything, no matter how minuscule, she would, just to get me back. Tit for tat. I wheeled the bike off the drive and beneath a shade tree.

"You're nuts, you know that?" Rick said. "Stark raving crazy, you are."

I unzipped my leather jacket, peeled it off, and draped it over the handlebars. "I may be here for a while. You staying or going?"

"I'm outta here." He paused, torn by two distinctly different needs. "How do you know the rogue vamp came through here last night?"

I decided on the truth, as far as it went. I had to practice it on somebody before I tried it out on Jodi. "I followed him partway. Saw him come through here but never saw him leave."

"You told the cops the place smells like dead meat. All I smell is fresh cut grass. And lady, I got a good nose."

The fragrance of the newly mown lawn across the street did permeate the air, but I had automatically filtered out every scent but the one I was looking for. Not smart. I should have walked around the house first. I really had to work on my lying. Going for surprised and innocent, I asked, "You don't smell that?"

Rick's eyebrows suggested I hadn't been entirely successful. He dug into his jacket's inner pocket and held out some folded sheets, paper-clipped together. "The property owners you asked for," he said.

I palmed the small wad, tucking it into my shirt. "Thanks."

"I'd like to stick around but . . ."

"But you have issues with cops?"

"Something like that. I'll see you later."

"Sure. Dancing at the club you play at." I offered him a half smile. "Beer'll be my treat." Nothing like a girl asking a guy out—looked like I was a modern-day gal, after all, or I just wanted to keep an eye on him and his acquaintances. Rick might be on his own rogue hunt, hoping to bag the creature out from under me, taking money out of my pocket. Maybe make a name for himself along the way. Or he might be on some other mission that could impact mine.

"Yeah. Well." Which didn't sound like a ringing endorsement for a date. But then he was probably too bruised to dance, from when I tossed him on his keister. Twice now. He turned a key; the engine of his red crotch rocket turned over and purred. I almost said, "Key starts are for wusses," but I managed to keep it in. My own bike's engine was running a little rough, so I had no call to be insulting someone else's. Still. A keyed start? Where was the excitement and mystery in that?

I watched him motor off. He didn't look back. Soon as he was gone, I redialed Jodi. When she answered I said, "You know a local Joe, Caucasian but Frenchy, olive skin, black and black, maybe six feet, slender? Name of Rick LaFleur?"

She hesitated. "No. Can't say as I do. But he may go by other aliases," she said. "Why?" It was the hesitation that did it. Jodi was lying to me.

"A source of mine claims he's doing some low-level work for Katie and a few other vamps. I was checking him out."

"Name's not familiar. But I'll keep my eyes open. ETA's under an hour," she said. "Stay close."

"I'll be here," I said. I closed the phone and tucked it into my pocket.

Was Rick running a scam on me and/or the vamps? Reporting to NOPD? A street source giving the cops inside information in return for help on a past legal problem? Was he ratting out the vamps? And if he was, should I care? Should it bother me? No, it shouldn't. But it did. It bothered me that he might be sharing secrets. It bothered me a lot. I'd rather he was trying to take my hunting gig. "Crap," I said. "I'm starting to like vamps."

Leaving my helmet and leather jacket with the bike, I circled around the house, into the woods, sweating in the humid heat. It wasn't even summer yet and it was in the high nineties. I tried to imagine what it would feel like in August. A steam bath was trite but it was the closest analogy, and sometimes trite just meant true. A city-sized—heck, a state-sized—steam bath.

For an instant, the urge for home swept over me. I stopped and closed my eyes as homesickness shook me. I wanted mountains, towering ridges and deep folded valleys. I wanted hemlock, spruce, fir, oak, and mountain maple, babbling brooks and streams spilling off hillsides and under small bridges that echoed hollowly off chasms when a bike clattered across. I wanted cool breezes and nighttime temps that dropped to the forties this time of year. I wanted icy spring showers. I wanted home, not this flat, muggy, wet, heated, miserable place. But here was where I was, and some people loved it with the same passion I felt for mountains. For now, I had a job to do and a way to put money in my pockets. I sucked up the need for home and started into the trees' shadow line.

A mosquito landed on my arm and shoved his proboscis into me for a blood meal, which seemed part and parcel of this job. I swatted it, leaving a bloody smear behind. Wiping it on my jeans, I muttered, "Damn bloodsucker."

A snake slithered away from my approach and I halted midstep. I wasn't afraid of snakes, but not being afraid didn't mean that I particularly liked them. If I got bit, and if it was poisonous, I'd have to shift to deal with the venom. And shifting, even into Beast, was hard by daylight, especially without my fetish necklace.

I wasn't familiar with local reptile varieties. The snake was three feet long and blackish, with a sort of diamond crosshatching down its length. Not a king snake. Not a garter snake. It rippled across the grass and turned its triangular, spear-shaped head my way. The arrowhead-shaped skull was the most common sign of a venomous snake. Maybe it was a diamondback, though its tail tip didn't seem to have rattles. It slithered off into the shade.

I moved on, watching my step. If I landed on a snake, the boots would only help if it bit below my knee; above that was skin. I saw no more wildlife and quickly found the place where the rogue came out of the woods. On the lawn there wasn't much to indicate the rogue wasn't human, but into the woods a bit, he had run through a muddy patch and left three nice, clear, weird-looking paw prints with claw marks, half human and half something else. Big Cat.

The prints were about thirteen inches long, eleven at the widest point, across the toes. Two of the prints had human-shaped heels, which made it look awkward, something a Bigfoot expert would point to with pride. Deep, slashing indentations indicated the length of the claws—way longer than Beast's. *Big* prints. Beast's paws were about eight inches across, nails about an inch and a half across the recurved length, depending on how they were measured.

Liver-eater, Beast murmured to me, awake, her danger radar active.

Whatever it was, it wasn't just a vamp. The term "rogue" wouldn't do anymore, and until I figured out something better, liver-eater it was. It bothered me that Beast knew more about this thing than I did. Would this creature put Beast in danger from the cops?

I had an instant instinct to obscure the tracks, hide the creature's trail—an instinct from Beast in survival mode. If I hid them, and the cops decided I had messed up a crime scene, I was going to have to start explaining, and that meant lying—lies that would eventually catch me up. So, against Beast's better judgment, I left the tracks pristine and went to wait on the cops. First, I bypassed around the window where the rogue had entered. The screen was ripped and hanging. Shattered glass in jagged shards jutted from the bottom pane. Blood had dried on the broken ends. As I watched, a fly buzzed through. It didn't come back out.

Stretched out in a lawn chair, distant enough from a fire ant hill to provide some safety, I pulled out the crumpled batch of property owner info Rick had given me. He had Googled up a map and drawn in the real estate, adding random notes on the taxpayers and owners on the bottom. The pages seemed to be compiled from several sites that collected personal information, most of which I used myself. On the map, the Jean Lafitte park and Bayou Segnette State Park were both colored in a verdant green, and until now, I hadn't noticed how close they were to one another.

Every predator has its own territory/hunting range. Beast's largest range had been over a hundred square miles. A large male mountain lion might have a territory of three hundred square miles. I guessed that a sabertooth might claim a proportionately larger range, and wondered if the park properties, as well as New Orleans city proper, fell within the liver-eater's range.

Long-distance running is problematic for big cats. Aside from cheetahs, most cats are ambush predators, waiting for dinner to pass by and dropping onto it, maybe with a short sprint to finish it off. To avoid building up body heat, we seldom pursue prey at a dead run. Occasionally we are stalkers, tracking prey by scent and print, but few of us ever run for any length of time.

The rogue had run an amazingly long distance last night. I remembered the sound of the shower running in the small house after the killing ended. Had the liver-eater needed to cool off? Had he taken a cold shower? Was that also part of the reason he slept underwater in the wooded lair, to stay cool?

On the map, I traced the distance between the vamp cemetery, the parks, and Aggie's house. It was conceivable that all of it was part of the rogue's hunting ground—and the French Quarter too. But I couldn't guarantee that the map was drawn to scale; it might all be different from what I was thinking. I'd have to study it later. I folded the papers to the property owner info. A large tract of land bordering Jean Lafitte park was owned by Anna, the mayor's wife—the woman who was sleeping with Rick and the liver-eater. I hadn't noticed how much land had been put in Anna's name. Goose bumps rose on my arms. Beast growled.

I pulled out the next sheet and found that ten property purchases had been made in the last year in Barataria, all single-family homes, most in the two hundred thousand bracket, on or near the waterfront. Many of the properties had been purchased by Arceneau Developments. Clan Arceneau? If so, why were vamps buying up property there?

I was studying the names when the cops showed up, an unmarked car pulling down the street, no crime-scene van in sight. But then, Jodi had only my claim that a crime had taken place. I refolded the papers and tucked them in my boot. I had a decision to make.

Jodi did the usual cop thing: knock on front door, walk around the house, knock on back door, check the outbuilding—which I hadn't even noticed—look at the broken window with the blood on it, knock on neighbors' doors, talk to the housewife across the street. My good ol' buddy Officer Herbert followed in her wake, shooting me glances of hatred that made Beast want to toy with him. I had a feeling that, eventually, she would get her chance. Then Jodi and Herbert went in, guns drawn. After that, a lot of cops went in, some in CSI clothing.

They stayed inside a long time, as the sun dropped lower

and shadows lengthened. I heard snatches of soft-voiced conversation through the windows, but I didn't bother to listen; I didn't have to—the rank odor of death rode the heated air. The liver-eater had indeed munched on the house's occupants. Yet I had seen someone exit the house and drive away, which made my half-contemplated and unvoiced speculation correct. The man I saw leave was more than a glamour; like me, the liver-eater must have the ability to shift into another shape, but in his case, he ate his victim, then shifted using the ingested DNA, and strolled out. Just like in the ancient legends of liver-eater. But this one didn't have a long fingernail.

Beast huffed. *Little cat steal Beast. Jane steal Beast. Thief-of-soul.*

Despite the heat, cold shivered through me like an icy electric shock. *What I did was an accident*, I thought. *What the* liver-eater *does* isn't *an accident*. It's black magic. Blood magic. Ancient Cherokee blood magic. And shifting changed his basic scent. The rogue could be anybody, anywhere, even someone I had spent time with, talked to. Sunlight might not damage him except when he was in vamp form—how the heck did I know? He could be vamp, witch, or human. Maybe he could look like one of the true-dead whose bones had been disturbed. Had he found enough genetic material to shift into an older vamp's shape? So, what did I know? He hadn't attended Katie's blood gathering. He'd watched and then come out to feed. Yeah. . . . I started cataloguing who had been at the gathering.

The whole time Jodi did her cop thing, I sat, relaxed in my chair, sunglasses hiding my eyes, speculating, letting my mind wander over impossibilities that might not be so impossible. I knew Jodi was letting me wait, hoping I was stewing, deliberately ignoring me. Her way of getting me back for my attitude. As soon as I worked through all the impossibilities, her ploy began to work. I had people to talk to, alive and dead. If I wasn't going to get inside—and I surely wasn't—then I needed to be on the move.

Instead, I sat as cop cars piled up in the street and as media vans with satellite dishes arrived. One van had a cherry picker mounted on top, allowing a cameraman a bird's-eye view of the crime scene. As the news crews set up, the neighbors began to come home to be informed and questioned by the cops. Across the lawn, I heard their shock and smelled their fear. And then the sun set and I started to get hot under the collar, which had to be Jodi's intent.

Beast, on the other hand, loved every minute of the cat and mouse. And unlike me, she liked lying half asleep in the heat of the sun, if not the fire ants and the mosquitoes that came out to feast. And she liked the game playing. Ambush predators were patient.

I have sharp claws, she thought at me. *Human female has only a gun she has been told she cannot fire. She is not Big Cat. She is not even alpha in dog or wolf pack. Not alpha in cop pack. She is nothing.*

"She's a cop who wants to lay a crime on me," I murmured back, my voice lower than a whisper, my eyes closed behind my glasses against the final rays of late-day glare. "She's a cop with access to the prints in the woods and the blood on the window and the forensic evidence inside the house. DNA evidence."

Snake that lies at heart of all things? Beast asked.

"Yes." Though Beast was unable to grasp the concept of DNA, she understood the snake. "DNA evidence that might prove skinwalkers exist."

Humans will not see truth. They will say blood is spoiled.

By spoiled, I understood that she meant contaminated. She was probably right. Unlike more primitive peoples, intellectual, well-educated humans just pretended the things they didn't understand didn't exist. It was how vamps had survived so long among humans.

Liver-eater is not skinwalker like Jane.

"Fine. So what is liver-eater?"

"Say what?"

I opened my eyes and shoved back the glasses. Jodi was standing in front of me, lips pursed. I'd been so intent on the inner conversation that I hadn't heard her walk up, but I knew I had spoken too softly for her to hear. I rolled my head around on my neck as if stretching from a nap, and smiled sleepily at her, letting Beast have her way. I extended my arms and laced my fingers like a pianist, pulling on muscles from shoulders to fingertips, cracking two knuckles, as if I had been asleep while she worked, sweating in the heated house. "Sleep talking. Can I go now?" Asking to leave was a sure bet for being made to stay. And leaving before I knew what she had found inside was not what I wanted.

"No. I want to know how you found this place."

I didn't bother sitting up, but dropped my sunglasses back over my eyes. I could see that brought all her instincts to the fore and so I smiled. "If you want to see my eyes while you question me, you can take a chair and not make me look into the sunset." I shrugged, the same in-your-face shrug I had perfected at the children's home to keep the girls off my back. Bullies need for their marks to care, and despite the fact that Jodi was a cop doing her job and that job was for the benefit of the welfare of the citizens of New Orleans, yada, yada, she was still trained to be a bully. And I just flat-out didn't like bullies. Not at all.

With ill grace, Jodi took a chair. "How did you find this place?

I shoved the glasses on top of my head. The sky was golden, fuchsia, and violet, the sun balanced on the horizon. It made me squint, but a deal was a deal. "I was tracking the rogue. It covered a lot of territory last night. It ended up here. There's tracks for it getting inside. No tracks for it leaving."

"What time did it get here?"

I shrugged, trying for cooperative. "Tracks in the mud in the woods suggest it was some time ago, before sunrise. When I got here, they were dried around the edges, starting to crumble in. Weird tracks, by the way. Like something a witch worked on. Like maybe he's got access to a spell that appears to alter the shape of his feet. Or something."

"I saw them. Witches can do that?" she asked. It was real curiosity. Real worry.

"Either that or the rogue can change his body shape. You decide."

Jodi looked over her shoulder at the crime-scene van and the techs who were walking from the house. "Since vampires came out of hiding, we've been speculating on what other nonhumans might be out there."

I chuckled. "Werewolves?"

"Maybe. Why not?"

"I guess there could be, but I never heard of any. No trolls, no pixies, no fairies either."

"Would you tell me if you did?" Her eyes were back on me, piercing.

"I would definitely tell you if I had ever met a troll, a werewolf, a pixie, or a fairy. Yes."

She seemed to accept that, and why not? It was the truth. I do truth pretty well. She looked back to the woods. "We're going to get casts of the tracks." When I didn't respond, she said, "So, you think he used a witch spell to alter the shape of his feet."

"Or to alter the shape of any tracks he left. *If* witches can do that. I never asked."

"I have a contact at a coven. I guess I can ask." She didn't sound real thrilled about it. Jodi was still staring at the woods when she said, "The house belongs to the Broussards—Ken, twenty-seven, Rose, twenty-four, no kids, no pets. A neighbor saw Ken's personal vehicle leaving this morning near sunrise, when she was nursing her baby. Looks like he broke in, killed them, and then stole Ken's truck." When I still said nothing, she looked at me, her head rotating slowly on the stem of her neck. "He ate them," she said.

I didn't change my expression. Didn't tense. Didn't react in any way. I just waited.

"He ate them just like he ate the cops. But this time he didn't try for subtlety. He hurt them. He tore them"—her words stopped as if her throat closed off, as if a hand choked off her air, but when she took up her narrative her voice was steady—"apart, like a wild animal. Like a pack of wolves." She shook her head and her neck muscles creaked, she was holding them so tightly. "The only thing left in any way intact was one head and the lower sections of the extremities. Elbows and ankles down. Even the brains were dished out."

That was new, but I didn't alter my stance. It seemed the only thing that made Jodi Richoux gabby was silence. I could do silence real well. I waited. "Why did he eat them?" she asked. "Why did he leave the lower limbs? What is he? It. It had fangs. Or a knife with dual blades, about eight inches apart."

When I realized that the questions weren't rhetorical, but were a request for knowledge, I said, "I can speculate." She nodded for me to go ahead and focused tightly on my face, as if to read my soul through the pores of my skin. "First, there isn't much meat in the lower extremities except for the calves. And that's only a few mouthfuls—" Jodi flinched, just the barest twitch, but I saw it. It was hard for her to accept that humans were being hunted and eaten. "—even on a well-built man. It—he—was looking for food. I'm guessing he has something wrong with him that makes him need blood and meat. A lot of meat. And human and vamp meat both work for him."

I sat up and Jodi's gaze followed me intently. I was ravenous when I shifted. If he was shifting several times a night, or if his shifting wasn't voluntary, but at the whim of his own body, he'd need huge amounts of protein, massive amounts of food. And humans were the biggest, most available, easiest-to-catch-and-kill food supply on the planet. That made perfect sense. But I couldn't say that to Jodi. I said, "I think maybe he's not just rogue, but sick. I think the meat he's eating is helping him to control his condition."

"I didn't think vamps could get sick. I thought that was the purpose of drinking blood for eternity—immortality and all that crap." Her tone was derisive. Jodi might be Katie's liaison at NOPD, but Jodi didn't like vamps. Not at all.

"Maybe it's rare." I watched her take that in and mull it over. I waited another beat and said, "I need to see the crime scene."

"Not gonna happen."

"Then I'll call Leo Pellissier. I figure he can pull strings and get me in."

"No." She shook her head and blushed slightly, startled. "I need you to wait on that."

I had just pushed a button. *Leo and Jodi?* Nah, not with her antipathy to vamps. Something else. So I pushed. "Yes. You can make it happen. It's the crime scene on your say-so or Leo." When she hesitated, I said, "I've hunted rogues before. I need to see the scene so I can tell if it looks like anything from past kill sites."

Beast rumbled deep inside, *Never hunted liver-eater.* Which was true, but not something I was ready to contribute to the conversation. More gently, I added to Jodi, "Leo can make it happen if you won't. But I'd rather work with you, not him."

"You're pretty chummy with Leo. He makes sure I call him Mr. Pellissier."

"I'm sure he'd like me to be polite too."

Suddenly Jodi smiled, a wry pull of lips. "You yank his chain like you yank ours?"

I didn't like being transparent, but I did like the smile, so I answered honestly. "More."

Jodi chuckled under her breath and stood. "My ass'll be in the grinder if it gets out you were on a crime scene. Try not to screw with the evidence or bring trace in. And you step where I say and not one step farther."

"Thanks," I said, standing slowly, trying for humble and appreciative. I was pretty sure it worked because Jodi led me to the crime-scene van and handed me paper and plastic PPEs. It turned out I needed all the personal protective equipment. The house was a bloodbath. Another trite term. But the only one that fit.

CHAPTER 21

The Lord of the Manor

I stood just inside the front door, the window where the rogue entered to my left. A trail of blood splatters marked the wall from the window for six feet, evidence that he'd wounded himself badly on the glass. It was the kind of splatter arterial blood makes, pulsing sprays, arcs that dribbled down the wall. Ten feet inside the door was a blood-drenched leather recliner where a man had once sat. His body had molded the chair to his form; now blood pooled in the depression. It still looked damp, tacky to the touch. There were two slippers on the floor under the footrest, which was up, the back of the chair pushed nearly flat, facing the TV.

The man, or what was left of him, was in several pieces. His torso, the largest chunk, was beside the chair, as if he had been pulled to the floor after the kill and feasted upon. The abdomen was gone, all the way to the spine, the pelvic bones exposed. The chest cavity was nearly as clean, ribs ripped up and out of the way, internal organs missing.

I felt gorge rise, a sick reaction to the butchery. I had slaughtered rogue vamps. I had taken down prey with Beast, so blood and butchery weren't foreign. However, even with that experience, this level of wanton carnage was hard to take.

Beast rose to the surface, taking me over with shocking swiftness. Holding me down, seeing through my eyes, she studied the kill from a predator's viewpoint. She focused intently on the scene. She parted my lips slightly, so she could pull in the scents, memorizing, breaking them down into their individual protein structures. Learning. Blood, feces, urine, all human. Blood from the liver-eater, rank and foul, old death and rot. And blood from something else. From what the rogue became in the process of taking on the form of the male victim. Some other scent, nearly familiar, tantalizing. Totally free from rot.

It looked like the liver-eater had taken the body apart by brute force, not the way hungry predators ate in the wild. In nature, a predator ate the soft tissue first: internal organs, fat, large muscle mass of buttocks and thighs. Later, feasting down to connective tissue. Finally, tearing at tendons and cartilage, separating limbs one by one.

Hard to tear ribs loose. Usually eat upward from abdomen, then tear ribs apart to gnaw later, or give to cubs to train to eat meat.

We stared. The head was against the wall to the hallway. He still had a thatch of short red hair on his scalp. His face had been eaten away, along with tongue and eyes. The empty cavity of the brain was visible through the sockets, yet the jaw was still attached. I understood from Beast that big cats got at the brain later too. After the soft tissue and jaw were long gone.

I spotted a leg and an arm under the kitchen table, well gnawed. The left leg was in the hallway. Well, two left legs were in the hallway, along with other parts of victim number two. I remembered the thumps I had heard from the house while in raptor form. The sounds made when a body was being pulled apart, tossed around, and consumed?

I became aware of Jodi watching me. I blinked Beast back down and closed my mouth, hoping I hadn't slurped air across the roof of my mouth like Beast did. I schooled my face into disgust. "This is the . . ." I let my words trail off as if shocked. Beast found that amusing. "This looks like a bunch of animals got to them."

"Yeah," Jodi said shortly. "That's what we thought."

"Are you bringing in dogs?" I asked. I was curious how trained scent-tracking dogs might react to the smells.

"Tomorrow. I wanted them today but they're on a bank robbery with shooting victims."

I nodded. "What did the psy-meter show?"

Jodi unclipped the device from her belt and switched it on, holding it to the room. The dial went wild, the needle flipping up and down, unable to settle. The clicking of the meter, so like a Geiger counter, was staccato and fast. Jodi swept the meter to me, and though it slowed, it was still a much higher psy reading than any human would give. I looked at the readout, amused. I had known it was only a matter of time before she measured me against the background psy levels of the room. "Wanting to make sure I'm not the rogue?"

"Something like that," she said, clicking off the meter. "This place reeks of leftover magic."

Yeah, it did. I had seen enough. I backed out of the house to the front porch, took off my PPEs and shoved them into the biohazard container. It and its bloody contents would go to the crime lab to be checked for trace, especially the paper shoes, which could have picked up important hairs or fibers. Then they would be destroyed. I hadn't stepped in blood, but I could smell it on me, in my hair, in my clothes, and beneath it all, the rot-stink of the liver-eater. The stench roiled around in me like oily sludge.

True dark had fallen. Security lights attracted swarms of insects, neighborhood windows bathed the night with light. The neighbors were inside, behind their closed, locked doors and windows. Lot of good that does a family if a liver-eater wants in.

Bike roaring, I let my hair blow in the wind, trying to clear the stench out of my nostrils, out of my clothes. I was halfway home when I passed a grocery store just off of 90 and pulled over. I bought a stack of steaks and two six-packs of beer, ignoring the stares of the other customers. I had seen my reflection in the dark windows upon entering. I looked pretty rough, a biker chick, attitude on steroids. Outside, the groceries stored in the saddlebags, I finally strapped on my helmet and kick-started the bike. It spluttered and coughed but eventually turned over. I really had to find time to do a little bike maintenance.

Inside Katie's freebie house, I dropped my clothes where I stood, still smelling the blood. To get it off of me, I took a long shower, standing under the hot water, letting it scald me. I was spending a lot of time in the shower. Too much. There was something almost religious about that, about the need to be cleansed. Afterward, I ate two steaks. Very very rare. With a couple of locally brewed beers. Louisiana beer was really good. I'd miss it when I left.

Near ten p.m., I dressed, tucked a few crosses into my clothes, twisted my hair into a sloppy bun, and secured it with three stakes. Not expecting trouble. But just in case. Suitably dressed, I slid my feet into the new sandals and jumped the fence to Katie's. Jumping fences in sandals is fine, but the landings can be less than graceful. I was glad the camera was gone.

I stalked around Katie's, checking windows and doors for security. Like most old houses in the South, it had been built for airflow, not safety. A system had been retrofitted, not that it had done much good. Last time, the rogue had come through the back door. Next time, he might pick a window on the second story. But why did the alarm not go off? Was it because the security system was switched off during business hours? Or did the liver-eater have a key? Or know how to disarm the system? Access. Like Leo had to my house. Could the liver-eater be Leo . . . ? No. Leo was at Katie's gathering.

Knocking on the back door, holding the doorbell down, I waited for Troll. I remembered my promise to tell Jodi if I ever saw a troll. I had a feeling that nicknames didn't count, and that she wouldn't be amused at my whimsy. I let the buzzer go when he opened the door.

Troll looked better, had more color in his face. Someone had given him some vamp blood to help him heal this fast, and Katie wasn't in shape to offer it. I stepped inside, drawing in the air. I detected Leo. He was here, along with Bruiser and another vamp. They had been here long enough to saturate the place with their scents.

"What's Leo doing here?" Not that I had to ask. He had been feeding. I could smell fresh blood on the air too.

"You have to tell me how you do that someday—know who's here and who's not." When I didn't rise to the bait, he said, "He came to feed Miz A and Bliss and me."

Something like shame swept through me. *Bliss*. She had been injured while under my protection, attacked by a vamp and bled nearly dry. And I had gone racing off after the culprit while the victim still needed care. I was an idiot. "How is she? And how are you?"

He gestured me toward Katie's office. "Better now. Bliss has had a hard time recuperating. She needs blood support to continue healing, and with Katie on holiday . . ."

Holiday? Is that what they're calling it? "And you called Leo."

"No. Leo came on his own."

"Oh?" That surprised me.

"Leo brought her home the night she was attacked in his club. He was pulling up to the Mojo when the attack took place."

Leo probably saw me leave the club, moving with Beast speed. Combined with the taste he took when he healed my arm, he should have known what I was, and he hadn't. Of course I now knew *less* about what I was. A skinwalker? Accidental practitioner of black magic? Troll sat down, releasing a pent breath, part exhaustion, part melancholy.

"You cleaned up," I said, looking around the office. "It looks new." I remembered the morning the liver-eater had attacked Katie. There had been a fair amount of blood. Not as much as at the Broussards', the house where Ken and Rose got digested, but enough. I smelled strong cleansers on the air. An air filter hummed in the corner. A big one.

Troll flipped a limp hand. "Lot of experience cleaning up blood."

I figured he did, living in a whorehouse with a vamp. But I didn't say it. I was getting better at controlling my natural rude instincts. "How're the girls?"

"Fine. A couple were patched up at the hospital after the attack, and Leo fed them too. They're right as rain, now."

"And Miz A?" In an overlay of snapshot images, I remembered the blood and the extent of the housekeeper's wounds. She had lost a lot of blood and a good portion of deltoid and other upper arm muscles.

Troll started to answer, but something changed behind his eyes, a flitting of reconsideration. "She's better. Still with us." It didn't smell like a lie, but the little telltale wrinkles around Troll's eyes suggested that he wasn't telling the complete truth either.

Better? Still with us? Had she been close to death? Drained enough to be turned? Was Miz A chained in the basement of Leo's house, a mindless bloodsucking machine? I almost asked. I opened my mouth to ask. And Beast caught the flavor of unfamiliar vamp. Close.

I whirled. Saw a blur of vamp speed. Whipped out a cross. Stamped my leg behind its knee. Twisted. Punched with my left hand, holding the cross. I struck it. Knocked it off balance. Rode it down. Trace of scorched vamp flesh.

Beast screamed. I ripped away the cross. Brought it down. An inch from her face. She howled and swiveled away. Her fangs were out. There was fresh blood on her mouth. It carried the scent of Indigo. The little blonde with blue eyes. I pulled a stake. A hand gripped my arm with steel strength. It stopped me. I growled, scenting Leo.

"Not her, little vampire killer," he purred. "She is mine. George."

Bruiser, moving faster than a human, knelt at the vamp's head and pushed my cross away. He slid his hands under the vamp's shoulders and pulled. Inside me, Beast slunk down into a crouch, watching as Bruiser removed the vamp. Amitee. Leo's soon-to-be daughter-in-law. Leo was out . . . *drinking* . . . with his son's fiancée. Now that was just sick. . . .

Then . . . had the vamp been at Katie's gathering? I didn't remember seeing her. Could a male liver-eater take a female form? I couldn't take a male's. I didn't think it was possible, but I was unlearning a lot of impossibilities.

I let Leo lift me to my feet, like a dance step. He lifted my arm, hand at my hip, turning my body, my feet following, across the vamp's body beneath me, three steps into Katie's office. Amitee took off fast. Nearly getting staked musta made her itchy.

Leo's eyes locked mine as we moved, dark and old, bled black, but controlled. Utterly controlled. Beast liked it. Beast liked the power that flowed over us like a warm hand. "Put that away, if you please," Leo said, his face so close his breath brushed my/our cheeks. No smell of fresh blood on him. He hadn't fed off the girls.

My heart pounded, the hard thump of danger, instant fighting, and faster cessation. I forced down adrenaline, fought to control the shakes quivering along my arms and legs; draped the cross around my head; tucked it under my clothes. I pulled my hand free and stuck the stake into my hair. I wasn't even sure why I was following his requests.

I could feel him pushing at me, testing the parameters of my mind, but this didn't feel like vamp mesmerization. Not exactly. But there was Beast, telling me to let him have his way for now. Beast, testing the waters for something I couldn't even imagine. "She'd been feeding. I want to see Indigo. Now," I said, still parsing the scents.

"Tom, would you please ask Indigo to join us," Leo said.

Tom. Troll. Right. I pushed Beast farther down. She let me, amused. Beast was playing, though I didn't know if she toyed with Leo or with me. Or with both of us.

Leo led me to the sofa and I sat where he placed me, in the corner, one knee up, sandal in the seat. One arm along the back, so I could push up and over fast if needed. Leo sat on a tall stool near the bar. He was wearing a suit. Tie. Fancy shoes. We waited. Moments later, I heard footsteps clattering down the stairs: heels, one pair; soft-soled shoes, also one pair, that gait Troll's. Indigo's voice, giggly, happy. I began to relax and felt my shoulders droop. Felt Leo's eyes on me when they did. Speculative.

Indigo came through the doorway, her big blue eyes blinking at the change in light. She saw Leo and she smiled. Saw me and stopped. I inspected her, not hiding my perusal. She looked fine, except for tiny dots from a recent feeding. They were closed, nearly healed. No torn throat, just nice clean punctures, the flesh properly treated so the wounds would constrict, the sign of a vamp in control of herself. Then why had Amitee attacked me? Troll stopped behind Indigo, standing framed in the doorway.

"The vamp who fed on you tonight," I said. "Is she a regular?"

Indigo raised a hand and her fingers brushed across her throat. A smile played across her mouth, lighting her eyes. Sexual awareness, pleasure, and something more. Fondness. I could tell she liked Amitee even before she spoke, answering more than I had asked. "She's nice. She don't"—she glanced at Leo—"*doesn't*—ask for weird sh— weird stuff. She pays well, tips better, and treats me like a lady." Her eyes and face went sly and taunting, as if hoping to shock. "A girl likes a little romance sometimes, you know?"

I didn't react, which seemed to disappoint her. "Thank you, Indigo," I said, polite.

"I got a client, at the Iberville," she said to Leo. "You want me to take a cab?"

That caught my attention. Why was Indigo asking Leo about business? Wouldn't Troll take over for Katie? I glanced at the doorway. Troll was standing stiffly in the shadows, his face a mask. Something was hinky here.

"Until the rogue is brought down, my driver will deliver you all to your assignations," Leo said. "Let George know when you will want the car. He'll make arrangements."

Troll looked down. He was not a happy troll. I grinned at my humor. When Leo raised a brow at my amusement, I waved it away. I had a job to do, and then I was outta here. I was so not getting into vamp politics. As long as I got paid. And as long as they didn't get me killed.

Indigo said thank you and Leo dismissed her. Actually dismissed her. Like a king or something. He said, "You may be dismissed." I didn't bother to hide my snort or the wider grin at that one. Leo did his brow-lift thing. The man was so smooth he wouldn't slide on an oil slick. He looked at Troll standing in the shadows. "Tell Ipsita to meet me at the door in an hour." Troll didn't look happy, but he nodded.

Ipsita was the South Asian girl, delicate as a rosebud, the girl who looked like she might be twelve. She roused my protective instincts. Knowing she was of legal age didn't help me to see her differently, and the idea of her going on a "date" with an old vamp made me grind my molars. *And anyway, why is Leo making off with one of Katie's girls?* I didn't realize I had spoken that last part aloud until they all turned and looked at me. *Crap.* Even Indigo stuck her head back in, a look of surprise and puzzlement on her face.

In for a penny . . . "It seems to me that until Katie gets back, Tr— Tom should be in charge." I looked at Troll. "Does Katie have legal papers written up about who takes over if she is"—*stuck in a coffin in a pool of vamp blood?*—"indisposed?"

Leo lifted his head. "I am Katie's master. It is fitting that I assume command for her while she is unwell."

"Maybe in the Dark Ages, but not in the United States and not now." So much for me not getting into vamp politics. "Tom? Where does Katie keep her legal papers?"

He entered, keeping well away from Leo, and knelt at Katie's desk. Using a small key, he unlocked a file cabinet cleverly tucked against the wall, in a shadow. Papers rustled, the silence charged with something volatile, explosive. Indigo disappeared. Smart girl. I wasn't so wise, however. I stuck around to see what happened to the hornet's nest I was currently kicking. A moment later Troll withdrew an expandable file and stood behind the desk, the folder in both hands, indecisive. Okay, scared to death. I could smell his fear.

I got up from the spot where Leo had placed me, which suddenly bothered me a lot more than it had, took the folder, and centered it on the desktop. I opened it. "Which ones?" I asked. Troll reached around me and tapped a tab about midway back. I couldn't read the tab's print; it might have been French. I withdrew the papers and opened them, scanning the first five sheets of legal mumbo jumbo, not understanding what I saw even though it was in English, but using the time to think. Leo was old. Real old. Maybe even feudal-times old. Back when honor meant something. I held the pages out to Leo. "What does she want?"

I thought I heard Troll smother a laugh, but it could have been a cough. If Leo was an honorable man, he'd read the pages and follow the directions in them. If not, then he wasn't honorable. Of course, the fact that he wasn't a man at all might complicate things.

Leo went still, that marble-statue stillness, not breathing, not blinking, not anything. It's eerie and unsettling to watch, and it probably foreshadows danger of a very messy and bloody variety, but then, my understanding of sane vamps was still limited, and I had three stakes in my bun and a nice selection of crosses on my person. Leo went on not moving. The silence went from unsettling to unnatural, to eerie, creepy, and then scary. His pheromones were pure rage. Behind me, Troll's breathing was unsteady; his heart beat too fast. The chemical composition of his sweat was bitter; Beast recognized the smell as death terrors. Finally, Leo pulled in a sharp breath. I nearly jumped. Beast flexed her claws. Troll stopped breathing altogether.

Leo slid across the room in a predatory slither, his eyes bled totally black with contained fury. He took the papers and read. Flipped pages. Read some more. He raised his eyes and looked from me to Tom and back again. "Katie has placed her holdings into Tom's hands." When he spoke, his words were precise, his voice neutral, so lacking in emotion it might have been an electronic, digitized voice—except for that vaguely European accent that would make starlets swoon.

"All of her accounts, properties, and assets are under his control, including this house and its employees. All business and employment checks are to be written and signed by him and cosigned by me. All have this legal proviso." He switched his gaze to Tom. "You knew this?" Tom nodded, the motion of his head jerky. "And yet you chose not to inform me. Why is that?"

"I . . . I . . ."

"He needed you," I said. "He needed your protection from the rogue for the girls, he needed your goodwill for Katie, and he needed your intercession with the vamp council. And he was grateful that you called the gathering and put her to earth."

Tom swallowed noisily under Leo's gaze. But the master of New Orleans slowly turned his eyes to me. "What do you know of *gatherings* and of one of us being *put to earth*?"

I shrugged. I wasn't about to answer that one. He'd smell a lie. He wouldn't believe the truth. Or he would believe it and think how handy it would be to have a skinwalker as a blood-slave. I wasn't eager to fight him. Not now. If I had to go stake-to-fang with the blood-master of New Orleans, then I wanted my chain-mail collar, studded clothes, and plenty of prep time.

"So," I said. "Back to the question that started all this. What are you doing making off with one of Katie's girls? Is she a date, does she get paid for her services, or are you pulling the dark right of kings on her? Because in my opinion, that's not gonna work for much longer."

Suddenly, Leo seemed to find me amusing. He chuckled, handed Tom the legal papers, and took the seat I had vacated on the leather couch. He rested his arms across the back cushions, looking expansive, a lord in his domain. "And why should my rights change?"

"Simple. The courts in the United States are already looking at citizenship laws, slavery issues, and interpretation of legal statutes in light of a being with an expanded life span. Eventually, the 'rights of a master' "—I made little quotation marks in the air with my fingers, just in case he missed the sarcasm in my voice—"will come under scrutiny. And they'll be thrown out, as will the dark right of kings. No doubt about it." Leo was looking at me, totally focused and unblinking, his mouth smiling, his eyes a deadly snake stare.

Snake poisons do not affect Beast, she reminded me, unconcerned.

"It seems smart for you to start adapting how you do business," I continued, "altering things from the way you vamps did them a thousand years ago. Good-faith moves, to make any future court take notice that you've been changing with the times."

"The term 'vamp' is insulting," Leo said.

"Get used to it." And why pick that one tiny part out of what I had been saying? I was tearing up his entire power structure and he gets his panties in a wad over the word "vamp"? I handed the papers to Troll. "I have work to do. Later, Troll."

He nodded, a single shuddering move.

I was halfway out the door when Leo said, "My time with Ipsita is not by command." I halted with my hands on either side of the doorjamb, and I didn't turn around. "I have paid her usual commission, plus a tip, in advance, according to my standing arrangement with Katie. I require an escort to a social function tonight."

I nodded when he finished speaking, trying to decide how to reply. I settled on, "I appreciate you telling me." Then I pushed off with my toes and headed toward the back door.

"You are dismissed." The words floated after me.

The Lord of the Manor just had to add that last bit in, didn't he. But I could have sworn that he was laughing.

CHAPTER 22

All that I wanted

I checked in with Molly, got her voice mail, and left a message. Bored, I checked my e-mail and spent some time on the Internet searching local society/gossip pages and a few online sites dedicated to local and state politics. I discovered that Anna was scheduled to attend an event in the French Quarter's four-star Marriott tonight. I pulled up maps, did a little math on distances, made notes, and hoped Beast could follow Anna home, or wherever she spent the night.

I took a nap until midnight, woke, and stripped down. Time to shift and go after the woman sleeping with Rick and the liver-eater in one of his shapes. The woman who was also involved with whatever was taking place in Leo's club. I wondered if Leo knew about that. I could have asked him—or maybe told him—about the meeting, but that info, on top of insulting him, might have been stupid. Even for me.

In the backyard, I dropped four steaks onto the ground and climbed, naked, to the top of the stones. The panther fetish necklace in hand, I checked that the small line of gold I had scored into the rock was still there. The rains had washed much of it away, and I again rubbed the gold nugget over the boulder's stone face.

Big? Beast asked, hungry for size.

"Not yet," I said. "But soon." Beast said nothing to the refusal, and I sat, lotus position, the travel pack and necklace loose on my neck. I relaxed, settled onto the cool stone, and quickly sank into Beast's snake. The shift was easy tonight, dropping down, into the quiet rhythm of drums. The notes of flutes. A pulling of muscles and bones, a sharp gray tingling, as if I stuck my fingers into a light socket, and faint nausea after. Almost painless.

I stretched and huffed at ugly man-smells: breath of cars, stink of garbage, mold on walls of man-dens, paint, plastic, upholstery, scent of dog urine. Yappy mutts, fast snack. Padded down stones, bypassed sharp broken stone from when she became Jane after bird. Smell of dead cattle made belly rumble. Huffed, pulling blood and fat scent into mouth. Cold meat, but hunger demanded. Steak was fast bites, swallowing down chunks. Beneath was larger piece of meat, thick. Paw on top to tear and rend. Better when hot and fresh. Needed fresh kill.

Soft thump sounded. Whirled. Cat on fence, hunched. I hissed. Fangs bright in night. *My territory.* Cat yowled. Fell off other side. I huffed with laughter. Stupid cat. Jane ate cat when bird. Not very tasty, but fresh. I wanted to hunt deer. Kill and eat.

Hunt for Anna.

She wanted to hunt female who had sex with man. I ignored command and finished last of dead meat. Licked paws, groomed face. Drank from fountain of stone vampire.

Hunt! Her command, urgent.

I jumped fence and padded around den, slinking through shadow. Down street, along walls, beneath ledges. Good place to hunt, sit on ledge, watch for prey. I jumped from man-path to chair, to upper ledge. Metal all around, to keep clumsy humans from falling. Made it hard to drop on prey. Stupid humans.

Hunt!

I huffed in disgust, dropped to smooth ground, still warm from hot day. Jogged down street, keeping to shadows, checking for humans and yappy dogs. Sitting still when humans drew near. Moving on after.

Hotel in view. Marriott. Too much man-lights. Faint trace of Anna-human on air, fresh, moving, in car with human man. Not Rick. Liver-eater? I raced down street, cornered into another. Saw/smelled Anna in car window. Headed toward liver-eater territory, over river. I crouched in shadows, watched for truck. Two came by, too tall. Another with picture of fish and crabs on side. Smelled wonderful. I licked mouth and gathered feet in tight. Truck moving like lumbering cow, slow, closer. Jumped to car trunk, raced up car roof, leaped. Landed on lumbering-cow truck. Settled to ride, crouching low. Claws on metal strip with bumps. Smell of seafood. Stomach rumbled. I lifted nose into air, smelling fish, crab. River drew near, with Anna-human scent, ahead. Lumbering cow–fish truck followed Anna-human across bridge.

Look! Remember!

I saw sign, WESTBANK EXPRESSWAY. Dropped into scent-bliss again, mouth open, face lifted into wind, taking in wonderful smells of fish, dead things, alligator, birds. Much prey here. Good smells. But watched signs, remembering. GENERAL DEGAULLE DRIVE. Cow–fish truck turned off, away from Anna-scent.

Hunt, she commanded.

I huffed and jumped from wonderful cow-fish truck to roof of parked car. Trotted back to General DeGaulle Drive. Found Anna-human scent. Trotted after. Her scent turned on new street, sign in man-words, WOODLAND HWY. New part of town, south and west of French Quarter. Far from the liver-eater's known hunting range.

Cut across overgrown, marshy land. To English Turn Parkway. Big human-dens everywhere. Stink of chemicals. *Golf course*, she whispered. I trotted over bridge, chemical-smelling water. Found house where Anna-human and male entered. Anna-human scent everywhere. In garden. Her den. Kit. Mate.

Daughter. Husband. The mayor, she whispered.

I paced perimeter in shadow of house. Lapped from fountain, water spouting from fish-mouth, but tasting of city water, not fish. House dark. Pool in back, man-lights blue in depth. I was hot, so waded in, cool water rising. I sighed, heat from run easing away. Paddled to far side and back, her pack floating. Refreshed, I stepped from pool, shook stink away. Tired, I stepped onto long chair, sank onto padding. *Lounge chair*, she said. I rested, tongue grooming smelly pool water from face, paws.

Inside, phone rang. Human-man answered, deep voice close, near door. "I know it's late," tinny voice said through phone, far away. *Rick?* Jane asked.

"I'm still up, Ricky-bo. What I can do you for?" Both humans laughed.

I coughed softly. No humor in words. *Fake Cajun accent,* she thought. Still no humor. No prey to play with.

"I need some info," Rick said.

"Of course, I'll do what I can. How can I help?"

"I ran into Anna at an event and she said you were helping a vampire clan buy up land along Privateer Boulevard in Barataria. I got me some friends who might like to sell, housing prices being so low and all."

"And you want the vamps to pay you bigger money than current market prices."

"And I'd like my name kept out of it, if possible. Put it all in Anna's name for now, like you're doing with your other land deal."

Silence for a moment. "She tell you 'bout my other land deal, my Anna did?"

"Yeah, right," Rick said. "Over pillow talk. I was down at the Notarial Archive Office on another case and came across her name on a dozen different land deals. I put it together. The Hornets need another stadium, a swamp land-use law is in committee, and you just happen to be buying up swamp property out southwest of the city, property that I figure will be drained by the Corps of Engineers in a year or two. Meantime, you're getting it cheap. No skin off my nose. I just want a cut of my friends' deal if the vamps will pay up. And you are the *man* when it comes to dealing with vamps."

Hornets? I saw hornet, stinger sharp, vicious. Hornet nest, round, vibrating, high in tree.

She chuckled in the dark of deep mind. *Basketball team,* she thought. *If I'd known about the Hornets, the land in the wife's name might have made sense. This is why I don't like to do business in a strange town. Not enough background info to put the pieces together.*

Inside, more speaking. "I can mebbe do you some good there, bro," the mayor said. "You come by the office, yes?" The deep voice moved away.

Night sounds grew loud. I wanted to listen, but voices

were gone. I rolled over, rubbing wet off, on chair. Paws in air, squirming, scratching itchy back. Felt good.

Footsteps paused inside house. Door opened, breaking silence. I rolled-leaped-landed in shrubbery, on front paws, back feet following, close together. Silent. Big leaf hid face. Something huffing, feet pattering. Running to far side of pool. I leaned out. Focused on little dog. Poodle. Male. Three-week-kit-sized. Curly, water-swimmer hair, puffy. Raised leg, let loose stream of aromatic urine. I pulled feet closer. Intent on dog. *Food.*

No! she demanded. Frustrated, I drew in air, faint hiss.

Dog looked up, sniffed. Put nose down, scenting. Hackles rose. Dog followed Beast scent-trail to pool, to splashes. Man-scent-perfume on dog, stank on wind. Dog raced to chair. Saw me in bushes. Started barking. *Danger! Danger! Predator hereherehere! Danger!*

"Sparky! Stop that!" deep-voice-man—mayor—shouted from door.

"What is it, honey?" Anna-human said.

Come out! Trespasser! Killkillkill! dog barked.

I gathered self for killing attack. Hissed, soft, full of threat. Eyes on dog.

No! She rose up, forced me down.

"Your stupid dog is barking," deep-voice said. "If he wakes the damn neighbors—"

"It's probably another possum. Come on, Sparky." Anna-human walked out into night, little shoes tapping.

I turned hungry eyes to her. *Not a possum. I am Beast!*

No! She held control tight. Forced down killing instinct. We fought. I showed killing fangs, white in man-light. Hissed. Little yappy dog yelped, ran to Anna-human. She picked up snack-dog and tap-tapped back inside. From safety, she said, "Look at all the water. I bet Sparky heard the neighbor's teenage kid out here again."

"Damn stupid dog. All we need is a drowning lawsuit," deep-voice grumbled. "I'll call the Demarcos in the morning."

Door closed. Outside lights went off. Pool lights still glowed. *Killkillkillkillkill!* Stupid dog barked inside, thinks it could kill Big Cat. I shook free of Jane's control. *Not possum! Not human child! I am* Beast*! Need to scream it to the winds!*

Not now, she thought. *Woods nearby. Hunt.* Image of fat rabbit. Blood, fresh meat. Killing claws sinking deep.

Yessssss. I turned tightly, slunk out of backyard, along property line, into trees. Strong rabbit smell. Nose to ground, filled entire head with rabbit-scent. And stalked.

I ate rabbit—blood and flesh and milk from her teats filling mouth. Then tracked back to rabbit nest, under fallen tree. Dug out young ones, screams and cries bringing pleasure with feast. Jane slunk back, away from blood feast. She was not hunter. Was not mother to kits. Was only *human. Kit-less.* She was only *thief.*

Satisfied, I allowed her to surface. She was silent. Unhappy. Pictured den. *Katie's freebie house.* She thought, *Let's go home.* I wanted long hunt. Smelled deer. Found tracks, small, dainty, smelled of doe. She commanded, *Home.* I growled. Turned toward city, grudging, not happy. She thought, *Maybe we'll find a deer on the way.*

I huffed with satisfaction. *Deer!*

Dawn was lightening the sky when I came to myself on the garden rocks, steaming in the cool air. We had found no deer and Beast had been obstinate, not wanting to let go, wanting to hunt, wanting blood and meat, wanting to remain in cat form after dawn. Beast had never been so difficult to restrain and now she sulked, her anger tainting my mood. Her claws opened and pressed into my mind, deliberately hurting. She had wanted to eat the dog.

Bird ate cat, Beast muttered, sulking, still mad because I had shifted into a bird, and the bird got to eat whatever she wanted.

"I'll let you hunt," I murmured. "Soon. I promise."

Bird ate cat, Beast repeated. *Saw in Jane's mind.* She slunk away.

I half crawled into the house, limbs so tired they quivered with exertion. I fixed a bowl of oatmeal and ate without tea. Clambered into bed, exhausted.

I woke slowly, the sun setting, sending slanted rays across the room, through cracks in the blinds. The mattress was soft under me, firm deeper down, a far better quality mattress than the one in my apartment near Asheville. Not something I could afford getting used to. I had money, but it was invested, not for creature comforts.

I rolled over, resettled, and pulled a pillow under my neck, letting my mind wander. Rick LaFleur called the mayor at home at night, probably with Anna's intervention. Anna who was sleeping with the mayor, Rick, and the liver-eater in an unknown form, unless the mayor was the liver-eater—but his smell wasn't right, so I didn't think he was the creature.

Rick was investigating the vamps, but what else was he doing? Not acting as the mayor's eyes, clearly; the mayor didn't know what Rick was up to. Maybe cop's eyes. Or he was after my bounty. Or investigating the vamps for an unknown third party. I'd have to keep him close.

Beast sent an image to me, blurred by sleep. Rick, on his back, her paws on his chest, claws nicking the flesh at his throat. I chuckled softly, happy just to have her talking to me. She sent me an image of a deer, and slid back into dreams. I rolled out of bed.

I had to hunt again tonight. If I wanted to win the ten-day kill bonus, I had to locate and kill the rogue within forty-eight hours. I repacked the contents of my travel bag, hanging the sour-smelling, pool-water-wet clothes up to dry, rolling a pair of gauzy pants, T-shirt, undies, and thin-soled shoes around the crosses and stakes and rezipping it.

I ate, set raw meat on the lawn, stripped, and climbed the rocks. I had never shifted so many nights in a row. I hadn't expected it to tire me this much. Hadn't expected it to give Beast so much control and/or make her so stubborn. Hadn't expected tonight's pain. It ripped into me, slashing, like claws at prey. Beast raced into the gray void, pushing the change, forcing. Rocks cracked and split, sounding like thunder.

I rolled from rocks. Broken rock rained down around paws. Big paws. Flexed them. Recurved claws slid from sheaths. Bigger. I was big. *I like big. Big Cat. Big as liver-eater.*

Jane was afraid of big. *What have you done?* she asked.

I snarled, angry; pressed paw onto her, pushing down, claws at her throat, her belly to sky, Jane beta, me alpha. Her necklace and travel pack were too tight. *Not good. But better to be big. Big Cat.* Jumped fence, raced from yard, into night. I found truck, rode across river, muzzle high in air, taking in scents. Truck swayed, motion soothing. *Hunt*, I sang. *We hunt.*

Moon was growing fat. Not yet pregnant hunting moon. Gave enough light to see water far below, moon reflection broken on river surface, like droplets of blood, scattered by wind.

Truck turned. Jane saw sign—BAYOU SEGNETTE STATE PARK. I launched off truck, to ground, moving fast. Hit. Rolled-rolled-rolled. Into ditch. Brackish water. Stink of dog filth. I sprang out, dog filth all over. Blood splatters showed tale. Dog hit on road, flung down. Dead dog—blood and entrails—spread up incline. Shook pelt, hissing, irritated. I raced into shadows. She was amused. I was not. *I do not smell like* dog. *Will not.* She comforted. I slunk along ground looking for water. Pools, fresh, free of dead dog, were ahead. *Look at sign*, she asked, properly beta to my alpha. I looked up. DRAKE AVE. Moved on; found water and splashed in.

Rolled to clean off dead dog. Something moved in water. *Get out!* she screamed. I pushed off bottom, leaped from water, forepaws spread, claws grasping. Landed. Spun. Drops scattered. From water, wide jaws reached. Wicked teeth rising from pool. I hissed. Hacked.

Alligator, she said.

Alligator bad.

I don't like them either, she agreed, fear in her tone. *Hunt the liver-eater? Please?*

Liver-eater bad. Long time since tasted liver-eater. Watched Jane in mind at words. She went still—fear-prey still. I jogged into shadows, watching her in mind. Cat and mouse.

Long minute later, she asked, tone fearful, *When did you taste a liver-eater?*

I hacked. Remembered. Image eased up from dark of mind, hidden from Jane for many seasons. Old woman. Long gray hair, chin and nose and yellow eyes like Jane, piercing.

Not old. A woman in her sixties, maybe, she thought, her mind uneasy. *She smells rotten, like the liver-eater we chase.* Fear swelled fast in back of Jane's mind, like belly of dead prey in summer sun. She thought, *I don't remember this. . . .* I hacked with amusement; shared past.

Crone held knife. Fire crackled near, smoke rising high, herbed and bitter. Night was cold with winter, trees bare like bones. A girl lay before old woman, bound, gagged, arms over head, tied to stakes at hands and feet, stinking with terror. Eyes blue in firelight. Blond hair. Girl wasn't human. Smelled of new thing. *Learned later, scent of vampire girl*, I thought.

Crone leaned in. Movement made liver-eater scent rise rank on air, rotten meat. She nicked girl with blade, a stabbing cut, pointed, deep. Girl screamed behind gag, face bleeding. Crone gathered blood on finger, carried it to mouth. Sucked it. Made another cut, another. Tasting each. Crone cut girl's clothes with knife, exposing belly and breasts. Girl squirmed, but stakes and ropes held her. Girl vomited. Unable to release it, she breathed it down. Her breath sounded wet. Her bowels released old blood stench, rising with herbs in fire.

I eased closer to ledge, claws extended, gripping rock as if gripping flesh to shred. Crone raised knife. Brought it down into girl's belly. Cutting. Bound girl screamed, keening sound, like kit in mortal danger, held in paws of male big cat, or under claws of rival female invading territory. Crone cut deep. Girl's squeals bounced off rock walls below. I exposed killing teeth. Eyes on knife. Crone lifted out chunk of vampire girl's liver. Steam rose from human-meat. Crone tasted raw flesh. Bit, tearing with teeth. Blood ran down chin, over clothes.

When meat was gone, crone reached into bloody hole. Cut more. More again. Still holding knife. Girl stopped screaming, stopped moving, yet her heart still beat. For a little time. Crone ate more. Kidney. Part of lung. Girl stopped breathing. Heart fell still. Crone reached into body cavity and pulled, tugged. Heart came free. Crone began to chant, eating heart.

I watched as energies gathered on crone, silver gray, full of sparkles. Power touched her. Fire that did not burn. Bones slid, twisted, flesh growing lighter. Hair growing pale, blond. She stole young girl. Took her form. Bad smell in air. *Much later, understood it was scent of evil*, I thought.

Anger erupted in my spirit, anger at evil I did not understand. I leaped, silent. Driving down liver-eater. Paws on back, killing teeth at neck. Biting. Breaking spine with snap of jaws. Flesh was rancid, oily, foul. Burning tongue. I spat. Turned body with swipe of paw. Ripped out throat. Spat foulness. Tore off head. Liver-eater was dead. I turned, padded into night.

Images faded. Memory was ended. Jane was silent. I placed paw on her head in joined mind. *You are liver-eater*, I thought, snarling. *You ate me as crone ate girl.*

No! She struggled. I shoved hard with paws, holding her down, claws in her spirit flesh.

I was stronger than blond vampire girl. Stronger than you. I did not die. I came into you. With *you. Now we are both, I and Jane. Better than Jane alone. Better than me alone. We are strong. We are Beast. And now we are Big Cat. Very big.*

She stopped struggling, fear shaking her spirit, thinking fast human-thoughts. *You took mass from the minerals in the boulders*. Her fear grew, skittering like squirrel claws. *You performed the mass to mass, stone to stone, of complex magic. How did you do that? How much mass did you take?*

I said, *Found place in snake for bigger. Gene for much bigness. I took all mass I wanted.* Jane fled, deep into joined spirits, hiding. I hissed, shook the last scummy water away. *Pelt is thick and rich and deep. Claws are sharp and long. Hunt liver-eater. Kill another one.* I padded into deeper shadows, mouth open, scent-searching for path of liver-eater. *I am Big Cat. I will kill.*

CHAPTER 23

Mass to mass, stone to stone

Moon was high when I padded into park land far behind Cherokee shaman's house. Liver-eater's scent was strong and hot, from upwind. It was running, sweat stinking with rot. Second scent floated on night wind—blood, fresh, potent with fear. Human. Liver-eater had hunted. Found man to drink and eat.

Deep in woods, on high ground surrounded by swamp, I found kill site. Paused. Studied clearing. Tent, latrine, shovel, lantern burning, guttering, latched cooler, string in trees, damp clothes hanging limp. Blood everywhere, slick, shiny in moonlight. Body parts, scattered. *A homeless camp*, she thought. *A drifter.*

I crouched, silent, sniffing, watching. Liver-eater was gone. With slow hunter steps I walked into camp—hunched low, back paws into space when front paws rose, no sticks or leaves to crackle. Sniffed chewed leg. *Old and scrawny. Sick human. Not good eating.* I moved through camp, scenting. Liver-eater was rank, rotten when he came. Scent changed as he ate.

Jane shuddered at thought. I hacked laughter. Padded around tent. Man-torso chewed in half at spine. Upper half near swamp. Lower half in water, pelvis jutting into air. Small fish fed at torn flesh. Gator swam close, eyes above water, tail moving like snake. I hacked warning. *Feed later. My place.* Gator slowed, stopped, sank. I jogged to tent opening.

Man-head inside tent, resting on cot. Liver-eater didn't eat face of this one. Hairy, scruffy. Pale blue eyes caught lantern light. Cheeks drooped, wrinkled.

I found path liver-eater took from woods. His scent changed again. I stopped. Pulled air over scent organ in mouth. Studying. Rot smell changing. Gone. Not liver-eater scent. Vampire scent. Vampire over all other scents. Scent change worried Jane.

Path reached blacktopped road. Truck headlights moved through trees, coming this way. I leaped into tree, crouched on wide limbs hanging over road. Dropped on pickup bed cover, denting weak metal. Liver-eater came this way, in vampire body. Moving fast. Air blasted hard, full of smells. Rich, strong scents.

He stole a car, she thought. *Or left a car here, planning ahead.* She urged, *Look at signs.* Truck turned onto Lafitte-Larose Parkway. Still south. Signs proclaimed BARATARIA. *Barataria*, she thought. *That's where property is being purchased by Arceneau Developments and by Anna, according to Rick's paper-trail search. But why?*

I sniffed with disdain. *No sense to humans or vampires.* Truck puttered along Jean Lafitte Boulevard, across Fisherman Boulevard bridge, down Privateer Boulevard, in Barataria. When truck turned on side street, I leaped onto low tree limb, into shadows. *Dark. Good place to hide, hunt.* Liver-eater's changed scent was fading. When headlights gone, I dropped to ground. Stretched, mouth wide, yawning. Shaking pelt into place after fast-truck wind. Jogged down street, following scent. She looked at signs, to remember. PRIVATEER BOULEVARD.

Liver-eater-vampire scent grew strong at small man-den, buried in overhanging trees, hidden behind shrubs, flowers blooming all around. Brick walls, hard, smooth walks between bushes. Lights on inside, spilling out windows. Car was dead in yard, parked on loose shells, car and shells both white in night. *Mercedes,* she thought. I trotted up to it, its roaring heart silent, but still pinging with life. Liver-eater had just arrived, his new scent on door handle. Scent was mingled, faint-faint liver-eater-rot. Mostly . . . vampire.

She thought, *A vampire turned a skinwalker and the transformation didn't take properly.*

Yesssss. And no. I dropped to ground.

She thought more. *He didn't take the drifter's form; he called up another one from memory. He has to eat a lot of protein to retrieve a form he wants. And his original form, is it old? Decaying? He has to steal another human or vamp and become him?*

Yes and no. Skinwalker and vampire. Together they are liver-eater.

Sorrow filled her heart. She grieved, as I grieve when a kit dies. *Foolish to grieve*, I thought at her. *Not your kit. Not kit at all.*

But my kind. And the only one I've ever seen, Jane thought.

Not *your kind. Liver-eater.* I spat in disgust, padding around house. Bayou water flowed close, silent, blacker than sky when moon is dead and gone. Loud crickets and frogs.

A car roared along road, headlights piercing. *Privateer Boulevard*, she said, trying to remember. Car slowed, turned down small street, slowed more, pulled into yard. I slunk through foliage, to front of house. Crouched in darkest shadow. New car parked beside liver-eater's Mercedes. Its roaring heart stopped. Anna-human got out, talking to phone. She wore white dress, her feet on tall spikes. *Easy prey.*

"I'll get his help," she said to phone. Mayor's voice growled, low, scratchy, words not clear. "Once we get Clan Pellissier's backing on it," Anna-human said, "we'll have enough vamp clout to push the project through the council. And enough money to disappear." More mayor growling. "Love you too." She ran to house, rang bell. Her perfume was strong on air, overpowering blooming flowers. Inner wooden door opened, then screened door. "You have no idea how hard it was to get away from the hubby," Anna-human said, lying.

"Come here," man said. Voice strange, not familiar. He smelled of liver-eater's vampire scent. Rot smell almost gone, even to my nose. Screened door banged closed. Wooden door was pushed to. But not closed. Light streamed out. I gathered feet in close to leap. *Hunt!*

No! she commanded. She tried to wrest away control.

Yessss. I am big. Big Cat tonight. *Big to kill liver-eater.*

Another car turned into small street. Into short drive. I

hacked with displeasure. Car died. Rick got out. He had followed Anna-human. Trailed her. *Hunted* her. I crouched, tight.

Rick raced to front door. Looked in window. His body went still, like predator in shock at size of large prey. Pulled gun from beneath arm. "Anna!" Rick shouted. He tore screen open. It banged against brick with sharp retort. Like gunshot. I flinched. Rick dove inside.

Big-cat roar echoed into night. Not mine. Not Beast.

Rick shouted. Words lost beneath roar. Anna-human screamed. Loud thumps. Liver-eater and Rick shouting, wordless anger. Fighting. Anna opened door, scuttled into darkness. Stench of liver-eater rot erupted out door with her. And hot smell of much Rick-blood. *Crack, crack, crack* of gunshots. Window broke. Rick screamed, choked off. *Go!* Jane commanded.

I leaped through door in one massive lunge. Landed, silent, behind couch, wood floor beneath paws. Lips pulled back to expose killing teeth. Rank, rotten-meat stench filled air. Slurping sounds were loud, coarse. Rose up on couch, claws half exposed. Seeing room.

Overturned furniture, candles flickering. Rick on floor, lying in spreading pool of blood. Face up, eyes open, arms out to sides, legs splayed, shirt ripped open. Chest poured blood from deep gashes. Liver-eater stooped over him, hunched, face at Rick's chest. Drinking.

Mostly human-shaped, wearing human clothing—slacks and belt, white shirt, all stained bright with blood. Long, tangled black hair tucked behind human ear, fell forward, hiding face. Flesh showed at liver-eater's forehead and ear, at forearm and bare feet. But liver-eater's hands were paws, claws flexed. *Huge* claws. Body shimmered with silvery gray light, danced with black motes. Energies of skinwalker shifting, half changed, yet held in check. Half human. Half cat. Liver-eater's face from nose down was tawny pelt and big-cat mouth. Huge fangs rose from upper jaw, smaller from lower jaw. Fangs bit, buried in Rick's flesh. Rick wasn't fighting. Unmoving, yet still alive. *He's in thrall, mesmerized,* she thought. *Break it.*

I leaped over couch, reaching. Screamed.

Liver-eater raised head. Bloody mouth open. He roared.

Big cats collided. Bodies slammed. Rolled into wall.

Glass breaking, falling. Energies of liver-eater's shift flowed over my pelt. My claws sank deep in liver-eater flesh. Teeth latched on, killing teeth at liver-eater's shoulder. Sinking deep. Foul taste, foul smell. *Rotten/dead/bad. Remembered taste.* Rolled, snarling. Clawed for purchase, to hold, to tear, to rend. I ripped muscle from enemy shoulder. Tore into wound again, again. Blood, hot, rank, splattered. Liver-eater arm went limp. Claws raked my side. Blood poured out. Strange energies poured over my wounds, energies of liver-eater, seeking change.

It's trying to take on mass, she thought, panicked.

I understood. Liver-eater needed stone, but there was no stone. Desperate, liver-eater's energies flowed over my pelt. Trying to steal Beast-mass, Beast-body. I bit deep in neck. Fighting. *Never give in to skinwalker again. Never!* I drew up dark energies, Jane's energies. Fought back with skinwalker magics, using her power, using gray place she went to, to shift. Surprised, she saw what I did, helped, fighting. We screamed challenge.

Liver-eater rotated hips. Slammed me down to floor, hard. Belly up like prey. I lost grip on its pelt. Its fangs latched near jaw. Vital blood spurted. I screamed prey sound. Fear and anger. Fangs twice bigger tore into flesh. But liver-eater mouth was wrong, still part human.

Can't bite properly, she thought. *And there's no stone to steal mass from. He can't complete the change.* She chuckled, full of malice. *We are strong. And smart.*

I faked weakness, going limp, withdrawing fangs. Screamed as if deadly wounded. Liver-eater snarled in victory and loosed hold. I raised hind claws and curled back. Reached. Dug into liver-eater's unprotected belly. Latched on to neck with killing teeth. Just as Jane did when she was little cat.

Liver-eater squeal was death scream. Deadly wounded. Liver-eater slashed fast, across face, single swipe, claws digging in, scoring deep. Toward my eye.

I rolled, curling, throwing body. Flesh tore along cheek. Liver-eater claws caught travel pack at neck, snagging leather. I bit liver-eater bare foot-paw, sank teeth deep. Skinwalker energies flowed. Buzz of pain stabbed deep into tongue. Liver-eater paw . . . vanished . . . into gray place. And back. Liver-eater vaulted up, breaking window. Out. Into night. Trailing gray light and blackness. I gathered tight to leap. To follow.

"Help. I need help." Gasping voice.

Glimpse of Rick, shaking head, rolling to side. Bleeding. Half lying on floor, half propped on overturned chair. Hand on neck, at ear. Metal of phone between fingers. Blood pouring across bare, wounded chest. Spreading fast. Dark red flood. No pulsing. Rick stared, eyes glassy with shock, wide with terror. Face white, bloodless. Spoke into phone, words slurred, voice low. "I'm at one-oh-two Walker Street in Barataria, just past A Dufrene Street."

I showed teeth, growled. Rick's eyes focused. Breath caught. He looked to side. Metal grip of gun lay under edge of rug. I shoved off with hind foot, spun in midair. Jumped over him, raced out door, from lighted house into dark. Smell of liver-eater rot was strong here. A car's heart started. I leaped long, from porch onto white car's hood. Growled at windshield. Liver-eater sat in driver's seat. Naked, in human form. Met eyes. Liver-eater face went bloodless. For long moment, world stopped. Jane surged to surface, seeing, thinking, *Cherokee. One of The People.*

His eyes on travel pack. His mouth moved, sound almost lost beneath soft roar of car. He knew me/us for skinwalker. "*Ani gilogi*," liver-eater said. *Panther clan.* Gray light sparkled over liver-eater. Face shifted into . . . something else. Blond-brown hair, narrow nose. Very young white man. She saw. She *knew*. Liver-eater spun wheel, hit gas. Car pivoted, bucked. I wrenched control from her, screamed with rage. My claws dug in, sliding, raked paint across hood. Slung off. Into air. Landed hard. Rolled. Snarled. Car sped off, spewing shells, pattered over pelt.

Shift. Now. Please, she asked.

Liver-eater runs. I snarled. *Want to follow, to hunt.* But car was fast. Gone. Away from territory. I huffed, satisfied. *Victor*. Padded beneath flowering bush full of blooms, long arms reaching from high, trailing over ground. I slunk into dark. Sat, panting. Thought of Jane. She reached into head, into thoughts. She took control. Remembered her snake, its twisted shape.

But Beast was big, had taken mass from rock. Jane

needed to send mass back; thought of boulder in garden. Thought of gold scraped onto surface, renewed after rains. Thought of gold necklace tight on throat.

Mass to mass, stone to stone. Sound of drums rose in night, heard only by me and by her. Soft whistle of flute. *Mass to mass, stone to stone.* Scent of herbed flame rose in memory. Shadows danced against stone walls. Shifting. *Pain. Painpainpain.* Mass decreasing, moving through earth, back to rock with gold on it. *Mass to mass, stone to stone.* Dark magic.

Complex magic, she thought, becoming alpha, becoming Jane. Weight and muscle, skin and bone, slid away, through the grayness of the place *between*. Back to rock. Back to yellow rock. In my mind, I heard rattle of old bones, and crack of boulders.

I came to myself under a bush, dirt and grass under me, something sharp stabbing my face. I brushed a shell away. I was itchy, sticky with sweat, and being dive-bombed by mosquitoes. I pushed to a sitting position, running my hands over my face, along my sides to my hips and down to my toes. Ten fingers, ten toes, five on each limb, and all where they belonged. I thought I was pretty much my usual size, too; I didn't want to add a hundred pounds of muscle and bone just so Beast could be Big Cat whenever she wanted. When I worked with mass, I was always afraid I'd come back all wrong, and this shift had been a first in many ways. Beast had never forced mass upon me, had never taken over and made choices against my will. And I had never given back mass through the gray place. I didn't have time to worry about all that now.

I remembered the memory Beast had shared, and I shivered in the heat. It had clearly happened before Beast and I joined. And it showed just how much I didn't know about her, how little control I might really have over her. It was another thing I didn't have time for. Not now.

My stomach growled with hunger. I pulled the travel pack off. There was a tear in the leather, a claw tear, long and lethal if it had caught on prey. As in me. I opened the pack. My clothes spilled out: tightly rolled T-shirt, undies, thin cloth pants. Shoes. I dressed in a hurry and raced into the house, still pulling on my shoes as I ran. "Rick?" I shouted, stumbling through the front door, into the mess. It was worse through my eyes than through Beast's, a lot more bloody. Rick lay in the center of a pool. I knotted my hair out of the way and knelt on the floor beside him, knees half in the blood, unable to avoid it. Rick was in bad shape.

I pressed a pillow against his neck, which was seeping. His eyes opened. He struggled to focus. "Mountain lion," he murmured. "Sabertooth lion." He worked to take a breath, his chest moving with obvious pain. "Lions fighting." I pressed, knowing I couldn't tie the pillow at his neck without cutting off his air, so I settled for minimal pressure, the cloth for a clotting surface. Not sterile, but infection worries were for later. If he lived. "Biggest . . . damn things," he said.

"Uh-huh." I found another pillow and laid it on his chest. The claw marks that scored across him had opened up from his left pectoral, laterally across his upper abdominals, and down to his right hip, deep enough that muscle had been ripped and white rib showed where the flesh had been torn away. "You've lost a lot of blood." I spotted a drapery tie and yanked it off, wrapping it around his chest. Ludicrous yellow pillow, stained scarlet with blood, and a buff-colored, silky tie, the tassel hanging from his side. Not very good for a field dressing but marginally better than nothing.

My stomach growled again, demanding. "I heard you on the phone. Did you call an ambulance?" When he didn't answer, I called, louder, "Rick!" and slapped his cheek. Not an approved medical response, but it had the right effect. His eyes fluttered open. His pupils were dilated, his face way too white. Shocky. I eased him down to the floor, and pulled an ottoman over, propping his feet on it.

"Jane?" he mumbled.

I met his eyes. "Yeah. Did you call for an ambulance?"

"Backup. Called for"—he stopped to breathe—"backup."

I considered his choice of words. Cop words. Without permission, I patted his pockets.

"Not a good time, babe. Not quite up to . . . wild monkey sex."

I chuckled, pulled his wallet and flipped it open, half expecting to see a badge, but there was only a driver's license and bank cards. No official NOPD ID. But there was an odd choice for his "in case of emergency" number hand-printed in a little clear plastic wallet window. I was pretty sure it was Jodi Richoux's cell number. I took the cell from his limp fingers and snapped it open, noting that he had called that number most recently. I tapped REDIAL. The call was answered almost instantly.

"Rick?" Jodi's voice demanded. I almost answered, but instead I held the phone to Rick's ear. "Rick?" she asked again.

"Yo, babe. I'm . . . kinda hurt."

"Help's on the way."

"Bleeding . . ." He passed out and I dropped the phone. Jodi shouted for him. I left the phone on the floor, her voice calling his name. My stomach twisted with hunger, begging for food. I was shaky, needing to eat, but no time now. I had covered Rick's wounds, but the pool of blood was still spreading. I stepped back, looking him over, searching for bleeders I had missed, and spotted it. Blood pumped from his arm to the floor, arterial bright.

Kneeling again, I gripped his torn T-shirt and ripped upward, exposing his right shoulder, revealing the tattoos that had been hidden there. Around his right bicep was a circlet of something that looked like barbed wire, but was twisted vines with claws and talons interspersed throughout. Recurved big-cat claws and raptor talons, some with small drops of blood on them.

I leaned over and tore his left sleeve, exposing the tat there. I rocked back, my fingertips barely touching him. Cold chills raced up my arms. On his left shoulder, from collarbone down his pectoral and around his entire upper arm was a more intricate tat. Much more intricate.

"Lion," he murmured, unexpectedly awake. He focused on my face, his eyes bleary. "I saw a lion. Half man . . . half cat."

"Yeah," I whispered.

"I like lions," he said.

The tattoos that I had noticed before, the black points that looked vaguely clawlike as they peeked from his left sleeve, were panther claws. The tattoo was *tlvdatsi*, a mountain lion. And behind the staring, predator face peeked a smaller cat face, pointed ears, curious and somehow amused, lips pulled up in a snarl to reveal predator teeth. A bobcat. My first two beasts. On Rick's shoulder.

CHAPTER 24

You should have come when I asked

Multiple emergency sirens sounded in the distance, each distinctive—several cop cars, at least one ambulance. Jodi had stopped yelling for Rick, though the line was still open and some of the siren sounds came through the cell, proving that Jodi was one of the cops nearing, tearing down Privateer Boulevard. Getting close.

"You're in danger," he mumbled. "From the vamps. I have to help you. . . ."

He seemed to know he was talking to me, so I nodded, tying an upholstered arm cover and a second drapery tieback around his arm, the fibers deep in the wound, slowing the bleeding. I rose, standing over him, my feet to either side, his blood pooled beneath and in my thin-soled shoes, squishing with every shift of weight. Blood had soaked into my pants, wicking up like thin fingers. It was under my nails, in the creases of my hands, splattered up my arms. The bleeding at his chest had almost stopped, though I had a feeling it wasn't because of my great bandages, but because he was nearly bled out. He looked half dead, yet was still breathing.

The cops were nearly here. I had to decide. Go or stay? If they found me with a bleeding cop, I was in trouble. If I took off and Rick remembered that I was here, I was in trouble. If Jodi had heard me while I applied dressings, I was in trouble. If I had left prints somewhere, I was in trouble. I wiped my fingerprints off of his phone, but people touched things all the time that they didn't remember. No matter what I did, I wasn't going to get the big meal I needed anytime soon. My stomach growled hard, cramping. I was light-headed. Blue lights flashed through the trees and bushes that covered the windows, growing closer. *Decide!* I told myself.

Beast does not run, Beast said to me, miffed that I hadn't figured that out myself.

"Yeah," I muttered. "Right." I picked up the phone and spoke into it. "Anyone there?"

"Who is this?" Jodi demanded over the sound of sirens.

"Jane Yellowrock. Who is this? Jodi?"

"What are you doing on this call?"

"Saving a man's life. What are you doing on it?"

"Stay put," she said, all business, her tone cop-demanding.

Beast bristled. "Not going anywhere," I said. Beast huffed with insult. "I see the lights. I'm going to the front door. Tell them not to shoot me."

Jodi gave a creditable snarl and Beast went silent at the sound.

I stepped to the door and pushed open the screen, standing in the doorway with my hands raised high, open palms visible, if they could see them beneath the blood. The first two cars swept down the short cul-de-sac and swung into the drive. The next car and ambulance bumped into the yard, tires sinking into loamy soil, headlights bouncing up and down, over me. The car doors opened, revealing cops drawing weapons. Beast snarled in warning.

"Do not fire," Jodi shouted, tumbling from her unmarked. "Repeat, do not fire! Don't move, Yellowrock. Keep your hands where we can see them." Like that hadn't occurred to me.

Jodi and her shadow, Herbert, reached the small porch, Herbert's hand on his gun butt, eagerness in his eyes. "He's inside," I said. "I did what I could for him but he's in bad shape."

Jodi pushed past me. Herbert said, "Looks to me like you mighta put him there." Jodi cursed, I assumed at the sight of Rick. I stepped aside for two stout EMTs and their stretcher.

"He needs blood," I said, my arms still overhead. "You guys carry units in this state?"

"No," the fatter of the two said, setting down his gear. "But we got volume expanders and if he needs faster transport, the choppers all got blood." He took a look at Rick and at the blood on the floor and swore.

"Call the chopper in," Jodi said. "Get 'em here fast."

"Yeah. You ain't kidding," he said, pulling his portable radio and making the call.

No one was watching me, so I put my arms down and stepped into the corner. The EMTs were fast, starting IV lines, taking blood pressure. Herbert was walking around, his thumbs in his belt, looking the place over. Jodi was talking to the medics, asking the kinds of questions a cop asked in the field, questions medical professionals had no answers for. Questions that cops asked when one of their own was injured in the line of duty. If I hadn't already figured out that Rick was an undercover cop, that would have decided it. He was spying on the vamps for NOPD. Did Troll know his relative was a cop?

It occurred to me that I had no car here, no visible means of transportation. I'd have to lie about how I got here when they questioned me. I'd have to tell the cops that I arrived with Rick. Or walked. The first lie would be easily disproved, the second wasn't likely. I really didn't want to have to lie to Jodi, especially such a bad lie. When Herbert's back was turned, I casually slipped out of the house. As soon as the shadows covered me, I broke into a dead run.

I called for a Bluebird Cab on my cell, and was lucky that Rinaldo happened to be off from work. I didn't expect to be lucky again, and so took extra precautions when I stripped and rinsed my clothes in the bayou. Squatting naked on the bank not far from Fisherman Boulevard Bridge, I was totally exposed in the moonlight, had anyone awake been looking this way instead of toward the flashing lights. I heard several neighbors talking and spotted them, standing on front porches and in the road, not getting closer to the action, but not letting it out of their sights either. I hoped the distraction would keep them from noticing me.

Mosquitoes nipped at me as I worked to get the blood out, and I hoped I was successful before I was drained by insects or attracted every gator within ten miles. When moonlight assured me that my clothes and shoes were mostly blood free, I re-dressed. Dripping, I jogged up Privateer Boulevard in my squishy shoes, keeping to shadows, watching for my cab, watching for anyone who might spot me and then report me to the cops. I was hungry, shaky, sticky with blood and sweat, stinking of bayou, and hot, even with the wet clothing.

I crossed Fisherman Boulevard and was almost back to the Jean Lafitte National Historical Park, my breathing coming harder than I expected, my stomach cramping as if Beast had her claws in me, before I spotted Rinaldo's cab. I flagged him down and waited, bent over at the waist, huffing and trying to control my hunger before I bit into him for a quick snack. Beast thought that was amusing and sent me images of a big cat attacking from the back of a cab.

"You look like shit, you do," he said, leaning out the open window, one arm on the door.

I huffed a laugh and tried to stand. My back wanted to spasm, and my legs were trembling. "And you're a sweet talker, Rinaldo."

"That what my wife tell me," he said, sounding increasingly Cajun the better he got to know me. "Lemme guess. You want stop at nearest fast-food joint for half dozen burger and three or two shake."

"Sounds delicious." I made it to the car. "I'm wet. Where do you want me to sit?"

"Up front fine. I got towel. What you do, go for a bayou swim? There gator in there, you know."

I eased into the car and quickly shut the door so the interior lights couldn't pick out the tinge of bloody red all through my clothes. I rested my head back and sighed, smoothing the edges of the towel to catch the spreading damp. "Home. Food. And not in that order," I said. Overhead, the moon passed behind clouds, and thunder rumbled in the distance.

Rinaldo made a three-point turn. "Best burgers in state coming up. And boudin balls."

"I'm not eating anything's balls," I said, closing my eyes.

For some reason Rinaldo thought that was funny.

I remembered what they were as soon as I bit into a fried boudin ball—spicy meat and sticky rice, shaped into a ball and fried in lard. They were totally wonderful; I had six, each as big as my fist, and only two double burgers. And two large shakes, one order of fully loaded fries with chili and cheese, and two fried apple pies. I treated Rinaldo to a burger and shake, and let him watch me eat as he drove. He was fascinated.

"Where you keep all that food?"

"I didn't eat dinner tonight," I said, shrugging, shoving a handful of fries into my mouth and licking the chili off my fingers. "Fast metabolism."

"Like a damn race car, you is."

I chuckled and drained one of the shakes through a straw with a long slurp of satisfaction.

Rinaldo dropped me off down the street from my house and I walked the rest of the way, carrying his towel. I had insisted that I be allowed to wash it for him, taking refuge in manners when I really just wanted to keep him from seeing the thin, washed-out blood soaked into it. He charged me an arm and a leg for the after-midnight fare, cash, and I paid it without demur. I also tipped him well, wanting to keep my safe transportation happy. As it was, if Jodi ever discovered and questioned him, Rinaldo would provide a lot of unusual information to the suspicious cop.

When I got inside, I showered off fully clothed, hung up the wet things, and re-dressed in vamp-hunting garb, human style. I had gotten a good look at the rogue vamp in his nonstinky form and I now knew enough to go hunting. The vamp that didn't stink had been painted on a mural once, decades ago. I recognized him from the naked vamps partying in the mural at Arceneau clan house—Grégoire, bloodmaster of Clan Arceneau, lately traveling in Europe.

When I left the house, my shotgun was slung over my back, the Benelli still loaded with the hand-packed silver-fléchette rounds. I carried a selection of silver crosses in my belt, which would be hidden under my leather jacket when I zipped it up, and stakes in loops at my jeans-clad thighs. I hooked the chain-mail collar over the necklace of panther claws and bones, the gold nugget necklace well secured. If I had to change again tonight, I wanted all the help I could get. Studded leather gloves protected my hands, steel-toed boots were laced up my legs. Vamp-killers were strapped in leather sheaths at waist and thighs. My hair was tightly braided in a long plait, close to my head and tucked under a skullcap. No vamp would be able to grab me by the hair during a fight. Into pockets went extras: extra crosses, a vial of baptismal water—not that I knew yet how it worked against vamps, but in a pinch I was willing to try it—a camera for proof of death, and extra ammo.

My cell rang five times while I dressed, all the calls from Jodi. Her voice mails went from nasty to threatening. The last thing I grabbed was the wooden box of Molly's witchy tricks from the top shelf. It was slightly dusty, free of fingerprints, proof that no one had touched the box through the obfuscation spell on it. I unlatched it and studied the charms: petrified wood disks hand-carved in bas-relief, scenes of the cross with a dead Jesus on them. I dropped them down my shirt collar; they slid down my belly to rest against my skin at my jeans.

This time when the cell rang, it was Molly's number. "Molly," I said, heading out the door. "It's the middle of the night. What's wrong?"

"You opened the spell box," she said. I thought about that for a span of heartbeats. Before I could reply, she added, "Be careful." And hung up.

I chuckled. "I'll do that." I kick-started the bike and took off. I was two blocks away, the bike roaring beneath me, when the first marked cruiser turned down the street, lights flashing, but sirens silent. I had gotten away just in time.

Even with the leather jacket unzipped and the gloves off, even at fifty miles an hour, the wind wasn't cooling. It was wet with unspent rain, heavy with fog, the artificial breeze I created as I rode smelling sour and ripe. I was sweating like a ditchdigger, trickles running into my hairline, under the skullcap, streams damping the silk shirt against my skin, pulling with every movement under the vest. I was so hot I was pretty sure I was melting, and the charms resting against my skin added to the sense of sweltering itchiness. As I sweated and drove, I dialed Jodi.

"Richoux," she answered. "Where the hell are you, Yellowrock?"

"Out and about. How's Rick?"

"Dying," she said, the single word brutal.

I felt a chill settle on me, like the chill of death, cooling the sweat that smeared my skin. I remembered the tattoos. I remembered his worry that I was in danger. "How bad?"

"They flew him to Tulane Medical. He's in surgery. They've given him four units of blood and most of that is on the floor. Where the fuck are you?"

I slowed and wheeled the bike off the road. Came to a stop and killed the engine. Into the phone I said, "I'm sending help. Tell the docs."

"Tell them *what*?"

I hit END and speed-dialed another number. Bruiser didn't answer. Leo, the head of the vamp council of New Orleans, picked up his own phone. "Jane."

I said, "I need a favor."

"And what do you trade for this favor?"

Beast growled. Leo, hearing the sound, chuckled. I thought fast. I had only one thing the blood-master of the city wanted. *Crap.* "You still want a taste of me?" I asked, hearing a tremor in my voice. Hating it. Knowing that Leo could hear it too.

"I want to drink of you in every way," Leo Pellissier said, his voice dropping into spellbind timbre.

I swallowed at the images his voice brought to mind, and managed to say, "No way. But . . ." I took a breath, not quite sure what I was promising. "I need a favor. And I'll trade a blood meal for it if I have to."

There was total silence for just an instant. Sarcasm lining each word, Leo said, "What a lovely proposal. I can take an unwilling Valkyrie to sip upon, without true blood exchange, without a true joining, in barter for an unnamed favor. No."

Blood exchange? True joining? What were they? I did *not* have time for this. "Look, you sorry, bloodsucking bastard," I ground out. "Rick LaFleur is dying in surgery at Tulane Medical from a rogue attack. He needs vamp blood. What do I have to trade to get it for him?"

"You should have said so. George," Leo said, his mouth no longer at the phone. "The car. Now!" The line clicked off.

I started to retort before I realized he was gone. I looked at the phone with its blinking CALL DISCONNECTED notice. "So, am I your dinner or not?" I asked it. Beast hacked with laughter. "Not funny," I said to her. She just laughed harder. Beast has a weird sense of humor.

I took St. Charles Avenue, tooled in to the Garden District, and entered on Third Street. I stopped three blocks in, zipped up, and went the rest of the way on foot. A gentle rain began to fall as I walked, pattering on the trees overhead, wetting the street where the canopy of leaves parted to reveal the cloud-covered sky. A dog barked inside a house, demanding, not alerting, probably needing to go outside to do his business. Thunder sounded, close now. My feet were almost silent on the street. Music and TV sounds were tinny, so muffled no human would have heard them. Air conditioners and electric wires whooshed and sizzled. Beast was on full alert, energy humming in my veins, my senses ratcheted up.

The house where I had visited with the blood-servant twins was palely lit, the light of candles or maybe lamps flickering between closed window draperies. I was certain whom I had seen in the moments the liver-eater's gaze and mine were locked, while he shifted. The Cherokee I had expected, but Grégoire was a huge surprise.

I had been in Clan Arceneau's house and I knew that no rotting liver-eater was using the premises as a lair, but someone there would know where he was. I stopped on the walkway, only now realizing that the iron gates were open and no one had come to the door . . . and the drapes were closed. Drapes closed at night seemed backward. Something wasn't right. Anxiety raced down my spine on little spider feet. Pausing, I stood in deep shadow, taking in the scents, letting my eyes adjust. The wrought-iron fence glinted in the streetlights like wet blood. The pattern of fleur-de-lis was like the pattern on Katie's grillwork at the freebie house, and oddly like the brand on Katie's arm. I wondered when some distant master of Clan Arceneau had turned a skinwalker. And how soon after that he had met his demise, to be replaced by the walker. And if anyone in his clan knew that Grégoire had gone rogue. Useless questions.

I lifted my face to the night, drawing the air over my tongue and through my nose, smelling, tasting the pheromones and subtle chemicals that permeated the night. Same as before. Chemical fertilizers, traces of yappy-dog and house-cat urine and stool, weed killer, dried cow manure, exhaust, rubber tires, rain, oil on the streets. And faintly, very faintly, the smell of the liver-eater when he wasn't all rotten and stinky. Well. How about that.

I dialed Leo. When he answered, I said, "I'm at Clan Arceneau. Turn off the house alarms."

"What?" he said, his voice haughty and offended, traffic noises in the background.

"Do it. Now. You got one minute." I closed the phone, turned it off, and tucked it into a pocket, hoping he or Bruiser would do what I needed. Finding my timing technique amusing, I counted, "One Mississippi. Two Mississippi . . ."

Sixty seconds later, I walked up the front walk, unstrapping the Benelli, not that I intended to fire unless I had to. Collateral damage, possibly killing a twin or another human blood-servant, would mean a prison sentence unless I could prove self-defense. My contract only covered me for accidentally or purposefully killing *vamps* helping the rogue. I checked the vamp-killers in their sheaths, settling the stakes as I walked. I pulled a cross, one of inlaid silver and wood. On the wide front porch, I rang the bell. Nothing like a frontal approach.

I heard footsteps inside, close together, unsteady, like an aged, human servant. Where the heck were the twins? I remembered the sight of the skull in the underground lair. The liver-eater had eaten at least one blood-servant. Why not others? I felt sick. I liked the twins.

When the footsteps inside paused, I reared back and kicked the door, just over the dead bolt. The bolt held, but the dry wood around it gave, a harsh, splintered sound. The servant screeched. An alarm went off. And was silenced. Cold air rushed out at me like a blessing, cooling my face. But the servant was still screaming.

I turned to the cringing, wailing human. She looked like she was two hundred years old, her face drawn and wrinkled, skin hanging like swags of old cloth from her jaw. "I'm not here for you," I said. Her screams didn't abate. She raised a hand. It held a derringer.

I knocked the little gun away with a swift slap of the cross, metal to metal clicking hard. Before it hit the floor, I grabbed her shoulder and shook her, holding the cross in front of her eyes, dragging her to the mural. This was not going like I expected. I ground out, "Shut. Up."

She did, her eyes on the cross. I pointed at a man in the mural. "Who?" When she looked puzzled, I said again, pointing to the blond man who looked like he was fifteen when he was turned. Wanting to make sure, to confirm my identification. "Who is he?"

"Grégoire. Blood-master to Clan Arceneau." Her voice wavered.

"Where's his lair?" I growled, Beast bleeding into my eyes.

"No." Her shoulders went back; her chin rose. "Never." It occurred to me that she saw a lot worse than a mountain lion in the eyes of her bosses.

Before I could respond, I heard from the stairs, "Correen?" The voice was grating, sexless. Beast flared through me, into my limbs. I raced down the hall and up the stairs toward the sound, touching the charms to make sure they were still in place. I reached the second story.

"Correen?" The voice sounded weak. Scared. Dominique, the blonde who had commanded me to call on her, tottered from a bedroom, a white nightgown fluttering around her feet. Metal bracelets clinked as she moved. The cross in my hand flared with vicious light. Dominique cringed, hissed, her fangs falling forward. I ran toward her. She wrenched back, her feet landing wrong. Falling, she hit the floor, her wrist catching her weight with a loud snap. Her face twisted into a grimace and she turned her eyes from the cross, holding up a protective hand. "No," she said. "Put it away. Please."

"Not yet. Where is he? Where is the rogue?"

She cradled her broken wrist, the hand sticking out at an odd angle. "No. I can't."

"You don't have much choice," I said, breathing in. "I can smell him. He's been here. The vamp council gave me authority to kill you without reprisal for harboring him." Beast rose higher, snarling.

"Harboring him?" She laughed, a wretched gurgling sound, hysterical and despondent all at once. Full of . . . despair? *Vamps can feel despair?* Dominique turned her face up to me. She was crying bloody, watery tears, trailing down a face so pale that her skin looked transparent. "I haven't been *harboring* him. None of us have. We're his prisoners," she spat. "You should have come when I asked."

She held up a foot, displaying a shackle around her ankle. The flesh beneath it was red and swollen, blistered with pustules, torn skin seeping watery blood that made little *ssss*ing sounds as it cauterized against the silver metal. The clinking I had thought was bracelets was a silver anklet, binding Dominique.

I knelt and examined her. She was pale and bloodless. Her skin was faintly yellow, like brittle parchment, and her eyes were hollowed with purple smudges. Her neck showed repeated vamp bites, the skin torn and ridged with scar tissue. She had been bled, often and without recourse to enough blood to restore her. Worse . . . I hadn't known vamps could break bones. "The silver," I guessed. "It's poisoning you."

"Yes. Me. Three others of my clan held prisoner here."

I pivoted on one knee and looked back into the hallway. At each doorway stood a vamp wearing nightclothes, looking haggard. I inserted the silver cross inside my leather jacket. Dominique sighed with relief and dropped her head to the floral carpet. "Your human servants aren't feeding you?" I asked. "Where are the twins? Why don't they just let you go?"

"Our young blood-servants were bled and taken away. I don't know if any survive. The ones remaining are old, their parents, or even great-grandparents, unable to fight, unable to help us for fear that their loved ones yet live and will be killed. And we cannot feed while exposed to silver. The poison taints the feeding." She tilted her head to see the man across the hall from her. "He's taking so much. There isn't . . ." She turned back to me, her head moving slowly on the stalk of her neck. An emptiness spread across her features, and I recognized a despondency so heavy it looked like death. A deep, daunting desolation. "There isn't enough blood in the world for him. Not even Mithran blood. And if he takes more from us, we fear we will rise rogue, that the old tales will be borne out in our flesh." Her eyes closed and she whispered, "Already each of us takes far too long to find our own sanity at sunset."

I reached for her shackle. "I can take care of—" Her eyes shot from my face to my neck; my skin went sweat slick. The magic charms instantly grew hot against my stomach, burning in the presence of the danger presented by a hungry vamp. I fought the urge to move away in fear. "If I free you, can you control yourself enough not to drain me dry?"

The man across the hall chuckled. "If you set her free, she will rip out your throat in joy. We all would." He sniffed the air, raising his head, licking his lips. "I remember your scent from the Pellissier party. Not quite human. Tasty."

"So much for being kind," I said. I stood and stepped away from Dominique. "You'll just have to wait until I kill your blood-master."

"No!" Dominique said. "Why would you kill Grégoire?"

The vamp across the hall laughed, derision in the tone. "You are a fool, you little 'not-quite-human.' Grégoire is not rogue. No! He is prisoner, and has been for these two months and more. He is shackled, as we, with silver. He still lives, though he grows weak. I feel his heartbeat, slow and weak."

"You should have come when I asked," Dominique said. "You should have come."

Understanding slid into place with an almost audible click. The rogue was bleeding Grégoire, which was why Dominique had commanded me to visit, back at Leo's party. And if she hadn't felt safe telling me at the party, then the rogue had been there, close by, listening. Could I be any more stupid? I pulled the cross from my shirt. "Where is the rogue keeping your blood-master? And why is he keeping you shackled—other than a blood meal? And most important, who is the rogue?"

The man across the hall laughed. Dominique wept. The vamps in the other two doorways rattled their chains. And Correen moved up the stairs, a butcher knife in her hand.

"Though it surely means the death of my human family, I called Clan Pellissier," she said to Dominique, as tears rained down her wrinkled face. "The blood-servant of the blood-master of New Orleans is on the way." Outside, lights drew up in front of the house. An engine died. Doors closed. They must have been close by. I saw my payment for bringing in the rogue's head flitting away. Correen screamed and raced toward me.

I threw Dominique to the floor of her room, stepped in after her, and slammed the door. Out in the hall, Correen banged the blade into the door, screaming, "Dominique! Dominique!"

I dropped to one knee, so close I was bathed in the sick breath of the vamp. I shoved the cross at her face, blazing a cold, bright light. "Where is the rogue keeping your blood-master? Why is he keeping you shackled? And most important, *who is the rogue*?"

When she answered, all the breath went out of my body.

By the time the footsteps made the top of the stairs, I was standing in an open window overlooking the back garden. Gathering Beast to me like a cloak, I jumped, hit ground, rolled into a crouch, and took off across the lawn. In a single leap, I took the six-foot-tall back fence and raced to my bike, still hidden in the shadows, three blocks away.

CHAPTER 25

Witchy power

I gunned the engine, crouching over the handlebars. Beast crouched with me, face to the wind, my/our mouth open for scents. I was heading out of town, along the Mississippi River. And I was about to do great damage to the entire vamp council in general, and to Clan Pellissier in particular. When I was done, I figured someone would kill me.

Lightning cracked overhead, throwing the world into jagged edges of light. Rain sliced down, beating me as I rode through the storm. I was soaking wet by the time I found the old house and turned down the drive between the rows of oaks, in the wake of two cars, moving slowly through the rain. I passed both, the people inside obscured by the night. Security guards? Not like it mattered. They'd never have time to react.

Lightning shattered overhead. I smelled the rogue's human scent, fresh on the wind. I gunned the engine and bent over the bike. I took the stairs to the porch with a grinding of wheels on wood and hit the front door, still moving fast. The door wrenched open and kicked back against the wall, the impact slamming through my bones. I rode the bike into the foyer, spun out on the slick family crest, and killed the engine. Glass tinkled as something broke.

An alarm wound up, the single tone starting low and climbing, getting ready to wail. I was moving so fast that the engine was still whirring with power and the alarm was only a hope of urgency. I kicked the stand into place while tossing the helmet, checked the M4 for firing readiness. Pulled the strap over my head so I wouldn't drop it. Rested the weapon on my chest. I wasn't going to use the gun unless I had to. I could smell humans in the house. I saw one at the kitchen, her mouth wide.

With one hand, I reached under my jacket and pulled my T-shirt free of the jeans. One of Molly's little charms landed in my damp glove, the tingling of its harnessed power hot even through the gloves. I had worn them close to my body, reactivating the protection portion of the spell they carried. Now, like the Benelli, they were locked and loaded. The bike fell silent. I retucked the shirt and rotated my head on my neck to loosen muscles tight from the ride.

I raced up the curving staircase on the right, my booted feet almost silent on the deep carpet, my motion throwing rainwater in spirals. The vamp scent of the rogue was strong. The alarm wailed.

Immanuel, Leo's son, raced into a hallway at the top of the steps, swathed in silvery light, already shifting. I had a single instant to see dress pants, bare feet, shirt hanging open, revealing his bare chest. I reached the landing. Pulled a stake. The alarm reached its pinnacle, wailing.

A paw swiped out, claws raking the air—so fast. I dodged, ducked. Chose my spot on his chest. Slid up under his guard. Stabbed him with the stake. Hard, up under his ribs.

He staggered back. I pulled the cross and advanced. There was only a pale glow. Immanuel fell against a tall stand. A statue tottered, started to fall. A marble statue. On a stone stand. He roared. Stone cracked. The statue exploded before it hit the floor. Marble dust and rock shards shot over me, shrapnel, cutting deep. Immanuel was drawing mass. I'd hit his heart. He should be dead, if he was a skinwalker turned by a vampire. . . .

Not a vampire, Beast said. *Skinwalker. Liver-eater. Took Immanuel's place.*

In an instant I understood what I should have comprehended earlier. Way earlier. The usual methods of vamp killing wouldn't work because this thing wasn't a vamp and never had been. A vamp hadn't turned a skinwalker and brought it in to a blood-family. If Immanuel had done that, Leo would have recognized my blood scent. Instead, a skinwalker had eaten the liver of a vamp and taken his place, subsuming his native scent; he had eaten Immanuel, Leo's son, and taken his place. The reek of rot filled the hallway.

Statue dust rained down. The marble pedestal exploded. The rogue/skinwalker was drawing more mass. I backtracked through a storm of stone projectiles. Immanuel lashed out. One massive paw. Claws fully extended. They ripped through my leather jacket. Sliced flesh beneath deeply. I sucked in a scream.

"Stop!" The word echoed with power. Witchy power. The walls rippled at the purpose and intent of the single syllable. Power bombarded me, hot prickles of pain, stealing my breath. Off balance, I fell to the floor and bounced, muscles frozen, *stopped*.

Immanuel, on one knee, at the apex of his swipe, stopped. I realized it hadn't been Immanuel's command. The alarm died. Lights flickered. A human I hadn't seen stood at the end of the hallway, immobile, panicked. Footsteps trod up the stairs, soft in the carpet. I remembered the cars I passed, people inside. Crap. The cavalry had nearly been here when I arrived—witches. "Stop," the voice said again, softer, closer, strengthening the spell. Beast raged in me. I held her down, resisted her need to *move*. To *fight*.

My hands sizzled with heat and electric agony. I'd been hit with a spell before, and I understood that to resist was to make it stronger. I ceased fighting against the compulsion and released my grips. My hands fell open. My body relaxed. The Benelli thumped softly to the carpet; the charm lay exposed in my palm.

"*Stop!*" Power flowed from the word like silvered light.

The rogue/skinwalker began to slowly sink to the floor, fighting the compulsion, his body moving a fraction of an inch at a time as his own kinetic energies were used to bind him. I looked around, able to move only my eyes. I couldn't even breathe beyond a shallow intake of air, not nearly what I needed in the interrupted aftermath of fighting. But at least the rogue was similarly trapped. Neither of us could move with conscious choice. The footsteps grew closer. I heard others behind them. One, perhaps two more witches.

"*Stop*," several said together.

The command was much more than a set of letters arranged into a single syllable. It was an intricate spell, a general, all-purpose, spoken word—a *wyrd*—wrapped around a spell, intended to stop all kinetic energy, except the speaker's own, within a predetermined radius. And it did. I lay on the floor, trying to relax, trying not to fight for the breath I so desperately needed. Everything around me took on a shimmering hue, bright and sharp, amplified by the spell's power. It was brightest around the rogue, where the silvery energies began to tighten and constrict as he fought the forces bearing down on him.

The witch moved into view. Antoine. Behind him was the woman I had seen in the Royal Mojo Blues Club in the secret meeting. They walked up the last three steps, moving easily, human slow. The woman stopped at the landing, her long skirt swaying. Antoine stood before her, his locks tied back, curiosity on his face. He was wearing sneakers, a button-down shirt open at the collar, and threadbare jeans. A half dozen or so wicked-sharp blades were strapped at his belt, blades with steel and green stone handles. *His cooking knives.* I wanted to giggle but I didn't have the breath. My sight was growing darker at the edges, a sign of oxygen deprivation. I needed to breathe. Soon. A glance at the liver-eater showed his face ashen. His eyes livid.

Antoine pulled a knife as he advanced on the rogue, who still wore the beautiful face of Leo's son. But, like the walls that had rippled at Antoine's *wyrd*, and the air that held too much power in check, his flesh rippled slightly. The rogue was tiring, his exhaustion draining his control; he was losing his focus. The rot stench intensified. His skull bones took on an odd fusion of features, part human, part lion, while his skin slipped from hue to hue, a coppery, olive, pale, tawny pelt patchwork underlain with sickly, yellowed skin and pustules. His hair slid from blond to ashy brown to black with scraps of pelt. His flesh—the snake in his bones—wanted to return to its Cherokee form, seeking the original pattern, while his intent and fear pushed his body toward other forms.

His skin darkened, lightened; his hair flowed black and long. His eyes went from a tint so dark they looked black, to a softer tone, yellowish, like mine. From above me, kneeling, he turned those eyes, those so-familiar eyes, to me. Recognition again flared there. He saw Beast within me, close to the surface, barely harnessed. He hissed in a breath so hoarse it sounded as if he breathed in through glue.

Antoine moved through the kinetic energies trembling in the air. He knelt beside Immanuel, one knee on the carpet, close to my face. I could see the frayed seam in the denim, and the two men just beyond.

In an instant I put it together. The rogue was trying to take over Leo's position of power, using Grégoire's form and monies to buy land for his new clan. In a perfect position to carry out his plan, he was the one creating instability in vamp politics. Like I said before, could I be any more stupid?

"We thought it might be you," Antoine said. Immanuel's eyes flitted to him. "But when Clan Arceneau was buying up all the land, we thought it was the woman Mithran, little Dominique, seeking control of her clan, or seeking to begin a new clan-family and expanded hunting ground."

Antoine shifted, blocking my view, his back to me, his body standing within the outstretched claws of the rogue. "Or, we think perhaps it was Blood-master Arceneau, eh? You lead us to think that, yes? The 'traveling in Europe' was ruse? You have him, Arceneau, bound in silver, stash him somewhere?" He chuckled at whatever he saw in Immanuel's expression. "And then Anna join us. Tell us something about you become strange. . . ."

The rogue, the liver-eater, twitched a claw. Only a fraction. At the movement, the charm lying in my palm grew hot, burning. *Oh crap. The charms.* They were reacting to my fear and Antoine's spell. They were intended to protect me. Clearly at least one of them had identified a threat to me and was trying to react. The burning increased, gathering, intensifying in the center of my hand. I wanted to scream. As my skin blistered I managed a gasp, soft, almost silent.

Neither of the two looked my way. Antoine reached out and touched the rogue's paw, one finger on the tip of a claw. "I don' know what you are, mon, but you not Immanuel. Not Immanuel, long time pass. Decades, maybe. You steal Immanuel shape, yes? And this sabertooth shape. How you do that? You kill a witch and take her power? Yes? No? No matter. Your time here done. I no miss de heart, like dis *petite chat*."

With a quick flick of his wrist he jerked the stake out of Immanuel's chest. Blood flew. Splattering me. A droplet landed on the charm. The crimson drop bubbled and spat, releasing the heating stench of rotten meat. It mixed with the reek of my burned flesh as the charm bristled with power. I gagged on the pain. Tears blurred my eyes. I wasn't supposed to hold it once it was activated. I was supposed to throw it at the danger. It was supposed to detonate, but only on the cause of the danger, not on me. Holding the charm was having an unexpected effect on the incantation embedded in it. *My hand is burning.*

Antoine flipped his knife, lowered it to Immanuel's neck. The blade pressed in. More blood spurted. I managed a strangled scream as the charm fully activated. Burning a hole into my palm. My fingers spasmed closed. Increasing the pain tenfold.

The charm detonated. Taking with it Antoine's kinetic spell. Everything happened fast, in overlapping images. The concussion of energies was a backwash of agony as I sucked in a breath, filling my air-starved lungs.

The liver-eater's outstretched arms ripped inward, closing on Antoine's body. The liver-eater slashed through Antoine's thin shirt. Tearing deep into the witch's back at waist and neck. A deadly embrace. With a violent jerk, Antoine's spine gave way with two distinct popping sounds. I grunted out a choked warning. Too late. The liver-eater fell forward onto four legs. Shimmering. Shifting. Fangs and pelt and massive musculature ripped through his clothes.

The female witch, half forgotten, screamed and rushed forward. The liver-eater slashed at her with one massive paw. Took off half her face, throwing her away, out of sight.

I gripped and raised the Benelli in my uninjured hand. Pulled an arm under me and levered my body up. Gathered my legs beneath me.

He roared. Leaped at me. The half man, half sabertooth landed over me, the weight a jolt I felt through the floor. *Moves and fights like a human,* Beast thought at me. *Not like Beast.*

I had no time to react. Except. My finger squeezed the trigger. Shots boomed.

Silver-shot impacted the beast's chest, neck, and face. The

fléchettes tore through him with brutal efficiency. Blood and gore back-splattered over me. The liver-eater jerked to the side. I stopped firing, watching as he fell, slowly. He hit the carpet, his body encased in silver energies, black motes of dark power dancing, red flames of heat whirling and gusting.

Belatedly, I threw the other charm at him. It hit him in the center of his chest. The explosion rocked me, rolling me, shoving me against the wall. Fire erupted out of the beast's chest. Witchy fire. He roared.

Statues along the hallway exploded. He shifted fully into the sabertooth cat. Striped tawny coat, with short, powerful legs, a stubby tail, and six-inch upper canines. His lower canines were shorter, only a couple of inches, if the word "only" ever applied to a sabertooth. Round, human-looking pupils stared at me, glinting with vengeance. He stood a good five hundred pounds of cat-fury, and . . . he was drawing in power from my charm, pulling it inside him. Using it. The fire of the spell went out. The charm plinked to the carpet, smoking, its energies used up. The sabertooth attacked.

Fights like human! Beast is better! Beast roared into my head, into my eyes. But there wasn't time to shift. No time to draw mass so we could fight on equal terms. The sabertooth leaped. I rolled against the wall. Gripped two vamp-killers. The sabertooth landed, jarring the house. Beast rolled me onto my back. Exposing my belly.

The sabertooth took the bait. Claws outstretched, it rose up and dropped down. Landed on my chest. Driving the breath from me with a *woof* of air and pain. A sharp crack of broken ribs. Stabbing me. The huge cat rose up again. Dropped. Batted me over. Straddled my body and dropped his head. To tear out my throat.

Now! Beast screamed. I thrust up with the knives, deep into his chest. The blades slid along his ribs, one catching and grinding to a stop. But the other slipped deeply, under ribs, slicing cartilage, cutting lungs. Finding heart. I felt it when the blade slid into the heart cavity, a slight give in the resistance.

The lion roared. I rolled as he bit. He caught my shoulder. His teeth punctured, cutting through leather into flesh. With my good hand, I shoved the hilt of the knife with all my might. Swiveling the hilt against and into his body. He shook his head. Rending and tearing. My entire body quaked and snapped. I thought my shoulder would rip free.

He slowed. Shuddered. Gasped, his nostrils fluttering. His eyes met mine, shock and understanding in the depths. His paws swept me up, claws piercing through my jacket, into my skin. Silver light blazed over him, the energies buzzing like sound waves, like the pressure of fast-moving water, over me. The black motes of power shocked where they touched me.

He was trying to throw off mass. He was trying to shift. He was trying to steal my form. Once again, Beast did . . . something. Deep inside my mind I felt her—saw her—an image of Beast twisting in midair, tail rotating, claws outstretched as if to grab prey.

Liquid gushed out of Immanuel's mouth, out of his nose, out of the holes in his chest, thick and viscous. Smelling like rotten meat, like old death, rancid and fetid as an open grave.

He backed up, dropping me. I landed hard, knocking my head, unaware that he had lifted me so high. I managed to take in a breath. Pulled the last of the vamp-killer blades. And the last of Molly's charms.

I rose to my knees in the slimy mess pooling beneath the sabertooth. Got one foot beneath me. And shoved with it, hard, shifting my weight, the power of my whole body, into the motion. Turned the blade point out as I moved. And pierced through his eye, into his brain.

He made no sound, just dropped to his belly, his legs gathered beneath him. But a back leg splayed free, sliding. He was losing control.

With my burned hand, I flipped Molly's charm at him. It hit his damaged chest. I hadn't wasted any of the spell's energies this time by burning my own flesh. None of its power had dissipated into the air in reaction to a spoken wyrd spell. And the creature was too injured to take the power for himself. It was all there, ready and contained.

It exploded inward, into the lion. It took apart every organ, the shaped concussion shredding and bursting every blood vessel, tearing his chest cavity apart. A magic hand grenade. Flesh and bone blasted away. Fluid flooded out of him, foul and choking. His remaining bone and muscle shifted, grinding into a different configuration. His skin split and re-formed, the pelt shimmering away.

I scuttled back, cradling my injured arm, unable to take my eyes from him. The silver energies darkened, forcing a change on him, compelling the shift. They seemed to shudder; the black motes blinked away for an instant. The rogue fell to the carpet, his head in the foul mess that had come from within him. The silver light bathed him in a soft fog.

And then, even that wisped away.

On the carpet was a half-naked man. Or mostly a man. His scalp was still partly cat, his hands still paws. But his torso and limbs appeared mostly human, though the joints were oddly turned, his knees bent the wrong way for a primate. He was a huge man. Larger than he had been as a human, still carrying the mass of the unfinished shift. Three hundred pounds of pure muscle. One side of his face was Cherokee. The other half was Immanuel. Both halves had long killing teeth in upper and lower jaws.

I toed him with my foot. He wasn't breathing. No pulse beat in his throat. There was no heart left to beat in the ruined chest. The liver-eater was dead.

I had exterminated a skinwalker. Perhaps the last one besides me.

I knew that I should feel grief. Shock. Sorrow. But for now, all I felt was Beast's triumph. *Killed Big Cat, I/we, together! Beast is victor!* she screamed into my mind.

Standing over the rogue, in the ruins of the upper hallway of Leo Pellissier's home, I stared into the face, noting the hair on its scalp had made the change to long black hair so much like my own. Noting the brown skin, slightly deeper brown than my own golden hue.

Beast said, *Escape. Now*. Details of the next few minutes, the next few hours, raced through my mind. First, stop my bleeding. I needed to apply pressure to my shoulder. Fumbling, I opened a pocket inside my jacket and pulled out my tourniquet. It took a moment to remember how to use it. Evidence of shock. With teeth and my good hand, I opened the loop and applied it above my shoulder joint, pulling it tight, securing the Velcro. The strap caught on the head of my humerus, exposed through the flesh. I nearly gagged with pain.

Beast stared at the blood running down my hand, off my fingers, onto the floor. *Shift*.

"I can't," I muttered. "Not now." She growled at me. But the tourniquet was working; the blood dripping from my fingers slowed. I glanced at Antoine. Dead. And I'd killed him. I was too numb to feel grief or shame or anything beyond the momentary ecstasy of surviving, a joy already blurring with pain and shock. I knew my charm had killed him just as much as the liver-eater, but I'd have to deal with that later.

I found the woman, also dead, her neck at an impossible angle. She was the woman I had seen, all right, the one in the long skirt, entering the meeting with Anna and Rick. They had indeed been tracking the rogue. And from what I had learned, using Anna to do it.

I had to get out of here. But first, I had to make sure I got paid. I needed proof of death to fulfill my contract. I pulled my camera out and took a dozen photos, then repeated the process with the cell, though these shots would be less clear. I e-mailed the photos to myself, pocketed the cell and camera. I pulled my knives out of the liver-eater's flesh and wiped them on my jeans. I limped past Antoine, down the stairs, to my bike, hoping to get out of here before Leo arrived and figured out that I'd just killed his son—or what had passed for his son. I didn't have enough energy or moxie to fight the blood-master of New Orleans.

I managed to get Bitsa back down the steps into the drive. Managed to kick-start the engine, mostly one-handed. There was only one car in the drive as I motored past. Empty. I wondered who had left. And why.

CHAPTER 26

Untender mercies of the human world

I made it home before I bled to death, grabbed steaks, and dropped them on the grass out back. Stripped and fell in a heap on the cracked boulders in the garden, fractured stone stabbing into me. I needed to shift to heal but there wasn't time to do it right, using the fetish necklace. Instead, I reached for the coiled form of Beast in my memory and pushed. Gray light and black motes flowed over me. The pain was heat like a branding, like being flayed alive, like being skinned while my heart still beat. I shifted, screaming.

I lay on broken stones. Panting. Rose and stretched, from back paws up spine, to front claws, to killing teeth, in a long, smooth motion. Leaped to ground in a single silky arc. Ate much raw, cold steak. Cold and dead, but full of life. Satisfied, I drank water from vampire fountain.

She asked, *Shift? Please?* Properly servile. Asking for alpha. I dropped belly to ground and gave her alpha control.

No longer bleeding, with all the visible results of the attack mended, I began to hide proof of my involvement. Just in case I was accused by human law enforcement after the fact in Antoine's death. Just in case there had been security cameras in Leo's hallway that I never saw.

I rinsed blood off the bike and the grass with the garden hose, mopped up the mud and blood from the porch and house floor. Carried my clothes to the shower. Standing under the spray, I washed and rinsed my clothes, letting the filth of the liver-eater flow away. The leather coat was ruined, rips in the shoulder where the liver-eater had chewed through to skin. The silk T-shirt was a goner, but the boots and jeans could be saved. If I managed to get off the slop that had dried to gluelike hardness on the way home. I'd take the boots to a shoe repair place in the morning. If I lived through the rest of the night. I washed myself repeatedly with soap and shampoo, rinsing between sudsings until the stench was gone.

I dried off on a fluffy towel, and left all the clothes hanging, plinking water. Most of my wardrobe hung there now. My phone rang. I checked the number and answered while dressing. "I'm alive."

"You could have called," Molly said, huffy. But I heard worried tears in her voice. "Call me when you can." She hung up.

I packed, knowing that I still had a lot of things to do to assure my safety. If I couldn't get them done in time, before Leo figured out what had happened and came after me in a vamp rage, then I had to be ready to run. I ate a bowl of oatmeal, finishing a big box with the last of the sugar and the milk. The shakes left me then, though I still felt a strange weakness deep inside. Something that could have been grief. I shoved it down deep. Locked it away. If I lived, I'd take time to look at and deal with the emotions later.

When I was pretty certain I could handle myself, I called Bruiser.

"Where are you, Yellowrock?" he asked, in lieu of a hello.

"At my house. You're at Leo's place?"

"Yeah. On the upstairs landing standing in a pool of putrefying sludge. What's Antoine doing dead? And this woman? You kill them? And what's this thing with him?"

"The *thing* killed Antoine and I killed the thing. It's what's left of the rogue. And Bru— George," I amended. I hesitated, softening my voice. "Look at the Anglo half of his face. The rogue was masquerading as Immanuel. I'm pretty sure it . . . killed Leo's son and took his place."

Bruiser breathed heavily, started to speak, and stopped. He took another breath, processing what I had said. I stayed quiet, letting him think it through. After what felt like a long wait, he said, "Where's the body?"

Great. Right to the heart of the matter. "I'm guessing the . . ." I couldn't call it a skinwalker, could I? Not when no one but the dead thing and I seemed to know what we were. ". . . thing ate it. Just like it ate the bodies of the other people it caught. It wasn't Immanuel."

"What was it?" No wasted words or questions.

And now I had to find a way around the truth. "It tried to take the shape of a sabertooth cat of some kind. It tried to take Immanuel's shape. And the shape of a black-haired human. I killed it before it could kill me. I'm guessing Immanuel has been dead for a very long time." Which was a lot of information, but didn't answer his question. I hoped he didn't notice.

"Weeks? Months?" he demanded.

"Years," I said softly, gently. Knowing I was dumping a lot of bad news on him all at once. "Maybe decades. It was dying, Bruiser." I tried to find a way of explaining what it was without giving my own dual nature away. "I don't know how it came to take Immanuel's place, but I think the melding between vamp genetics and its own wasn't working, hadn't been working for a long time. That's why it needed so much blood and protein. Only massive intakes of blood and tissue kept it looking and smelling like Immanuel." *That's why it stank so often,* I thought.

"In the last weeks it had started needing more, stronger blood. When the blood-master of Clan Arceneau came back to the States, the *thing* took him prisoner. He was draining him nearly dry. Forcing Grégoire to sign financial papers, using clan monies to buy land for . . . whatever it planned to do. Take over as blood-master of the city, at a guess." *So it could use the city's vamps for feedings as it wanted? Maybe. . . .*

When he said nothing to my observation, I went on. "It imprisoned the rest of Clan Arceneau in silver in their clan home." I paused. "Tell Leo he needs to find Grégoire and send him to earth. And look for the blood-servants of Clan Arceneau. They'll need rescuing, if they're still alive."

"Was it some kind of were?" he asked.

"I don't think so," I said. Not lying. Not telling the truth.

"It handled silver?"

I remembered the stench of burning meat when I tracked it at dawn on Aggie's land. It had taken on some of the vamp characteristics, just as I had taken on some of Beast's. Black magic. I had done magic as black and foul as the liver-eater. I took a breath and went on. "It could touch silver. It could drink blood. But, though it had a vamp's reaction to sunlight, it wasn't a vamp. It was only masquerading as a vamp."

"I don't . . . I can't believe this," Bruiser said.

"I think if you go into his room, you'll find some . . . let's call them fetishes. Leg bones, skulls, big stuff like that, as well as teeth and smaller mementoes, like trinkets from his kills, using the bones to take different forms." I heard footsteps, sloshing, as if through the blood and goop in the hallway at Leo's. The tone of the background noise changed, as he entered a smaller room. Then the sounds of things being moved, dropped, shoved. Bruiser was searching a room, with no regard to neatness or care.

"There's a skull in his room. On the top shelf of the closet."

"Human?" I asked.

"Yeah. And some . . . looks like femur bones. And other stuff. Not human."

"The skull is probably Immanuel's," I said, even more gently. "Something for Leo to lay to rest."

George swore, his voice breaking. In the background I heard Leo shout, his voice ringing, full of command and power. "I'll get back to you if I live through the night," Bruiser said, echoing my own worries.

"Call the vamp council," I said. "I can report to them before dawn, before this gets around as something it isn't. I have to call the cops in too. Tell them what happened."

"Yeah. Sure." The phone clicked, the display showing CALL DISCONNECTED.

The next call, to Jodi, went about the same, with a few variations, all of them along the lines of "Why didn't you call me?" When she interrupted the third time, with the same question, I said, "Jodi, I don't work for you. I didn't call you. Get over it."

She made a little choking sound. "I'm going out to his house," she said stiffly when she could speak again.

"Leo's?" I squeaked. "Are you out of your mind? You

ever see a vamp lose it? A real honest-to-God vamp rage? As far as he can feel and tell, his son just died. He's grieving, the way vamps grieve, the way vamps do everything. Think about it. If he's out of control, and you show up, he'll rip off your head and drink you dry. George is the only one who might be able to survive the experience. You show up and the balance changes. *Stay. Away*."

After a moment, she grunted with agreement. "I don't like you, Yellowrock."

"It's mutual," I said with a smile in my voice. "I may have to address the vamp council before dawn. Want to come along?"

"Yeah?" She sounded marginally happier. I wondered how many cops had ever seen the members of the vamp council all in one place, let alone ever seen a council in action. "Let me know the details. I'll be there."

I closed the cell. I had me a new best pal cop. Oh, goody.

I braked my bike as I turned into the circular drive, moving slowly through the gathered limos, all black and sleek, some sitting heavily, an indication of armor. Each driver looked me over as I rode past, eyes following me the way professional muscle would, a look that was half assessment, half threat. If I hadn't been so tired, I'd have reacted, but I just didn't have the energy to care. Let 'em look.

At the front door, I pulled to the curb and cut the engine, lowered the kickstand, and unhelmeted, letting my hair fall in a single long black wave. I was wearing jeans and boots, a T-shirt, and the gold nugget necklace, my weapons at home on the kitchen table; I was carrying nothing to pose a threat to the council. To carry a weapon into the council chambers was tantamount to taking a weapon into a foreign embassy or a federal courtroom. A good way to get jumped on and locked away, if not killed. Of course that left me in danger if I did need to protect myself, but there wasn't anything I could do about it except not show.

Bruiser had called me at two a.m. with info, orders for me to talk to the council, directions and details. He sounded weak, but in control and alive, if not exactly healthy. He'd informed me that going before the council meant formal wear, but my only little black dress was more suited to cocktail parties than ambassadorial and embassy functions, and my other clothes were all wet. Boots and jeans were the best I could do on short notice.

Inside, they patted me down, very thoroughly, and sent me to a small waiting room with wood-paneled walls, two couches, a small refrigerator stocked with bottled water, a TV set high on the wall, and one table. No windows. A human blood-servant stood guard at the door.

Jodi, when she joined me in the small waiting room, was in cop dress blues. She looked pretty spiffy and she raised an eyebrow at my casual attire when they showed her in. I shrugged. There wasn't much I could do about my wardrobe at four in the morning.

"The chief wanted to come in my place," she said by way of greeting. Her eyes were sparkling, and there was an air of repressed excitement about her, maybe nervousness. "But George Dumas specified me when he called HQ with the invitation. Thanks."

"Your boss ever been before a council?"

"Nope." She smiled slightly. "I think he's ticked off with me."

"It's good for a cop's career to get an invitation?"

"Don't know." She smoothed down her skirt with anxious hands. "This is a first. The boss just gets a phone call with instructions."

"Ah." I hid my smile. Jodi would soon be moving up in the world. "Where's Herbert?"

"Beats me." She glanced at me from the corner of her eye. "You like Jim? Want me to set you up on a date?"

It took a second to realize she was razzing me. "Cute. No way, no thanks." I stretched out on the couch, feeling the hours, the constant shifts, and the burn in every muscle, nerve, and skin cell. I wanted to close my burning eyes but I was afraid I'd fall asleep, so instead I spent a half hour in small talk with Jodi, which wasn't as painful as it might seem. She was okay when she was nervous, even invited me to go shooting with her, which made me wonder about the twins, if they were alive or dead. If they had survived the liver-eater, maybe they'd like to . . . not double date, exactly.

The thought was somehow unsettling, but before I could figure out why, Bruiser walked in, wearing a formal-looking black suit, black tie, and a white shirt—average business attire, if the average businessman spent four thousand bucks on a suit. His clothes had obviously been tailored specifically for him. The man himself was pale as paper and wore a bandage around his neck. When he sat down beside me, it was with a sigh that sounded like a cessation of pain. "Long night," he said, looking at me. His flesh was unnaturally warm, feverish; I could feel it across the two inches that separated us. The heat made me want to move over, but I held my place. "Nice outfit," he added.

I couldn't think of an appropriate reply or welcome, so I said, "Looks like you lived." *What an inane comment.* I wanted to slap myself, but he just smiled.

"Yeah. It was a near thing. Leo . . . Leo's not doing so well."

"Oh?" Jodi said, a cop tone in her voice.

"His son died tonight, Detective." Bruiser touched his bandage with uncertain fingers. "He's in mourning."

"His son died a long time ago," I said.

"Yeah. Well." He studied me a moment. "You're an interesting woman, Jane Yellowrock." I wasn't sure what that meant, but it sounded like a compliment, sorta, so I smiled.

A woman stuck her head in the door. "Miss Yellowrock, Detective, they're ready for you now." We stood and I raised a hand in a casual wave at Bruiser, who watched us go, his face expressionless. Jodi followed me down the corridor, our footsteps silent. The human blood-servant opened a door at the end of the hallway and stepped inside. "New Orleans Police Department Detective Jodi Richoux and Jane Yellowrock."

Sudden nerves grabbed me and I wanted to giggle. Wanted to say, "What? No title for me? Like, famed vamp killer?" But I didn't. And I stifled the titter in the back of my throat. Me? Nervous about speaking to one of the most powerful vamp councils in the United States? Oh yeah.

The door closed behind us with a swish of air, a soundproofed thump, and a final click. Two muscle-bound bouncers took their places in front of the door, motions choreographed, eyes on us. Armed to the teeth and not trying to hide it. Unhappy at being locked in with vamps, sane or not, Beast rose and studied the scene, muscles bunched and breath hot in my mind.

The vamps were seated in carved black chairs on a dais, at a narrow, curved, half-round table that was probably ebony, a black rug under their feet. They were dressed in black, the men in tuxedoes, the women in floor-length gowns. It was a lot of black. Playing to the stereotype? There were little brass plaques on the table's front edge, engraved with clan names. This wasn't a full council, apparently, but an executive session, with only clan heads present. I identified the blood-masters or heirs of Clans Mearkanis, Rousseau, Desmarais, Laurent, St. Martin, and Bouvier. The chairs for Clan Pellissier and Clan Arceneau were vacant, but I figured they had a quorum. If vamp councils needed a quorum. The titter tried to rise again, but I wrestled it down, and studied the woman at the center of the table, Sabina Delgado y Aguilera, the priestess—a vamp I was not supposed to know, I reminded myself.

Jodi and I stood two steps down from the dais, shoulder to shoulder. I felt like a kid standing in the principal's office. My near-hysterical titter made a third bid for freedom. The vamps turned to us, nostrils flaring, scenting.

Rafael Torrez, scion and heir of Clan Mearkanis, leaned forward, his black eyes on my face. He got in the first sally. "You were hired to kill the rogue vampire, yet we understand that the creature you killed tonight was *not* one of us. Why should we pay you?"

Anger zinged through me. These creeps were going to try to cheat me. The world slowed down into distinct images of survival and death. Beast rose into my eyes. Growled low in my throat. A threat.

Instantly, the whites of Rafael's eyes and his face blazed with blood flush. His pupils widened to black. It was a young-vamp loss of control.

The other council members drew back in shock at his gaffe. But Rafael didn't back down. His fangs snapped down with a soft click. Pheromones of violence filled the room. Vamp menace has a smell, sharp and spiky. Intense in a room full of them. Beside me, Jodi froze. Two other vamps fought their own reactions to Rafael's scents. Jodi stepped away, her hand going for her gun, which she no longer had. Her fear spiked. Human prey smell. As one, the vamps turned to her. Predator eyes. For a moment, danger churned in the air like poison.

The vamp priestess, sitting beside Rafael, placed a hand on his arm. "Be still," she said, her voice infused with power. It was almost witchy in its strength. But her eyes were on me. Hawk eyes, seeing too much.

I couldn't help it. I started to laugh. The vamps all turned to me, swiveling their heads in unison like a circus act. The scents changed to outrage and insult, violence of a different kind. I extended a hand in apology, as if waving away my amused eruption. The vamps simply stared. Jodi took a breath, the sound shaky.

When I got my laughter under control, I said, "The thing that took over Immanuel had been living among you for years and you never guessed. Never knew. Not till he went nuts and started killing off and feeding on humans and his vamp friends. You trying to tell me he didn't smell like a vamp? Feed like a vamp? As far as the world is concerned, he *was* a vamp who was morphing into something else. Something even worse." I saw several eyes blaze at the insult. Well, tough. Beside me, Jodi's fear increased, her body tensed in indecision.

"My contract specifies that I was to 'dispatch the rogue who is terrorizing New Orleans.' I did that, within the ten days allotted me for the bonus. Which I want. The fact that he had eaten a vamp and assumed his identity is not my problem." Their chins went up in a collective reaction, and I realized I had called them vamps several times. How rude of me.

"I've already uploaded the photos of the dead rogue. One is a good, clear shot of his teeth, which has a caption of 'sabertooth vamp.' They're on my Web site with details of the kill. You'll pay or I'll bombard the Internet with the fact that the New Orleans vamp council is not to be trusted in contractual matters. I'll post the contract on my Web site right next to the shot of his teeth. Let the world decide if I fulfilled my contract."

The reek of enraged vamp pheromones saturated the air, sharp as pepper and vodka. Three of the clan heads were gripping the table, their eyes vamped. Jodi's breath and heart rate were fast. Fight or flight. Prey response. Not very smart of her. The head of Clan Desmarais, calmer than most, opened a thin laptop and tapped some keys. "She speaks the truth," he said, his eyes on the screen. Desmarais glanced at me. "The composition of the shots is quite unprofessional. And what are the shadows on the corners of the photographs?"

"My blood," I said, bluntly.

He leaned toward me and drew in a breath through his nose. "You are not bleeding now. I smell no open wounds at all."

"Lucky me." Let them wonder why and how.

"I told you she would not allow us to renege based on such flimsy wording," Bettina, blood-master of Clan Rousseau, said. I had met Bettina at Leo's soiree. She was beautiful, and knew it. She had asked me to visit her and I hadn't gotten the idea that it was for a platonic chat or tea. Even now, her eyes warmed when they touched me. She liked me way more than I wanted, like for dinner and bed, me providing both. "She is a creature of her time," Bettina said. Beast thought that was funny and I let her humor shine through my eyes.

"Pay her, and be done with it," Laurent said.

"If she takes down the photographs," Desmarais demanded.

Though my knees quaked at refusing, I couldn't negotiate away the pics. "No deal."

Jodi edged away, toward the door and the bouncers stationed there, her eyes going from me to the dais and back. She wet her lips with her tongue and one hand made a little twitch again, reaching for the missing gun. To keep the vamps' attention off her, I said, "I make my living killing rogue vamps. The ownership and use of the photos weren't covered in the contract." I wondered how far I could push, and decided to go for broke. They could only drain me once, right? "They make good advertising. They stay on the Web site."

"Enough," the priestess said. "I saw the creature when it attacked me. I inhaled its scent. It was not of our bloo[illegible] and yet it was. I was unable to identify the species o[illegible] creature, but it intended to kill me. And now *it* is d[illegible] spirit of the contract has been fulfilled. Pay her[illegible]

The table fell silent, that total could-ha[illegible]

vamp stillness. Seconds ticked by. There were no other objections. Eventually Desmarais opened a thin file on the table in front of him and removed an envelope. He slid it across the table. "Your payment and bonus. Certified check, as per the contract."

I kept the victory off my face, took the check, folded it over, and slid it into the waistband of my jeans. The priestess said, "Jane Yellowrock, it is hoped you will remain in New Orleans for a time." My mouth opened in surprise and I halted in mid-money-stuff.

Rousseau took over the invitation. "Perhaps for several weeks, until Katherine is recovered and returned to us. We have an additional problem that needs your"—she paused, as if picking her words carefully—"your talents."

Ungraciously, Desmarais said, "Some low-level Mithran is making scions and leaving them at the untender mercies of the human world."

I remembered the two young vamps killed in the public housing area. To me, it had looked more like the human world had been left at the merciless fangs of untender vamps. I didn't say it aloud, however. I figured I had pushed the limits of the council's own untender mercies as far as I could. Besides, I needed another job. Might as well be here. "I'll consider it."

"You will be contacted with details and our offer, after the funeral for Pellissier's heir," Bettina Rousseau said. She focused on Jodi before I could reply. "You are commended," she said. "Your subordinate and undercover officer did well. Richard LaFleur was not detected until a blood-servant at the hospital informed us. We will reimburse the city for his medical bills."

Jodi blanched at hearing her officer outed. I looked at the toes of my boots and hid a grin. Vamps were sneak attackers.

Desmarais took up from Bettina. "In appreciation for his services and yours, we have placed official commendations in your files, and arranged for the psychometer on loan to your department to become your equipment permanently."

Jodi looked like she would rather chew through shoe leather than accept the compliment or the device from the people outing Rick, but she knew it was a coup, and logic overrode pique. She managed a simple, "Thank you."

"You are dismissed," Desmarais said.

At the dismissal, Jodi looked like she wanted to choke, but I just turned and went to the door. A bouncer unlocked and opened it with an ear-popping change of air pressure and a little swish of air. Airtight, soundproofed. If they had wanted to snack on us, no one would ever have known. I went out, my knees releasing the clench I'd held to keep them from knocking. The relieved breath that whooshed out was more noisy than I'd have liked, but Jodi didn't comment as she followed. Silently, we traipsed through the house to the front door, followed and led by the bouncers, our muscle-bound escorts. We didn't see Bruiser.

Outside, the air was moist and heavy from the storm. I blinked at the cloudy sky, seeing a sudden overlay of the death of the liver-eater and Antoine. My breath went unsteady. For the first time I let myself react to the fact that it could have been me on Leo's floor, dead. Or me on the floor of the vamp council, dead. I'd come close to being dead several times tonight. Real close, real dead.

Jodi's cop shoes followed me to my motorcycle, little clip-taps of sound. "Looks like you'll be sticking around for a while," she said to my back. "Give me a call. We can do coffee."

Hiding my surprise, schooling my face, I picked up my helmet, thinking as I straddled the bike. I faced her, studying her expression, which was a little belligerent, as if she expected to be rebuffed and maybe thought she should be. "You just want to know everything I know about vamps," I said, giving a half smile to take the edge off.

"Yeah. You got a problem with that?" When I shrugged, she added, "I like you. I'm not asking to do a spa day together or a sleepover or anything. Coffee. Maybe some beignets."

"That would be nice," I said, carefully. "My friend Molly may be coming to town. You got anything against earth witches?"

"Nope." She turned and walked down the curving drive. Over her shoulder she said, "My mother is a witch. So are two of my sisters. Later, Jane Yellowrock. I'll call."

I made it back to my freebie house just before dawn, left Bitsa in the yard, her engine pinging, and climbed the steps to the back door. I was so tired my teeth ached with each footfall. As I rattled the key in the lock, all I could think about was the bed. Without turning on the lights, I entered and tossed the keys on the table next to the weapons I'd left piled there. And stopped like I'd been punched.

My crosses were faintly glowing—all of them—not with the brightness of the full moon, but the soft greenish phosphorescence of minerals in a cave, in the deeps of jungle pools, a pale warning of distant danger. My heart tripped and sped. I went still, breathing in, Beast rising in me, sending out her senses, questing. The house *felt* empty, as if nothing else alive was present. But that didn't mean I was alone. Too tired to notice when I entered, I now scented anise and papyrus and the peppery taint of vamp on the air. Leo was here. Somewhere.

He didn't know what I was, didn't know I could smell him. Or he didn't care, which was infinitely worse. Beast drew in tight, quivering through my veins and nerves. *Predator in my den*, she thought, a snarl in the words.

Silently, I picked up two stakes, holding them left-handed, one sharpened end forward, the other pointing back, and pulled two crosses over my head to dangle on their chains. There wasn't time to better outfit myself for a fight; without my jacket and gear there was nothing to shield me from vamp fangs and talons. Remembering Katie's grief, I knew it sometimes took their sanity away. It wasn't enough to protect me in a hand-to-fang battle against an aged, deadly powerful vamp—even assuming he was still sane.

Lastly, I picked up my favorite vamp-killer, its blade eighteen inches of heavily silvered steel. The blade brought me luck, but I felt nothing when I gripped the elkhorn hilt except my own slick sweat.

I had no doubt that Leo knew exactly where I was; vamps could see in pitch-black dark, better night vision than Beast, and for once Beast didn't contradict me, just growled low in my mind. I took a steadying breath and spoke to my silent house. "I didn't kill Immanuel, Leo. What I killed wasn't [illegible]r son." I heard a breath drawn . . . in the living room? [illegible]re he could use the air, I stepped to the opening, curs[illegible] booted feet on the wood floor.

"I saw him," Leo said, his voice gravelly, as if his vocal cords had been damaged by a knife wound . . . or screaming. "I saw his face." He took a breath; it sounded wet, torn, and came from a different spot—the bedroom doorway. Beast quivered, knowing we were stalked. My skin rose to tight, icy peaks. The crosses around my neck brightened with his nearness, allowing me to pick out a shadow across the room. A hunched shadow with wide black pupils in bloodred eyes. "You destroyed him," Leo said, hissing his anguish. "And you will pay the blood debt."

My throat went dry as stone dust. The urge to run settled into me like claws. "I destroyed a creature, yes, but not a vampire," I said, with grave politeness, holding on to my runaway fear, praying to keep from being attacked alone, in the dark, by the blood-master of the city. "If the thing masquerading as your son had been a vampire, he would still be alive."

I felt Leo pause, the utter stillness of the dead. I didn't know if he was gathering himself to pounce or hearing my words. Feeling like I was running through the bottom of a ravine on a moonless night, I said, my words trembling, "I left him his head. A vampire could have been brought back; enough blood would have healed him." In that moment, I knew that Leo had tried to feed his son, had tried to bring him back. And failed. In some part of his mind, he had to know that what I was saying was true and right.

Beast forced in a deeper breath, not letting fear's claws paralyze me. "But the thing I killed wasn't a vampire. It had taken on some of the qualities of one . . . but he wasn't Immanuel." I adjusted my grip on the weapons, firmed my tone and gentled it all at once. "He wasn't Immanuel, Leo. He was Immanuel's killer. He had stolen his way into your house. Into your family and clan."

"You killed him," he said, but his voice was softer, rougher, less certain.

"I killed Immanuel's killer." Remembering the words Leo had just said, I took a chance, adding, "I avenged his death. I paid his blood debt and left you the body of your enemy." The silence stretched, my breath strident, my heart beating hard. The air conditioner came on, adding its chill to the air. I shivered, smelling my sweat and the adrenaline coursing through my veins.

Leo whispered, "He wore the face of my son. You killed him. You will pay for this."

Faster than I could see, the front door slammed open. Its window shattered. Tiny, antique panes of glass dinged across the floor. One shard tinkled between my booted feet. Dawn wind blew in. And Leo Pellissier, blood-master of Clan Pellissier, head of the New Orleans' Council of Mithrans, and blood-master of the city, was gone. Relief slumped my shoulders.

I wasn't stupid enough to think it was over between us, however. No freaking way.

EPILOGUE

I kicked high, hitting the padded glove, but holding back on the strength and speed gifted to me by Beast. Landed and twisted all in one move. Kicked the other glove. Punched hard, not putting my body behind it, but searching for and finding the perfect form. Again. Again.

"Enough." Instantly, I stopped. Backed away. Put my hands to my thighs. Bowed. The padded man beside me bowed as well. "You should compete," he said. I raised my body and cocked a brow at the sensei. He was trying to be funny. Everyone who trained with him knew he never competed. He thought competition was for sissies.

"Your cell rang. See you tomorrow," he said.

Class was over. Dripping sweat, I went to my travel pack and saw Molly's number on the screen. I hit REDIAL, and she answered. "Hey, Big Cat. Want company?"

I laughed, wondering if she would ever really come. It had been a whole week and she was still procrastinating. "Sure. How soon can you get here?"

"Angelina, Little Evan, and I are about a half hour out of New Orleans, with your address plugged into the GPS. Hope you got an extra bed in whatever dump you're staying at."

Joy blossomed up in me like light. My breath stopped, blocked by a heart that didn't want to beat properly. I clutched the cell. Turned to the wall and ducked my head to hide my expression. I didn't want my sensei to see me tear up. I managed a single breath against the pressure in my chest. "I got clean sheets on all the beds upstairs. Bought foodstuff y'all like."

A small voice said into the phone, "Aunt Jane, you need a shower. You been fighting."

"Yeah, Angie. I do. See you in a few minutes."

"You got my doll?"

"I got it," I said. I had found a doll maker on the backstreets of the French Quarter and ordered a Cherokee doll with long hair and yellow eyes. The porcelain, hand-carved doll wore traditional Cherokee garb and carried a bow and arrow just like Angie wanted. An entire wardrobe was being hand-stitched by a local woman, both modern clothes and more traditional garb. "It's a beauty. She looks like this Cherokee girl I saw in a mural. Her name was *Ka Nvsita*, which means dogwood."

"Yes!" the little girl said. I could picture the fist in the air, a gesture she had picked up from her dad. "I love you, Aunt Jane."

"I love you, too, Angelina."

Beast purred. *Kits* . . .

The phone clicked and I saw the CALL DISCONNECTED message. I raced outside for my bike, helmeting up as I ran.

About the Author

A native of Louisiana, **Faith Hunter** spent her early years on the bayou and rivers, learning survival skills and the womanly arts. She liked horses, dogs, fishing, and crabbing much better than girly things. She still does. In grade school, she fell in love with fantasy and science fiction, reading five books a week.

Faith now shares her life with her Renaissance Man and their dogs. She is the author of the Rogue Mage novels: *Bloodring*, *Seraphs*, and *Host*.

To find out more, go to www.faithhunter.net.